THE INTERN TRILOGY

THE COMPLETE SERIES

usa today bestselling author
BROOKE CUMBERLAND

The Intern Trilogy
The Complete Series

Cover photography: Wander Aguiar
Cover designer: Designs by Dana

MAD ABOUT YOU

INTERN TRILOGY #1

PART I

PROLOGUE
CECILIA

EVERY LITTLE GIRL HAS A HERO, someone they look up to. To little girls, their dad is everything to them. My dad was my everything. My hero, my role model, my best friend.

I was eleven years old when my world shattered—came to a crashing halt. Laughing and living a carefree life was easy when you were oblivious to the world's cruelty. That was when I had my first real life lesson. The world is a cruel place.

My little brother and older sister were outside with me jumping in and out of the sprinklers on a hot summer day in Omaha. It was our favorite thing to do together, something we couldn't fight about. My dad was sitting at the patio table reading his newspaper and drinking his coffee like he did every Saturday morning. From the outside, we were the perfect suburban family.

On the inside—lies, hatred, and secrets.

I witnessed something that day that'll always be imbedded into my mind. I also have the evidence to prove it...on my very own skin.

CHAPTER ONE
CECILIA

AFTER SEVEN YEARS, the memory is still seared into my mind. Everything about that day. That moment.

I rub my shoulder as I always do when I think about him. That's where I have the scar—the memory—of what that day entailed.

I engross myself into every crime and detective show possible. I'm fascinated with everything relative to murder or criminal cases. I know it's an odd fascination, but it's all I know. It's all I've wanted to know.

I'm not your 'typical' high school girl. I don't wave pom-poms around, wear short skirts to get boys to notice me, or even bury my head in a book studying. I'm not any of those, so if that's what you're hoping to get, it's time to adjust your expectations.

I'm that girl in Chemistry getting an ear full right now. I'm the one that was so damn distracted that I blew up my Bunsen burner and nearly the entire school. I'm the one that's fascinated with everything I shouldn't be. The one who doesn't have to work to get a guy's attention or cares about popularity. The one distracted by my past, and it won't ever go away until I know the truth of that day.

"Miss West, what a surprise to see you in here." Principal Jamison smirks at me from across his desk. I cross my arms and legs as I prepare for another lecture.

"It was an accident," I begin to explain.

"I'm sure it was, Cecilia. But you've been having quite a few accidents lately."

7

I shrug as if I'm bored, which I am. I've heard it all from Mr. Jamison.

"Seeing as you didn't intentionally blow it up, and you didn't harm anyone I'm going to let this slide. But—"

I roll my eyes. There's always a freaking but.

"I need your mother to sign this form." He hands me a typed out form explaining what I've done and what matters are going to be taken for my actions. I grab it from his hands and stuff it in my purse.

"Fine. Anything else?"

"No, Miss West. But please, try not to burn anything else. I'd rather like to keep this place in one piece."

I stomp up and grab my bag that's hanging on the chair. I turn my back and head for the door without saying another word—instead I flash him the bird.

"Good day, Cecilia," I hear him say with amusement.

I'm sure you're wondering how a teenage girl like me gets away with shit like that, but when the principal is your aunt's husband who knows exactly the childhood you've had, you tend to get the sympathy card.

The tragedy of losing my dad—my hero, idol, and best friend—has forever altered me. I'm no longer his little girl—his princess. I'm a cold shell of a person forced to grow up and deal with the new complexities his absence left of my upbringing. I was forced to grow up much faster than I should've had to and face the realities of what the world was really like—cruel and unfair. I don't know who I am, or who I should be, but I know one thing's for sure—I can only rely on myself to find out the truth of that day.

"I heard what you did." Simon appears next to my locker with a grin.

"Yeah, and what's that?" I snap back as I turn the lock code on my locker.

"That you about burned off Montana Greyson's fake eyebrows."

I laugh. "That should teach her to be ninety-five percent fake then."

"I could hear her screaming from outside the girl's bathroom. She was cursing and crying."

I roll my eyes. "What a fucking drama queen."

"Well, to be fair, she wasn't blessed with your perfect skin and naturally straight hair," he teases, pretending to give her an excuse.

8

"True." I smirk. "But I don't care about those things."

"It's a shame you don't see how freaking gorgeous you are." I scowl as his eyes wander up and down my body like a dog in heat.

I quickly look in the tiny magnetic mirror that's hanging in my locker and shrug unapologetically. "I see it. But I only care when it gives me an advantage," I respond playfully.

If he only knew that's exactly what my plans are…

I slam my locker shut after putting my bag away. "Well, I'm out. Tell Cora that I'll call her later if you see her."

He flashes me a disgusted face. "Yeah, like I'm going to purposely run into Cora."

I laugh at his expression. "Fine, whatever. I'll talk to you later, babe."

After this morning's incident, I'm ready to get the hell out of there. I have somewhere else to be anyway.

My older sister, Casey, is living at home while she attends college. It's cheaper and that way she has our mom to do her laundry still. If it were me, I would've gotten the hell out of here long ago.

She's only three years older than I am, but we look a lot alike. At least I hope people think we do, because I'm hoping to be her for the next sixteen weeks.

After showering and getting dressed, I peek into her room where she's studying on her bed.

"Hey, Casey. I need your student ID."

Her eyes never lift from the book. "It's in my wallet."

I walk over to her purse and pull out her tiny Coach wallet. I've been in it numerous times, usually to borrow her license to get into clubs or to buy alcohol. She never questions it, either.

"Thanks, I'll bring it back later."

I wasn't dressed in my usual clothes. Instead, I'm wearing a navy blue pencil skirt, white silk blouse, and nude pumps. I look like a librarian, but I need to look the part.

My hair is up in a tight bun with a few loose curls. I wrap my late grandmother's pearls around my neck for added effect. My face is naturally pale, so I add a touch of makeup—nothing extreme. My body is slender—a gymnast's body—but I haven't trained in years. Not since I was fourteen and could no longer deal with the memories each practice brought.

It used to be a passion of mine, but now it was only a reminder of my dad and the times we spent together every Sunday afternoon at the gym. I loved it before dad died and now it was only a painful memory —a painful passion.

Who the hell dresses like this? Someone who needs to pretend to be someone else, I suppose. And that's exactly what I'm doing.

I walk into the building marked Leighton Enterprises and then take the elevator to the third floor. Confidently, I step off and walk straight to the secretary's desk.

"Hello, may I help you?" She looks up at me bored.

"Hi, I'm Casey West. I'm here for an intern interview."

"Welcome, Miss West. Mr. Leighton and his colleagues are a few minutes behind. Please take a seat, and they'll be with you shortly."

I nod. "Thank you."

I hold the manila envelope in my lap as I take a seat. It contains my 'college transcripts' along with a lengthy essay on why I deserve this unpaid internship.

I forged all of it, of course. It wasn't hard at all, actually. I used all of Casey's college scripts and found her school schedule to look up her professor's names. A few phone calls and I had my fake transcripts and recommendation letters. Add in Casey's student ID, and I was now a makeshift college student.

I made sure to do extensive research on this company. It's one of the largest investigative criminal reporting companies in the Midwest. They do a little of everything, but the part I'm interested in is the criminal cases. They hold files to every unsolved murder in Nebraska, which is exactly my reason for being here in the first place.

"Miss West? They're ready for you now."

I stand up and smooth my skirt. I thank the receptionist as I walk down the short hall to a boardroom.

The internship process is extensive due to all the private information held here. I had to go through an extensive questionnaire online as well as a phone pre-interview, but I'm prepared. I'm going to nail this interview head on.

One thing my dad always said about me was that I was a real charmer. I've had the ability to manipulate and deceive people for as long as I could remember, and I fully intend to use that to my advantage. Using charm and seduction—my two secret weapons—I confidently walk in.

"Welcome, please take a seat."

Three men sit in a row behind a long cherry table. They all have files lying on the table and shuffle through them as I make my way to the chair.

"Hello, gentlemen." I lean over and urge my hand in front of them, quickly shaking the first two men's hands. I shift my body, so I'm angled toward the last one whom I assume is Mr. Leighton from the pictures I found.

Oh my God. He's intimidatingly stunning. I try not to stare, but it's impossible not to when I'm trying to put on a show of confidence.

He hesitates, but grabs my hand anyway and shakes it. It sends a chill down my body, and I immediately jerk back.

I smile as I slowly sit down and set my folder on top of the table.

"You are Miss Casey West, correct?" The one in the middle asks.

"Yes, sir." I remind myself to keep eye contact while controlling my facial expressions.

"Excellent. Well, welcome. I'm Paul Landers, and this is my colleague, Logan Sommers, and this here is Mr. Bentley Leighton."

I glance at each of them, but my eyes halt on Mr. Leighton. As I get a better look at him, I swallow as I take in his face, mouth, and biceps. Little butterflies appear in my stomach as his eyes make contact with mine.

Paul and Logan look like typical businessmen. They're the most engaged, whereas Mr. Leighton looks bored and irritated that he's been called into these interviews in the first place. He shifts uneasily as our eyes make contact.

He also doesn't look the part. Where Paul and Logan wear the clean-cut look—short slicked hair and clean-shaven face—Bentley looks straight out of a motorcycle ad. He has shaggy dark blonde hair that has a little curl to it and a week's worth of trimmed facial hair. It's actually a good look for him, but it definitely is not what I expected a future CEO to look like.

"It's a pleasure," I say as I make sure to keep my smile seductive. It's a talent I nailed down years ago.

"Can you tell us what you know about Leighton Enterprises? And why you think you'd benefit from the intern program here?" Paul asks right away with a pen ready to start taking notes on everything I say.

I clear my throat and sit up taller. "I know all the basic information that is on your website, and honestly, it's just the tip of what this company is really about." I notice all three are now staring intently at me. "What is not on your website is that Leighton Enterprises is one of the largest charitable contributors in the Midwest. You give the most to foundations that support Amber Alerts, Missing Children Programs, and unresolved cold cases to name just a few. You truly believe in the justice of finding missing persons, and giving justice to the families of the victims. Besides your charitable contributions, you also hold the highest record in the country for reporting the most open cases from over ten years ago. And I think I can benefit from all of that."

Paul and Logan's jaws drop as Mr. Leighton's expression remained unchanged. I'm unsure if he's impressed or pissed off, but I continue smiling as I make eye contact with each of them.

"That's very impressive," Logan finally says.

"Thank you. I did an extensive background search, but I'm very fascinated with this line of work."

"What do you see yourself doing in the future?" Paul asks.

"I'd like to be a journalist. Perhaps a news reporter. I want to dig into open or even seemingly impossible cold cases. I want to make a difference to someone's family, even if it's years later. I want to do the unthinkable."

This earns an eyebrow raise from Mr. Leighton. Well, it's a start. I'll get him to warm up to me before I walk out that door.

"Excellent choice," Paul nods as he writes his notes down.

"What do you think you can offer Leighton Enterprises during your internship?"

"I hope to offer my skills, but mainly, I hope to make your lives easier. I want to be the middleman that helps get you whatever is needed to help you do your job better." I know I won't be working on any cases, so I won't even pretend that's an option, but I can definitely use the advantage to get my foot in the door. Once I am in, I can do my own digging.

"Sounds very ambitious." My head jerks to Mr. Leighton, who finally speaks. His voice is low and stern. It takes me by surprise.

I smirk and cross my legs. "I guess you could say that." I like the attention he's finally giving me. It makes me feel like I'm cracking him.

"What can you tell us about your college experience thus far? What major are you?" Logan asks as I tear my eyes away from Mr. Leighton.

"I'm a double major in journalism and criminal justice. My plan is to find a career where I can merge both of those since they both fascinate me," I answer honestly—well, as honest as I can be. I do plan to double major in college when I attend next year.

"You sound very busy," Mr. Leighton interrupts. "How do you plan to juggle it all?"

I pull my bottom lip in between my teeth just before releasing it and answering. "I'm very skilled at juggling."

CHAPTER TWO
CECILIA

I WALK OUT with confidence and feel optimistic that I nailed the internship. I had Paul and Logan eating out of the palm of my hand. Mr. Leighton was impressed. I could tell—and feel it, but he didn't let it show to his colleagues.

While I was researching Leighton Enterprises, I came across many pictures of Mr. Leighton himself. He's gorgeous on screen, but in person, he's trip-over-yourself-just-to-lick-him gorgeous. His hair is a shade of light brown—golden, almost—but purposely messy. I could tell his suit fit him just perfect. I imagine his body is rock hard, chiseled to muscular perfection. It was hard to tell with him sitting down, but from his pictures he looked tall—well over six feet. The thing that tripped me up was his age. He's certainly successful and extremely smart for only being twenty-six.

After doing more research, I learned it's a family owned company. After the interview, I can successfully assume he's just getting started, and his family is now forcing him to be a part of the bigger decisions like interviewing and being involved in the mechanical aspects of the corporation. He certainly acts as if he belongs there, yet he acts completely bored and irritated for having to waste an afternoon.

My mother pays little to no attention to my antics anymore. After dad died, and the insurance money drained from expenses, she started working full-time to keep up with Casey's tuition. And with three kids, she has a lot to balance.

She used to take me to therapy after the incident, but after thousands of dollars and no results, she was finally convinced I wasn't going to participate anyway. Best decision she ever made. All I did was sit and stare at the wall anyway. I didn't want to talk. It didn't help. It didn't bring my dad back. And it sure as hell didn't take the memories away.

"Why are you dressed like that?" my younger brother, Nathan, asks as soon as I walk into the kitchen.

"None of your damn business." I open the fridge and grab a can of soda.

"Cecilia," my mother warns, "be nice."

She only calls me by my full name when I'm in trouble, which is actually, most of the time.

I slam the fridge shut. "That was me being nice."

I turn to walk away before remembering I need her to sign that form. I spin back around and grab it out of my purse. "Here, sign this."

She eyes me suspiciously. "What did you do this time?"

"It was an accident," I defend. "No one got hurt."

"Oh my God! Hurt? What the hell, Ceci?" She unfolds the note and reads the note Mr. Jamison typed out. "Jesus, Cecilia." She shakes her head in disapproval before scribbling her signature on the line. "I don't work forty plus hours a week to save up for your bail money," she scowls. She assumes I'm going to get in enough trouble some day, or that I'll smart off to the wrong person, and end up behind bars.

I wasn't worried about it.

"You're not invincible, Cecilia," she warns after I roll my eyes at her lame lecture.

"I don't know why I need your damn signature anyway. I'm eighteen."

"Doesn't matter. You're still living under my roof. Mr. Jamison and I have a deal."

I snatch the letter from her hand. "Yeah, yeah, whatever." I turn on my heel and head back upstairs to my room.

I watch my phone like a hawk wishing they'd call me today and just tell me I got the internship. I know they said a few days, but that's going to be torture waiting.

I grab my lock box from under my bed and place it on top. I have the key in my bedside dresser underneath My Little Ponies and Barbie's I used to play with when I was a child. The only reason I keep them is

15

that they are the last thing I could find that was from my dad. Mom went crazy and started throwing all of his shit out that would remind us of him. She said it would help us 'heal' and 'move on'.

I didn't want to heal. And I sure as fuck didn't want to move on. I couldn't.

Not until that bastard was caught and sentenced to death.

"Oh my God, that was brutal!" Cora giggles as she slams her body into the locker next to mine.

Cora's been my best friend since we were in elementary school. She's the only one who knows all the gory details of that day.

"You're a drama queen," Simon spits out who's standing on the other side of me. Those two are always fighting for my attention and never getting along.

"Go away, Big Brother," she spat back, waving her hand back at him.

"Okay, you two…just go hump in the closet already. Your pretending to hate each other is driving me insane."

"Oh, it's not pretend, babe. It's as real as Montana Greyson's nose job," Simon snorts.

I laugh at his remark.

"Okay, well I have class. See ya guys at lunch," I holler over my shoulder. I know those two are secretly crazy for each other. I'm just waiting for both of them to figure it out.

I check my phone every five minutes for a missed call or voicemail. Nothing. I know I'm impatient, but I can't help it. I'm fidgety as hell.

My whole life is weighing on this internship, and although, it's technically not counting for anything, I just need to get into their system long enough to find what I'm looking for.

The position wasn't a typical college internship. Most students that needed internship credits didn't take any college classes during the semester because they worked at least forty hours a week. However, Leighton Enterprises was looking for a weekend intern—someone they could train and mold into a future employee.

It was a rare occasion that they held internship interviews since most were found from within—someone's son or daughter, niece or nephew—but not this time. And this time, it would be mine.

It's spring semester for college students, meaning many are getting ready for graduation soon. And although I'm preparing for mine as well, mine's a high school graduation. And this would be my one and only chance to get into this company.

I'll need to learn a lot about their software system, and how to crack into the private and restricted information—for my own personal research—but Simon is a computer genius. He teaches me anything I want or need to know. He doesn't know the extreme measures I'm about to go through, but I know he'll help me if I ask him.

I don't pretend to be an expert, but it doesn't take a rocket scientist to find out information and piece them together. Given the right tools and details, I know I can find out more about my dad, and at least with that, I can have closure.

To distract me from checking my phone, I decide to search Bentley Leighton during computer time. Okay, so it's not the best distraction, but it doesn't hurt to know more about my potential boss.

The second I click on images my entire body heats. Apparently, he was into modeling before he started working at Leighton Enterprises. There are professional shoots and magazine spreads of him shirtless… though, I am definitely not complaining about them.

He's completely ripped and lined with tattoos on one arm and his chest. That, I wasn't expecting to see under his suit and tie, but the more I dig into his past, the more sense it makes. He wanted to be a model. He was getting his career off the ground, booking shoots and ads, when his parents told him it was time to become involved in the family enterprise.

Explains his damn attitude.

My entire body tightens and butterflies reappear in my stomach. It's a foreign feeling—it's nothing I've ever felt before. There was no denying I was attracted to Mr. Leighton's looks, but his attitude sure could use an adjustment.

Interestingly enough, he majored in English with a minor in criminal justice. So he has the background to be a reporter or journalist. And from the reports that I found online, he's damn good, too.

I grab my lock box that I left on my bed and open it. I have numerous files, pictures, and 'evidence' from my dad's death. I wish I could put the memories in there as well, lock them up, so I don't have to be constantly reminded of them.

I look through the newspaper clippings that are all headed with

Murder on Maple Heights and Man Shot Down in Front of House. Let's not forget about his three innocent children standing in the front yard. Who fucking does that?

I rub my scar as I close my eyes and remember. It's hazy, and I wish I could remember more. I wish I could remember the man who was driving the old '79 Cadillac. It was like slow motion—his car slows right in front of our house, he pulls out his gun and aims for my dad. As soon as my dad falls to the ground, the car speeds off.

And then nothing. All I remember are sounds. Screaming. Crying. Sirens. That's it. My memory is literally useless.

Perhaps it was because a bullet nicked me in the shoulder, and I blacked out, waking up a day later in the hospital.

We had cops and detectives flooding the house for days after. They checked into my dad's background trying to link anything to a gang or a business deal gone wrong. It made no sense. My dad wasn't a bad guy.

"What book are we reading tonight, Princess?" my dad asked as he tucked me into bed.

"Hm…" I pretended to think aloud, but he knew which one. My favorite one. "Sleeping Beauty." I smiled.

He smiled and shook his head. "Of course."

He grabbed it from my bookshelf and sat next to me in bed. I leaned against my pillow as his arm wrapped around me.

He was the best at reading stories, always making the voices match the characters. I giggled every time he read it.

"The End," he said as he turned the last page and shut the book.

"One more time?" I pleaded. "Please, Daddy?"

"Not tonight, Princess."

"Will I ever find my Prince Charming?" I asked stalling, not wanting him to leave just yet.

"Yes, of course. And when you do…you'll know he's the one. You'll know."

I crinkled my nose. "I'm too young to be rescued just yet. I don't need a hero." I giggled.

He leaned in and kissed my forehead. "Be your own hero, Princess. Worry about finding the one that makes you happy. That's all that matters, anyway."

"You'll always be my hero, Dad."

. . .

The few memories I have left of my dad are priceless. He was a great dad, and I feel lost without him. I owe him this—not just for me, but for my family, too.

After six months, the detectives called to say it was a cold case. They had no leads, no evidence, and without a full license number to track the vehicle down, they had nothing.

My sister had limited information. She remembered the license plate vaguely. She remembered a QL on the plates, but it wasn't enough. And although she explained what the car looked like, and they had narrowed it down, nothing in the system matched. It was probably stolen and sold for parts.

Even after asking the neighbors and finding a couple maybe witnesses, it never led to anything. Nothing did.

The only thing I can do now is find some information out on my father. That's my ticket. Find out whom he was associated with, his past, his job—basically anything my eleven year old self didn't know.

My mother wouldn't tell me anything more about him. She said he was an insurance broker—simple nine to five job. However, she hadn't worked since before Casey was born, so I found it very unlikely that we could afford to live in one of the most expensive parts of town. I was a kid, but I wasn't stupid.

CHAPTER THREE
BENTLEY

"CAN someone please explain to me why the fuck I'm wasting my afternoon looking at intern applications?" I pace my office overlooking the floor to ceiling windows. "This is why I have Paul and Logan," I scream into my earpiece.

"You need to learn all aspects of the job, Bentley," my father replies calmly. "If you wish to take over some day, this is all part of the training process."

"I don't want to take over. You fucking know that!" I spat back. I rock back and forth on my heels, trying to contain my temper. "I told you I'd go along with this damn charade if I got to do what I wanted."

"And you will, son. But even bosses have to do the dirty work sometimes. It's all part of the business. You're a Leighton."

I scowl every time my father says that. You're a Leighton. Yeah...not by fucking choice.

"Fine," I agree through clenched teeth. 'This is the first and only time I do this."

"Well, do a good job and you won't have to." Before I could retaliate, he hung up.

I whip my earpiece out and throw it on my desk. "Fucking interns."

I unhappily drag my feet into the boardroom where Paul and Logan are already seated. I take the chair next to them and open the folder of applicants in front of me.

I hear them talking and wonder if I should say something, but before I can, the first applicant enters.

Shit.

And then another.

Shit.

And another.

Shit.

They're all shit. Every single one of them. They can barely make eye contact with me, yet they want to work for me?

I about give up and say to hell with it before Erika, my assistant, beeped in through the phone and announced there was one more.

Fucking great.

I grab the last applicant's form and study it before she enters. Casey West. 21. University of Nebraska. Senior.

I look over her letter of recommendations and see several from professors and assistants. Fast-learner, above average student, and dependability are all her glowing raves.

Well, she better fucking be, since she's basically my last hope.

My jaw ticks the moment she walks in the room. I try to hold in a laugh as I take in her librarian-wannabe wardrobe. I know most girls don't wear that. Hell, I was in college only four years ago. I know for a fact girls her age wear a lot less clothing.

She smiles and takes a seat as she greets us. Her voice is filled with passion as she begins talking about the company. She has sure done her research and then some. She's the only one to go into depth about our charitable foundations, and I'm hit with an immediate attraction to her capabilities.

Her face is genuine and soft as she talks about herself and how she'll make a good asset to the company. Her hair is light brown with blonde peeking through. Her skin looks silky and soft...and holy shit...I'm describing her looks as if it matters for the job. It doesn't.

But it sure as hell doesn't hurt.

She's the most intriguing of all the applicants. Her self-confidence is obvious, but she's also one of the smartest we've interviewed all day. The way her body shifts easily between the three of us to the way she passionately speaks about my father's business has me feeling an uncanny attraction to her.

Once the interview is over, I sneak a glance at her ass as she walks out. Bad habit, I suppose, but damn if I didn't like what I saw. I shift uneasily in my chair as I watch her leave, needing to tame my cock before I can stand up and walk out of here.

Truthfully, her application and her interview were by far the best I've seen all day, but I'll need to dig into her background to double check she isn't a fraud or a secret Russian spy.

"All right, I'm out for the day," I announce to Erika.

"Sir, you have a message here from a Professor Hennings."

"Oh, shit," I groan. It's Casey West's guidance counselor. I had called to verify all the information she gave us was correct.

"Do you want me to call back and schedule a time?"

"No, thanks. I'll just call back tomorrow."

I'm not in the mood to do anything else intern-related. I don't even care for interns, yet it was 'part of the business' as my father said.

We're a teaching company, son.

I didn't need a damn intern, but since it'll keep my dad off my back, I have to play nice.

We're a team.

Be a team player.

And yadda fucking yadda.

If I have to deal with an intern every Saturday for four months, she should at least be hot—give me something to look at.

Before you go judging my character about noticing pretty girls, you should know I work in an office with seventy-five percent men. That's a lot of sausage to be looking at. My college party days are way over, and even if I wanted to party, I wouldn't have the time. The second I graduated, I was forced into working here and learning to 'take over' so my dad can eventually retire.

It isn't that I hate working here. I love what I do, but I'm not ready to give up my life yet. I would've eventually joined the family business but at my own pace. I hadn't been given the chance to live my life my way or make decisions on my terms.

The only thing that keeps me from jumping off a bridge is that I actually do love the job aspect of reporting and writing—case files are a close second—but reporting about the solved ones are the real highlights of this job. And my life. But now, there's no intermission for girls in my life. The occasional hookup isn't uncommon, but the last thing I wanted at my age was to be tied down.

To anyone.

I pour two fingers of whiskey before taking a seat on the couch. I grab the remote and flip through channels until something interests me. Nothing does, so I pour two more fingers of whiskey. I do this about two more times before I stumble into my room and pass out on my bed, fully clothed.

The week flies by, and I completely forget about calling all the interns references. It's already Thursday, so I say fuck it and tell Paul just to pick one.

"You can't seriously just say pick one? She'll be working mainly for you."

"Fine, the hot one." I wave a hand in his direction as I continue typing away on my computer.

"And that would be?" He stands eagerly in front of my desk.

"I don't know...Cathy, Corrine, Casey something. The last one," I ramble.

"Ah...Casey West," he offers.

"Yeah, she was the best one for it anyway."

"And that ass wasn't bad either," he responds dryly.

My body ticks at the way he's describing her. I know I'm not much better, but hearing it from another guy—especially Paul—fuels my urge to punch him in the face.

"Don't say shit like that," I growl as I slowly raise my head to look at him. The expression on his face turns from supercilious to one of being baffled.

"Relax man. Did you call her counselor or references?"

I want him out of my office so I can finish reports, so I tell him what he wants to hear.

"Yeah, yeah. All good."

"Great, I'll call her this afternoon and have her begin this Saturday."

"Good, fine. I'll be here, I guess." I come in every Saturday, so I'll be training her.

Fucking hell.

He leaves without another word, and I continue typing hard against the keyboard. There's a huge case that's just had a breakthrough. I hurriedly type it out so I can get it online ASAP. Most of our customers are online. We try to get our reports out first before anyone else can.

"Casey West will be here eight a.m. this Saturday," Paul informs me over the phone. My body tenses up at the sound of her name. "Do you want your assistant here just in case?"

"In case what?" I scowl. "She can't figure out how to work the coffee maker? No, I think we'll manage."

The truth is I want her alone without interruptions. Her personality and confidence have me completely captivated, and I want to know more about her—without my assistant getting in the way.

"You have to teach her more than just how the coffee maker operates," he warns. "She could potentially want to apply here after graduation. By teaching students the ropes of the job, they're already pre-qualified to work here."

"Yes, I know, asshole," I snap. "You don't need to repeat everything my father tells me, you know?"

"Oh, you mean you don't want to have the talk about the birds and the bees?"

"Screw off, man. I'm not a child."

"You're twenty-six," he laughs. "You may as well be." And then he hangs up.

Working here is a joke. No one takes me seriously being the son of the CEO. Everyone thinks I'm here because of daddy, and technically, I am, but I could've scored this job without his help. I double majored in college, earned above average grades, and did a lot of community work. I was no one's charity case. I could fend for myself.

I'm browsing through emails on my phone as I ride the elevator down to the lobby. It halts on the third floor, and I back up to let more people on. I don't lift my head up as the elevator starts again, but suddenly I'm hit with the sound of laughter.

It's innocent, young, and vibrant. I'm intrigued, so I shift my body to get a better view of her. My eyes find the young girl in the front by the doors. I watch her from the side and notice she's on her phone. She's smiling wide and laughing with whomever she's speaking to on the phone. The doors slide open, and I walk around a few people to exit, except the girl doesn't move and I crash right into the back of her, pushing us both out of the elevator before the doors close. Instinctively, I wrap my free arm around her waist to catch her from face planting the floor. Her back is pressed against my chest and for a moment, I don't want to let go.

Her phone isn't as lucky. It slips out of her hand and lands on the lobby floor.

"Shit," she curses and my arm frees her to bend down and grab it off the floor.

"I'm so sorry," I begin apologizing as I step back. My eyes wonder to her bare legs and up her tone thighs to a pair of black workout shorts. She's wearing a baggy sweatshirt as if she'd been running or working out. I can smell the fresh sweat on her, but it doesn't turn me off. In fact, it does the exact opposite.

"That's okay." Her voice cracks as she turns around, and I finally get a good look at her. "Oh, Mr. Leighton," she says surprised, and I immediately curse the bad luck that brings me to my new intern—Casey West.

"Miss West?" I finally say as she stares up at me in silence. "I thought you weren't coming until Saturday?"

"Hide your disappointment, Mr. Leighton." The corners of her mouth perk up into a cocky smile. "I was just picking up the paperwork and doing all the background check questions." Her witty personality is spot on just like the last time.

Everyone that works or interns at Leighton Enterprises goes through an extensive background check for security reasons. All of the files are confidential, and only journalists reporting on the stories can know the exclusive information.

"Ah, yes. Of course, the paperwork."

Paul failed to mention she'd be here today...

She continues eyeing me, and I wonder if she feels the electricity between us as much as I do.

"Well, I'll see you Saturday, Mr. Leighton," she says as she is seductively smiling up at me. She quickly turns around and begins walking toward the lobby doors.

I put my phone in my pocket and shake the thoughts of Casey out of my head. This is crazy. I can't think of her like that. She's my goddamn intern. And yet, my mind is complete mad about her.

Being a model all through college and graduate school, it was never hard to find hook ups. Hell, they came to me. It was a much different lifestyle than I have now—everything was handed to me on a gold-lined platter. The clothes, partying until four a.m., limos, drinks, endless amounts of girls throwing themselves at me—it was all part of the lifestyle.

And now?

The partying has stopped. The limos, drinks, and endless girls stopped. Suit and briefcases became my new wardrobe, and my modeling career vanished as if it never even existed.

I work sixty plus hours a week, take shit from my colleagues who have no faith in me, and have become a walking/talking puppet for my father who wants to mold me into the future CEO.

The family enterprise isn't what I have an issue with, but the fact that I'm twenty-fucking-six years old and the last thing I'm thinking of is settling down. A part of me wishes for my old life back, just to give me some sense of clarity, but that's no longer an option for me.

By Friday, my mind is fully consumed with thoughts of Casey. Since the interview and bumping into her the day before, my mind has been places extremely inappropriate for someone that'll be working for me.

I realize I need to get the hell out of this office and clear my head. I call Ryan, another colleague of mine, and tell him to go out with me tonight. He doesn't argue, so we plan to meet up at ten p.m. at the Dusty Row bar.

I change into jeans and a fitted t-shirt before heading out and meeting him. The only thing on my agenda tonight is to get drunk and hopefully, lucky.

I wake up to the blazing sound of my alarm clock. Six-forty-five a.m. is flashing in bright red lights on my iPhone.

Oh, fuck.

I slowly roll over on my bed and smack into someone on the other side. I quickly rack my brain for memories of last night, but there isn't any—well, not many at least.

I remember beer.

Girls.

Shots.

More girls.

Liquor.

Naked girls.

That about sums it up.

"Hello?" I shake her until one eye peeks open. "You need to leave, sweetheart. I have to go to work."

I grab a sheet and wrap it loosely around my waist. I walk to my closet and pull out my suit for the day, partially excited that I get to 'train' my new intern—my hot as fuck librarian-looking intern.

"On the weekend?" she asks lazily as she shuffles around on the

26

bed. "Mm..." she moans and pats the spot next to her on the bed, "come back to bed."

"I can't. I have to get in the shower. See your way out?"

Her expression tells me she's offended, and her loud stomping on the floor clarifies that I'm right.

"Do you even remember my name?" she asks angrily as she scoops up her clothes that are scattered on my hardwood floor.

I smirk as she inches closer to me. "Do you remember mine?"

She scowls. "You're an asshole."

"Take a number, sweetheart. You aren't the first one to think so," I call out after her. She's stomping down the hallway, and I just shrug.

Walking into work feels different today. I know it's because I'll be seeing her again and that she's my intern. And knowing that she's completely off limits.

I'm already in my office logging in reports when a soft knock is at my door.

"Come in," I answer without looking up. I vaguely see her out of the corner of my eye. She's not in her Grandma-wear, but she's dressed appropriately for an office job—black, sleek skirt and a red shirt. I vaguely take in her shirt, noticing it reveals much more skin than before.

"Good morning, Mr. Leighton," she says confidently. I finally look up and curse myself immediately for doing so. Getting a better view of her, I notice her clothes are clung tight to her, showing off every curve and her taut nipples. She's smiling ear to ear and resting her hands in front of her.

"Good morning, Miss West. Welcome."

"Thank you." She smiles at me, and I swallow. "Oh, I forgot to say thank you for this opportunity. I'm absolutely grateful."

"Sure, well, you deserve it," I reply kindly.

"Oh, and please call me Ceci. I mean if that's okay," she stammers nervously.

"Ceci?" I raise an eyebrow.

She giggles, and it nearly kills me. That sound. The sound of her laugh is probably the best sound I've ever heard.

"Yeah..." she begins shifting back and forth on her feet, "it's a nickname," she explains. "My younger brother couldn't pronounce my name when he was a toddler and ended up calling me Ceci. And well, it's just stuck all these years, I guess."

"Sounds good. Ceci it is." I roll her name with my tongue, and it feels so good…as if I could say her name over and over again.

"What would you like me to do? Do you have some kind of list or agenda that you'd like me to follow? A schedule perhaps?"

That was supposed to be on my to-do list last night. Shit.

"Well, first. Do you know how to operate a coffee maker?" I grin.

She gives me a confused expression, and I'm afraid I might have scared her off already.

I smile and grab my wallet out of my back pocket. "Never mind. There's a Starbucks one block west from here. I'll take a dark coffee, two sugars. And whatever you'd like." I hand her my company credit card and her hand briefly grazes mine before taking it.

"Absolutely, sir. I'll be right back." She spins on her heel and is out the door in ten seconds flat.

While she's gone, I try to think of things she can do when she returns, so I don't feel like a goddamn babysitter, but it's so hard to concentrate when all I can think of are her damn legs.

Note: No allowing skirts at work.

On second thought…

Only short skirts allowed.

CHAPTER FOUR
BENTLEY

I WAIT IMPATIENTLY until she walks back in, sashaying her hips with ease. She gently places my coffee on my desk and smiles up at me.

Now what do I fucking do with her?

Shit...there's a lot I'd like to do with her.

"Dark coffee, two sugars, sir."

"Thank you," I breathe out. I give my attention back to my computer, hoping she'll take the hint and leave.

"Sir?" Her voice cracks. "Where would you like me?"

My jaw twitches at the innuendo she's just put in my head. I try not to stare at her, but the way her soft, pink lips are perking up at me makes it hard to tear my eyes away.

"I've made a list—you can start with that," I respond coldly. She doesn't deserve it, but I need to remind myself of the situation we're in currently.

Boss.

Intern.

Off limits.

She inches closer to grab the list from my hand, slowly brushing her fingers over my knuckles. She keeps eye contact with me the entire time, completely pissing me off. This girl wasn't a scared little intern, and she wasn't intimidated by my authority. Hell, I bet she even takes charge in the bedroom.

"You can go now," I toss out.

This girl was either messing with me, or completely oblivious to the way she could attract men. Either way, I couldn't have that in my office. This was strictly business.

Or so that's what I'm trying to tell myself.

"You can use the office across from mine for now. Mr. Baumann doesn't come in on Saturdays," I add before she turns on her heel and walks out. She needs to be far away from me right now.

I grab my coffee and bring it to my mouth. The smell on the lid grabs my attention before I take a sip. I bring it up to my nose and smell her scent—a mixture of fruity lip-gloss and expensive shampoo—as if she took a sip of my coffee first.

I instantly adjust my pants at the thought of her lips on my coffee lid. It's an innocent gesture, but smelling the scent and imagining where I'd want those perfect, warm lips is anything, but innocent.

I bury my head in case files all morning. Leighton Enterprises is a full-round corporation, meaning we do many things under the same scope. We investigate criminal cases and report our findings. We also report on major murder cases in the US, such as the case of Caylee Anthony. Leighton Enterprises worked day and night on that one, keeping up with new information and building reports from it.

Often, the police reports are included in the cases we receive, but sometimes they go missing or aren't filled out accurately. It then becomes our job to try to fill in the missing gaps to write a full, thorough story.

I became interested in criminology after a huge murder flooded the headlines when I was seventeen. My dad worked night and day on that case, making sure to keep up with the news and report anything new that came in. To be the first to report it and to update it added to the Leighton Enterprises' name. We pride ourselves on being accurate and efficient—all while being number one.

Unfortunately, all we could report was case updates and news from the investigation—the case was never solved. It's one of the biggest unsolved cases in Nebraska.

I shuffle through files sitting on my desk and don't notice that my office door is opening. She walks in with ease, smiling as she walks up to my desk.

"Yes?" I snarl, not making eye contact with her.

"I'm all done," she replies simply. "What else can I do for you? Is there anything maybe…" she pauses, biting down on her lower lip, "more challenging that I can do?" Her voice is higher as she anticipates my response.

I look down at my desk pretending to stack papers and smirk at how her innocent questions suddenly sound dirty in my head.

"Well…what can you do, Miss West?" I clear my throat. "I mean Ceci. I know you have high achievements, so you tell me. What do you want to learn?" I look up at her this time and watch her squirm at my words.

She grins and steps closer. "What can you teach me?"

I adjust my pants again—my damn cock can't behave. This girl is a twenty-one-year-old naïve college student, and I'm her boss, I remind my cock, but it does nothing to tame itself.

"Are you okay?" she asks leaning over my desk to where my hand is trying to hide the tent I'm now sporting.

"For someone so well-educated, you're sure a curious little thing," I respond nervously trying to get her eyes off my junk.

She giggles.

She actually fucking giggles.

"Sorry, sir. It's just…you look very uncomfortable. Like you're trying to scratch your skin off or something."

"Excuse me?" My eyes meet hers.

"Oh, shit." She covers her mouth with her hand. "I'm so sorry. That was really inappropriate." I can tell she's still smiling.

I pull my chair back and stand up, towering over her tiny size. "I think it's best you go home for the day."

She checks her watch quick before speaking. "It's not even noon, sir. Please, I'm so sorry. It'll never happen again. I really want to be here. Just tell me what to do. Anything. I'll do it."

I sit back down and think about her request. She looks at me pleadingly and like the sucker I am, I give in. "Fine." I breathe out. "I'll show you the software we use. You'll need to know how to operate it."

She clasps her hands tightly together and thanks me over and over. I nod, hardly acknowledging, and then I tell her to bring a chair over to my side.

I move my chair over to give her enough room, but with the way my computer is angled, she has to lean over me to get a good view.

"All right, so…" I clear my throat as I try to concentrate on the screen and not the fact that I can feel her warm breath on my neck, "it's pretty easy once you get the hang of it."

"Don't worry, Mr. Leighton." She interrupts. "I'm a fast learner." I can hear the seduction in her voice and immediately realize how bad of an idea this is. Her body is close to mine as she leans over her chair. Her breasts are rubbing against the back of my arm, and I can tell her skin is silky smooth just from the contact.

My cock twitches and I move forward to avoid her body against mine. I swallow hard as I continue. "Here is where each case is located. They are categorized by date, location, file number, and last name. You can do easy searches by this icon up here, as well as typing in the first couple letters of the name. It's very user friendly."

Just when I think I'm home free, and my cock tames itself, she leans off her chair and puts a hand on my shoulder as she reaches a finger to the screen. My body immediately tenses at the touch of her hand. Even if it's an innocent gesture, she knows what she's fucking doing.

"What's this icon down here?" she asks, oblivious to the mini heart attacks she's currently giving me.

"Um…" I clear my throat as I adjust myself on the chair. I can't have her this close to me. "It's for transcripts. You can read them right on the screen instead of digging the files out. Most have been electronically scanned in."

"Wow, how awesome. I mean, for the journalists."

"Yeah, it's definitely a time saver." She finally sits back down, so I turn and face her. "I could have you do something like that, but it's not very challenging. You seem too smart for something like that." I grin.

Expecting her to agree with me, I'm surprised by her reaction. "That's perfect!" She sits up straighter. She is giddy at the fact that she'll be scanning in documents all day? This girl was a basket of crazy. "I'd love to do it."

I scratch the back of my neck trying to think of something that might keep her in my office instead. Too bad the only thing I have in mind is her kneeling in front of me.

I stand up and tell her to follow me out. There are only a handful of other journalists who come in on Saturdays, so the office is relatively quiet.

I lead her to another room where the transcripts are kept. I show her how they are categorized and documented. Then I show her to another room where the scanner and computer are for organizing the transcripts in the system.

She nods her head the entire time, not even bothering to ask me any questions. She smiles confidently as she speaks. "No problem, Mr. Leighton. These are all safe with me."

I give a weak smile back. "Great. Just let me know when you need a break, and you can leave for the day."

"No problem. This looks like Heaven to me, so I'll probably get lost in here for a few hours."

I give her a confused look. "You really aren't like typical college girls, are you? You're actually excited about this?"

Her smile turns seductive as she eyes me carefully. "No, I'm not like other college girls. In fact, I'm very, very different. I'm driven by success, and I don't allow failure into my vocabulary. If this is what will get me experience, and into a career that I want, I'll do it. Anything you ask me to do, Mr. Leighton. I will."

She speaks as if she's promising me those very things. She's determined, and I like that.

She inches closer to me so I can feel her breath on my skin. It's rapid and quick like mine—she's thinking the same thing I am.

"Well...enjoy," is all I say as I slowly back up and walk out the door. She keeps her eyes on me the entire time until I'm out of view.

That girl...her personality and confidence completely captivate me. She's different from any intern I've ever met. Or girl. Most act vulnerable and ditzy to gain my attention. However, this girl is anything but that. Not to mention how stunning she is.

And she's one I haven't gotten out of my head since the moment she stepped into that boardroom.

CHAPTER FIVE
CECILIA

I FINALLY FEEL as if I'm doing something for my dad's injustice. It may not be much, but getting into those transcripts is a step closer. Even being around the software and learning about the files gives me an advantage to dig around and find the information I need.

Although I'm only eighteen years old, my soul has far surpassed that. My whole life altered in one split-second, leaving with me no choice. Leaving me with the harsh reality.

I know I can do this job. Minus the professional experience, I have the passion. I have the drive and desire more than anyone else I know. Most girls my age are only worried about fashion, prom, who's dating who, and reality television—and I could care less about any of that.

I nearly screamed when I got the call that I had been picked for the internship. I begged to come in to finish the paperwork that day, so I could start right away. I didn't even care that I wasn't dressed up or anything, I wanted to start right away.

Bumping into Mr. Leighton—*literally*—was an unexpected surprise. The way my heart raced at the sudden contact of our bodies being slammed together was something that had me shaking the entire drive back home. I knew the way my body responded to him was unusual, but I wasn't going to let that stop me from doing what I had to do.

"Hey, we hanging out this weekend?" Simon asks as we walk to lunch together.

"Sure, um, Sunday?" I suggest.

"What about Saturday? We could catch a movie," he says hopeful. Simon and I usually hang out on the weekends, except the times I'm with Cora. Those two refuse to spend any time outside of school together.

As I said, they secretly love each other.

"I can't Saturday. I have something going on already." I try to sound vague, so I don't give myself away.

He opens the door for me and lets me walk in before speaking again. "Well, fine. Sunday. But tell that bitch she's not to beg you to sleep over or something so I can't see you."

I laugh at his assumption. "Yes, Dad," I scowl. "You two really need to get along. I don't even understand why you hate each other. It's childish."

I grab a tray and begin walking down the lunch line.

"Humph. Childish? She's the one that acts like a child."

"Ooh…good defense." I roll my eyes. "I think you guys hate each other so much because you secretly want each other, and until one of you fesses up, all your sexual tension is just going to continue burning until one of you finally combusts," I say matter-of-factly. "That I'm certain of."

"Okay, Veronica Mars," he scowls. "You couldn't be more wrong."

We both pay for our lunch and walk to our table. "Okay, well then spell it out for me." Before he can answer, Cora plops her ass next to me. I turn and look at her. "Why are you smiling like that?"

She tries to hide the overwhelming grin on her face, but fails miserably. "Lance Kingston just asked me to prom." I can tell she's trying to act calm, but the constant tapping of her foot tells me just how giddy she really is.

"Prom?" Simon shrieks. I notice he instantly tenses up, and the burning stare he's giving Cora right now reassures me I'm right—he's jealous.

"Yeah…isn't that like four months away?" I ask taking a bite of my food.

"Mm hmm…" She grins, shuffling her food around on her tray.

It's all I need to hear to know just what that means.

They hooked up.

I can't even concentrate on her right now. Bentley is flooding my mind, and it's all I've been able to think about since Saturday. And I get to see him again in two days.

When I was there, I felt like a different person. I was playing a role. Acting. And I was damn good at it.

But operation *charm and seduce* is in full blown mode. I'm doing what I have to do to get the information necessary. I need to know as much as possible about my dad's case. Otherwise, I know I'll never be able to move on.

I'm not faking my attraction to him. He's definitely a guy I'll break my rules for, even if just for one night. But from the way he was responding to me, I could tell he'd take that one night and demand more.

He has no idea what he's getting himself into.

I wake up feeling anxious and excited Saturday morning. I have two things to look forward to—seeing Bentley again and to get one step closer to finding my dad's murderer.

I arrive promptly at seven-forty-five a.m. with Mr. Leighton's coffee and for good measure, a plain bagel. He looks like a plain bagel type of guy. I have to kiss his ass as much as I can without making it too obvious.

Although, I'm sure I'm going to fail miserably.

"Good morning, Mr. Leighton," I say politely as I place his beverage and food on his desk.

"Good morning, Ceci. You are bright and cheerful today," he says with amusement. He grabs the hot cup of coffee and brings it to his mouth. I get lost in his lips for a split-second before I remind myself I have to speak.

I knew going into this I'd have to tell him to call me something else besides Casey. I was worried I wouldn't respond on instinct if he said Casey instead of Miss West—I couldn't risk him thinking anything was unusual. And although Ceci is a nickname for Cecilia, he completely bought it.

"Of course, sir. It's a pleasure to be here. What's not to be cheerful about?"

He studies me carefully, letting his eyes wander up and down my body, paying close attention to the tight fabric I'm wearing today. I borrowed Casey's clothes since I don't have anything 'work' appropriate. I'm sure the ripped-up jeans and band-tees would be a dead giveaway.

"I guess that's an honest trait." He studies me carefully, and I know my plan is working.

"I sure hope so," I reply quickly. He doesn't need to know how easy it is for me to lie, especially when it's something that I desperately want. "Where would you like me today?"

He cracks his jaw slightly, and I notice how uncomfortable he easily gets when I say things like that.

"Where I would like you and where you should be are too very different questions, but ironically, they hold the same answers."

I shift from one foot to the other as his come-on's become stronger, more tangible in what he's after.

Part of me knows it's wrong, but I'm eighteen—I'm legal. And I do find him intriguing. He's attractive, and I'm willing to play along in this little game—whatever it takes to stay in this building for as long as possible.

"That sounds like motive." I smirk back. "Which one would you like to answer?"

I'm throwing him a bone, because it's obvious he's struggling just as much as I am. Part Angel says it's morally and ethically wrong and Part Devil says to go for it...*he's fuckable.*

I agree with Part Devil.

Being here...with him...I don't feel like a naïve adolescent. Rather, he makes me feel grown, as if my thoughts actually matter. However, making him beg for it and practically coming in his pants is just as amusing.

He shifts in his chair as if he's shocked by my response and needs a minute to think. "Miss West," he pauses, but doesn't correct himself. "Go do your job. Please."

His voice sounds pained, as if he's pleading with himself. He's fighting between what his body wants and what he knows is wrong. And although I'm having the exact same battle...

His body will win eventually.

I walk past a couple of open offices. I glance inside as I slowly tread by, getting a good look at the other journalists working there. I need to make sure I keep a healthy distance, but still be aware in case I ever have to sneak around for something later.

I begin digging through the transcripts, skimming over them as I scan them in for anything that could possibly resemble my dad's case. Perhaps the shooter had done this before and gotten away with it, or perhaps he's been caught for a crime long after. I would never know, but I was willing to try to find out.

It's hard to concentrate on scanning when my body is trembling at the thought of him. Bentley's mouth keeps popping into my mind. His face. His hands. His eyes. Everything about him. I realize I'm falling deeper in the trap, the sexual tension that is so obviously between us.

After four hours of continuous scanning, I stand up and stretch. My legs are cramping, and my neck is getting sore from staring at the same thing.

I let out a moan as I stretch my arms over my head. "Ah, God," I moan again as my body completely melts into the stretch, feeding my muscles the relief they need.

"Jesus. Christ." I hear a growl from behind me. I quickly spin around and see him standing casually in the doorway, his arms and legs are crossed as he studies me. "I never knew a moan could sound so fucking hot."

I grin as I move the chair out of my way. I imagine his coming at me like a wild tiger filled with hunger and need, as he grabs me and then places me on top of the desk. I get lost in the thought of him running his hands up my legs, and soon up my skirt. The thought makes me forget reality, and soon I'm just standing there staring at him as I clench my legs tighter together.

"Are you hungry?" he asks, changing courses from the very dirty fantasy I was having.

"Um, yes. Sure," I stumble. I mentally kick myself for sounding weak in front of him. I need to stay in control, keep my ground if I I'm going to continue doing this.

"Why don't you take a break and I'll order us in some food."

"Sounds great. Thanks." I continue smiling up at him like a fool. I really need to keep my cool.

"What are you in the mood for?" His voice is low, almost a whisper.

On top. Doggy style. Bent over the office desk. Reverse Cowgirl. Basically, anything that involves him…

"Um…" I clear my throat, feeling uneasy. "Anything is fine with me." I nervously shuffle some documents around, pretending to organize them.

"Sounds good." His face is expressionless as he turns and walks out.

Ten minutes later, I walk into his office, unsure if I should be there or not. He welcomes me in, and motions for me to take a seat across from him, as he sits behind his desk.

"So what made you interested in journalism and criminology?" he

asks suddenly. He's staring intently at me as if he can see right through me, as if all my secrets are transparent.

"I've always been fascinated with them both, but for different reasons," I begin, sinking lower into the chair as I make myself comfortable. "Writing is something that comes natural to me, something that has been very therapeutic in the journey my childhood has played out. And criminology, well, what's not to love?" I smirk, crossing my legs to expose the bare flesh. I want to get off this topic as soon as possible.

"So what are your plans for after graduation?" He eyes me curiously. I tense up at his question, knowing I need to be convincing in my lies.

"I hope to get a full-time job in something that merges both of my majors and interests together," I say vaguely hoping he stops grilling me.

"Hm…and what's that exactly?" He tilts his head up, and I know he's not going to quit anytime soon.

"Why don't you tell me how you got here, Mr. Leighton? I know you're only twenty-six and fresh out of grad school with a master's in English. Is this what you planned for after graduation?" I speak with a lace of seduction, hoping it keeps him from asking about me anymore. And it works as I watch his eyes stare at my lips, as if he's thinking hard about them.

"You're sure a little investigator," he muses, licking his own lips. "My guess is you already know the answers to that."

I laugh aloud at his cockiness. "No, the only thing that comes up when I researched you was chicks in bikinis on your arm and information on Senior Mr. Leighton. Anything personal about you was zipped tight."

That comes out much harsher than I mean for it to, but he doesn't seem to mind. In fact, he laughs.

He fucking laughs at me.

"If that's all you found, then I guess I have nothing to worry about."

Now I'm curious what secrets he's possibly hiding. It's not easy for someone in the spotlight to keep personal demons unknown, but apparently, he's managed to somehow.

"So what's your story? You have a Google page I can snoop through?" he asks with a cocky grin as he leans back in his chair and folds his arms. "Any stalker ex-boyfriends I need to be aware of?"

I raise my eyebrows at him. "I'm pretty certain that breaks about a hundred employment codes asking about my relationship status."

He smirks. "This is hardly a job—I mean you come in on Saturdays." He laughs before adding, "for free."

"So?" I quickly defend. "Not all of us have a trust fund for financial security for the rest of our lives. Some of us have to work the hard way, and in most cases, work for free to learn and work our way up."

He leans forward in his chair in complete seriousness. And it's not until he speaks that I think he's about to chew my ass off. "Wait…wait a fucking minute! You mean to tell me that you don't have a trust fund? I was sure all kids do."

I scowl at the way he's teasing me. "Since this isn't a 'real' job, I don't feel threatened to say that you're a real asshole." I grip the chair and stand up. He laughs loudly as I make my way to the door.

I don't need his condescending shit.

"Wait." He's still laughing. I continue as I storm out and feel his hand on my arm as I reach the door. I freeze in my tracks, my back to his chest. I can feel his heartbeat racing—it matches mine. My skin heats as his touch sears my flesh. The way his hand is still gripping my arm sends a shiver down my body making it nearly impossible to not relax against his body. My body tremors and I know he can feel it.

"Ceci, I said wait," he growls. His voice is no longer light and playful. It's as if he's turned a complete 180.

He spins me around, and I gasp at the closeness. My eyes skim his body, going from his hips to his chest, and up to his face. He looks much bigger close up, his muscles more defined as I get a better look at him. He's built, and his biceps are about to pop out of his baby blue button up shirt. He's dressed more casual this week, not in his usual suit and tie.

"I'm waiting," I manage to say. I don't want him to know how he affects me, but part of me knows it's too late—he knows.

"I was only kidding," he says genuinely, and I feel bad for getting upset. "I don't know your past, so it was really arrogant of me to shove my wealth in your face."

This guy is unreal.

I jerk my arm out of his grasp and lock eyes with him. "I don't care how much money you have or lack of money I have, it doesn't make you any better than me or anyone else. And I stand by my first observation—you're an asshole."

Instead of getting angry like I had hoped, he flashes a genuine smile and places his hand on my cheek. The connection instantly sends goose bumps over my skin—suddenly making it feel cold in here, but I know it isn't. It's evident the way my body reacts to him—the dual attraction and feelings. I only wanted to flirt and mess with him, but it seems my own body has betrayed me.

"Don't go. Our lunch will be here shortly," he pleads.

His eyes go soft as he speaks. I feel paralyzed to his voice, so all I can do is nod. He grabs my hand and leads me back to the chair in front of his desk. I watch intently as he takes his seat back, and soon, we're playing a game of cat and mouse—who's going to stay away the longest and who's going to break.

If I play my cards right, he'll be the one breaking, but I have a feeling I'm no longer in control of my emotions.

CHAPTER SIX
CECILIA

THE MOOD LIGHTENS once our food arrives, and Bentley begins telling me more about the company. I ask him questions, and he happily answers them. I dig for as much information as I can—anything that will help lead me to the answers I want.

"This is starting to feel like an interrogation," he says once we've finished our food. "I think it's time for twenty questions—lightening round style."

I flash him a confused look, and he laughs. "I'm going to ask you questions as fast as I can, and you have to answer them all as fast as you can."

"That sounds painful." I giggle. "But I'll try it."

He smirks as he casually places his arms on top of his desk in front of me. "Okay, ready?"

I nod. "Bring it."

He locks eyes with me as he begins his questions. "Favorite food?"

"Italian."

"Favorite color?"

"Red."

"Favorite thing to wear to bed?"

"A tank top and shorts."

"First boyfriend's name?"

"Malcolm."

"Age when you lost your virginity?"

42

I try not to laugh at the absurd questions because he's taking this so seriously, so I match his expression. I fold my hands on top of the desk and lock eyes with him as I answer.

"Sixteen and a half."

He smirks.

"Favorite position?"

"This doesn't sound very job related."

"No breaking the rules, Ceci." Bentley rolls the sound of my name with seduction, making sure I listen to his made-up game.

I swallow.

"The roller coaster."

I read an article about it in Cosmo, and it sounds like something that'll get his attention.

And it does.

He raises an eyebrow at me, and I can tell he wants to ask me what exactly that is—because only girls really know names of positions—so I'm assuming he's clueless on what exactly I mean.

"Don't think we're not getting back to that one." He cocks a grin.

"We'll see."

He laughs.

"Worst grade you ever got?"

"B+."

"Goody-to-shoe," he jibes. I just shake my head at him.

"The most interesting place you've ever had sex before?"

I see the game he's playing. One or two innocent questions before he pops in a sexual one.

"At work."

I instantly close my eyes the second the words come out. Now he'll get ideas in his head for sure.

I hear him swallow. Hard.

I open my eyes and see he's adjusting himself. Now he's hard.

Fuck, that's hot to see Bentley all sexually frustrated. I never noticed a guy adjusting his pants as much as Bentley does, and for some reason, it turns me on.

It's hot seeing what I do to him, and suddenly my body and heart are no longer fighting. They're on the same level—matching heartbeats and sexual desires.

I grin and lean over the desk to where his hands are resting. "Are you all right over there?"

"I'd be better if I wasn't rock hard getting blue balls," he responds bluntly. I can't help but notice how thick he looks under his pants. I can feel my cheeks heat up, but I quickly remind myself I can't show him that side of me.

I keep my stance, not wanting to show how much that affects me. "Hm…I could Google some of those bikini bimbos and get their numbers. I'm sure one of them could help you out with your… um…issue."

Bentley walks around the desk and aggressively grabs my hand. "You want to feel what you do to me, Ceci?" He wraps both of our hands around his thick, growing erection. "Do you want to know what you've been doing to me since the second I first met you?"

My eyes halt on the firm bulge our hands are now grasping. I swallow in anticipation, but fear isn't too far behind. I'm not used to boys—rather men—coming onto me so strong.

"You're blunt," I blurt out.

"Well, why shouldn't I be? When I know what I want—who I want —I go for it," he says in all seriousness. My heart practically stops at his confession, I'm unsure how to handle him—if I can handle him.

Then again, I'm insanely attracted to him. I mean, who wouldn't be? And if I make a scene now—something a young, inexperienced girl would do—I'd lose any chance of coming back and finding the information that I need. I couldn't let him see that side of me.

Not that I want to make a scene, but I'll do anything to get what I need—to find the truth.

I surprise myself when I allow him to move our hands up and down his thick length. My breath hitches as I feel his shaft stretching under the heat of my hand. He's so close, making my body burn and my mind spiral out of control. I moan as our hands stroke his shaft together. He's just what I imagined—*thick and large*—larger than I've ever felt before.

"Do you feel that, Ceci?"

"Mm hmm," I moan, my eyes closing on their own accord. My entire body is trembling. My skin is covered in goose bumps, and my pussy is throbbing as I feel the fabric of his slacks around my hand.

I can feel Bentley's face close to mine. I lick my lips in anticipation, but before his mouth can meet mine, his cell phone rings, alarming both of us and making us immediately come apart.

"Fuck," he growls.

He searches for his phone in his pocket and curses again when he sees the name on the screen.

"What?" he barks. "This is not a good time."

He turns and faces the window as he shifts his pants back into place. I can tell he's trying to tame himself, and I take that as my cue to get the hell out.

I need to stay focused. On task. I'm here for one reason and one reason only.

Or so I keep telling myself.

I sit anxiously as I continue reading through open cases and scanning in transcripts. I'm not sure what I'm looking for, but when I see it, I'll know.

I feel Bentley behind me before I see him. My body instantly shivers and feels cold when he walks in. I continue what I'm doing and ignore the fact that his body continues to get closer to mine.

"I apologize for that earlier," he begins in a more natural tone. He doesn't sound as tense, but he's not demanding, either.

"It's fine." I wave him off, not turning around to look at him. "It was a weak moment. It'll never happen again."

I hope that he accepts that and walks out so I can continue reading through files.

He grabs my chair and jerks it around, so I'm forced to face him. My eyes widen on instinct as I brace myself for what's to come.

"I wasn't apologizing for that."

I look up at him, and his eyes are no longer soft. He looks angry, hungry almost.

"I was apologizing for having to take the fucking phone call."

"Oh." I sound weak, but I can't help it. I don't know what I'm supposed to say. My mind and body are at complete odds right now, and all I can think of when he stares at me like that is how good it would feel to have his hands all over me.

Shit.

Focus.

Stay focused.

"Ceci," he growls, leaning his face in closer to mine.

Fuck focused.

"I just want you to know, in case your mind is racing a thousand miles per hour like mine is—that I don't do this. I don't go around groping my interns or people I work with."

I swallow.

I know he's trying to be genuine, but I just can't take how serious he's being. It's making me uncomfortable and antsy.

"Oh, so I get to be your first?" I taunt.

He grabs me harshly and pulls me up, so we're now standing chest to chest.

"Perhaps you didn't hear me correctly," he barks. "I've never been like this with someone I work with, and definitely not someone I just met. I was trying to be nice instead of a fucking asshole and tell you so you wouldn't think I was just using you."

"Well, aren't you? I mean, for your…" I look down at his re-appearing bulge, "needs."

"I don't need interns to take care of that for me," he spits back.

"What makes you think I'm not using you? You think you're the only person capable of doing so?" I challenge, and I see the amusement in his eyes. He thinks I'm full of shit. So I continue playing. "Women like sex just as much as men do."

"Is that so?" He grins. "I have yet to meet another woman who can keep up with me."

I may not be as experienced in the world of sex, but I don't let that scare me from accepting his challenge.

"Let me be your first one."

Bentley's mouth slams to mine before I can react. Right before our lips make contact, he stares at me as if I'm his last meal. He's devouring me as such, but his hands are firm and gripping me tight. I reciprocate his moves, dancing my tongue with his, and grinding my body against his.

I can feel him growing harder and hungrier with need. I'd be lying if I said I wasn't feeling the same way. I've never been with a guy before that knew what he was doing, and I have a feeling Bentley knows exactly what he's doing.

His hands wrap around my waist as he pulls me closer to his chest. Our mouths explore each other, both fighting for the control that we crave, but I surrender and let him take the lead. My body is seizing in about a hundred places as I melt into his touch and lips. Being with a guy that I feel physically attracted to is something new, something I was oblivious to. I've liked boys before, but never felt this way and to this extent. This must be the difference between a boy and a man—Bentley gave no apologies for his domineering behavior, he took what he wanted, and I willingly gave it.

This was new, but now that I've had a taste, I was more than willing to dive in.

He quickly breaks the kiss and pants against my lips as he rests his forehead on mine. His eyes are closed, and I can tell he's having an inner battle with himself just as I am. Part Devil and Part Angel are having a full-out wrestling match in my head.

The throbbing in between my legs proves which one will eventually win. I've never felt such a desire before. It's something that's been awakened…and now it wants to be fed.

He backs away while licking his lips. He never takes his eyes off mine as he makes his way out the door and soon out of sight. I stand there wondering if that really did just happen.

Before I leave, I knock on his office door to let him know it's time for me to go.

He's sitting in his chair casually as if he's been waiting for me.

"I'm…um…heading home now. I scanned in transcripts and decoded some of the files. Perhaps you can teach me something new next week?"

I really meant it as a teaching question, but soon realize he would take it as something else.

"For the job, I mean," I clarify and he laughs.

"Absolutely. I'll teach you whatever you want to know."

"Great." I smile weakly. "Well, I'll see you—"

"Wait," he interrupts. "I set up an email account for you. In case, I need to get ahold of you before next Saturday."

He holds out a business card where he's written down the information. I walk toward him and grab it. I study it carefully and ask, "Why would you need to get ahold of me? I mean, it's not like I do any real work around here."

"That may be true, but you are scanning in files that haven't been evaluated in years. I might need some of your new, profound knowledge."

He's eyeing me carefully, and I know he's full of shit. However, I take it willingly and thank him.

"I'll see you soon, Ceci." His voice is filled with amusement, but for some reason, I don't think he's joking.

In fact, I think he's dead serious, and that scares the living shit out of me.

CHAPTER SEVEN
BENTLEY

I WAKE up Sunday morning with the taste of her still on my lips. I don't want to go another week without talking to her, so I start thinking of things I can email her.

My mind is pre-occupied the entire time I'm having brunch with my parents. It's a tradition we do every Sunday, and although it makes me feel like a child that I'm 'told' to go, I like that we make time for each other since the rest of the week is busy with work.

"So, Bentley, did you hear about the Montgomery's?" my mother asks, breaking me out of my trance.

"The Montgomery's?" I rack my brain quick. "Oh, you mean how Mrs. Montgomery smuggled millions of dollars out of the country? Of course, I heard about that." I just shrug at the story that's headlined most of the local news.

The Montgomery's are like royalty in Nebraska. Mr. Montgomery's the state senator who married a woman half his age.

"Well, anyway, sounds like they're going to brush it under the rug and keep it tight-lipped." I hear the annoyance in her tone.

"I don't doubt that. I've written a few news pieces on it, but if they'd ever get the damn police files, I could write an actual report on it. People like her shouldn't get away with shit like that."

"Enough about work, son," my father interrupts. "What's going on with your new intern? I haven't heard a thing, and it's been what...two weeks?"

I shift uncomfortably in my chair at the mention of Ceci. My mind has been wondering about her since yesterday, and she was the last thing I wanted to talk about with my parents.

"Ah, it's working out great, I guess." I try to sound casual, so they don't suspect anything. "I've been showing her how to use the software, scanning in documents, reading transcripts, and teaching her the basics. It's only been a couple weeks, so as time goes on, I'll teach her more," I reply honestly, because there's a lot more I want to teach her.

"Excellent." He smiles wide. If there were one plus to this whole being forced to work in your family's company, it was seeing him proud of me. I love knowing he's happy with my work. "I knew you'd figure out how to train someone underneath you."

I grin to myself as I imagine her underneath me.

After the not-so-brutal brunch with my parents, I head back home and pace the living room until I finally build up the nerve to email her.

To: cwest@leighton.com
From: bleighton@leighton.com
Subject: Company Policy

Ceci,
I apologize for interrupting your Sunday. I forgot to give you the necessary paperwork while you were here. It's company policy that I give you these.
Attached below is the company handbook. Please look it over.

Mr. Leighton

I don't know why I'm so eager for her to respond, but it'll make me think she's thinking of me as much as I'm thinking of her. After our kiss, my entire body has been tense, and all I want is to feel her lips against mine again.

My phone beeps signaling I have a new email.

To: bleighton@leighton.com
From: cwest@leighton.com
Subject: Re: Company Policy?

Mr. Leighton,
Do you ever take a day off?
I've been there two Saturday's now.
Ironic how you forgot.
I will familiarize myself with the company handbook right away.

Ceci

I smirk as I read her email at least three times. Such a cocky-mouthed, smart ass. And I love it. She's not intimidated by me, yet she has to submit to my demands in order to keep her internship.
And that is driving me fucking insane.
I want any excuse to keep talking to her, but I know I have to keep my distance before I become too obvious.
Oh, fuck it.

To: cwest@leighton.com
From: bleighton@leighton.com
Subject: Re: Company Policy?

Yes, I'm aware. I was a bit distracted.

Mr. Leighton

It's a risky move, but I hope she gets what I'm saying. And now my cock wakes up, begging for attention as I think of Ceci and the way she teases me without even knowing it—or perhaps she does.
I need to do something to get her off my mind. Anything.
I grab my gym bag and decide to go for a work out. Lifting and burning my sexual frustrations off will give me a clear head. Yes, that'll work.
And then my phone beeps again.

To: bleighton@leighton.com
From: cwest@leighton.com
Subject: Re: Re: Company Policy?

I noticed.
Enjoy your day, Mr. Leighton.

Ceci

I smile as I hear her seductive voice although her email reads so professionally. I don't know why I read her email over and over as if there's some secret code I'm searching for, but I do.

I work out harder than I have in weeks. I run myself until my legs feel like jelly. I lift until I can no longer lift. I completely sweat through my shirt before leaving. And my mind is still running of thoughts of her...except, now it's worse. The sound of her voice, the way her shapely legs walk in that skirt, the way her fingers carelessly brush *against me*—it's all too consuming, and I have no idea why.

By Wednesday, my mind hasn't cleared at all. If anything, it's even more clogged than before, and I come to the conclusion that I need to see her and know more about her. I don't care what it takes.

My condo is twenty minutes from work, and by the time I arrive at my office, I've already called in a favor—my secret weapon to seeing Ceci.

To: cwest@leighton.com
From: bleighton@leighton.com
Subject: Invitation

Ceci,
There's a criminology presentation with special guest speakers taking place at the Windhover Center tomorrow evening that I think will benefit you greatly in your major and the internship. I have a ticket for you.
It starts at 7PM.

Bentley

I decide to sign as Bentley—hoping she notices the transition from boss to date.

I grin as I hit the send button. I don't want it to be obvious that this is my way of seeing her again, but if I request her presence for learning purposes, there's a better chance of her coming. I can tell how much passion and interest she has in criminology, so it's my best bet of seeing her outside of work.

I wait impatiently until I hear the sound of a new message.

To: bleighton@leighton.com
From: cwest@leighton.com
Subject: Re: Invitation

Bentley,
Thank you so much for thinking of me. Sounds like something I'd greatly benefit from. Please have the ticket waiting for me at check in.

Ceci

She's either extremely naïve or playing hard to get. Either way, I'm going to play.

CHAPTER EIGHT
CECILIA

I IMMEDIATELY GET ONLINE to look up tomorrow's presentation. My eyes bulge out of my head as I see it's for elite members only. Bentley must've pulled some strings to get me that ticket.

I rub my shoulder anxiously as I wait for the response of his email. I can't understand why he's going through so much trouble for me, unless he truly believes in me enough to give me this chance and opportunity to learn more from him, which in that case, makes him about a hundred times hotter than he is already. I've never met someone like him—someone so intimidating, yet weak. Perhaps he's just weak when he's around me, but if that's the case, that's exactly the angle I need to get into the files of my dad's case.

I sit nervously in my last class waiting for my phone to vibrate with a new message. And then finally, it does.

To: cwest@leighton.com
From: bleighton@leighton.com
Subject: Re: Re: Invitation

You'll be accompanying me, Ceci.
Meet me at Sebastian's Steakhouse at 5PM.

Bentley

Holy shit.

Now we're going to dinner first? This guy was horrible at asking for things. Instead, he took them...no...he *demanded* them.

I clench my thighs together at just the thought of being alone with him in a restaurant. Sebastian's was a fancier restaurant—much more romantic than a boss-intern dinner should be.

My mind floods with nerves as I anticipate seeing Bentley again— outside of work this time. Bentley wasn't a boy. He's a man. An older man who could make or break me. A man who could give me everything and more. A man I could see myself falling hard for.

I could barely focus on Simon as we hung out the following day. He ranted for hours about Cora and how could she hook up with Lance, and blah blah. Like I said, I couldn't focus and really have no idea what he said.

My mind and body were still in an aftershock from the events of kissing Bentley. The more I thought about it, the more I wanted more of it. I didn't care how wrong it was or that I was lying to him about who I was. I didn't want to let that get in the way of being around him. Even if it could come back to bite me in the ass.

"Why are you so giddy?" Cora asks me in between class periods.

"I'm not giddy," I retort. "I'm always this way."

She looks down at my books and takes notice of the newest Cosmo magazine lying on top.

"You are so not always this way, Cecelia Rose West. Something is up with you." She eyes me curiously, and I can't stop the stupid grin from forming on my face.

"Okay, fine. I met a guy. And we're going out tonight for the first time," I blurt out, and it feels so good to get that off my chest.

She screeches to a halt. "WHAT?"

I decide to leave out that it's with my boss where I'm working on a fake internship.

"Tone it down, Cora," I hush at her. I bump my hip with hers to get her to cool it. "It's not that big of a deal," I lie. Inside I was screaming.

"This is a huge deal." She links her arm with mine as we continue walking. "Give me the details, right now, woman."

"Well, he's older, so that's why I haven't said much. And it's new and weird and—"

"Hot?" she finishes, raising her eyebrows.

I laugh as she teases me. "Yes, he's hot. The kiss was pretty hot, too."

"Damn girl. You are smitten."

"I am so not smitten. Have you ever seen me smitten?"

"Nope, that's exactly how I know that you are. You have never been this way with guys before."

"That's because guys our age are immature and annoying. There was nothing to be smitten about," I joke.

"So true," she breathes out and laughs.

"I'll tell you more later," I promise, because I know she's going to beg for answers. And I usually tell Cora everything, so she knows I'll come clean eventually. I just need to make sure to cover my bases, so I don't get either of us in trouble for lying.

I can't stop the smiling, as I get dressed and ready for my 'work' event tonight. I find a classy but simple black dress in my sister's closet with some red heels, making my whole outfit pop. I don't want to be over-dressed or look like I'm trying too hard, but I want to look good for Bentley.

I'm sweating as I drive anxiously. I arrive at the steakhouse promptly at four-fifty p.m. Being around him at work is different. It's business. But now, this feels much more intimate. We're going to be in a date-type setting and the butterflies in my stomach won't quit. I'm obviously attracted to him, but the part of me that wants to let go and let him in is fighting against bricks to keep him away. Deep down, I know it's a bad idea, but my body doesn't agree. My body craves every inch of him.

I tell the host who I am and that I'm waiting for Mr. Leighton. He gives me a head nod as he grabs a menu and says, "This way, Miss West."

I nervously follow behind him taking in the setting. The lights are dim, and every table is full of couples sitting in a very close, intimate way with candles lit in the middle.

It feels as if I've lost my voice as I thank the host for escorting me to my table where Bentley is patiently waiting for me. His face is intense, barely showing any emotion.

I swallow nervously as I eye him. The host goes to slide my chair out, but Bentley stops him.

"I'll do that." He stands up quickly, and the host backs away.

Bentley doesn't say a word to me as he grabs my chair and motions for me to sit down.

The host places my menu in front of me, and I quietly thank him again.

In the office—work setting—I feel confident and invincible. But not here. I feel intimidated, weak, and hopeless.

"You look beautiful," he finally says sitting casually across from me.

"Thanks." I gulp as I take in his intense stare. He's eyeing me, not giving any part of what he's thinking away. "This place is really nice." I try to make conversation in order to ease my nerves, but the still way he's sitting and staring at me is putting me on edge.

"Have you never been here before?" he asks with amusement.

This was a five-star, top-notch restaurant that took weeks to get reservations for—certainly, something not a typical college-aged student has ever been to.

Rather, I shrug off his amusement and try to relax. "Oh, sure. I come here whenever I feel the need to drop a few hundred."

That earns a small grin and finally, my body eases into the chair.

"Only a few hundred?" he muses. "Clearly, you aren't ordering the right wine then."

My heart stops as I realize he's going to want to order alcohol. I don't have Casey's ID with me...*shit shit shit*...how could I not think of that?

I laugh, so he doesn't see my mini heart-attack. "I guess so."

"Are you excited for tonight's presentation?"

My eyes widen as he brings up lighter conversation about something that makes me more comfortable. "Yes, absolutely! You must've had to pull some mad strings to get those tickets," I gush.

"I have a friend," he responds casually and shrugs as if it's no big deal.

"A friend who apparently can pull some strings." I grin.

He flashes a cocky smirk. "Something like that."

I feel like an idiot as it finally registers in my mind. He's fucking Bentley Leighton. He probably gets whatever he wants whenever he wants it.

And that should scare the hell out of me.

The power he has...holds...controls. A sudden chill radiates my body as I think about what I'm doing—what game I'm playing.

I grab my menu and stare at it intently to get my mind to calm down. He sits with one leg propped up on his knee as his body is angled toward mine. He probably comes here so much he has the damn thing memorized.

"So what's good?" I ask simply smiling at him over my menu. He's watching me as if he's waiting for something magical to happen.

"Everything, of course." He grins and then it hits me.

"Let me guess. You own this place. Or your family does? Or a friend of the family?"

He laughs lightly and shakes his head no. "You have six food options plus the couple of specials they offer. So really…everything is good here."

I was staring so hard at the menu to distract myself that I hadn't even realized. He's right—there are literally six things to choose from, what the hell? This is the weirdest restaurant I've ever been to before.

"A little different than my McDonald's tradition," I joke as if I live on a college student's salary.

He doesn't even crack a smile, and I see his mind spinning as he eyes me with concern.

"I'm kidding," I finally say. His face relaxes a bit, but it's still tense. "It's between that and ramen noodles." I cock a smile, so he finally loosens up.

"That makes me feel a whole lot better."

"Oh, come on. That's like the college lifestyle." I smile and finally feel comfortable with our easy-going banter. "Well, for poor students," I add getting him to laugh.

"I guess I deserved that."

I smirk and shrug unapologetically. A waiter greets us finally, and before he can ask us our order, Bentley rambles off some kind of bottle of wine. I'm fully ready to turn down the offer and tell him I don't drink as he asks for ID, but he never does. He simply nods and accepts every word Bentley says.

"I think you'll enjoy the house steak with the red wine."

"Sounds good."

I rest my menu down as the waiter soaks up every word and says he'll be right back with our wine and bread.

He grabs our menus and walks away, leaving me alone with Bentley with nothing to hide behind.

"So, um, do you go to these presentations often?" I cross my legs and keep my eyes locked on his. I have to take back the control. I can't let myself be intimidated by him.

He waves his head back and forth before answering. "No, not really. I did in college, but not since I've started at the company."

"Well, what should I expect?"

"You should expect to see a lot of old men."

I burst out in a laugh. "Is that so?"

"Nah, just kidding. There might be some college-aged and some professors."

"Well, I'm intrigued. I'll take any opportunity to learn more."

"I can teach you anything, Ceci." His voice is low and deep as if he's completely serious. "Anything you want to know about journalism and criminology—consider me your endless source of information," he continues genuinely. I see the confidence in him, and I know his words have a double meaning.

"You're pretty egotistical for a guy that just graduated a couple years ago."

"I prefer confident." He grins.

"I bet you do." I try my best to hide my smile, but he notices.

The waiter returns with our bottle of wine. I watch as he pours my glass first and then turns to pour Bentley's. He stands and waits as Bentley sips it before giving the waiter a nod of approval.

"I'm guessing you don't drink wine much." He held his glass up and swirls it.

"I love how you have me pegged with barely knowing me," I say sardonically.

"Well…college honor student, works for free on the weekends, lives off ramen noodles. I'm guessing you're the typical poor college student —you study too much to work and seeing that you work for free on Saturdays and study all week, you have no life outside of college, which means you don't have a boyfriend. Or any that know how to take you out."

"Hmm…very observant." I grab my glass and close my eyes as I inhale the scent. I swirl it before bringing my lips to the glass and taking a sip. I moan out slowly as I enjoy the taste burning down my throat.

"Jesus…" I hear him growl before opening my eyes. His face is pale, but his eyes are wide and hungry with need. "Or you have dated a winemaker," he jokes.

"I saw that in a movie once," I say honestly, laughing. "I've always wanted to try it."

The corners of his lips curl up in a smile.

"What?" I ask feeling self-conscious as his continuous stare becomes more intense.

"There's just something about you, Ceci. You're bold and fearless, yet there's such an adolescent side to you that makes you adorable." He's playing with his glass as if he's nervous about being honest with me.

"Adolescent side? Are you calling me a baby?" I tease.

"Well, if baby's what you like to be called." He places his foot on the ground and sits up leaning closer into the table and bringing his face closer to mine. "Otherwise, there's plenty of other names I can call you," he threatens in a teasing tone.

I swallow and smile at his flirty attempt. "Is that normal for a boss to call an intern?"

"No." He doesn't move.

"Breaking your own rules?" I lean in toward him challenging him to his own game.

"What rules?" His eyes give me a questioning look.

I get lost in Bentley's face and start studying the curves of his features. His hair is brushed back slightly—purposely messy, as his groomed beard is perfect in length. His sideburns are thicker and run into his facial hair. I imagine my fingers intertwining in his golden locks as he wraps me up in his arms assaulting my lips as our tongues tango together.

"Ceci?" His deep, pained voice shakes me out of my fantasy.

I clear my throat before speaking. "The company handbook," I remind him. "Any relationships formed within the office are strictly forbidden," I quote right from the handbook that he emailed me.

His lips form a cocky grin as he shifts in his chair. "You read the company handbook, did you?" he asks surprised.

"Well, it's company policy," I quip.

"So you aren't a rule breaker?" I can tell he's testing me, but I know what he really wants to know—am I willing to break the rules for him.

"You've seen my portfolio. Does it say I am?" I ask with seduction laced in my voice.

"It says you're a fast learner and that you're willing to learn new things."

"That I am." I wink, and I can tell I just gave him the green light.

CHAPTER NINE
BENTLEY

WATCHING her squirm is one of the hottest things I've ever seen. She acts so confident and cocky on the outside, but on the inside, she's a timid girl not wanting to show her true self to anyone. She's hiding something.

Once our meal arrives, she relaxes a bit. Her open, edgy, carefree attitude returns as we ease into simple conversation. She continues to ask me about my work and favorite cases I've worked on, and I ask her about her family and classes.

"What happened to your dad?" I ask as I cut into my steak.

She fidgets a little before responding. "He, um, left when I was eleven years old. I haven't seen him since." Her eyes are glued to her plate, and I know I've hit a sore topic.

"I'm sorry." Instinctively I reach across the table and grab her hand. "You don't have to talk about it."

She finally looks up and smiles weakly. "There's not much to say." She shrugs.

I continue holding her hand and rub my thumb over hers in comfort. It seems to help, and she relaxes again.

I take care of the check and escort her out of the restaurant. She begins fidgeting in her purse and asks, "Should I just follow you?"

I grab her hand to stop her from searching for her keys. "No, I'm driving."

I want Ceci next to me for as long as I can get. A part of me knows she's too good for me. She's smart, funny, and I can tell she's a genuinely good person. But the other part is too selfish to back off. I want her.

"All right," she says letting me grab her hand and hold it as I lead her to my car. Her small hand fits perfectly in mine, and I'm already dreading having to let it go. "You drive? I'd figure you'd have a 24/7 chauffeur."

I guide us to her side of the car and back her up into the door without opening it. "Do you even know what kind of car this is?"

She glances over her shoulder and looks. "A black one."

I smirk at her innocence. "It's a Range Rover 4th Edition. No way in hell I'd let someone else drive that."

She looks over one more time before speaking. "Looks roomy."

"You want to see how much room there is?"

"I assume you paid extra for that." She grins confidently. "The extra-large package."

I can feel the intense heat between us and know she feels it, too. Her skin pricks in goose bumps every time I touch her, and she's arching her hips toward me, begging for me to press my body against hers.

"Okay...you've gotten enough money jabs at me for one night, don't you think?"

She pulls her lips in as if she's thinking hard about it. "I may or may not have a few more," she challenges.

"I guess I'm going to have to find a way to shut that pretty mouth up." I lean into her body like she's secretly begging me to, resting one hand behind her and one hand around her waist.

"That's a very backward compliment," she breathes out, and I can tell she's fighting an inner battle with herself, which, if I do this right, she'll soon be losing.

"Backward? Are we talking positions already? Because we have yet to go back to that roller coaster comment." I lean my body into hers only holding us up with my hand behind her. Her body stills as she sucks in a breath. She's focusing on my chest, and I can't tear my eyes away from her mouth.

She arches her hips into me and feels the hard bulge now formed. She gasps lightly as her body squirms to start a rhythm with mine.

"Ceci," I growl, tilting her chin up to make eye contact with me. Her expression isn't fear, but desire, and I can tell she's feeling the same way I am—desperate and hungry for more. I lean in and bring my lips to her ear. "As much as I want to fuck you against this car, I promised you a presentation tonight."

I lean back and kiss the corners of her mouth. She simply nods, and reluctantly, I pull away to grab the door and escort her into her seat.

As soon as I begin driving, I grab her hand and place it in mine. She rests it on my leg, which is probably the worst fucking spot for any contact.

The drive is comfortable and quiet as we listen to music. I watch her out of the corner of my eye and see her sinking into the seat as she patiently waits for us to get to our destination.

Walking in with a beautiful girl like Ceci doesn't go unnoticed by the rest of the men sitting nearby. They're like vultures ready to jump on their prey and rip her apart for themselves.

I rest one ankle on my knee as I wrap my arm around her, claiming her. I dip my face into her neck and whisper, "You better stay close before you are eaten alive by the rest of the audience."

Before I pull back, she turns her head and responds, "Maybe I like being eaten alive." She cocks a smile.

My head falls back as I groan. "You're killing me," I growl close to her ear. "I'm going to sit here the entire time with a hard on."

Her eyes immediately go to the noticeable tent in my pants, and she laughs. "It must suck to be a guy," she teases.

"You think you're the only one that can play this game?" I breathe into her ear, and she shivers against me. "That's what I thought."

The lights dim as the speaker walks on stage, welcoming and thanking everyone for coming. Luckily, no one is sitting close to us, giving me a green light for what I'm about to do. I casually move my arm and lay it against her bare thigh. I squeeze tightly as my fingers inch up her leg, pushing her dress up with them. I can tell how aroused she is from the way she squirms under my hand. Heat radiates between her legs as my fingers continue rubbing against her.

Her hand grabs mine as she tries to force it off her leg. She barely has any strength against my hand, and it's comical as I watch her try. "What's the matter, sweetheart?" I whisper, letting my tongue vibrate against her ear. "You think it's funny now?"

I slip my pinky inside the lace of her underwear and her breath catches. She sinks lower into her seat, no longer fighting me. Another finger slips in and pushes her panties out of the way.

I lean in as I whisper, "Tell me to stop, Ceci. If this breaks your rules, tell me to stop."

Her eyes are closed, and I can tell she's fighting with herself to say the words. Her mouth parts slightly as she sharply inhales. I work my fingers harder against her, making sure that I'm not obvious as to what I'm doing to the people behind us, but that only gets me harder knowing we're in a public place.

"Bentley," she finally breathes out. Her tiny voice whimpering my name just about makes me come undone. I'm ready to sweep her out of here and fuck her against the nearest wall.

I feel her body tense up, ready to explode around my fingers. I bring my lips back to her ear as I aggressively pull my fingers out. "I want to hear you scream my name when you come...so until then, you'll have to wait." Her eyes flash open as she intently stares me down, obviously shocked by my quick exit. "Now we both suffer in sexual frustration."

"That's cruel," she spits out in a hushed tone.

"No, sweetheart. What's cruel is getting me all worked up with no outlet." I kiss her cheek softly. "You'll be paying for that later."

I feel her shiver under me, and I know she wants it as badly as I do. But the anticipation is killing me. Knowing she's interning for another three months puts me in a really hard position.

I watch as Ceci is completely captivated by the speaker and their presentations. It's everything I already know and have learned from working the past couple years. He speaks about past case studies, cold cases, and some of the big headliners that roamed Nebraska.

"One of the biggest unsolved murder mysteries in Nebraska is from Omaha seven years ago. An All-American father and husband was gunned down outside his home on a summer day in broad daylight, yet the evidence never matched up to find the shooter."

I hear Ceci's breath catch as she inhales sharply. Her hand covers her mouth and her eyes are glued to the speaker on stage.

"You okay?" I lean in and ask curiously, oblivious as to why she has this kind of reaction.

She immediately drops her hand and nods her head. "Yeah, fine. I just...I think I heard about this one before."

"Yeah, it was pretty big news in Nebraska for a long time. My dad worked night and day on that case."

She turns and faces me, and her expression is unreadable. "Really?" She swallows.

"Yeah, almost killed him to write that final report."

"What was that?" she quickly asks.

"That the cops were calling it a cold case. No suspects. No witnesses. Little to no evidence."

"Are you all right? You look flushed."

"Um, yeah. Just tired. Would it be okay to leave early?"

I lean in happily and answer, "I was ready to leave fifty-five minutes ago."

She lets out a small laugh. "It's only been an hour."

I smile back. "Exactly."

I grab her hand and lead her out the back without disturbing anyone. What I want and what I should do are two different things, because right now, I want to take her to my house and fuck her six ways to Sunday. But what I should do is drop her off at her car and kiss her goodnight.

My cock agrees with the first.

"Thank you," she begins as we sit in the car outside of the restaurant where her car is parked. I can tell that she's still upset about something as she fiddles with her fingers in her lap. She nervously continues, "I appreciate you letting me tag along for the presentation."

I lean over and grab her face, tilting her chin up so she'll finally look at me. I close the gap between us and kiss her softly on the lips. I feel her body relax against mine as I wrap an arm around her waist. I so badly want to roam my fingers across her skin and through her hair, but I don't. I can tell her mood has changed since we left, and the last thing I want to do is push her.

"You didn't tag along," I say as I lean my forehead against hers. I move my head back so I can look directly in her eyes. "And it was my pleasure, Ceci."

I sit back in my seat and let myself out of the car. I close my eyes briefly as I fight with myself before opening her door. I want to slam her body against mine and beg her to stay the night with me, but something in me stops the words from coming out.

I grab her hand and escort her out, shutting the door behind her. She leans against the car in a way that tells me she's battling with it, as well. I stand, so she's in between my legs and wrap both arms around her waist. I pull her in closer, so our lips are just barely touching. Her body is still but relaxed as she places her hands on each of my arms.

"Do you work out, like 24/7? Isn't this like abnormally muscly?" Her light tone shows me that she's back to herself, and I laugh at her sudden change of topic.

"Muscly?"

"Yeah...I've never seen a guy with arms like this."

I shake my head as I try to hold in the laugh that's threatening to escape. "I fear for your lack of ex-boyfriends. Not only did they serve you ramen noodles and cheap wine, they didn't even bother to work out for their girl."

Her head falls back as she laughs whole-heartedly. I'd do anything to bottle up that laugh—it drives me fucking mad.

"You sure are a cocky son-of-a-bitch. What if I like puny guys who make ramen noodles and poor guys that can only afford cheap wine? See...you aren't my type at all," she muses.

I press my body into hers to show her how wrong she is. My cock is firm against her, and I know she feels it. I dip my head into the nape of her neck and kiss lightly all the way up to her ear.

"You lie," I whisper. "You haven't stopped eye-fucking me since the day you met me. Every time I'm near you, your body is begging for my attention. Say it," I demand.

She whimpers against me, not saying or denying it. I know she's holding it in. She wants to let go. I just have to convince her it's okay to give in to what she wants.

"I said say it, Ceci." My mouth wraps around the lobe of her ear, and she moans against me. Her body becomes limp under my lips, and it's just a matter of seconds before she comes undone.

I slowly kiss up her jaw as I tilt her head back. She arches her body for me, giving away how badly she wants it, how badly she's willing to take whatever I have to offer.

"I want to hear you scream my name, Ceci. I want your sexy, little legs wrapped around me so tight that you'll have no choice but to let go as I press hard into you."

Her body is trembling against me with each word I whisper, and I know it's not because of the chilly weather—her body craves the exact thing mine does.

"Bentley," she finally whimpers. "God...yes..."

I pull on her arms and yank her body into mine. "Yes, what, sweetheart? I'm going to need you to say it," I command.

She flutters her eyes back open and stares intently into mine as she says, "Yes, I want you."

CHAPTER TEN
CECILIA

I IGNORE every alarm going off in my head as Bentley speeds to his place. He had me dripping wet against his car. I can't even imagine what he's going to be doing once we're behind closed doors.

I struggle to fight with my head, and my heart—Part Angel and Part Devil are screaming at me, and all I can think of is how good it feels to have Bentley's mouth and body on me and how much I want more.

I hardly pay attention to where we're going and soon realize Bentley is parking in his garage. He quickly gets out and opens my door, grabbing my hand eagerly and pulling me out.

He barely yanks the keys out of the lock before slamming me into the wall, pressing us firmly against it.

"I hope you aren't disappointed if we skip the tour." I feel him grin as his lips run up and down my neck. I shiver under his touch, and then respond with a mumbled moan.

He shimmies my jacket off and aggressively grabs around my thighs, wrapping them around his waist and holding us up against the wall.

He presses hard into me as our mouths attack each other, roaming hands and tongues begging for control. I can feel how hard and thick he is under his pants. It ignites an electric charge within me, making me realize what I'm about to do.

Meeting Bentley has awakened something inside me. Rather, it is Bentley who is the reason I want—need—this. My body feels as if it's on fire as I crave every part of him. I want him inside me—teasing and torturing me. I want his mouth on my skin, kissing every bruised and broken memory. I want him more than I ever thought I needed someone.

"Bentley," I breathe out. "I want you," I confess. "So fucking bad."

"Do you have any idea what you just said? What you just told me?" he growls as he presses his hard-on deeper against me.

"Well, I hope it translated to that I want you to fuck me...*now*."

He pushes us off the wall and starts walking us down a hallway. His lips never leave my body—moving from my ear, neck, and mouth—he's devouring me.

"I hope you don't have a close attachment to these panties." He lays me on top of his bed. Before I can slide them off he rips my panties in two. My legs are lying loosely off the bed, and his body is in between them kissing up one leg.

"No, they were from an ex-boyfriend anyway," I lie humorously, but he doesn't laugh.

Bentley's head jerks up, and his body is suddenly pressed on top of mine. "Are you trying to piss me off? Because if that's the kind of guy you like, you just say the word, sweetheart. I can do this sweet or I can do this rough. Say the word," he threatens.

"We need to work on your sense of humor."

"I don't ever want to hear about another guy fucking you, understand? As far as I'm concerned, there was never another guy before me. I'll make sure to erase any memory of them—that I *promise* you."

If he only knew that isn't going to be much of an issue, but I can't let him know I've only had sex with two guys before him. They weren't well-experienced or memorable. So as far as I'm concerned, Bentley's the only one that matters anyway.

I reach for his shirt and begin unbuttoning it, no longer wanting to have this conversation—or talk at all, for that matter. My body is burning with anticipation, and I'm done waiting. I take in his tattoos that appear perfect on his skin. They are amazingly detailed, inked into his raw flesh.

He firmly grabs my wrist, taking me by surprise, as he jerks my body up to level our faces. His eyes are dark, and his voice is deep as he says, "Do we have an understanding, Ceci?"

There's no humor in his tone, and I know he's dead serious. "Yes. I understand."

"Good girl." He kneels between my legs and continues, "Now lay back. Put your arms above your head and spread your legs. I want to see all of you."

I nervously do as he says. I've never been told what to do before, but I'm positive I like it. In fact, I love it. The way his mouth demands me—intensifies the fire within me even more.

His hands are loosely roaming up my thighs as they make their way under my dress, pulling it up with his hands. His head dips down to my stomach, feathering kisses against my heated skin. I'm dying with anticipation as his tongue teases and tortures me.

I'm desperate to put my hands through his messy locks, but I know he'll stop if I do—and that's the last fucking thing I want him to do.

"You taste more incredible than I imagined," he moans as his mouth lifts up briefly to push my dress all the way off my body.

"You've been imagining, have you?" My voice is laced with amusement hoping he'll play along. I need to get my confidence back, but his lips on my naked flesh are making that pretty damn hard.

"You have no idea," he growls. "My cock's been hard for weeks."

I giggle at the image. "Perhaps you need to see a doctor."

He aggressively yanks my bra down and pulls my nipple into his mouth. All humor gone.

My body arches to greet his mouth. His free hand begins rubbing my clit as his tongue sucks my breast hard. The double sensation is overwhelming, and I can no longer control my breathing or the excessive moans releasing from my throat.

"You keep moaning like that and I'm going to come a lot sooner than I want, sweetheart."

"Then stop torturing me already."

He plunges two fingers deep inside me. My body convulses on impact as he drives further inside me.

I let out a puff of air as I try to even my breathing. He's relentless in pleasure-torturing my clit and nipple at the same time. I'm not used to the invasive pleasure, my body unfamiliar with the contact. I'm trying to hold in the screams that desperately need to come out.

"Release," he demands. "I want to hear you and feel you at the same time." His voice is seductive as he mouths my other breast and works it in the same fashion as the first—aggressive and eager.

My body unhinges, arching more and shaking harder. His fingers work inside me harder as I peek into an intense orgasm. My hands flock to his head, pulling and squeezing his locks.

"Oh my," I breathe out. "God!"

My body lays flat on the bed again as he pulls his fingers out and releases my breast. He's hovering directly on top of me, and I can feel his heavy breathing on my face.

Hesitantly, I open my eyes and look up at him. His face is intense, and I know he's feeling the same thing I am—passion and lust.

Slowly, he brings his mouth down on mine and genuinely kisses me. It's slow and controlled as if he's asking permission, easing me into what's about to occur.

His hand cups my cheek, his thumb rubbing softly against my skin. It's a sweet and caring gesture. My eyes snap open as I see the power he's taking over me. He knows I want it. I know he wants it. This isn't supposed to turn into something more than that.

I push hard against his chest and force him on his back. I straddle his waist and grab his wrists in my hands.

"I don't want you to make love to me, Bentley." I can see the conflicted expression in his face. "I want you to take me as I am. Fuck me, but don't make love to me," I warn.

I release the grip on his wrists, and his hands immediately grab my hips. He forces my hips to grind against his cock that's rock hard against his pants.

"If you keep talking like that I'm not going to make it that far."

I smirk. "Then. Take. Off. Your. Fucking. Pants."

I roll off his body and watch as he stands up next to the bed. I lay back casually on the bed as he removes the rest of his clothing. My eyes wander up and down his chiseled chest, admiring his tattoos and muscles again. His arms are definitely built, but the pictures don't do his body justice. His tattoos are the first thing I notice along with the V that goes from his hips down to his legs. He's fucking breathtaking, and I'm completely mesmerized by him.

"You're staring."

"You have a lot to stare at."

He looks down at his fully erected cock with a smug grin. "Then by all means, stare away."

"Did they even have to Photoshop your pictures in the magazines? I mean, seriously?"

He lets out a light laugh as he shakes his head as if he's embarrassed. "You're a grade-A detective, aren't you?"

I shrug unapologetically. "It's not the first time I've been told that." And it wasn't. I was always good at finding out the information I needed. And I was hoping that snooping around Leighton Enterprises wouldn't be any different.

"Is that right?" he asks as he begins crawling on the bed and right over my body. I lean back as his body presses into me. I can feel his hard cock pressed against my thigh and then up against my pelvis, begging for entrance.

I panic as I soon realize he's not wearing a condom. "You should know I'm not on birth control," I blurt out and my eyes immediately shut tight with embarrassment. I can't even believe I just said that.

His head falls loosely on my chest in surrender. "Seriously?"

"Sorry," I say softly. This is so embarrassing.

He brings his head up and smirks at me. He lays a playful kiss on my lips. "So you're saying all this time you've been using condoms without any other protection?"

If I were a twenty-one-year-old college girl, hell yeah, I'd be on birth control. But I wasn't. I had just turned eighteen, and there was no way I was going to have that conversation with my mother. I had planned on going to the clinic to get on the pill before I left for college.

"Yeah, my mom—" oh shit, shit, shit.

Fuck me.

"My mom," I continue as I try to think of something to save my slip up. "Never allowed it while I was on her insurance. But I just got my own, actually, so it was on my to-do list." He looks at me as if I have a third eye. "And now you think I'm crazy."

He laughs. "No, not at all. I was just thinking I better start buying condoms in bulk." He flashes one of his infamous smug grins.

"You are overly-confident."

"And you are overly-cocky. Sounds like we're a match made in Heaven," he jibes.

I begin laughing but am soon gasping as he drives inside me suddenly—with no fucking warning.

Bentley pushes through my tight walls. Inch by inch, his thickness breaks through, and suddenly, my body relaxes giving into exactly what I want.

"Shit," he growls. My back arches to push him further inside me, but he pulls back out and drives back in again. "Fuck, Ceci. You're so tight. I want to fuck you, so bad…you have no idea."

"I-I think I can feel how bad," I pant out. My arms wrap around his neck pleadingly, not wanting him to stop.

"That's a problem, Ceci. I need to get a condom on."

I watch as he walks to his dresser and quickly grabs one from the drawer. He smoothly rolls it on. I enjoy the view again as I take in his rock hard body and messy golden locks. He looks like more of a rocker than a CEO's son, and I think that's what I like best about him. He's not what you'd think he'd be—he's better.

He strides over to the bed and clasps my hands, pulling me close so we're chest to chest. He looks into my eyes, and I swallow as I take in his intense stare.

"Ceci…" he says slowly. "I want to be able to feel you, all of you…" One of his hands slides down and grips my waist. "I want to be able to fuck you anytime, anywhere, and I want to be able to feel you throbbing directly against me…"

I nod in understanding and he grips me a little tighter. I feel his hot breath vibrate against my flushed skin. I can hardly concentrate on my own breathing as I take in every soft gasp that escapes him.

He brings his face to mine and gently kisses the corners of my mouth. It's sweet and soft, and soon I'm lost in his touch again.

It doesn't last long. He whips my body around, so I'm facing away from him.

"Bend over and spread your legs," he growls in my ear.

I do as he says, clenching my hands to the mattress. He grasps my hips as he plunges back inside me. I gasp at the contact, clenching the sheets in my fists. It takes a moment for my body to stretch open for him as he fills me again, inch by inch.

Once he's fully inside, he controls the rhythm—rocking my hips against him harder and harder. I moan and whimper as he goes from fast to slow and slow to fast. He's filling me completely, stretching my walls with every demanding thrust.

"Mm, yes, Ceci…" he moans, as he's close to his release. I can feel it because he tenses up as he controls the movements. I open my legs wider to give him better access. It feels so damn good. I'd do anything for him not to stop. The rhythm, the pace, the way his head slams against my g-spot has me going over the edge.

"Oh my God…oh God…*yes*…" I moan over and over. "Just like

that…yes." I clench my eyes tighter as I feel my climax approaching. He slams into me harder as he feels my body react.

He leans over me, wrapping an arm around my stomach. His other hand goes to my clit as he begins rubbing relentlessly with each thrust. "I want to hear you scream my name, Ceci," he demands.

I can't focus on much as his body is pressed against mine, and his fingers are working my clit. He shifts in deeper, taking me over the edge for several seconds.

"Oh, God…Bentley…yes…" I pant and moan at the same time. He doesn't slow down. He continues harder as another one builds up inside me. "Fuck, Bentley…oh, God…" I can barely make a coherent thought, nevertheless a coherent sentence.

"That's my girl…" he whispers in my ear as he waits for my breathing to calm down.

He backs off me and pulls out without his own release. He twirls me back around to face him and slowly drops me on the bed. He bends to his knees and spreads my legs. He brings his mouth in between my legs, licking and sucking up my juices. His tongue plunges hard inside of me hitting my sensitive spot. I can hardly take it as I've barely come down from the first two.

I grab fistfuls of his hair to stop him, but it only makes him work harder. He grabs both my wrists and pins them to the mattress all while his tongue continues its tortuous play.

"Bentley…stop," I beg. "I can't take it." He shakes his head, and I know I'm fighting a losing battle. "Ah, God. Ah, Bentley. Yes…oh my God!" I scream with no embarrassment or shyness. He licks and sucks up my climax once again. My body is shaking from the hardest orgasm I've ever had.

"My name sounds good on your lips," he muses as he finally rises and towers over me.

I swallow as I even my breathing. "That was…intense."

He grins as he grabs both of my legs and places them on his shoulder. "Don't surrender on me now, Ceci. You had no idea what you were getting yourself into." He winks as he positions himself over me with both of my feet in the air.

I chuckle as he plunges back inside me. "I use to be in gymnastics, Mr. Leighton. There isn't a position I haven't done." His eyes widen. "I promise I won't break."

It's all the permission he needs to hear. He rapidly speeds up the pace as he bends my body in half, taking everything I'm willing to give.

We moan and pant together, barely able to contain the inaudible sounds that are forced out. He thrusts hard inside me until he finally releases.

"Oh, God…Ceci…fucking amazing."

He holds us in place for several seconds until he's released every last drop. He slowly puts my legs down on each side of him. He leans over and captures my mouth, kissing me into an oblivious bliss.

"Better than I ever fucking imagined," he says into my neck as he lays soft kisses. "So much fucking better."

CHAPTER ELEVEN
CECILIA

I COULD STILL SMELL the popcorn when I woke up in the middle of the night. Friday was always family movie night, and Nathan, Casey, and I had all shared a bag. We snuggled on mounds of pillows and blankets on the floor as our parents snuggled up on the couch watching some Disney animation movie.

The three of us fell asleep on the floor, and I vaguely remembered Dad carrying me back into my bed. He kissed my forehead and covered me up. *"Goodnight, Princess."*

The sound of yelling woke me up hours later. It was still dark out, and my eyes were blurry, but I rubbed them open as I got out of my bed.

I crept to my door and slowly opened it. The hall light was off, but I could see the kitchen light on in the distance. I tiptoed as quietly as I could down the hall and peeked around to the kitchen where my parents were arguing.

"Goddammit!" my mother cursed. Her hands were flailing at my dad as she continued. *"How could you spend all that money? How could you when we have a family to support?"* she scowled.

He hushed her and went to reach for her, but she pushed back. *"Claire, please. I'll take care of this. I promise."*

I could hear her crying through her hands that were covering her face. I was tempted to walk to her and hug her. I wanted to comfort her and ask her what was wrong, but I could tell it was something that my dad had done.

"How, Brock? How the hell do you plan to pay back seventy-five thousand dollars? We don't have that kind of money!"

He fell to his knees in front of her and wrapped his arms around her waist. I could see she was trying to fight him off, but after a few seconds, she gave up.

"I'll ask for an extension. It'll be fine," he promised. "Ramiro will get me some extra time."

My mom's hands finally released her face. Her eyes were red and blotchy. I knew it was something really awful if mom was crying like that.

"We'll have to sell the house," she deadpanned. "There's no other way we'll come up with that money."

"No...we can take out a second mortgage or something, Claire. We can't sell our house."

"And how are we going to pay on that steep of a mortgage, Brock? With one income and three kids?" Her face was stern, and I knew that look meant serious trouble. "You gambled our life savings away!"

"I'll get back in the business. I'll get more money." He stood up and promised her. He cupped her cheek and kissed it softly. "I'll do anything."

I wake up rattled, draped in Bentley's arms. My mind quickly analyzes the dream I just had. Ramiro. A name I don't remember ever hearing. But it gives me something I didn't have before.

I look over to Bentley. He's breathing quietly next to me, as we both lay naked in his bed. He looks relaxed as he sleeps, not a worry wrinkle in sight.

I carefully wedge out of his grip. I grab one of the loose sheets that had landed on the floor and wrap myself in it. This was my chance to snoop around for anything I could use. If his dad worked on my dad's case, it's likely that the information is somewhere.

I walk to the door and slowly open it. I quickly look behind my shoulder to double-check he hasn't woken up.

I creep down the hallway to look for his office. I find a linen closet and bathroom before I spot the door that opens to a desk and filing cabinets lining the walls.

I close the door behind me and sit at his desk behind the computer. I move the mouse and his home screen pops on. I have no idea where to look or how I'm going to get in, but I have to try.

I browse his files and one pops out at me: Dad's Cases. I double click and a password code box pops up. Shit. Password.

I try Leighton.

Denied.

Bentley.

Denied. Too easy.

I tap my fingers restlessly as I try to think of possible passwords. This is Bentley's personal home computer, so I imagine it's something closely related to him—something he's passionate about.

I can tell from the pictures and articles I found on him online that he was very passionate about one thing. The one thing he's unable to do anymore—modeling.

I try again.

Denied.

Shit. I'm running out of time. I shuffle through the papers on top of his desk for any kind of clue.

Nothing.

I open up the first drawer and spot a bunch of magazines. Men's Fitness. I move them around and look underneath for anything and then as my fingers brush against the glossy pages—it hits me.

I grab the magazines and flip through them. Men's Fitness is a fashion and health magazine—models. Bentley use to model for a variety of magazines and photographers, but he was only represented through one agency—the most popular agency in the US—*Elite Storm*.

With nothing to lose, I try one more time.

E-L-I-T-E S-T-O-R-M

Access granted.

I squeal quietly to myself as I gather myself back together and begin searching.

Docs, files, and scanned images pop up in the folder. There are hundreds of them. They are all organized from month and year. I look for the month and year of my dad's death.

My heart is racing as I spot it finally. I double click and browse through the names on the folders.

Anderson.

Easton.

Hunts.

Rodriquez.

West.

I double click the last one and up pops all of my dad's information on his case. I'm so stunned. My fingers are shaking as I move the mouse around.

The folder marked police files is the first one I click on. The police report basically says what I already know from the newspapers and from the little of what my mother told me. Drive by shooter. No helpful witnesses. Found six bullets.

I try to think of how many times my dad was shot and how many shots I remember hearing. He was hit twice, which means four were missed—one grazed my shoulder, but I was nowhere near my father, which means the shooter barely slowed down as he drove past our house and shot out his window. He didn't slow down as I originally thought—he could've cared less that there were three kids outside and in the way of his target.

It makes sense as to why my sister only partially saw the license plate and how the neighbors hadn't seen anything. Drive by. No stopping to make sure they even hit their target.

I exit out and click on the witnesses' folder. I know they spoke to my mother a few days after I was home from the hospital. She was a sobbing mess, but tried to keep it together for our sake.

A friend of my mom was over when the detective came over to ask her questions. She took us out of the room, so I didn't hear anything my mother told me, but this report outlined the conversation.

She confessed that my dad was in debt to another man, but she claimed not to know who. My father had gotten into some financial issues and was working on re-paying him. She said it was months ago, and the report said police weren't sure if they were linked or not to the shooting.

Another part of the report said the bullets were analyzed by technicians and were being put through the database for any matches to another crime. I know from my previous research that this was to cross-analyze to other shootings, but the results weren't posted in the report.

I click out of the folder to search through the evidence folder when I hear footsteps in the hallway. I quickly click out of everything and hold in my breath, but my heart speeds up as I start plotting my way out of this.

Without making the chair squeak, I quietly push backward and dip down underneath the desk. I squeeze under the desk and pull the chair in as much as possible. He can't know I'm in here.

BENTLEY

I wake up with the taste of her still in my mouth. The way her body tastes drives me insane. Everything about her makes me want more. The firmness of her breasts, the taste of her arousal on my lips, the way her body tightens around me has me desperately craving more of her.

I'm thirsty as hell and decide I need to get up and grab something to drink. I roll over to kiss Ceci, but feel the cold bed under my hand instead. Her side is empty, and I start panicking that she's left.

My memory starts flashing back to the night's events. My heart beats faster as I think about Ceci and her body pressed up against mine —her stunning face, mouth, and legs. She's fucking gorgeous.

The way she gave in to me, screamed for me, and released with me starts getting my cock hard again. If this is what being with Ceci is going to be like, I'm going to have a permanent boner.

I find my briefs on the floor and put them on before going out the door. I stumble to the kitchen and grab a bottle of water. I chug the entire thing before throwing it out and start walking back down the hallway. I expect to see the bathroom light on, but it isn't. I drove her here so she couldn't have possibly left.

Unless she snuck out purposely.

The thought makes my blood boil. Leaving me like a one-night stand when I have clearly made her mine... My hands turn to fists as I walk down the hall to look for her.

I open the bathroom door, but it's empty.

"Ceci?" I call. No response.

I continue walking down to my office. The door is closed, but I step in anyway.

The room is still and silent as I expect it to be, but I call for her again anyway. "Ceci, you here?"

Nothing.

Fucking A.

Rage builds inside me as I imagine the worst. She fucking bailed.

I start storming out of my office when something on the floor catches my eye.

Part of my white sheet.

It's peeking underneath my desk. I look up at my office chair and see it's not pulled in all the way.

She's hiding.

PART II

CHAPTER TWELVE
BENTLEY

I WAS BORN into a driven household. Failure was never an option. I was taught to work hard for what I needed and work *harder* for what I wanted. And what I wanted was hiding under my desk as if I were some predator. I hadn't known until now that she was what I wanted —*craved*.

I stop moving as my eyes roam the floor and spot the white sheet crinkled against the carpet.

Is she hiding from me or is she hiding from being caught?

"Ceci," I growl.

No answer.

I know girls respond to sex differently. Some make it an emotional experience while others are all about the physical. Ceci's a mixture of both—*the worst combination.*

After no response or movement, I decide to walk out as if I didn't know she was sitting under there. I walk to the other end of the hallway to where my sitting room is. I walk to the bar and grab a glass.

I try to think how I want to handle this, but only rage consumes me. My mind is filling with questions and until I know the answers to them, my body isn't going to settle down.

I hear the creak of my office door opening and slow, faint steps against the carpet in the hallway. I hear another door open and I know she's only walked far enough to reach the bathroom.

So this is how she wants to play it.

I pour a finger of vodka and suck it down before I slam the glass down against the bar. She's going to know I was looking for her. She can't deny that she didn't hear me—I checked the goddamn bathroom, for Christ's sake!

I pour more vodka…and another…and soon I know I need to stop or I'll be passing out before I even get to confront her.

I stumble my way down the hall and see the bathroom light is off. She must've wandered back into my bed. I slowly walk in and see she's curled up back on her side as if she never even left. I huff at myself, almost laughing at the stupidity of it all. Perhaps she was just emotional and needed a moment, but why do that in my office?

Fear, doubt, and rage continue to churn inside of me as I think about Ceci being a traitor or worse—an outside job. My mind is thinking of worst case scenarios and quickly, I convince myself she's working for someone else to get inside information. I couldn't let her make a fool out of me, or Leighton Enterprises.

Not again.

It wouldn't be the first time a girl used me for inside information. The thought brings me back to two years ago when *she* almost destroyed me. Leighton Enterprises holds exclusive and confidential information that other reporters wouldn't think twice about stealing.

I walk to her side of the bed and tower over her. I watch her sleep— breathing in, breathing out, breathing in, breathing out. She looks like she is asleep, but it's hard to know for sure.

Her eyes jolt open and her body jumps from the sight of me. I look down on her wondering who the girl I just fucked really is.

"What are you doing?" she asks hurriedly, grabbing the sheet for comfort.

I look at her through glazed eyes, and I can see the fear on her face. What's she thinking right now? What is it she's really after?

"Get up," I demand. The room is pitch black, but the outside streetlights are beaming through the windows. I can see her hesitation and fear immediately, but I'm only a shadow to her.

"What?" she croaks out.

I lean over the bed and hover over her body. "You heard me. Get up."

She looks at me as if I've betrayed *her*, or as if I've done something to invade *her* privacy.

She sits up, taking the white sheet with her and covering up her chest. I laugh to myself. I had my tongue all over that chest. What exactly is she hiding?

I grab her forcefully by the upper arms and pull her body up to mine. She looks me in the eyes, and I can see she's trying to not show the timid girl she really is. She's putting on a show.

"Drop the sheet," I order, keeping my eyes locked with hers. Her eyes stay locked on mine as if she dares me to order her again. "I'm not going to ask again, Ceci."

She releases her clenched fist that's holding the sheet in place. I watch as it drops to a pool at her feet. The light behind me shines through just over her body, giving me a perfect view of her silky, soft skin.

"Now what?" she challenges.

"On your knees," I snap. "Hands behind your back."

Her breath hitches at first, but she willingly obliges. She slowly looks up at me through her dark lashes as she waits for my next command.

"Open your mouth."

I pull my briefs down and stroke my already hard cock. I groan as I take it in my hand and plunge it into her mouth. She willing accepts my full length, not giving up until the tip has reached the back of her throat.

"Oh, fuck," I moan as soon as her lips wrap around me. She licks the length from the base all the way to the tip before taking me completely. "Jesus, Ceci," I growl. She moves her head up and down my length several times without stopping. She's a fucking pro.

I dig my hands into her hair, guiding her slowly just where I want her.

"Mm," I hear her throaty moans. It's enough to get me pissed off that she's enjoying this. She's not acting intimidated or fearful. She begins to speed up the pace and soon, my entire body tenses as it waits for its release.

"Stop."

I grab her hair and pull her head back. She continues anyway, licking and sucking where she can.

"I said stop," I order firmly.

"Mm…so good," she purrs, obviously not listening to my demands. I pull her hair tighter, but it does nothing to stop her.

"You like it when I'm rough, don't you, Ceci? Is this the kinky shit you're into?" I nearly yell as my body betrays me and it fully releases into her mouth. She accepts it willing, sucking me harder as it makes its way down her throat.

I'm beyond pissed. One—she didn't fucking listen to me. Two—I didn't want to come in her pretty little mouth. And now, three—she thinks she holds all control over me when her lips are wrapped aggressively around me.

"Do you have a hearing problem?"

Her face tilts up to look at me as she licks her lips clean. "No."

My blood is boiling at the way she's challenging me, pushing me to my end.

"Then you have a listening problem?"

"We're not in the office, Mr. Leighton. I don't *have* to listen to you," she counters.

"If I hadn't already filled that goddamn smart mouth of yours…"

"You'd what?" She glares at me. "Why are you acting like a controlling asshole?"

"Controlling asshole?" I muse, laughing. "Seems to me you like it, don't you, Ceci? I see the way your nipples perk up. I feel your hot breath all around me. You're aroused. And even more, you're aroused that this arouses you."

"So what if it does?" she challenges.

I grab her and force her up so we're eye level. "What else do you like?" I whisper. "What else are you willing to give me?"

"Anything you want, Bentley. *I'm yours.*"

My mouth instantly crushes to hers. My hands aggressively cup her face. Her arms wrap around my body, her nails clawing at my skin as her hands make their way down to my ass.

"You are the most intriguing and confusing person I've ever met," I breathe out as I continue to hold her.

"Likewise, Mr. Leighton."

"You want to tell me who you *really* are, Ceci? I know you're hiding something from me," I growl deeply, letting her know how serious I am.

"I'm exactly who I told you I was. I have nothing to hide," she answers confidently.

Too confidently.

I quickly grab under her ass and hoist her up against me. Her legs wrap around my waist and her arms lock around my neck in a death grip.

"How far are you willing to go to prove that?" I whisper in her hair. I nip the skin just below her ear, showing her how deadly serious I am.

"I already told you, Bentley. *I won't break.*"

The way her voice lingers sends a chill down my body. She's not kidding. She's willing to do anything I ask. The way her body melts to mine as if she's daring me to do with it as I please, which instantly grabs my cock's attention.

I'm filled with a mixture of rage and passion, and all I want to do is fuck her senseless until she tells me the truth.

Our naked bodies are molded together, and I know I have the upper hand here, yet it feels like she's controlling everything when it comes to my emotions.

Fuck. *Emotions?*

This was exactly why I didn't allow myself to get too close—like last time.

Emotions. And then *attachments*. But now it's me fighting those feelings off. However, I'm not sure I can.

I kiss her once more, nipping at her lips with an uncontrollable desire. I can feel her body heating against mine—she wants it as badly as I do.

"Bend over the bed," I say breaking the kiss. I drop my arms and allow her feet to land on the floor. "Keep your hands planted on the sheets."

She spins around and willingly bends her body over the bed with both hands above her head. I lean over her and squeeze her breasts in my hands. My cock springs torturously against her ass, signaling her to spread her legs farther. She releases a moan, parting her legs for me.

"Let's play a game," I whisper.

Her body writhes underneath me, yet she doesn't say no. I release one of her breasts and roam my free hand down her flat stomach to her clit. I rub aggressively, not slowing down as she starts screaming and moaning. Her hands are still above her head, but I can feel her struggling to keep them there.

"Bentley…" she finally says. "Please. Oh my God." I feel her struggling against me. Her body convulses as I bring her to orgasm. I rub her nipple hard in between my thumb and forefinger as I work her clit in the same rhythm. My cock is still pressing hard against her ass, trapping her against the bed so she can't move. Her hands are balled into fists as she struggles to control her breathing. "Oh, God….I can't take it. Bentley, please." She continues begging and it's the sweetest fucking sound. "Stop…it's too intense." As the alcohol surges through my blood, the more daring I become.

"Sweetheart, we're playing a game here," I remind her, my voice laced with amusement. "Tell me a secret."

"I-I don't have any secrets, Bentley," she forces out. "Ah…yes. Oh, God." Her body is shaking against me, and I know she's close.

"Tell me, Ceci," I demand in her ear. "I'm going to torture every part of your body until you tell me the truth."

"Tell you what?" she pleads.

"Tell me who you really are," I growl, pissed off that I even have to say it again.

"I swear, I'm telling the truth," she insists. "Ahh…oh, God…yes…." I feel her releasing around my fingers, but before she does, I remove them and kneel down in between her legs. I force them apart and like a hungry animal, my mouth is on her pussy, licking up her juices as she releases around my tongue.

I keep working her. I don't let her come down. She's pleading for it, yet she's begging for me to stop.

I run my hands up her legs and spread them as far apart as possible. I catch her with one hand as she loses her balance—unable to keep up with the pleasure-torture my tongue is giving her.

"Bentley…I swear…my name is Ceci. Everything I told you is true," she forces out right before I force two fingers inside her. My tongue and fingers work her into another frenzy, her body ready to collapse around me.

I stand back up and slap her ass before leaning back over her.

"Why don't I believe you?"

Her breathing is rapid, her body pulsating up and down as I allow her body to rest.

"Why do you doubt me? I've been nothing but honest with you, Bentley. Why are you—"

"Why am I what, Ceci? Why don't *you* tell me what you were doing in my office?" I glide my tongue up her spine as my hands slide up her arms. Her breathing hitches and her body stills.

"Yes, I saw you," I answer her silent thoughts. "So you can either tell me the truth, or I will fuck you until you do. Either way, it's a win-win for me." I grin selfishly. I know what I'm doing…yet, I can't stop. Rage and passion fuel my actions as I continue thinking about her betrayal.

She doesn't answer me, and it's all the confirmation I need to know that I'm right.

"All right. Have it your way," I warn.

I slide my hands back down her arms as I stand back up behind her. My hands grip her hips before I take her from behind. Her body dips to the bed in a perfect forty-five degree angle. I can see all of her this way —she's fucking beautiful the way she's laid out for me.

I thrust inside—her body jolts with my entrance. Her pussy opens up willingly around my length as I tease her clit with one hand. My other hand squeezes her hip to keep the pace.

"Ah, fuck, Ceci…" The feeling of her bare body against me is almost too much for *me* to handle. She's so damn tight. I know I'm not going to last long if I don't concentrate on the task at hand.

Her body jerks forward as I stroke deeper. Her moans and screams get louder as my hips rock against her.

"You ready to tell me now, Ceci? Who are you working for?"

"Shit," she curses in a half moan. "You, Bentley. I work for you." Another lie.

I free my hand from her clit and start rubbing her ass. I lick my finger before putting the tip of it inside her. She immediately tenses, jerking away from me.

"How about now? You ready to tell me now?" I threaten, forcing my finger deeper inside her ass. I can tell she's not experienced there from the way her body rejects me. It only makes me want her more—my finger and cock grinding deeper inside her. "I told you—I'll torture every part of you until you tell me the truth," I threaten.

"Oh my God…" she breathes out. "I am," she forces out. "Bentley… holy shit…" I can feel she's ready to give in and answer me, but instead, she presses her ass harder against me. "Yes, God. Ahh…*more*," she pleads.

This is fucking turning her on.

I soon realize I'm not wearing a condom…again. *Fuck.* If she keeps moaning like that, I'm going to come before I'm ready.

She grinds her body against me and begins circling her ass against my finger that's half a finger deep inside her. She's not intimidated…I haven't crossed any lines….*she's fucking enjoying this torturous act.*

Suddenly, I'm pissed that my plan isn't working and aggressively pull out of her.

"Ah…" she moans at the sudden exit. I flip her over and lean over her body.

"What were you doing in my office?" My tone is deep and serious. I lock my eyes with her so she can see just how serious I am.

"I was checking my school email," she explains. "I-I panicked when I heard you. I thought you'd be mad that I was on it without asking."

Oh, this girl is good.

I smirk at her as I tower over her body, her hands trapped by mine on either side of her.

"Checking your email?" I repeat doubtfully. "Why would you hide for checking your email?"

She shrugs lightly, her eyes maintaining eye contact with me. "I wasn't sure how you felt about people touching your stuff."

It's a simple response. *Almost too simple.* But as the alcohol wears off and my mind releases the rage, my heart actually *wants* to believe her.

"Why are you letting me treat you this way, Ceci? Don't girls want to be loved, cherished, and all that girly shit?"

"I told you…I'm not like other girls." The tone in her voice is seductive, challenging almost. I grab her legs and wrap them around my waist. I lift her off the bed and slam us both against the wall behind me.

"Is that so?" I growl against her ear. She nods as she clenches tightly onto me. "Good, because what I want to do to you requires a lot of trust. Something I've never asked of another girl. Think I can get that from you, Ceci?"

Her head falls back as I take her raw flesh in my mouth. I suck her neck hard, showing her just how much she's mine.

"Yes," she finally breathes out. "I'm yours."

"Those are the sexiest words I've ever heard." I move my mouth to her lips and kiss her softly. "I want to trust you, Ceci."

For the first time in my life, I feel vulnerable around someone else. Feeding the rage and passion wasn't too much for her, rather she gave into it—she liked it. She willingly gave me just what I needed.

"You can. I promise."

CHAPTER THIRTEEN
CECILIA

THE SIGHT of Bentley's body towering over me sent me in panic mode. I was pretending to sleep, hoping he'd crawl in next to me, and we'd spoon until he fell back asleep. What I hadn't counted on was Bentley catching me...or his games.

I allow Bentley to use me until he's satisfied I'm telling him the truth. I keep eye contact and never flinch at his abusive tone. I let his aggressive hold take control as he controls my body.

I'm convincing in my lies—I told you I was a master manipulator. It's not hard, considering every scenario he's thinking about is wrong. I don't work for anyone and technically, my name is Ceci—well, nickname. Too bad he never thought of a high school student turned makeshift college student would be out to attain information for personal gain—because that would be a bitch to explain. Or deny.

I laugh to myself at the irony. When it's said like that, it sounds ridiculous. What I'm doing *is* ridiculous. But I don't care. If I don't take the risk and at least try, I'll never know. I already live with regrets. I didn't want to live with the *'what if's.'*

There's no denying that my body craves Bentley. I want everything he's giving me...and more. I let him do everything to me because I want it. *I love it.* I don't want him to treat me like a little girl that can't handle it. I can.

And I did.

Bentley slams us into the wall—my bare back pressed against the cold drywall. It's chilling on my overheated skin, but much welcomed. It feels good.

"I want to, Ceci. I want to trust you so fucking badly," he confesses. His forehead is pressed against mine, and I can feel his hot breath against my mouth. He's battling with himself. He's torn between letting me in and keeping me at a distance.

I inhale the alcohol that he's exhaling, a strong vodka aroma. I thought I had smelled it on him earlier, but now I know for sure he was drinking.

After my dad died, my mom hid in her room a lot. Casey was left to cook and take care of me most of the time. She took advantage and watched mostly adult shows and movies on TV. I'd sit with her and ended up learning *much* more than I should have. By the time I was seventeen, I had lost my virginity. I was more curious than in love, but once I lost it, I didn't feel the need to protect it. It was the only time I ever felt anything besides anger and sadness. It was the only time I didn't think about my dad and how much I wished I had died right along with him that day. It was the only time I wasn't numb to the pain.

When I was seventeen, I met Jason. He was a year ahead of me, but we hooked up my entire junior year. He was never more than that for me—a hook up. After awhile, he wanted more. He wanted to start going on dates, holding hands, being a couple. I told him I couldn't and that I wasn't wired that way. I hadn't felt that *need* to have that with him. I kept him at a distance, not wanting to let that part of my heart open for him. I didn't want to be in love. I never felt like I deserved it. How could I allow myself to love when I was still mourning my dad's death all these years later? I just knew I could never give him what he wanted.

We stopped talking after he graduated. And my heart never skipped a beat in missing him. I always felt I was incapable of caring that much for someone, so much that I wanted to let them in. And this is how I knew Bentley was struggling with the same thing. Between letting me in, trusting me, and pushing me away. It was too late for the both of us. We were both *way* too far in, and now I had to cover my tracks before he found out the actual truth.

"You can trust me, Bentley," I say again. Because it's true. Besides the lies I'm forced to hide, my feelings are real. I'm ready to give Bentley anything he wants to prove it.

He presses his hips into me, binding us together. He grabs my ankles and forces them on top of his shoulder so the only thing holding us against the wall is my ass and his hips. I'm literally folded in half between Bentley and the wall.

He smirks as he sees how flawlessly I bend. "I told you I was in gymnastics."

He grins before saying, "At least I can believe that much."

He thrusts inside me deeper. My head falls back against the wall as my body opens up willingly for him. He's completely hard and thick, stretching me out farther than I've ever been before.

The tight sensation is intense. I can feel every thick inch of him—the way he grinds into me makes everything go away. I don't feel numb anymore. I don't think about the dangerous territory I've gotten myself into—it's just him and me.

He's moans and pants into my neck as he continues rocking into me. I feel his hot breath against my blistering skin. My head can't concentrate on anything but the deep pleasure he's giving me, the connection between us, and how good it feels to be with him.

"God, Ceci…your body…I can't ever get enough." He breathes against my skin. "I could never get enough of you." He bites the raw flesh of my earlobe, sending shivers down my body.

He presses deeper inside me, his hands clenching my ankles to him. His mouth wanders up and down my neck, ear, and jaw. His tongue traces my jawline igniting the raw, but real, feelings I have toward him.

I wasn't even looking for someone when I padded into that boardroom. It was the farthest thing from my mind, but now that I'm here with him, I don't want to let go. I don't want to let go of this feeling—alive, invincible, real.

I couldn't tell him the truth now. It'd destroy him. Destroy us.

"Bentley, God…you're amazing," I confess, unable to keep the feelings from spilling out of me. "So damn amazing."

His head backs up and makes eye contact with me. He slows his torture-pleasing rhythm and looks deep into me—*through me.*

"I hope you mean that, Ceci. God, I *really* hope, because this isn't easy for me. It's been a long time since I've let someone in…and I want to let you in. I *crave* letting you in." He leans his forehead against mine. His breathing slows matching our rhythm.

"I do," I whisper, a tinge of guilt leaves my throat. I hope he doesn't notice, but I can't help it. My heart and mind are in the middle of world war three, and there's nothing I can do about it because I already know my heart will win. I won't be able to say no to him, nor do I want to. But I can't lose focus on what I really want—what I'm really after.

He releases my ankles, but they stay placed on his shoulders. His hands wrap my face, cupping my cheeks as he crushes our mouths together. I immediately submit to his lips and tongue wanting everything he's willing to give me.

He speeds back up, rocking his hips forcefully against mine. I take in his moans and panting in my mouth as I release my own. I can feel the sweat between us, the lust releasing out of our skin as he rides out my intense orgasm.

"Bentley...ahh, yes..." I mumble against his lips. My head falls back on its own accord as his mouth drops to my neck. He licks a path from my collarbone to my ear as I scream out his name one more time until I come down.

"Sweetheart, as much as I want to fuck you hard against this wall and release everything I have in you, I'm not wearing a condom." I can hear the slight agony in his tone. He's disappointed but knows it's the right thing to do.

"Drop me," I demand.

"What?"

"Put me down."

He slowly releases each leg off his shoulder. I submit to my knees immediately and take him into my mouth.

"Sweetheart, what are you doing?" His fingers flock to my head, clenching his hands in fistfuls of my hair.

I release him and say, "I doubt I need to spell it out for you." I smirk up at him once before grabbing him and wrapping my lips around him again.

"Oh, God, baby," he growls and I can feel him leaning back, pushing deeper inside my mouth. "You look fucking amazing like this."

I use my hand to stroke him as I continue sucking him off. I use my other hand to keep his legs wide, giving just enough room for my knees to bend in between him.

"Yes...oh, God...baby, I-I—"

I want him to release inside me, so I stroke and suck even harder. "Ceci...God, yes..." I continue working him until he's completely filled my throat. I close my eyes and take it willingly, wanting every part of him.

He begins to come down and loosens his grip on my head. "*Jesus Christ*," he growls.

I back up and let him grab my arms to lift me up. I lick my lips and smile up at him.

His stare is intense as he says, "Bed."

CHAPTER FOURTEEN
CECILIA

I WALK into school Friday morning with a smile on my face and a limp in my step—a constant reminder of being sexually tortured the night before—not that I argued.

My mind is spinning on last night's events. Almost being caught. Bentley's darker, more *dominant* side. A side I should've expected.

I was sure he had passed out for good. I hadn't expected him to see me, and I especially hadn't expected him to react the way he did —*aggressive and vulnerable*. Two very different emotions, but I knew it was what drove him, and I willingly gave him anything he asked for.

"You look like death," Simon says casually as he leant against the locker next to me.

I'm sore, exhausted, and not in the mood for his shit. "Thanks, asshole. You always know how to make a girl feel good."

He narrows his eyebrow at me. "Would you prefer I tell you or some jackass that you hate?"

"I prefer you say nothing at all."

He puts his hands up in surrender. "So, where the hell have you been lately? Every time I call you, it goes straight to voice mail."

"Oh, my bad. Just shit going on at home. You know... the usual." I shrug nonchalantly so he doesn't question me. He's well aware of the love-hate relationship I have with my mom, but I don't meet his stare just in case he tries to break me of the truth.

"Have you seen Cora?"

"She's in the locker room las—" He clears his throat as his face turns an interesting shade of red. "She's probably in the gym or something."

I examine his disheveled look—messy, tousled locks, red scratches on his biceps, wrinkled shirt—all the signs of a heated make out session.

I smirk as I gaze down his body and back up to meet his suspicious eyes.

I take a mental note to drill Cora for details later. She'll never admit it was Simon, but she'll at least tell me about some guy she hooked up with—even if she lies about who it was.

"Okay, I'll just catch up with her later then." I grab my pre-calculus book and slam my locker shut. "Let's hang out next week, okay?"

He nods in agreement as we walk to our next class. I hate deceiving Simon, but I have no choice if I want to keep this secret a secret.

After school, I dig through my closet for something to wear at my internship tomorrow. I have to keep up my appearance for the other journalists that are also there, yet I want to look nice for Bentley.

Butterflies rise in my stomach as I think about him. A queasy combination of anxiety and fear build up as I think about being at work with him all day. Would we go back to boss and intern or would he treat me differently now?

However, as much as I *want* him, I want the truth about my dad more.

I shuffle through my closet and come across an old sweater I had forgotten was stashed in here—a purple one. It's been my favorite color ever since I was a kid. I don't even know why I still have it. It hasn't fit me in years. It brings me back to my dad immediately. Soon, the tears well in my eyes as I rub my thumb and forefinger over the fabric.

"How's it going, Princess?" my dad asked. I was sitting on my bed with my knees pressed against my chest, my head dug into the gap, as the tears streamed out.

He sat down next to me and rubbed my back until I calmed down enough to speak.

I wiped the tears off my cheeks and cleared my throat before speaking. "Today was the third grade spelling bee," I choked.

He sensed my disappointment immediately and wrapped his arms around me.

"What happened?"

"I was doing really good," I started to explain. "But then I guess I got nervous and froze up. I spelled a really easy word wrong and lost."

It might not have been a big deal to most kids my age, but I had studied day and night on that list of words. I was prepared.

"I even wore my lucky sweater." I look down at my favorite purple sweater.

I could feel my dad's body tense around me. He wasn't sure what to say to console me. I wasn't the easiest person to console.

"You're smart, Cecilia," he began. I turned and looked up at him. His eyes lit up and a smile crept on his face. And soon, I was smiling with him. "You're the smartest girl I know. Don't let one mistake keep you from taking on the world."

"You really think so?"

"I know so." He leaned in and kissed my forehead. I smiled. He always knew what to say to make me feel better. "So what was the word?" He leaned back and asked.

I sighed. "Honesty."

Thoughts of my dad surface randomly since his passing. A smell, a shirt, a color—all types of things will bring the memories back.

As I stand in the doorway of my closet, I think about the words my dad said to me that day.

Don't let one mistake keep you from taking on the world.

It's the most powerful thing I've ever heard and up until now, I hadn't realized just how powerful. He's right. Absolutely right. I shouldn't let one incident keep me from doing what I plan on doing—finding justice for my dad.

I walk to my mom's bedroom, peeking in before I plow right in. She should be working, but just in case, I double check.

She must have something in here. Some files, information, documentation on my dad. She always told me she got rid of everything, got rid of the memories, but something inside me knows she has to have something. There has to be a reason she wanted to get rid of everything so fast.

I dig around her vanity, dresser, and closet.

Nothing.

I look under her bed, moving around all the old shoes and water bottles that must've slipped under there.

Again, *nothing*.

I sit on the floor and think for a moment as I slowly take a look around.

Nathan barrels through with no consideration that I'm sitting in the middle of the floor, almost knocking me over.

"Whatcha doing?" he asks, spontaneously jumping on top of the bed.

"None of your damn business," I snap, irritated that he's made me lose my concentration.

"Mom said you can't say that to me. She said you had to be *nice* to me!" he taunts.

"Mom's not here. So deal with it."

He's laughing, jumping up and down on the bed trying to touch the ceiling. "You're going to break your damn neck. Get down," I scowl.

"Make me."

"One punch to your shin and you're going down. You really want to test me?" I stand up showing how serious I am.

"Na-na-na-na-na," he sings. *God*. I can't stand him sometimes. I know he's begging for attention, but right now, I can't deal with his shenanigans.

I watch as he jumps, arm straight up as he aims for the ceiling. He almost touches it. I watch annoyed as he jumps deeper into the bed making one last attempt to touch it.

It's like slow motion—his knees bend, his lips curve up into a smile as his arm slowly reaches up until his body can't go any higher. And then finally, his hand touches the pale-colored ceiling.

It's not until he lands back down shouting out in victory that it hits me.

It's not under the bed.

If my mom were hiding something significant about my dad, she would hide it somewhere people wouldn't think to look.

"Nathan, off," I demand. I snap my fingers at him to get off the bed, and he finally listens. "Go tell Casey to start dinner. I'll be right down."

He skips happily out of our mom's room, *finally*, and I begin ripping the sheet off. I feel around the mattress for a slit or opening. I round the corner and still don't feel anything. Frustrated, I finally lift the mattress up as high as I can. Adrenaline and determination feed my strength to flip the entire thing over, and then I see it—a white envelope taped to the bottom of the mattress.

I run over and grab it, ripping the tape off with it. It's sealed shut with nothing written on the outside. I rub my fingers over it, wondering if it'll give me any information that I've been craving.

I rip the envelope open and spot a small piece of folded paper. I pull it out and hold it firmly in between two fingers.

My breathing quickens as I unfold it, delicately as if it'll break. I unfold it once more before it's completely open, exposed.

Samuel Anderson.

42-19-36

No. 6

I stare at it and realize it's some kind of lock box code. Number 6 and this was the lock combination. *But for what?* And where? And who the hell is Samuel Anderson?

"Cecilia!" I hear my sister shout up the stairs. "Get your ass down here!"

"Hold on, I'll be right there!" I shout back unhappily.

I clench the piece of paper in my fist as I push the mattress back on top of the box spring. I quickly put the sheets and pillows back on before leaving the room.

As I walk down the stairs, I think about the secrets my mom must be hiding—*hiding for my dad.* Were we always unsafe?

After dinner, I go on a Google hunt for a Samuel Anderson. I have no idea what I'm looking for, and considering it's an extremely common name, I end up with thousands of Google links. But if it's important enough for my mom to hide, it has to link to my dad somehow. I can feel it.

I narrow it down and search Samuel Anderson + Nebraska.

No matches.

I try again, this time adding in my dad's old job title. Samuel Anderson + insurance broker.

Nothing.

This is going to be so much harder than I thought.

BENTLEY

My room still smells like her. Well, a blend of her anyway. Mixed with me. *And sex.*

Lots and lots of sex.

After last night's events and the alcohol finally wearing off, I can finally think straight. As much as my body craves and desires Ceci, I need to start thinking with my *other head.*

As soon as I arrive to work, I tell Erika to get me Ceci's file and her guidance counselor on the phone. I was supposed to check her references three weeks ago. And with the suspicion building up inside me, I have to know. I need to know *for certain* that she is who she says she is to get over this huge lump in my chest. I can't let my need for her take over my ability to protect my father's company.

"Here you are, Mr. Leighton. Everything's in there." Erika gently places the file on my desk and quietly leaves without another word. Let's just say, she's been well-trained. I don't do small talk and chit-chat.

I immediately open it up and rack my brain about the details of her interview. It wasn't that long ago, but for some reason, it feels longer.

Casey West. 21. Senior. University of Nebraska.

I remember the exact way she looked the day of her interview. Sophisticated and put together on the outside, fearless and strong on the inside. A deadly combination…

I look over her transcripts, her letters of recommendation, and college awards. It's obvious she's extremely bright. Her professors rave about her skills, her ability to learn quickly, and her desire for journalism and criminology. It's perfect.

Perhaps a little *too* perfect.

Thinking back to *her*, I decide to do a Facebook and Google search on Ceci. Something I don't typically do on my colleagues because I don't need to. Everything is usually broken down in the criminal background and security check. Yet, nothing popped up for Ceci. Her record was spotless.

I find Google records of her license, registration, and insurance. I find a Twitter account that looks as if it has never been used, and a Facebook account that's set to private. However, I notice the profile picture isn't of her face. Her back is angled to the camera as her shirt falls off her shoulder, her body turned away. Her hair is a darker blonde and swept to one side with light curls.

I stare at it and notice how vulnerable she looks—unlike how she acts in real life. There's so much I don't know about her, so much that she could be hiding.

My phone rings and distracts me from my thoughts. I quickly exit out of all the screens before answering it.

"Yes?"

"Sir, Professor Hennings is on line one for you."

I thank her and quickly switch the line over.

"Hello, this is Bentley Leighton from Leighton Enterprises," I greet. "Thank you for calling me back, Mr. Hennings."

"Hello, Mr. Leighton. How may I help you?"

I can tell it's an older gentleman by the raspy tone in his voice. I only plan to get a few details about Ceci because now all I can think about is she and that pretty little mouth of hers.

"Yes, I was wondering if you could give me some information on one of your students. A Miss Casey West. She applied to an internship program here a while ago and actually received it. My apologies for not contacting you sooner on this matter, but I thought we should at least communicate about her references."

I hear him clear his throat before responding. "Uh, Casey West, you say?"

"Ah, yes, sir. She's one of your students?"

"Yes, she is. I wasn't aware she was even looking into internships, nevertheless applying for them."

I hear the confusion in his voice and wonder if perhaps he's getting too old for his job.

I smirk to myself before replying. "Well, sir, I actually have a letter of recommendation from you. It says you acknowledge her skills as a student and that she would be a valuable asset to our company." I try not to sound rude, but I'm annoyed at how he can't even keep his students straight. "Casey West, she's about five feet-three, maybe a hundred and ten or twenty pounds. Um, brownish-blonde hair?" I ramble off her looks as if it'll matter.

"I'm aware of what she looks like, sir. I'm not aware of any internship she's applied to." His tone is harsh, and I'm immediately pissed off. "Or any letter of recommendation."

I run my tongue along my lower lip as I take in this new information. I'm not sure what it all means, but one thing's for sure—she lied on her application.

CHAPTER FIFTEEN
CECILIA

I SPEND the better part of Friday night trying to research Samuel Anderson and what connection he could possibly have to my dad.

I end up falling asleep at my desk with all my lights still on. By the time I wake up, I'm already late for work.

"Shit!" I frantically rush to get ready and drive faster than I should. I finally arrive at 8:27 am.

I don't have time to feel nervous anymore. All I can think about is how mad he's going to be. And how I have no idea what we are...or how I'm supposed to act around him.

I smooth my skirt with my hands as I walk down the hall to Bentley's office. I walk in slowly and watch him intently to gauge his mood. He sits tall as he continues writing something.

"Good morning, Mr. Leighton," I say as I stand in front of his desk with my arms folded in front of me. I don't have his coffee either...*fuck*, he's going to fire me.

"Good morning, Miss West." His voice is deep and smooth. I nervously stand there, anticipating him yelling at me soon.

He finally lifts his head and makes eye contact with me. There's an amused grin on his face as he takes in my outfit. I wonder if he's going to mention Thursday night, but after sneaking out early, and taking a cab to my car Friday morning, I haven't heard from him since. And I haven't tried to contact him either.

I watch as he squirms in his chair as if he's fighting an inner battle.

His eyes aren't as soft, and suddenly, I feel butterflies in my stomach, as I fear something is wrong.

"I have a project for you this morning," he says as he hands me a thick manila folder. "In order for me, as your boss, to know your abilities, we have all interns and out-of-college grads complete a practice case file."

I nod in understanding, but inside I'm completely dying.

"It's a simple junior college-level case, something similar you've probably already covered in one of your class projects." He smiles back at me, and I feel as if he's challenging me.

"Great, I'll get started." I smile wide as if it'll be no big deal and turn to walk out the door.

"Oh, and Ceci." His voice jerks me back around to face him. "You have *one* hour."

I nod and hurry out of his office and into the one I've been allowed to use. My body is shaking with nerves as I realize the task he's given me—something a college senior should be able to do in their sleep.

I adjust myself in the office chair and flip open the file. I read over the notes, the case information, and the evidence.

Victim: Mark Philips

Background information: 34-year-old Caucasian male, never returned home after work on Thursday, March 19. Wife reported him missing the next day.

Case Notes: Police followed up with his job at Tillman & Tillman, a sausage processing company. He worked 6AM to 6PM Monday-Thursday.

It was confirmed that he punched in at 5:57AM and punched out at 12:35PM for his lunch break. He then punched back in at 1:35PM but never punched back out for the evening.

Detectives interviewed the company owner, his supervisor, his line partner, and five other employees that said they saw him that day.

Ty Neumann, his line partner, claimed he left work early. Records proved he punched out at 5:02PM.

Randy Huntington, his supervisor, claimed to not have seen him after lunch, as he was in a business meeting from 1PM to 4PM and then left immediately after to pick up his daughter from daycare. Detectives confirmed his daughter was picked up at 4:17PM.

Jerry Sullivan, Heath Tyner, Joseph McMillian, Lenny Johnston, and David Winters were also interviewed—they noted that Mark always worked twelve-hour days. Jerry was known to not get along well with Mark, and

David was currently in anger management (both unrelated, just an observation.)

His car was found undisturbed in the parking lot. No video surveillance.

I read over the rest of the papers that are included in the file, all made up notes and interviews.

With one minute left, I shuffle the papers back in the manila folder and head back to Bentley's office.

I knock softly, and he tells me to enter. I cautiously walk to his desk, his body language unreadable. A shift has occurred since we were together the other night, and my increased heart rate tells me it's from him finding me in his office. The alcohol that once flooded his blood veins is no longer doing the thinking for him—*he's suspicious.*

"Well?" he asks as I approach him. He's leaning back all the way in his chair, his hands resting behind his head. "Do you have a conclusion?"

I can hear the amusement in his tone. It's as if he's expecting me to get this wrong, expecting me to not know the answer.

"I believe I do." He gestures for me to keep going. I clear my throat, stand up a little taller, and respond, "His wife is the suspect."

His eyes widen as his lips curve up into a smirk. "And what makes you think that?"

If I told him how I knew—the truth—it'd give too much away. When the shooting happened, my mother was inside. She had no idea what had happened, who was hurt, or where the shooting was coming from, but her first reaction? Get help. She didn't waste time finding answers. A wife and mother's first reaction should always be to get help.

I clear my throat again, stalling. His eyes wander up my legs to my chest and meet back up to mine. I smile confidently and continue. "She waited too long to call the police. Her alibi is improbable at best. Any concerned wife would've called his cell phone several times or the company phone, and after that, the police. Except, she didn't. She waited until the next day. She also made sure it was a Thursday, his last work day of the week. I found the likelihood of her coming into his place of work much more plausible than any of his co-workers having anything to do with his disappearance. She had distracted him before he got the chance to punch out, which was her sole purpose in getting the attention off her."

His lips form into a half-sided grin, a cocky smirk that could melt the panties off any girl. But right now, all I want to do is impress him— wash away any doubt that he's feeling.

"That's very impressive."

"You look surprised."

"Well…this case is used in many trial interviews and internships. It's been used as an extensive training guide due to the fine details that often get overlooked."

"And you didn't think I could do it." It's more of a statement than a question because I can hear the doubt in his tone.

His jaw ticks as he smoothly rubs a hand over it. "No."

I take a step back, shocked by his confession. "Then why even give me the task if you expect me to fail?"

"Let me make myself clearer. I *didn't* think you could do it…because it takes most people *three* hours to come to the same conclusion you just did."

"And you only gave me an hour," I whisper, confused.

"Correct. I wanted to challenge you."

"Why? I've done everything you've asked me to do. Do you doubt my ability to work here?" I ask with anger in my tone, but I quickly control myself—I have to remember he's still my boss.

"You're very bright, Ceci. Extremely smart and confident. Trust me. I don't *doubt* those qualities at all."

"Well, I can sense it's something, so why don't you just come out and tell me?" I snap reluctantly.

He leans forward in his chair and crosses his arms over his desk. His intensity makes me nervous, but I try to shake it off before he can sense it.

"All right." He looks me over once more before continuing. "I was finally able to speak with your guidance counselor, Professor Hennings."

My body stiffens as I hear his words. I assumed he had done all that before I was accepted. I didn't know I still had to worry about it.

"Did he even know who I was?" I smirk, trying to play it as if he's losing his memory from old age.

"He did."

I swallow. His face is firm as his intense eyes burn into mine. I suddenly decide to switch my plan.

"I guess he doesn't remember writing the letter since you're bringing it up?" I ask, trying to keep my voice strong.

"That'd be correct." I can see he's thinking the worst in his head, and I know I need to come up with something plausible.

"Okay." I clear my throat and blink a few times. "He didn't write me that letter of recommendation. Professor Hennings and I don't have a good relationship. I-I might've come on too strong around him when I was trying to ask why he gave me a B instead of an A. He made a pass at me and I told him off. Ever since then, he keeps his distance. I was too afraid to ask him for a letter of recommendation, so I asked his TA."

"His TA?" His eyebrows lift as if he's skeptical.

"Yes, Jordan Walsh. He's a friend of mine and I asked him for a favor. It was a letter I deserved, but I didn't want to approach Professor Hennings because of what happened last time."

I try to sound believable and look the part. I feel pathetic. *This* is pathetic. But I have no choice. I'm too far in. If I tell him the truth now, I'm ruined.

"You understand what could happen if I told your professor? Not to mention what would happen to your internship?"

I swallow hard again. Because I do know. I know very fucking well what will happen. This game—this strategy—will have been all for nothing.

I nod. "Yes, Mr. Leighton. I do understand."

CHAPTER SIXTEEN
BENTLEY

I WANT to believe every *fucking* word she's telling me. I want to believe her because I *want* her. But I need to remember what I'm doing here.

You're a Leighton, son.

My father's words echo in my head as I stare at the beautiful girl in front of me. She's strong, determined, and bright. I can't keep the thought of her out of my head for more than two seconds—the way she presents herself, the beauty in who she is, and the way she gets under my skin are all reasons I *want* to believe her.

Not many women try to use their brains to get my attention. And it's the fucking hottest thing in the entire world watching her use both —brains *and* beauty. But she's so much more than that. Her personality, witty sense of humor, and her ability to act professional when it's needed are all screaming at me to believe her—forgive her for lying about one damn letter.

"All right. I'm not going to say anything to the committee about it." She exhales a breath of relief. "*This time,*" I emphasize. "Is there anything else you need to tell me, Ceci?" I ask, but deep down, I'm unsure I want an answer. I don't think I can handle having to let her go, telling her to walk away from this internship, since I can tell how important it is to her.

"No, Mr. Leighton. Nothing else."

"Good."

I watch intently as she shifts from foot to foot. We've slept together, and yet I make her nervous still. She swallows slowly, taking in whatever I'm about to say. I want to scream and yell at her for being in my home office and demand the truth, but I know that'll backfire. She's given me a reasonable explanation, yet it still isn't sitting right with me. And I'm not sure that has anything to do with Ceci, or the fact that I need to keep her a safe distance. The closer she gets, the worse it could be.

I have her do a few errands for me. It's not work related, but I need to get her out of my office. I need to clear my head.

Except I can't. Flashbacks of the other night resurface—the softness of her body, the aching moans she screamed, and the way her tight pussy clenched around me. It's all too distracting when I need to be thinking about my company—my future.

Being burned before—and almost ruined— I know I need to be cautious, but part of me refuses to believe she's anything but genuine. She's in college. She's twenty-one years old. She's smart. All those reasons should tell me I'm over-paranoid. But part of me is still unsure.

She walks into my office with my dry cleaning, extra bold coffee, and transcript files I asked her to find. I didn't really need them, but I needed to keep her busy. I needed to keep her distant.

I stand up and take the dry cleaning from her, softly grazing her hand. "Thank you."

She scowls. "You're welcome, *Mr. Leighton*."

"Is there a problem, Miss West?" Her eyes drop to the floor, her body tensing at the firmness of my voice. I know she's pissed that I sent her on an errand run instead of giving her something to do here.

"No, of course not," she insists, but I can see right through her.

I place the hanger on my coat rack. She places my coffee and files on my desk and steps back cautiously waiting for her next order.

As much as she fights it and demands control, she submits nicely. Always willing to please and give me exactly what I want.

I smile at the thought.

In the office, I'm still her boss and she's my intern, but that doesn't mean I can't have some fun with her.

I sit back down with my arms behind my head and grin at her. "Take a step back," I demand.

Her eyes meet mine as she does what she's told. "Unbutton your blouse."

"What?"

"I won't repeat myself, Ceci. You're a college senior. I'm sure you're capable of following directions."

She swallows hard as she questions me with her eyes. She begins unbuttoning her blouse until each one has been undone. She drops her arms to her sides, breathing heavy as she waits again for my orders.

I take her in—her perfectly fit, athletic body. She's petite, but she's not small. She's flawlessly proportioned in every way I love—curvy and tone.

"Unzip your skirt."

Her hands go behind her as she reaches for the zipper. She slowly—and torturously—unzips her skirt. I watch intently as it falls to a pool at her feet. She's standing in fucking black stockings that end mid-thigh.

Goddamn stockings.

My cock stands at attention at the sight of her. I'm not going to be able to control myself for much longer. *Send her away. Send her home.*

Fuck no.

"Open your blouse so I can see you."

Her breath hitches, but she continues to do what I tell her.

"Beautiful," I say softly. "Now let me see your breasts. Pull your bra down."

She hesitates, holding her hands on her bra but not moving. "Why are you doing this?" she asks weakly.

My mouth curves into a cocky grin. She has no room for questioning my motives. I won't give in that easily.

"Don't ask questions."

She sighs and jerks her bra down, exposing her perfect pink erect nipples.

"Fucking gorgeous."

I can hear her breathing quicken as she watches me touch my cock through my pants. The sight of her makes me ready to toss all my plans out the fucking door, but I don't. I can't.

I stare at her, taking in every inch of her fresh, silky skin. I didn't get a chance to see her like this the other night. It was too dark and I was too hungry to wait. But now…now I was going to see exactly what was driving me insane.

"Touch yourself."

"What?" she gasps.

"Your breasts. Touch them."

"This is humiliating. I'm not doing that. You can't make me." She's trying to stand her ground with the seriousness of her tone, but I can see her quivering from all the way across the desk.

I stand up and round the corner of my desk. I step behind her, her back to my chest. I wrap an arm around her, squeezing her bare breast in one hand, and grabbing her hip with my other hand. I pull her toward me so she can feel exactly what she's doing to me, exactly what seeing her like this does to me.

"Good," I whisper in her ear. "You deserve it."

"Why?"

I rub her nipple in between my thumb and finger, pulling aggressively and squeezing her breast in my palm. She yelps at the pain.

"You're not as confident as I thought you were," I taunt. "If you can't handle it, just say the word and I'll stop."

"Just tell me why you're doing this."

I grab her blouse and pull it down her arms. I toss it down next to her skirt. I unsnap her bra and add it to the collection.

I palm both of her breasts in each hand firmly. She moans as her body leans into mine, her body arching deeper against me.

"You left yesterday morning without a word." I squeeze her breasts harder.

"I had class."

"You bailed like a one-night stand would."

"I'm sorry."

"Are you?" I free one hand and lower it down her stomach.

"Yes," she pants out.

"You humiliated me, Ceci." My hand slips under her panties, a finger making its way inside her. "Leaving me like that."

"Like you're humiliating me?" she counters. I begin rubbing her clit as I palm her breast harder. I synchronize the moments together, teasing and torturing both sensitive areas at the same time.

"You don't think having that conversation with your professor humiliated me, Ceci? I'm the soon-to-be CEO and you made me look incompetent."

"You acted like you understood," she breathes out, trying not to react to how she is really feeling.

I spin her around and push her until the back of her thighs hit my desk. I lean over her until my lips are barely touching hers.

"I said I wouldn't tell, I never said I wouldn't make you pay a price."

"I apologized." Her breathing quickens, but her eyes are strong, determined.

"I don't appreciate being made a fool." I lean harder against her so she can feel me through my pants. I run both of my hands up her legs and grab hold of her thighs. I spread them wide and fit my body inside. "Do we have an understanding?"

She leans back on her hands and arches her body up for me. "Yes, Mr. Leighton."

"Good girl."

I lower my mouth and kiss my way down her neck and chest until I reach one of her breasts. I pull it into my mouth and devour it. One hand rests on her back, holding her in place. Her head falls back as a deep moan escapes her throat. As much as she wants to fight it, she can't.

"You're going to need to keep it down," I warn as I move to her other breast and suck on it harder.

She gasps on contact. Her body relaxes against mine as her back arches again, fully giving herself to me.

I smirk at how hopeless her body is to my touch. My mouth makes its way lower toward her panties that are utterly useless in the first place.

I grab her panties and slide them to the side. I rub a finger up and down her pussy, curling a finger deep inside her. She's slick and dripping with want. "*Jesus*…you were waiting for me."

I kneel in between her, kissing up her exposed thigh. Her body already begins trembling and I've barely touched her yet.

"I guess your body doesn't agree with your mind," I say amused. "Or you secretly love being humiliated."

I look up at her as she bites her lip hard— preventing her from screaming at the pleasurable torture I'm causing her. It fucking turns me on to see her like this—greedy and ready.

I close the gap between us and devour her pussy. I continue rubbing her clit as my tongue circles inside of her. Her body jerks at the intensity of my mouth and finger working her. Her hands are holding her up behind her, but the way her body arches into me, she's practically falling flat on the desk.

"Oh, God…I-I can't—"

"Hold yourself up," I demand. I curl two fingers inside of her, making her hips buck forward.

"Bentley...yes..." she moans, her eyes closing as her head falls backward. "Oh, God...yes...oh my God..."

"Sweetheart..." I say in a firm tone. I stand up while keeping my fingers in place, bringing my face to hers. "You're going to let the entire floor know what you're up to."

"I don't care...let them."

"You want to test that theory?" I ask, curling my fingers inside of her harder and deeper. "How loud can you get?"

"Fuck...Bentley...God, yes!" she all but yells. I didn't think she would—she's testing me just as much as I'm testing her. I close my mouth over hers, kissing her fiercely as she lets her moans rivet down my throat. The vibrations are intense and keep up the rhythm my body has against hers.

"I love when you scream my name," I break the kiss and whisper against her ear. "However, I'd rather hear it with my dick inside of you."

"I don't remember that being in the company handbook."

I lick a trail up her neck and ask, "Do you want me to stop?"

"God, no," she immediately responds. "Oh, God...yes...so fucking good."

"Lean back," I tell her. She drops her elbows and lays flat on my desk. She's perfectly laid out for me in just her panties and stockings.

"Jesus, Ceci...I'm tempted to take you just like this."

"I'm not stopping you."

CECILIA

Bentley grabs me, pulling me up to his chest. He tells me to wrap my legs around him, and I comply willingly. He carries me to a sidewall that isn't visible from the door. He's eerily silent as he crushes his body to mine as he kisses my neck and grinds against me. I wrap my arms around his neck, pulling him in closer.

One arm releases me as he reaches for his back pocket and pulls out his wallet with a condom. I watch as he unzips his pants and rolls it on. He aligns our bodies up perfectly and moves my panties out of the way before entering inside of me.

"Oh my God…" I gasp at the size of him pressing inside of me. My body takes him inch by inch, opening up wide for him. It's only been a couple of days, but I already missed the way it felt to have him. It feels like nothing I've ever had before and now that I have it, I don't want to know what it's like to not feel him.

His tongue licks a path from my chest to my neck. He sucks lightly as he thrusts inside me, over and over again. My thighs tighten around him, begging him for more. He spreads his feet farther apart, stretching my walls wider for him. He grinds deeper, reaching all the way inside of me. My fingers claw at his back. My nails dig into his skin, marking him as he fucks me harder.

"Ahh, yes…Bentley…oh, God…fuck, yes." I can't control the random screams that escape my throat. My mind is beyond coherent thoughts.

He palms my mouth, muffling the moans and screams. "You have to stay quiet," he warns.

"I can't…" I pant.

He smirks, proud that he pleases me beyond control. His mouth grabs mine—his kisses fast and raw as he brings me to climax. I orgasm all around him as I moan deeper into his mouth.

His body begins to tense, his release not too far behind, when a loud knock interrupts us. He palms my mouth again and leans into my ear, "Don't move."

I breathe heavily into his hand, nervous that someone's about to walk in and catch us.

His hips don't get the memo, though. He continues a slow, sensual rhythm. My eyes widen at him in question—*what the hell is he doing?*—but he ignores me. His free hand grips my hips as he continues driving deep inside of me.

The knock continues as my heart beats loudly. So loud that I'm sure the person on the other side of the door can hear it.

"Don't tense up," he says softly. "I'm not going to stop fucking you."

I try to relax my body as he stretches my walls again, pumping harder inside me. My hips beg to move with his, but his firm grip securely holds me in place.

The door opens and my breathing stops. I lean firmly against the wall, hoping to God that this person doesn't round the short hallway in his office.

"Sweetheart…" His voice breaks me out of my panic attack. "You feel so fucking good. I'm not stopping until I'm done with you." I swallow, hearing the seriousness of his words. "It's the evening cleaning crew…" he informs me. "That's no reason to stop."

I want to laugh and cry at the way he doesn't seem to mind that we're about two seconds from being busted. Apparently, it was turning him on because I could feel him stretching wider inside me.

"Mr. Leighton?" A woman's voice asks.

"Shh…" he moans against my ear. "She'll just grab the trash and vacuum. Less than five minutes." I can tell he's trying to reassure me, but it's making me panic even more.

Both of his hands secure me in place on my hips as he jerks hard and fast inside me. My head falls back as he moves smoothly inside me, my eyes closing as he brings me to another orgasm.

The vacuum sounds just as another one ripples through me. I cup my mouth with both hands, trying to hold in the moans of pleasure that sweep over me. I try to bite my lip and keep it in, but the feel of him releasing inside me puts me over the edge.

"Oh, God, Ceci…fuuuuuuuuuck…" he moans hard against my ear. He's much quieter than I am, but as soon as the vacuum stops, I force the moans down my throat instead of releasing them.

We stand there until we finally hear the door slam shut. He releases me, slowly dropping my legs to the floor. He rolls the condom off and adjusts himself back in his pants before walking back to his desk.

I follow behind, feeling sore and exposed. Bentley and I haven't exactly talked about our 'situation' but I'm not so sure I should question it either. Before he found me in his office, I could've swore he wanted more from me, but now I'm not so sure he does anymore.

I watch as he disposes the condom in the trash and I go in search of my clothes that are sprinkled across the floor.

"Oh my God!" I squeal. Bentley turns toward me immediately as I take in my clothes—perfectly folded on top of his desk.

CHAPTER SEVENTEEN
CECILIA

As soon as Bentley told me to search for a certain transcript for him earlier, I knew it was my opportunity to search for Samuel Anderson. I hadn't known what to look for the last time I was in there, but this time I knew.

However, I still came up empty handed. No record of a Samuel Anderson and nothing linking him to any cases.

Shit.

This isn't getting me anywhere.

Once he confronts me about Professor Hennings, I know I have to come up with something quick. That'll be two strikes against me, and soon he'll be putting the pieces together. I have no choice but to lie, *again*.

Relief washes over me when he says he won't tell the committee, but part of me knows it's not over. The intense heat between us hasn't faded since Thursday—if anything, it's multiplied—escalating at even a faster rate than before. It's dangerous territory, I know, but I can't stop it now. My body gives into every command, no matter what my mind says—Part Devil and Part Angel has given up on me completely.

I grab my neatly *folded* clothes off his desk and quickly dress before anyone else can burst in. It's 5:30 PM and way past my internship time. I walk out with what dignity I have left without a word to Bentley.

My hair is a complete mess from being slammed against the wall repeatedly, my clothes are wrinkled, and my face is completely flushed.

There's no way I can go home like this. I need time to cool off.

Instead, I drive to Cora's and decide to have that chat I promised her.

"Holy shit!" she shrieks when she answers the door. "She's alive!" She grins.

I roll my eyes at her melodramatic tone. "Barely," I quip. "Are you going to let me in?"

We walk to her room where she finally takes in my wardrobe. "You are a hot mess. Where have you been?"

I clamp my mouth shut, unable to keep eye contact with her. I may be good at lying to Bentley and my mom, but Cora was someone I couldn't. Ever. I've tried.

And failed miserably.

"All right, spill it." We both sit on her bed and face each other.

"You first," I counter. "Are you and Simon hooking up?" I ask bluntly.

"WHAT?" she gasps. "That's a big fat no."

I look at her suspiciously, eyeing her closely to see if she's telling the truth.

She's not.

I grin at her fake disgusted expression.

"Why don't I believe you?"

"I don't know. It's the truth. I hate Simon."

"You might hate him, but you were definitely making out with him yesterday."

"Who told you that?" she spits out before realizing it. Her hands cover her mouth, her eyes wide. "I mean, who said that?"

"I knew it." I laugh. "Totally called it, by the way."

She sighs. "Shut up. It was a one-time thing. Not happening again."

"Sure." I smile.

"Okay, so now tell me. This new guy—who is he?"

I spend the next hour telling her about Bentley. I leave out the whole internship/boss thing, because I know she can't handle that, and I don't want to hear her freaking out over it. I tell her that after meeting him, we've been randomly hooking up.

It wasn't a lie. But it wasn't the full truth.

Honestly, I don't even know what's going on. I feel this whole situation is slipping away from me before I even have a chance to firmly grasp it.

After finding nothing on Samuel Anderson, I begin to wonder if he's even connected to my dad's death. However, I can't stop thinking that if my mother hid it that he had to mean something. I just have to figure out how.

I change as soon as I get home, trying to take in the day's events. Everything happened so suddenly. I'm not even sure how it happened. One minute, I was getting his dry cleaning, the next he was fucking me against the wall in his office with the housekeeper ten feet away.

I need to get my head back on. Focus on what I'm doing there in the first place. Bentley's a major distraction—a nice distraction—but I have to remember my priorities.

I decide to corner my mom and see if she'll tell me anything. It's a long shot, but I have to at least try again.

"Mom?" I peek in the living room where she's watching TV.

"What is it, Ceci?" she asks, yawning.

"I think we need to talk," I begin as I sit on the other end of the couch.

She sits up with a panicked expression. "Oh my God! Are you pregnant?"

I cock my head and grimace at her. "Yeah, you're going to be a grandma. My baby daddy and I are running away to Paris," I taunt with a straight face. "Congratulations."

She points her finger at me and scowls. "Seriously, that's not funny." She puts a hand to her chest in relief. "I'm too young to be a grandma anyway."

"I'm glad that's what you'd be most worried about." I roll my eyes at her.

"What is it, Cecilia?" Her face tenses. "Are you in trouble?"

"No. I want to ask you about Dad."

She shifts uncomfortably and stares at the ceiling hesitating before responding. "What do you want to know that I haven't already told you?"

I cross my arms and ankles at the same time. "Well, how about dad's lock box for starters. What's in it?"

She gasps, her eyes widen in surprise. "H-How did you know about that?" she asks in a demanding tone.

"I've been searching for answers, Mom. For *seven* years, I've asked. I've prayed to God to just tell me. I haven't been able to move on with my life. *Every day* my scar reminds me, making sure I *can't* forget that day. It's *consumes* me."

She swallows hard, shocked at my confession. "Who have you been talking to? Do you have *any* idea what you're doing? You could be putting us in danger, Cecilia!"

"By who, Mom? Why won't you tell me?"

"Who are you talking to?" she asks again.

"I have a…a friend who helped me. I found the note about Samuel Anderson under your mattress."

She shakes her head in disbelief. "You should've never done that. You have no idea what you're doing! You're going to get us killed!"

"Then tell me, Mom!" I shout, my cheeks burning with anger and resentment.

"We're not having this conversation. You're…not ready," she proclaims. "It's to protect you."

My mom runs out on me with absolutely no answers—except that I know for sure that the note *does* have something to do with my father. Which means I need to find out who Samuel Anderson is myself, since she clearly won't give me any answers.

My mom not telling me could be more dangerous than disclosing. I deserve to know the truth, no matter what. And I won't stop until I have it.

Casey comes into my room shortly after. She sits on the end of my bed silently. I pretend to read a magazine, but I'm watching her intently.

"We haven't talked in a long time," she begins. "Like really talked." I hear the pained regret in her voice.

I match her tone. "I know."

"How's Simon?"

"Good. Still longing after Cora but neither will admit it." I laugh. "And you? What's up in Casey-land?"

She narrows her eyebrows at me. "Casey-land? Oh, it's ultra-hopping, let me tell you. My semester is packed with back to back classes plus working part-time on campus. It blows."

I wrinkle my nose at her. "Something to look forward to."

"Yeah, right." She laughs. "Nah, it ain't so bad. College is awesome. You're gonna love it."

I shrug, not really agreeing with her.

"Can I ask you something?" I say softly.

"Yeah, sure." Her face flashes a look of concern.

I instinctively rub my fingers over my shoulder, feeling the scar with my fingertips. "How much do you remember about that day? I know you've told me before, but…do you remember anything else? Like any conversations between Mom and Dad before?"

Her lips form a straight line. I know it's a hard topic for the both of us, but I needed to ask her.

She looks down and her voice is pained. "I remember them fighting a lot. Mom crying. Dad begging her to forgive him. I remember he made her a lot of promises." She finally looks up at me with sad eyes. "I guess he never kept them."

I nod in return. I can feel my throat tightening up, becoming scratchy at just the thought.

"He loved us, Cecilia." I look into her eyes as she continues. "Dad loved you so much. Always gloating about how smart and talented you were." I smile weakly. "If he only knew what a hot mess, troublemaker you turned into." She laughs playfully.

"I prefer badass, thank you very much."

She smiles. "Either way, he'd be proud of you."

I reach across the bed and grab her hand. "Thanks, Casey. He'd be proud of you, too."

It was the first time in years Casey and I had talked about Dad. It was always a sore subject in our house, Mom never wanting to discuss it or allowing us to ask questions.

CHAPTER EIGHTEEN
CECILIA

AFTER THE FIGHT with my mom, talking to Casey really calmed me down. I still have a thousand questions, but at least Casey was willing to talk to me about Dad.

I shower and get ready for bed, but first check my email and see one from Bentley. My heart begins racing as I click on it.

To: cwest@leighton.com
From: bleighton@leighton.com
Subject: Employee Conduct

Miss West,
Don't think I didn't notice that you were over a half hour late for work today. Surely, you do not intend to make this a habit, as I'll have no choice but to fire you.

Mr. Leighton

P.S. Clearly the other night was too much for your body to handle, so next time we'll be skipping the fucking foreplay— there's not much use for that anyway.

I respond immediately.

To: bleighton@leighton.com
From: cwest@leighton.com
Subject: Re: Employee Conduct

Mr. Leighton,
I am fully aware that I was half an hour late to work today. I am also aware that HR received notice of my aforementioned tardiness *last week* as I knew I had a morning appointment scheduled for today a while ago.

Miss West

P.S. The other night was definitely not "too much" for me to handle. I handled it quite well, from what I remember—even slammed up against your wall. However, your assumption that there will be a "next time" between the two of us—after today—is rather laughable.

I lie about my morning appointment, but he doesn't have to know that. And after today, I'm not so sure things between us should escalate —but who am I really kidding?

To: cwest@leighton.com
From: bleighton@leighton.com
Subject: Re: Re: Employee Conduct

Miss West,
It's good to know that you're capable of contacting HR about your tardiness in advance, but last time I checked being late still means "being late."
Make sure it doesn't happen again.

Mr. Leighton

P.S. I went rather easy on you today. Next time, I won't give in to your loud ass moans. And yes, I did say "next time," because it's not an assumption. It's a fact.

I spend the next half of the week in a haze. As desperately as I want answers for my dad, I'm coming up empty. If I'm going to find anything, it'll be in the company database. But that's not going to be an easy task.

Unknown: Be ready by 7PM Friday.

Cecilia: And this is?

Unknown: 2100 E. Grand Ave.

Cecilia: Who is this??

Unknown: Don't be late. Wear those stockings.

I didn't know whether to be giddy or pissed off. I know I've given him reasons to doubt me, but now he's just acting like a cold and distant asshole.

Cecilia: I have plans.

Bentley: Cancel them.

Cecilia: Fuck you.

Bentley: That's what I'm hoping for.

I look up the address and see it's for the Hilton Grand Hotel of Omaha.

Cecilia: I'm not staying at a hotel with you.

Bentley: No one said anything about staying over.

Cecilia: You are impossible. At least tell me what I'm supposed to wear.

Bentley: Preferably nothing. But since this is a public affair, I suggest something elegant.

Cecilia: I don't appreciate being told what to do with no clue as to what's going on.

Bentley: I don't appreciate being deceived, Ceci.

God. This man is infuriating. Clearly, he's not going to give that up. He's the one that fucked me up against a wall with another person in the room! Yet, I'm the one in trouble for 'lying' about who wrote my recommendation letter.

Sigh. I know what I have to do now.

I'll have to put the digging around on hold until I gain his trust back.

Cecilia: Fine. 7PM.

Bentley: Friday. Be on time.

I lean back on my bed, sighing. How was I going to get out of this without blowing my cover?

I'm completely in over my head with Bentley. As much as I want to fight the attraction, it's obvious I can't.

And neither can he. Knowing Bentley craves me as much as I crave him, I'll use that angle into getting what I need.

I'm wearing one of Casey's favorite dresses—a dark purple sequin cocktail dress that lays mid-thigh with dark black stockings—just as he requested. She'll kill me if she finds out it's missing, but I ignore the thought as I refocus on my main mission here. If he's going to use my mistakes against me, I'm going to use his cock against him. It only seems fair.

I arrive at 6:54 PM and hand my keys over to the valet. I have no idea what I'm doing here, but I'm ready for anything he throws my way. If he wants to fuck the truth out of me, *I'll play.*

"Good evening, Miss West." I hear Bentley's deep voice behind me before I even enter the hotel. I turn around and gasp as I take in his crisp black tuxedo. His hair is gelled back and he's trimmed his face.

I can practically feel my panties combusting into flames, melting away at just the looks of him.

Focus, panties. Stay intact.

His hands are shoved in his pockets as he eyes my outfit. He gives me a nod of approval before closing the gap between us.

"You look exquisite." He places a hand on my lower back as he leans in and kisses me softly on the cheek.

"Thank you," I say softly. "You look stunning."

"All part of the job," he says matter-of-factly. "Let's go in."

I swallow as he wraps his hand around my waist and guides me inside. I still have no clue what we're doing here, but I go with it for now.

I've never been inside the Hilton before, but it's everything I imagined a five-star hotel to look like—bright lights, exceptional details on the walls, modern furniture too immaculate it doesn't even look used. And that's just the lobby.

He guides me to the elevator and hits the twenty-fourth floor button. "You mind telling me what we're doing?"

He presses me into the wall, his hips firm against mine as he nuzzles his nose into my neck. I inhale his clean scent mixed with his cologne. My body molds into him but before I can react, he responds, "Just go with it." He kisses my cheek tenderly before the elevator dings and opens wide.

He guides me out into a large ballroom. The lights are dim, but I can still see every intimate detail.

"Wow…" I gasp, taking it all in. "This is beautiful."

"Come." He grabs my hand and leads me further inside.

The ballroom is surrounded with people—mostly middle-aged people, but I spot a few younger couples.

"Good evening, Mr. Leighton," I hear several men say to him as we pass by. He stops for a second to nod and greet them back, but never long enough for introductions.

"Would you like a drink?" he leans in and asks.

"Sure," I reply quickly.

He grabs a server's attention with champagne glasses on a tray and grabs two of them.

He hands me one and says, "No getting tipsy on me now."

I grab it and smirk. "No promises."

I take a sip as I look around and try to figure out what kind of event we're attending.

"Bentley!" I hear a woman's voice echo across the room. We both spin around to an older woman flailing her arms at us.

Bentley leans in and presses his lips against my ear. "Play along."

"Darling, you made it!" She wraps her arms around him and he returns the gesture.

"Of course, Mom." He politely kisses her cheek, and I wonder how this man can have so many different sides. This one I actually like.

"You look fantastic. Perfect."

"Thank you," he replies embarrassed. "Can I introduce you to someone?"

"Oh, yes!" Her eyes light up excitedly.

I swallow hard as they both turn toward me. Bentley places a hand on my lower back and introduces me. "Mom, this is Emily. My date."

My eyes widen as my lips curve up into a surprised grin. *Emily?*

She immediately takes my hand. "Emily, darling. A pleasure."

I smile wide. "Likewise, Mrs. Leighton."

"She's stunning, Bentley. Just stunning," she gushes as if I'm not standing right there.

"I agree." His lips curve into a small grin. I smirk back as I take note that he just *lied* to his own mother.

"Your father is around here somewhere. Do you want me to go find him quick?"

"Not necessary, Mom. I'll run into him later."

She begins smoothing his tuxedo, brushing away invisible dirt off his chest and shoulders.

"Stop being nervous. It's going to be fine," he says calmly, grabbing her wrists and pulling them down. "My speech is ready."

She breathes a sigh of relief and says a quick goodbye before turning on her heel to find her husband.

I flash a knowing grin as Bentley turns toward me. "What?"

"Just taking in what a hypocrite looks like."

He licks his lips and brushes a hand through his hair. "I'm not a hypocrite."

I step toward him and say softly, "You've been punishing me for lying to you. You just lied to your own mother…"

He looks amused by my stern voice. He leans in close, looking around us closely to make sure no one can overhear us. "Would you rather I inform her that I'm fucking my intern instead?"

"Then why even bring me?"

"Because you look good on my arm," he says with no shame. I jerk back, irritated by his response. "Because you want to learn. What better way to learn about a company than attending its recognition ceremony."

"Well, you could've told me."

"And where's the fun in that?" He cocks his head and smirks at me. "Come on. We need to take our seats."

We run into more people before sitting down. I feel a dozen set of eyes on me the entire time. I try to not let the nerves get to me, but I have no idea what's going on and that makes me even more anxious.

Eventually, we're all seated and all our eyes are facing the front where an older man is giving an introduction speech. I try to keep up with what he's saying, but the paranoia of being here distracts me.

I look around and notice Bentley's mother sitting in the front with Mr. Leighton. She's squeezing his arm tight with a wide smile on her face. She's obviously very proud.

"And now, to present the award we're all here for tonight." The gentleman on stage begins speaking.

Bentley leans over and whispers, "That's Mr. Lyle, Chairman of the Business Board."

"Leighton Enterprises—not only do they have the highest record of most solved cases in investigating and reporting, but also hold the highest in charitable contributors throughout the Midwest. They are being recognized for both tonight, but I must add—they are the strongest team of investigative reporters Nebraska has ever seen. And that's why they are receiving the *Golden Bridge Business and Innovation Award* six years in a row!"

The room echoes in applause as Mr. Lyle holds up the clear, scripted award. Bentley's father takes the stage, shaking hands with him. Everyone stands up as Mr. Leighton takes the podium, myself included. I watch Bentley as his face beams with pride. His eyes are locked on his father as he sets the award down to showcase.

It's a different side of Bentley—watching him watch his father like that. His facial features soften as his eyes lock on his dad.

After Mr. Leighton gives his speech, Bentley rises and takes the stage. My eyes widen as I take him in—business and sex appeal wrapped into one deadly combination.

Watching him talk about how proud he is of his dad warms my heart. The way he praises his dad for a strong upbringing, being a powerhouse CEO, and intense work ethic makes me realize how proud Bentley really is of his father's company. Blood, sweat, and tears go into running Leighton Enterprises—failure and accomplishments all a part of the journey to get where they are today. His speech is heartfelt, and I cannot believe I'm even here tonight to witness it all.

"Stay with me tonight," Bentley whispers as we approach the valet.

"I can't."

"Yes, you can."

I turn toward him and eye him cautiously. "If I'm late to my internship again, my boss is going to fire me," I say matter-of-factly.

He rubs the stubble on his jaw and smirks back at me. "Sounds like an asshole."

"He very much can be."

He closes the gap between us and softly kisses my lips. It's not rushed or eager, it's sensual and sweet. "I guess he has a lot of making up to do."

CHAPTER NINETEEN
BENTLEY

"Thank you for coming with me tonight."

"I wasn't left a choice," she fires back. "But...I'm glad I did. It was definitely an experience."

She's sitting casually on the couch, trying to sit properly, but she's fighting a losing battle. Her dress is hiked up, and no matter what sitting position she's in, that thing is not getting any lower.

I sit across from her, twirling my drink around in one hand as I watch her intently. All the doubt flooding in my mind and the answers to the questions still not settling with me are both reasons why I shouldn't be with her right now.

But my body doesn't agree. It aches for her. Craves to touch every inch of her. There's just something about her, and I just can't seem to get enough.

"Are you hungry?" I finally ask. "Surely, that salad didn't fill you up."

"Are you offering to cook for me?" Her eyebrows rise in anticipation.

I stand up and hold my hand out for her to grab. She lets me pull her up and lead her into the kitchen.

"I do cook, actually." I smile back at her and she eyes me cautiously. "Well, I can cook pasta. So as long as you eat pasta..."

She laughs. "Yes, I eat pasta."

She props herself up on the counter as I gather the pots and ingredients. Finally being alone with Ceci without the distraction of work or other people around feels natural. I still feel like I'm fighting all the emotions unraveling through me, but I know I don't want to anymore.

"I think my mom likes you."

"She only met me for a few moments."

"Trust me." I grin. "She does." I place the cover on top of the pan as I wait for the noodles to boil.

"She won't once she finds out I'm her doting son's weekend intern," she mocks. "Or that my name isn't Emily." She laughs.

"I think she'll get over that. At least the name part." I grin.

"Well, at least she has a nice impression of *Emily*," she responds in a slightly higher pitch.

I walk over to her, settling myself in between her legs. I cup her face in my hands and dip my mouth down to hers, softly grazing her lips.

"Well, next time, you can give her a full dose of Ceci. She's the one I want anyway."

"You have an odd way of showing it, Mr. Leighton," she responds formally.

"I guess I deserve that." I smirk.

I caress a finger slowly up her arm, making goose bumps rise in my absence. Her eyes follow, and I feel her breath hitching as her body immediately responds to me.

"Would it help if I said you could introduce me to your mother as someone else?" I jibe as I continue brushing a finger up and down her arm, making her extremely aware of how close we are.

She swallows and responds, "Anything would be better than introducing you as my boss, Mr. Leighton...so how's Frank, my conquest?" I can hear the amused tone in her voice—she's uncomfortable discussing her parents with me.

"Frank? I'm not a seventy-year-old man."

"And I'm really not introducing you to my mother." She shivers as I blow cold air over the goose bumps that are now apparent over her entire body.

"All right..."I begin, unable to take my eyes off her. "So no meeting the parents."

"Just my mom, actually," she blurts out. Her eyes immediately lock on mine. "Since my dad left," she clarifies. I see the hurt in her eyes, and I know she doesn't want to talk about it.

I continue skimming my finger up her arm and land just below her shoulder. I place a few soft kisses on her burning skin and her head falls back on contact.

I gasp as my lips feel a large scar over her right shoulder. I brush a finger over it, silently questioning where it came from.

"You have a scar." I gently lay a kiss over it. She inhales as I feather kisses around the mark. "What happened?" I finally ask, needing to know.

"Car accident when I was younger," she says right away. I lean back to look at her. "A piece of glass got stuck in my shoulder. No biggie. Just left a scar, that's all." She shrugs casually, but doesn't continue.

My lips brush up her neck and slowly to her ear, gently sucking on the lobe. I'm losing myself in her, *in us*. The doubt, fear, and suspicion all take a back seat—no longer willing to let that set me back.

Her body quivers again. A moan escapes her throat as my lips get more aggressive, licking and sucking every fleshed surface I can.

I kneel in between her legs, moving her dress up and over her hips.

CECILIA

My dress lies on the floor as I sit on the kitchen counter, my legs spread wide for him in just my panties and stockings. His hands grip the back of my knees as his mouth devours me, captivating my every thought. The way he expresses himself to me shows me how *badly* he wants me, scares the hell out of me.

I know I should be keeping him at a distance, yet my body constantly betrays me.

After tonight, I feel even worse about lying to him. The last thing I want to do is get his company in any legal trouble, but I don't know how to walk away anymore—my chances of getting the information I need will never happen. My chances of being with Bentley will be nonexistent.

My heart bleeds in remorse because I know I'm deceiving him—every part of me screams to just tell him the truth and beg him to forgive me, yet my heart fights to protect him. I'll be crushed if he lets go of me completely, but he'll be *devastated* by the secrets and lies.

My stomach growls as Bentley kisses his way up my body, landing on my breast. His hand roams freely over my hot skin, revealing the goose bumps that lay underneath it.

"You're hungry." I feel him grin as his mouth wraps around my nipple.

I lean back with my hands flat on the counter and moan. "Well, only one of us ate…I'm starving."

He grins as he releases my nipple and finally stands up. He presses a small kiss on the corner of my mouth and smiles down at me.

"So clever."

"Are you going to feed me now?" I raise an eyebrow at him.

He licks his lips and eyes me carefully. "Absolutely."

I grab my dress and pull it over my head as he finishes preparing our meal. Two plates, cups, and silverware are all on his kitchen table, lined with candles. I narrow my eyes at him as I watch him set up a romantic dinner.

"What?" he asks.

"You're setting the mood."

"And?"

"I didn't peg you for a candlelight dinner type of guy, that's all." I grin sheepishly. "It's very…*un-Bentley*."

He presses a hand to his chest in disagreement. "I happen to know that chicks dig this, okay? This is the ultimate getting laid set-up."

I burst out laughing at how serious, yet sardonic he sounds. "Because *that's* going to be an issue?"

"I know girls watch chick flicks …you all secretly want to be wooed."

I shake my head at him, grinning. Not only is he *trying* extremely hard, but also he's letting his guard down around me—letting me in to see the type of man he could be.

My heart races as I realize he's doing this for me…thinking that it's what I need. The sex, chemistry, connection—it's all amazing and there's no denying that, but now this was crossing over into relationship territory.

"Favorite movie?" I ask, swirling my fork around in the pasta. "And it can't be porn."

"Well, then what's left?"

"Um, comedy, action, romance, thriller, horror…" I ramble off as I take a bite.

"Okay…comedy is anything by Steve Carell. Action movie is

definitely anything with Bruce Willis. Horror movies—love them, especially Friday the 13th. But the 1980's version. Always the original. "

"You forgot romance."

"I don't watch romance."

"Everyone watches some kind of romance. I'll tell you mine." I take a sip of my water quick before continuing. "50 First Dates. It has a mixture of romance and comedy. Plus, it's sweet the way he fights for her." I smile down at my food, too embarrassed to look him in the eye. "Every girl wants to be fought for," I say softly.

"I haven't seen that one," he admits.

I drop my fork dramatically. "Are you dead? It's Adam Sandler!"

He laughs at my melodramatic tone. "Sorry, I'm not a high school girl who sits in her room all weekend watching chick flicks. Hell, I didn't even do that with girls when I *was* in high school."

I swallow hard. My eyes widen. My body starts shaking, and I start to wonder whether or not I could be having a panic attack.

"I was just kidding…" he lingers off, but I don't move. I can't move. Every nerve in my body is on alert. My heart is beating so hard I'm afraid it will beat right out of my chest and plop on the table in front of me. My fingers are tingling, and I'm sure the blood has completely drained from my face.

"Ceci?" His tone is filled with concern. "Are you upset?"

I swallow again and shake my head to bring myself back together. "No, of course not. I know you're just joking."

I need to stop being so paranoid.

He rubs his hands against his legs soothingly and asks, "Do you want to watch a movie tonight? We can order pay per view."

I smile so he doesn't think anything is wrong. "Sure."

CHAPTER TWENTY
BENTLEY

OUR WEEKEND SLEEPOVERS evolved into weekday sleepovers. Sometimes even multiple nights, something I had never allowed before. She was consuming more of me, and I was powerless to fight it anymore.

I roll over to an empty space next to me. The smell of Ceci still potent in the air and sheets, the scent of our sweaty night still lingers in the room. I nuzzle my nose in the pillow on her side and inhale deeply. God, I could never get enough of that. *Of her.*

I hear the shower running and know she must be getting ready for her class. She studies in between her classes and sometimes stays late to finish up, yet she always finds time for me, time for us.

I swing my legs off the bed and grab my briefs that lay on the floor. I bite my lower lip devilishly as I think of a better idea instead. I toss my briefs back on the floor as I strut out of the room and down the hallway toward the bathroom.

I slowly walk in and can see her shadow behind the glass door. Her body is pure perfection—curves in all the right places, soft, smooth skin, long, gorgeous hair. I find it hard to believe another man hasn't placed claim on her before me.

I tiptoe to the edge of the shower and slowly open the door without disturbing her. Her head is fully under the spray of the water, her hands rinsing her long locks. I step in and slowly shut the door back just as her body jerks, but I wrap my arm around her waist pressing her back against my chest. She gasps and jerks her head back until I bring my lips to her ear.

"Shh…baby, it's just me."

"Jesus, you scared the shit out of me."

I grin against her neck and begin pressing kisses against her wet flesh. One hand roams free across her flat stomach as the other reaches to cup her breast.

"Sorry about that…but I just couldn't resist touching you the moment I woke up." I press my hand harder against her stomach, forcing her body to press against my growing length that's come to life. I slide my hand down and rub a finger over her clit making small circles around her.

"Mm…" she moans, her head falling back against my shoulder. "I'm going to be late for class," she whines, but doesn't stop me.

I playfully nibble her ear and kiss her under the lobe. "Is that a problem?" I tease.

She chuckles lightly. "My business teacher gets pissed when I'm late. It's a shock he hasn't kicked me out of class yet."

"Business? There's nothing you can learn about business in the classroom that I can't teach you…"

"Oh, yeah? What's that? How to seduce your interns? Was that part of business 101 or human sexuality? Perhaps I missed the memo…"

And with that, I force my finger inside her and squeeze her breast harder with my other hand. I push my cock against the flesh of her ass as she gasps out a sharp moan.

"Actually…" I begin, rubbing her harder and deeper. "It's psychology 101—learning to manipulate the human mind and body— how to possess the desires you really crave," I say matter-of-factly.

Her body melts into mine as she mumbles a groan of a response. Her hips rock with my finger in rhythm as I continue aggressively fucking her, torturing her—*owning her.*

"Mm…Bentley," she hums. "Oh, God…yes," she moans. Her hips rock harder demanding release. I force another finger inside her as I allow my cock to press into her ass. I rub it in between her cheeks as her body grinds hard against it.

"God, I love it when you say my name, Ceci," I growl against her ear. "Drives. Me. Fucking. Insane." She continues moaning and panting hard until she's close to release, but I don't let her just yet.

I quickly take my fingers out and spin her around so we're chest to chest. She gasps in disagreement, a smirk playing on my face.

"That's torture…" she whines as she grabs my hardened length and strokes it between her forceful fingers. "Is that the kind of game we're playing…" she muses, adding her other hand to fondle my balls as she continues stroking with the other. "Because you know how I feel about games…"

"God, yes…" I pant out, my head falling back as her precious fingers mold around my cock. "Baby…"

She strokes harder on command, my body building up with tension and craving release. I can barely take it, needing to feel her body against me right now. I cup her cheeks hard and crush our lips together. She continues pumping me, torturing me with her powerful hands.

"Good God, Ceci…" I growl, barely separating our lips from each other. I stroke my tongue with hers, begging to taste her. "Yes, baby…*Jesus Christ*…"

I can feel her smile against my lips in satisfaction as she feels my body tense harder around her.

"Stop…Ceci, stop," I demand. She slows her pace as her eyes look up at me. "I need to be in you, sweetheart. Bend over."

I assist in turning her around, her fingers wrapping around the towel bar that sits in the middle of the tile wall. She arches her back as I grab both of her hips in alignment with my length.

The view is perfection, her petite figure laid out for me, soaking wet and ready. I rub my length playfully along her ass as her anticipation of my entrance drives her insane. I can feel her body buck up against mine as she begs for me to give her exactly what she wants.

"Ceci, I need you to trust me," I say softly. "Can you do that, sweetheart?" Her body tenses slightly at my words. "Do you trust me?" I ask again as my fingers make their way to her clit. I rub in circles until her body relaxes against my soaking wet fingers.

"Yes," she moans out. "I trust you with my life," she admits. It's all I need to hear to know that what I'm about to do will be something she's fully trusting me with.

"Good girl… whatever you do, don't move until I tell you to."

"Okay," she responds softly. Her body molds into mine, giving me complete control and access to her.

I rub my length up and down her ass a few times. She moans in eagerness as I tease her pussy with the tip, but not giving into her silent plea.

I align our bodies and rub my hands softly against her ass. I spread her cheeks and work a finger inside her, letting her get use to the feeling. She grinds against it, moaning, and begging for more. *Fuck... she's into it.*

My cock presses slightly into her. She tenses up immediately denying me access.

"Ceci...trust me." I try again and on instinct, her body jerks. "*Don't. Move.*"

I see her head nod and wait until her body melds against mine once again. I take my opportunity and rub against her once more, this time pressing inside her. She's so goddamn tight I nearly lose my balance as I stretch her to fit my size.

"Oh, fuck, Ceci..." I groan. Her body opens up wider for me. I press further into her slowly inch by inch. "God, yes..."

"Holy shit," she screams out. I feel her grasp the shower bar tighter. Her body begins relaxing and moves in motion with me.

I ease into her slowly, inch by inch I dive deeper inside her perfect, tight ass.

My movements become harder and with each deep thrust, I feel her body contract against me.

"Ahh, Bentley...my God..." she moans. "Don't stop. Please, God, don't stop."

It's all I need to hear to grind balls deep inside her, giving her exactly what she's begging for.

CECILIA

Our routine progresses like this for weeks—comfortable banter, intense attraction, and spending more time together naked than clothed. The sneaking around at the office, weekend sleepovers, and texting continues despite the risks of being caught.

No matter how much we're together, it's never enough. I crave more of him—*of us.* My heart and mind are fighting a battle—stop letting him get close, stop letting him in—but I don't.

I break down his walls and walk right into his heart. Something I tried to get a handle on, but I'm afraid I'm no longer in control.

I've gained little information and I'm starting to wonder if it's worth it. Worth breaking his heart, shattering mine, and exposing who I really am.

I walk into his office and set another coffee on his desk. He's on a conference call, so I make sure to stay quiet. He mouths, 'thank you' but before walking out, I get an idea.

I round the desk and drop to my knees in front of him. His chair spins toward me, putting me perfectly in between his thighs.

He continues talking as I slowly unzip his zipper. He squirms in his chair, but I press my hands against his thighs to signal him to stop. I look up at him and lick my lips, showing him exactly what I plan to do to him.

He finally eases into the chair as I stroke his cock—long and hard— my palm wrapped around him firmly. His head immediately falls back as he tries to stifle a moan. I can hear the other person on the phone talking, but Bentley isn't listening to a single word.

I wrap my mouth around his cock, slowly and torturously bobbing my head up and down his length. His body tenses underneath me as his hand fists in my hair. I can feel him struggling against me as he tries to talk to the person on the phone. His hand holds my head in place, telling me to slow down, but instead, I begin stroking him with one hand as I suck him harder and faster.

His body soon unravels under me, his throaty moans evident—no longer being discreet. I hear him fighting against it as he continues rambling to the person on the other line. As soon as his cock convulses inside me, he slams the phone down and moans loudly without caring who hears him.

"God, Ceci…" He clenches his lips, but is powerless. "Jesus Christ," he growls as he releases inside me.

I lick him clean and tuck him nicely back in his slacks as if I hadn't just distracted him.

I round the desk in front of him and organize a few files on top. "Would you like me to do anything else for you before I head back to my office?"

He doesn't respond as he brushes a hand through his messy golden locks. He busies his hands as he grabs the files and piles them on top of each other.

He looks up at me, licks his lips, but doesn't say anything.

"I do believe you're speechless, Mr. Leighton."

He gets up from his chair and comes toward me like a pouncing lion. He cups my face with both hands before crushing our lips together, stroking his tongue against mine, passion filled-kisses emerging between us.

"I don't have a way with words around you, Ceci. With you, I am almost speechless." His hands soften their grip as he continues. "With you, I don't know how to act because I've never felt this way before. It's like a blend of lust and fear. A mix of wanting to protect myself and letting my guard down all at the same time. It's almost unexplainable, but the constant beating of my heart lets me know it's a feeling I can't ignore."

His face is soft and genuine. I can feel his steady breaths against my blistering skin. I don't know what to say...I don't know how to react.

I swallow slowly as I take in his words. They're so...honest. And raw. I've cracked him—he's *falling* for me.

"I've been having the same inner battle," I respond honestly. "But it's a battle I no longer want to fight." I smile up at him, hoping he understands what I'm saying. "I don't just want to be an office relationship, I want *more*."

"It is more, Ceci. Much more." He rubs the pad of his thumb slowly over my lips before leaning in and kissing me once more.

He takes a seat back behind his desk, trying to recover. I offer to help him sort out the files and bring them back when I'm finished.

He gladly agrees since he needs to make a call again—and apologize for his sudden 'disruption.'

I smile wide as I grab all the files off his desk and walk out his office door as if I've just stolen a million dollars.

An inner battle of motive and desire are fighting inside of me—struggling on what I'm doing—desire to get them without him knowing what I'm about to do.

My father's files sitting only a couple of feet from me feed my motive to distract him. Anything to get him thinking about something else, divert him of what he was doing previously.

I overheard his phone conversation with his father last night while we lay in bed. He thought I was passed out, but I wasn't. I heard every word.

"I want to work on some old cases. I think it'd be good for press."

He stayed quiet while his father spoke, but from the excitement in his voice, it was easy to assume his father agreed.

"I want to look into cases over five years old. Get some fresh eyes on them and see if I can follow up on anything. Imagine if a breakthrough exposes a case that was never solved. The press would go crazy. Not to mention, branching out would be next."

"Yeah, yeah." He listened to his father speak some more. *"I'm going to start with the ones you personally worked on,"* he stated with amusement, *"just to see if I can find anything."*

He laughed with his dad, obviously joking around with him, but I knew for a fact his father worked on my dad's case.

This was my chance.

I slam the files on my desk. I scatter them until I spot the *West, #178376* on a thick manila folder. Everything they used in his case is locked up in evidence, but this was a general run down of everything they found and how they had come up empty-handed. I peek out of my office before tiptoeing to the transcripts room.

I tap my foot anxiously as I photocopy everything. There're a good one hundred plus papers, but I'm not leaving until every piece has been scanned.

After lunch, I place the files back into his office all neatly organized. He has a lunch meeting downtown and told me to order something if I wanted.

I eat my Chinese takeout while reading over scripts of my dad's case —trying to make sense out of anything that happened that day.

Bentley is gone the majority of the afternoon. He's texted me several times apologizing for the delay and finally told me I could go home if I wanted. Considering there isn't much for me to do without him, I take him up on the offer.

I start walking down the hall toward the elevator when one of the reporters stops me.

"Hi."

"Um, hi."

"So you're Mr. Leighton's weekend fling, huh?" He licks his lips, as his eyes look me up and down. I shudder with disgust.

"I'm his intern, Ceci. Who are you?" I scowl.

"Oh, my apologies." He puts a hand to his chest, pretending to act sincere. "I'm Mr. Littleton. You can call me Toby." He continues eyeing me. "I just wanted to meet you."

"Great. Well, now that you have, I need to get going."

He looks at his watch, confused. "It's not five 'o clock yet. I believe that's when you're allowed to leave."

"Actually, Bentley is running late from a lunch meeting and said I could leave."

"Bentley?" His eyebrows rise in suspicion.

I clear my throat quickly. "Mr. Leighton." I swallow as he flashes a cocky grin. Shit. This guy is a complete creep.

"Do we have another Hannah on our hands?"

I raise my eyebrows in question. "Who?"

"Oh, *Bentley* hasn't told you?" he asks, amused.

"Clearly, he hasn't if I just asked who she was," I snap back. "Excuse me, you're in my way." I try to walk around him, but he steps in front of me again.

"She almost took this entire company down. Piece by piece, she dug her greedy little fingers into Bentley and stole insider information. The moment she went public with it, it almost ruined us for good. Not to mention what it did to Bentley."

My eyes glaze over at his words. I had no idea. Of course, how would I? Bentley never told me. I never asked about previous girlfriends. I only knew about his modeling career based off the search I did beforehand.

"Well...thanks for the info. I'm not sure why you felt the need to tell me, but now I'm really leaving."

Anger—at myself—fuels my power to push him hard enough and out of my way. He gasps and reaches out for me, but I'm already two feet ahead of him and fleeing to the elevator.

CHAPTER TWENTY-ONE
BENTLEY

I CHECK my watch constantly as I sit in my lunch meeting that runs three hours over. I normally schedule my conferences for during the week, but Mr. Welter flew in specifically for me.

I invite Ceci over that night. Although, I saw her that morning, I already miss her—miss touching and kissing her. I hadn't ever missed a girl like that before. Never.

No matter how many times I see her, it's never enough. I want more. *More of her.* Everything inside me screams to stop—stop letting her get close, stop letting her in.

But I don't.

I let her sledgehammer my thick walls, step over the debris, and get right under my skin. Something I swore I wouldn't do again after my life was almost destroyed before, but I don't feel in control of it anymore. My heart has completely taken over, ignoring all the flashing red warning signs around me.

We've fallen into a comfortable routine—cooking dinner, foreplay, eating dinner, and end up either on the living room floor, the shower, or sideways on my bed.

I wake up the next morning with my arms and legs wrapped up in Ceci. Her back is pressed against my chest and all I can think about is how breathtakingly beautiful she is. Her messy locks are spread wildly on the pillow and her bare skin glows in the sunlight that's shining through the windows. Her face looks soft and pure as it relaxes against my arm that's wrapped under her. She looks absolutely...*stunning*.

She's an addiction I never knew I wanted, a feeling of never having enough, never touching enough, never smiling enough. She made me *that* person. That love-sick puppy dog that craves her like my last meal. That person I swore I'd never be—that person I never *wanted* to be.

She startles awake, and I instinctively wrap her in closer to me, not wanting to let her go.

"Good morning." I kiss her shoulder softly. "Did you sleep well?"

"Mm hmm," she moans, squirming against me. "I don't even remember falling asleep..."

I smile lightly. "You passed out pretty quickly after—"

"Oh my God...my body. My legs," she interrupts. "They feel like jelly."

I rub a hand up and down her arm, feeling the goose bumps rise as I touch her. "Sorry about that." I grin.

She turns around, not even self-conscious about the sheet falling off her exposed chest. "You are so not." She smirks.

"Well, you're the gymnast. Perhaps you just need *more* practice."

She slaps my chest and wrinkles her nose—the most *adorable* fucking thing she does. "I don't think my body could handle more *practice*. I think it needs rest. And perhaps a massage." Her eyes light up, signaling exactly what she wants.

I lean down and kiss the tip of her nose. "I would love to, but I'm out of lotion."

She bursts out laughing and it takes me a moment to think about what's so funny.

"Oh my God...no...not...stop laughing," I laugh with her. "That sounded really bad."

"Sorry," she apologizes, continuing to laugh. "I hang out with really immature guys. It's not my fault I find that funny."

"Wait...you hang out with guys?" I narrow my eyebrows at her, only teasing, but wanting to know the truth.

"Yes...is that a problem?" she counters.

I cup her breast aggressively making her wince. "Not at all." I grin. "As long as they're gay."

I shift on top of her and kiss the corner of her mouth. She smiles weakly, keeping her eyes closed.

I lick a trail up her body, stopping at each breast to pull in her nipple. She moans as the pressure increases.

"You like that?"

"Yes, more," she pleads. She arches her back, exposing more of herself for me. I mouth her breast, sucking harder as my other hand moves down her stomach and don't stop until I reach her juicy slit. I curl a finger inside, synchronizing the rhythm with the movements of my mouth.

"Oh, God! Yes! Don't stop."

I increase the pressure, adding a second finger inside of her. My mouth moves up her chest, licking a trail up to her lips. She moans in my mouth as her hips buck at the intensity. My fingers ride her hard and quick, curling up deep inside her.

"Harder! Yes! Yes, oh, God!" she screams as I continue finger fucking her.

"What do you need, baby?" I encourage her. "Tell me."

"You, please! God, I want more!"

I grind my fingers in her as hard as I can, deep and slow as she arches her hips harder into me.

"Bentley! Don't stop."

"Jesus…" I growl against her ear, edging her on. "I love it when you scream my name, sweetheart." I push a third finger in. "The sound of your voice when you come could cure cancer."

I kiss her softly as she rides out her climax. She's completely beat, so I tuck us back in and fall back to sleep.

I hear ruffling in the distance, but my eyes are too heavy to open them. I tighten my hold on Ceci, double-checking she's still next to me. Her body is warm and molds just perfectly against mine.

"Oh my God!" A high-pitched squeal jerks my body into overdrive. My eyes widen at the sight of my parents in my bedroom doorway.

I grab the sheet and quickly cover us up. Ceci frantically presses back against me, shielding her naked body from my parents' eyes.

"What are you doing here?" I scold. Ceci covers her heated face with one hand, keeping her head down. Her cheeks heat as her eyes close in humiliation.

"You never showed up for brunch," my mother scowls. "We were worried about you when you didn't answer your phone."

"After the tenth time calling you," my father adds in.

"Can you please give me a minute to get dressed? I'll meet you in my office."

My mother clenches her pearls as she flashes me a disapproving look. My father grabs the door handle and pushes them both back into the hallway. I wait until the door clicks before finally exhaling.

"I am so sorry."

She uncovers her face finally. "Well, there's a first time for everything. Getting caught by your parents." She swings her legs off the bed and begins looking for her clothes.

"Are you angry?" I sit up and watch as she frantically searches for her clothes that I know are lying on my living room floor.

"No, I'm just embarrassed."

"I know. And I'm so sorry. I should've remembered to call them and let them know I wasn't coming. I'll go speak to them and ask them to leave. Okay?" I grab a pair of shorts and shirt from the closet. "Your clothes are in the living room, by the way." I kiss her gently on the forehead before heading out to scold my parents.

I brush a hand through my hair as I prepare for a lecture for missing Sunday brunch.

I close the office door behind me as I lean back against it. Both of my parents are standing and staring at me—practically glaring daggers in my direction.

"It's not what you think—"

"It's exactly what we think," my mom huffs, cutting me off. "Is she another Hannah?"

"NO! She isn't like that *at all.* She's not just a one-night stand," I defend. "You met her already," I remind my mother.

My father grins wide and my mother takes notice, jabbing him in the gut with her elbow.

"Yes, but after what happened last time, your dates don't usually last longer than one night."

"Thanks for making me sound like a pig." I cross my arms in disbelief. Most parents would approve of their son being in a *relationship.*

"We're still dealing with Hannah," she reminds me. "What did we tell you?"

"Patricia," my father warns, but she ignores him.

"Did you at least do a background check on her? Make sure she's not another one?"

"Oh my God…" I groan, brushing a firm hand through my hair. "Not every girl is going to be like Hannah. She's not like that."

"And how do you know, Bentley? You need to be careful. You aren't just a typical guy—"

"Yes, I know." I roll my eyes at the same lecture she's been giving me for two years. "She's an intern," I spit out needing to get her off my case.

My father's eyes go wide. "*Your* intern?" he asks slowly, and I know I really fucked up now.

"Yes, but it's not like that," I say quickly.

"Do you have any idea what you're doing, Bentley?" he scowls. "Apparently you aren't ready, son, putting the company at risk. Not to mention breaking a hundred company rules."

"It's *not* like that," I say again more firmly. "She isn't Hannah. I've checked her out already. She attends the University of Nebraska. She's a senior and is graduating this semester."

My mother walks toward me and places a hand on my cheek, her eyes finally going soft. "Just be careful, son." My father follows suit and doesn't even look me in the eye as I step out of the way for them to leave.

I exhale as I hear my front door closing. Flustered, I pace the floor until I regulate my breathing. This couldn't have been worst timing.

"Ceci?" I call out as I walk down the hallway back to my room. "They're gone now. It's safe to come out." But she doesn't respond. "Ceci?"

I push my bedroom door open and look around, but she isn't in here. "Ceci?" I call out again with fear laced in my voice.

I run to the door and whip it open to see that her car is gone.

She left.

CHAPTER TWENTY-TWO
CECILIA

I CRY myself to sleep every night until it overcomes me, and I have no other option, but to pass out. The hurt, the betrayal, the lies—I've caused it all.

I overheard Bentley's mother yelling at him. *Hannah.*

Why did she do it? Did Bentley love her? Who was she exactly? Answers I didn't deserve to know. Answers that would soon force my lies to crumble down around me.

I can't hurt him. Not after what he's already gone through. I don't know anything about this Hannah chick, but I know enough from Toby and his mother's screams to know she's bad news and that she royally fucked Bentley over.

I ignore every call and email from Bentley. I know I have to deal with my consequences soon. I know he won't just let it go. *Let me go.* But I'll have to convince him, though.

It's taking me days to read and dissect everything in my dad's files. Although it's a summary of it all, I find myself Googling the terms to even know what they mean. I don't want to rush through, it's my only piece of hope—I'm reading it thoroughly, word by word.

Simon knocks on my door Friday afternoon with a suspicious grin and a grocery bag. I narrow my eyes at him as he lets himself in.

"Come in," I mock. "What are you doing here?"

He spins around and eyes me carefully. "I've known you for years,

Celia. Long enough to know when something is wrong. You've been off all week."

I tilt my body forward, chancing a glance inside his bag. "And you've brought me cookie dough and ice cream?" I tease.

"I'm not a chick," he retorts. I raise my eyebrows at him and he sighs in defeat. "But you're a chick, so of course, I brought you junk food."

"I knew there was a reason I keep you around."

"Well, I'm kidnapping you. Pack a bag and meet me at the car."

"Wait, what?"

"You haven't told me to fuck off all week, so that's when I know there's something wrong." I laugh at his bluntness.

"Fine," I groan. "Meet you in five."

Simon lets me dig into the cookie dough on the ride to his house. I've been sleeping over at Simon's for years. His parents are super laid back, and I secretly think they are hoping something happens between us, but it's never going to happen. Simon is like a brother to me.

I had shoved the file in my purse before we left, because, at this point, I'm out of options. Simon's extremely smart, so if there's anything to be deciphered from my dad's case, Simon will figure it out.

"Okay, girlfriend. I've sugared you up, gave you caffeine and ice cream, and even let you walk around in those hideous yoga pants. Time to spill."

My spoon stops mid-way to my mouth just as I was about to devour another spoonful. "Hideous?"

"Well, they aren't exactly *attractive*."

I shrug, shoving a spoonful of ice cream into my mouth. "Good thing I've turned lesbian. Girls dig yoga pants."

He rolls his eyes and laughs at my dramatic speech. "You couldn't be a lesbian if you tried. You enjoy dick too much."

I spit the ice cream out, shocked at his words. "Simon!"

"You and Cora think you talk quietly at lunch when you discuss your little girl shit. I can hear every word," he confesses.

"Oh my God, that's so embarrassing." My face heats at the thought of Simon hearing all the juicy details from last year when I dated Jason. "No, I'm erasing this whole conversation out of my head. Never happened."

"Whatever you say, sweet bottom."

I gasp loudly as my eyes dramatically bulge out of my head at the words he just said. *Sweet bottom.*

"I so hate you right now. I cannot believe you heard all that last year."

"Every word, baby," he taunts.

Sweet bottom was Jason's nickname for me. At the time, I thought it was cute, but now I cringe just hearing it aloud.

For the next hour, I tell Simon everything about my internship at Leighton Enterprises. I leave Bentley out of it, but I explain how I applied, interviewed, and used Casey's transcripts to get inside. He was both impressed and worried about me, knowing the serious repercussions if I were to get caught.

"You are insane. Seriously."

I also describe the dreams and flashbacks about my dad. I tell him everything I remember about that day, and how my mother never seemed bothered that it ended up a cold case.

"Wow…that's intense, Celia."

I tilt my head toward him, silently begging him to understand my reasoning. "Simon, I need your help."

"You know I can't say no."

I smirk. "I know."

I spread out some of the papers that I want him to take a closer look at—the evidence, the background history of his job, and his financials.

"What exactly are you hoping to do, Celia?"

I shrug, feeling hopeless. "I just need to know, Simon. I know my mother is hiding secrets from me. She won't tell me anything. She hid that piece of paper about Samuel Anderson on it. I need to know that my dad was a good person and that whoever did this gets the justice they deserve. I know I'm in over my head, okay. I'm not *that* crazy. But I can't just walk away. I have to at least try."

Hours go by and eventually, I fall asleep on Simon's bed. When I wake up, he's curled up on the other end with papers in his lap. I notice the energy drink in one hand as he holds a piece of paper in the other.

I glance over to his clock on the dresser. It's after 4AM.

"You're still up?"

"Yeah," he says excitedly. I adjust myself on his bed, sitting upright. From the looks of it, he's completely wired.

"Read anything good?"

"Celia…this is *all* good stuff. Like, I think I'm finally figuring it out."

"Figuring what out?"

"Your dad's finances—they're all over the place. One month he deposits thousands of dollars, the next he's in the negative. For someone with a steady job and salary, it doesn't add up."

"So what's that mean?"

"Well, it explains why your mom and dad were fighting about money, why your mom was hysterical about the money he spent."

"So you think it has something to do with his death? Like maybe he owed someone a lot of money and he couldn't pay them back?" My heart begins racing as I try to put the pieces together.

"I don't know. Maybe. It's too soon to know for sure. There's a lot more in this file I have to go through yet."

"But what if does have to do with money. I mean, we live in a nice neighborhood, and always had nice things. We lived on one salary and yet never went without."

"Perhaps there's a reason for that." He looks at me sympathetically, silently telling me what I've feared this whole time—my dad *wasn't* a good guy.

BENTLEY

The last thing I was prepared for was Ceci leaving me—again. I wasn't sure if she was upset about my parents coming in or if it was something else.

Having my parents bring up Hannah's name again stirred my emotions up. It's not something I enjoy thinking about.

The very girl who screwed me—over and over again. I believed every word she said to me, every word laced with lies and deceit.

I was fresh out of graduate school when I started working exclusively at Leighton Enterprises. Saying goodbye to my modeling career, my father slowly taught me things throughout my college years. It wasn't until I had my master's degree that he finally gave me access to all the files and confidential information. Information news reporters and magazines would do anything to get their hands on during a big story.

Enter Hannah Whitman. Twenty-two year old college graduate from Penn State. Education major with dreams of teaching first graders. Sweet, sexy, and full of complete shit.

Enter the real Hannah Whitman AKA Hannah Winters. Twenty-five year old post-graduate student in journalism.

I've been known to think with my cock before my head. Shit, it happens. Especially, when beautiful, young girls throw themselves at you. Especially, when you're a high-profile model with nothing to lose.

She made a fool of me. I let her in—too close. She stole all of my files and sold them to another company. They were later recognized for solving the case. Not only did they report on it for months after—my mistake constantly shoved in my face—but it almost ruined Leighton Enterprises. New security measures were taken and the battle of taking Hannah to court began—still in the process of making her pay for all that, but more than likely, she'll make a plea bargain.

It's been hard to let anyone in after that. I went back to one-nighters and emotionless sex—that was until I met Ceci.

I curse the second I realize she's left. I text her how sorry I am and beg her to come back and talk with me. I know she's humiliated, but my parents are the last thing we need to worry about right now. As long as no one in my office finds out, we're in the clear until her internship is over, and then I don't fucking care who knows.

I've called her thirty-six times in the past six days. No answer. I've emailed nine times. No response.

Nothing.

By Friday, I can barely take it. I don't know if she'll show up for her internship on Saturday. I don't know if she'll ever talk to me again, and I hardly understand why.

I'm filled with so much rage, I don't know if I'll be able to stand seeing her without slamming her against my desk and fucking her until she comes to her senses. I wouldn't even stop if my own mother walked in.

I'm agitated the entire day. I snap at everyone who tries to speak to me. Even my own secretary flipped me off when I told her where to shove that piece of shit stapler.

I need to see her. I can't wait another fucking night. It's killing me. I don't know what she's doing, what she must be thinking or who the hell she could be with.

I dig into her intern application and find her home address. If she's going to insist on hiding from me, I'm just going to have to find her.

After showering and getting dressed, I head out. I anticipate she'll be pissed, but I don't care. I'm not letting her walk away without giving me answers first.

I pull up to her house and notice it's in a nice neighborhood, mainly filled with families and children. I begin sweating nervously, unsure if I should get out or not. This isn't where I expected a college-aged student to live with a household of roommates. Perhaps they were renting from a family or she was living with hers?

I wipe my hands on my jeans and get out. I walk to the front and knock firmly on the door. My nerves eat at me until a young woman opens the door, her eyes bulge out of her face as she scans my body.

"Good evening, I'm sorry to bother you—"

"Yes." She licks her lips seductively. "Whatever you're selling, I'll take it." Her lips form a flirtatious grin.

I grin and stifle a laugh before responding. "Um, sorry I'm not selling anything. I'm actually just looking for someone. Ceci? Ceci West. Does she live here?"

Her smile instantly drops and she frowns. "Ceci?" Her eyebrows rise in question. "Sorry, she's not here."

I exhale, disappointed. I shift uncomfortably before asking, "Do you know where she is? Or when she'll be back?"

She cocks a hip. "Who are you? And what do you want with my little sister?"

"Little sister?" My eyebrows narrow. "Like a sorority?"

She laughs. "No...like I'm *her* big sister." She puts her hand out in front of me. "I'm Casey West. It's nice to meet you—"

My body tenses. No, freezes. Hell, I don't know what the fuck it does, but I'm stunned shocked. My body's autopilot takes over as I grab her hand in mine and shake hers.

"*Casey*, it's nice to meet you. I'm Bentley."

"Pleasure's all mine." She continues her seductive tone. "I can let her know you stopped by. She's hanging with Simon tonight. She'll probably get in late, but I can—"

"No, it's fine. I'll just, um, catch up with her later." I nod pleasantly and make my way back to my car.

I can't control the emotions flooding in as I take in what I just learned.

Casey.

Shit.

It's not even her fucking name!

And who the hell is Simon?

My mother's words reluctantly re-enter my mind... *Make sure she isn't another Hannah.*

Fuck.

ONLY WANT YOU

INTERN TRILOGY #2

PART I

CHAPTER ONE
BENTLEY

MAKE sure she isn't another Hannah. Why did my mother have to be right? Right about her. Ceci. That isn't even her goddamn name.

Emotions flood my mind the moment I get back behind the wheel. Hearing her sister as she says her name—*her* name—is like a knife slicing right down my spine. Rage, lust, and confusion all ripple through me.

How? Why...

So many questions, but no answers.

I slam my fourth shot and sit back in my office chair as I think about how to deal with this situation. How did this become my life? How did I let one girl consume me so much that I fucking missed what was right in front of me?

West.

I should've known.

I flip the file in front of me: West, #178376.

Brock West (36). Male. Insurance broker.

Husband to Claire West.

Father to Casey (14), Cecilia (11), and Nathan (2).

Son-of-a-bitch.

Cecilia West. *Ceci.*

How did I miss this? I look down at my cock and know. She consumed me. Took every rational thought and made me give her the benefit of the doubt.

I curse and slam another shot as I read over my father's old case notes. I haven't looked into this case before. It was filed under cold cases long before I arrived. But knowing what it did to my father at the time, I thought if I could come up with any new information, he'd be proud. Or at least it'd give him some closure on the whole thing.

Case notes in the file that have been sitting on my desk when she was here last week. Wasn't it obvious? She got what she wanted and fucking bailed.

I'm onto her little scheme.

I'm not about to let her win. Not again. Not like Hannah.

I'm still hung over by the time I arrive to work early Saturday morning. But it doesn't matter. I won't be here long today. Just long enough to watch Ceci leave.

Or rather…*escorted.*

"Erika, I need security on standby." I beep through to my assistant who's just down the hallway. "Please let me know when Miss West arrives."

"Of course, Mr. Leighton."

Forget pissed off. I'm raging with steam coming out of both ears. I've cracked my damn knuckles so many times, they've turned white. My face feels flush and my whole body is heated with anger. I don't think I've ever been this mad before in my entire life—not when my father told me to quit modeling, not when Hannah dug her dirty, scheming little fingers under my skin, and not even when some asshole drove drunk into my brand new Lexus. Nope. This tops everything.

"She's walking in, sir."

"Thank you. Have security ready in exactly five minutes."

Show time.

"Good morning, Mr. Leighton." She walks in with a bright, wide smile holding my bold, dark coffee. She struts over in her off-white pencil skirt and navy blue top. Her hair is wildly wrapped into a top bun. She looks more disheveled than she's ever been.

"Rough night?" I raise an eyebrow, eyeing over her outfit.

"Just woke up late. My apologies. My alarm didn't go off." She sets the coffee down in front of me and steps back, her hands laying flat in front of her as she waits for her itinerary.

I should make her do something awful, something mind-numbingly degrading—the same way she's made me feel. She's degraded my entire company, treated it as a playground for her to use as she pleases.

"I guess that's what happens when you stay at someone else's house the night before you have to be to work the next morning." I grab my coffee and bring it to my lips. I notice her shocked expression as she takes in my words.

"What are you talking about?" She swallows hard, trying to remain calm.

"Simon, is it? That's where you were last night," I say matter-of-factly.

"Are you stalking me now? You have no right—"

I raise my hand, cutting her off. I stand up and quickly round my desk. She stares at me intently as I walk behind her. I press her back to my chest, gripping her shoulders and securing her in place.

I lower my lips and whisper against her ear, "You're just like the rest." I keep my hold on her, feeling her body shiver against me. I rub both hands down her arms and grip her wrists. "It's a shame."

"Bentley, please. You're freaking me out," she pleads, her chest pumping up and down. "What are you talking about?"

I spin her body around so we're facing each other. I cup her jaw firmly in my hand and grip her hip firmly with my other hand.

I lower my face to hers, just grazing her lips. Her breath hitches.

"You're a goddamn liar. Whoever the fuck you are." I clench my hand around her hip tighter. "At least I found out now before you took my company to the cleaners."

"I-Is this about last week—"

I force a finger over her lips as she stumbles backward. I don't want to hear anymore fucking lies. I don't care anymore. She's taken that ability from me.

"You're *eighteen*."

She gasps loudly, taking another step backward. Her eyes widen as disbelief flushes through her face. I step forward into her space, not letting her get away just yet.

"EIGHTEEN!" I yell, making her jump. I can feel the veins popping out of my forehead as I yell, my face heating with anger the longer I look at her. I get as close to her as I can without actually touching her.

"Bentley, I can explain."

"I don't need an explanation, *Cecilia*. It's pretty fucking clear, don't you think?" I mock. I turn away so I'm no longer facing her. The longer I look at her, the more pissed off I get. "You've been lying since the moment you walked in here. You used me to get what you wanted and now that you have it, you were planning to throw me out like yesterday's garbage."

"No, it was never about—"

Her pleading voice is like nails on a chalkboard. I can't fucking stand it. No more fucking lies.

I turn around and stride toward her, pushing myself right in her face. "Eighteen…" It comes out more like a pathetic plea—begging her to tell me it's not true. But I know it is. I can do the math. It's why she had to use her sister's ID and college information in the first place. She lowers her head, clearly guilty of everything she's done. "Goddamn liar," I growl.

Tears begin falling down her pink-tinted cheeks. She's upset she's been caught, but perhaps more upset about losing me. Losing us? It didn't matter anymore—this is unforgivable.

I take a step backward as I see the two security guards at the door behind her. I lick my lips and lean in to kiss her, but I stop just before our lips meet.

"Let's make this quick and painless, shall we?" Her face tilts up, her watery eyes looking up at me is pitiful. "Cecilia West, you're fired. Get the *fuck* out of my office."

"Wait, what?" She frantically looks around, noticing the guards before screaming, "NO!" Both guards grab an arm and start pulling her to the door. "Bentley, you have to let me explain! Please!"

"The police will be in contact, Miss West. I wouldn't go far." I grin selfishly at her.

Her face turns red as more tears stream down her guilty face. "Please, no! I swear I'll tell you everything!" She begins kicking as the guards exit my office and shut the door behind them. I can hear her screaming and fighting them all the way down the hall.

I've turned off every emotional outlet inside—or at least the alcohol is assisting in making sure it stays that way. That's what got me in this problem in the first place. I couldn't let that control my actions anymore.

Now it's time for damage control.

I need to figure out what information she got away with. What information she got from her dad's case and anything else she found while scanning in transcripts.

My father is going to kill me.

Not a tinge of guilt ripples through my body as I imagine the guards kicking her off Leighton Enterprises property. I only wish I could've witnessed it myself. The look on her face when I revealed her real name was priceless. She knew her lies were now exposed.

I grab the West file and pack it into my briefcase. I need to examine everything before the press gets ahold of anything. Either she has a buyer on standby already or it's for her own personal investigation—either way, charges will be made.

"How the hell did this happen? What the fuck were you thinking? Have you lost your damn mind?" My father's been screaming at me for the last twenty minutes. I've basically tuned him out now. Of course, I know he's be pissed. I'm pissed. But he's beyond anything I've ever seen him before.

Bentley—0.

Girls-who-fucked-me-over-for-information—2.

I surrendered to my dad's screaming match. Basically, he'd been yelling to hear himself yell by this time. I wasn't even fighting back. There was nothing I could say to defend myself. I fucked up.

"Ashton!" my mother scolded, breaking him out of his rage. "That's enough."

"It's fine, Mom. Let him get it out."

"Is that what this is to you? A little game that's just going to go away?"

"No, not at all. I'm going to do everything in my power to keep anything from being leaked. I'm already on it. You don't need to worry. I don't think she was looking to sell anything. She's West's daughter. She wanted information for herself or her family. I don't know for sure, but I'm on alert."

"You better be. This could cost you big time."

"That's enough now." My mother grabbed his arm and forced his body to jerk toward her. "Yelling at him isn't going to change anything now."

"Perhaps you're in the wrong business, son," he mutters just before my mother drags him toward the door.

"Perhaps you're right," I mumble.

CHAPTER TWO
CECILIA

I DESERVE everything Bentley is handing to me right now, but fuck if it still doesn't hurt. The look on his face—empty and distant—makes me want to run up to him and beg him to give me another chance. I want to wrap my arms around him and remind him of what we have—how we feel for each other. I want to go back in time and fix this.

But I can't.

And truthfully, I'm not even sure I would. I came in with the intention of finding information out on my dad, and although I was able to get his file, I'm not sure it's going to help me much, but I had to at least try. I couldn't let the opportunity pass without at least knowing I did what I could.

I sit in my car and sob. I cry for the pain I've caused Bentley, for the lies and secrets I've held, and for the loss of him. I cry because I'm going to miss him and there's nothing I can do to win him back. I know that what I've done is inexcusable.

I don't even know what he knows, or how he knows it, but it doesn't matter anymore. It was only a matter of time. Had I not ignored him all week, perhaps he wouldn't have found out, but the truth would've came out eventually. It was just a matter of time before the bomb went off.

I realize this.

I should've known better. But the way I feel for him...*falling* for him, clouded all my better judgment.

Usually, I'd be on the phone with Cora planning something to keep my mind off Bentley, but what was the point? I hadn't told her much about him and nothing would ever get my mind off him. He was the first guy I've ever connected to, the first guy I've ever really given myself all to—the first one I wanted to be around, to have *more*.

I feel completely helpless. Everything taken from me at once, everything I never deserved in the first place. I wish I could feel sorry for myself and cry about how unfair it is, but I can't. I'm not that girl. And rationally, I know this isn't unfair. It's everything deserve.

I drive home in a haze, still in shock and filled with questions of what Bentley knows or how he found out. Answers I'll never find out, but that doesn't stop me from wanting to know. My dad's file is completely confusing to me, but at least it'll answer some of my questions—but first, I need to get home and tell Casey.

I knock softly on Casey's door with his file under my arm. I know she's going to freak out, but she's the only one that can understand my frustration and how I'm feeling. I have nothing to lose at this point.

"Case, can I come in?" I hear light sobs so I cautiously enter. She's lying down on her bed with her hands covering her face. "Why are you crying? What happened?"

I sit next to her and wrap my arms around her. I've never seen her like this before. Casey is always so strong and hardly shows emotion. This wasn't usual for her.

"Go away, Celia."

I hug her tighter. "No, just tell me what's wrong."

"I caught Elliot cheating on me. And yet, he denies it! Who does that?" she sobs, yelling into her hands.

I look at her in confusion—she's dating someone?

"Asshole," I mutter. "H-How long were you guys dating?"

"Like six months…"

"Why didn't you ever tell me?"

Her head pops up, she wipes under her eyes that are bright red and watered with tears.

"You tell me about every guy you date?"

"We never talk about guys, Casey."

"Exactly." She sniffs and sits up next to me.

"You've never brought a guy home before," I remind her. "I was starting to think you didn't swing that way," I tease, hoping to make her smile.

She scowls at me before replying, "There's nothing to take a guy home to. Mom's never home. You're never home. And really, what's going to happen? Not like Mom would take time out of her work schedule to cook dinner for us all. I guess it worked out for the best though since he's apparently a cheating bastard."

I hadn't thought much about bringing home guys to meet Mom or Casey. When Bentley introduced me to his mom as *Emily*, I knew he'd never be able to meet my mom. Not without some kind of explanation at least.

"Well, either way, I'm sorry you got hurt. Guys can be unpredictable douchebags."

She turns toward me with a small smile on her face. "Oh yeah? Care to share anything?"

"Uh, no. Trust me. You don't want to know."

"C'mon. It might make me feel better." She grins widely, waggling her eyebrows at me like a cat in heat.

"Oh…I can guarantee you'd forget about Elliot if I told you my story. But it'd get me into too much trouble, so I'm keeping my lips sealed." I twist a lock over my lips to emphasize I'm not spilling.

She frowns and her eyes bow down to the floor. "Fine. Make a girl suffer alone then."

"Stop it." I knock shoulders with her, getting her to smile. "The plus side of both of us down at the same time is we can wallow together. Ice cream, trashy magazines, and reality shows."

"Oh my God." She laughs. "Sometimes I forget you're not an eleven-year-old brat anymore." I smile back at her. "Now you're an eighteen-year-old brat."

She laughs loudly as I push her over, making her fall to her side. "Okay, you're only like three years older than me."

She sits up and looks at me sincerely. "I know. We should do more stuff together."

"Agreed. Now…time to raid the kitchen."

"So what was this boy's name?" she asks as we both sit against the headboard watching reruns of some reality show and scooping chocolate ice cream out of the container.

"Bentley…"

"Oh, he even sounds hot."

"He is." I eat another mouthful of ice cream, hoping it freezes my brain, and I forget everything perfect about him. "I screwed up though, not him."

She turns to me with a shocked expression. "I guess he didn't forgive you."

"Oh, hell no. He was *mad* to say the least. I deserved it."

She's looking at me with a careful expression as if she's wondering if she should go there or not. We don't share a lot of personal information about each other. Just seems easier when you're in an unreliable family.

"Well, whatever you did, I'm sure it was with the best intentions." She shrugs, clearly trying to make me feel better.

"Yeah…it was. But it doesn't matter. I screwed up and have lost him forever."

"You're only eighteen, Celia," she offers. "You have plenty of time. Plus, guys are going to be tripping over each other to date you in college." She smiles and curls her feet underneath her. "Like, I worry about your safety. Perhaps you should hire a bodyguard just in case."

"You're so dramatic." I laugh. "But then what if the bodyguard starts coming on to me. Who'll protect me then?" I mock.

"We'll make sure it's a woman."

"And what if *she* hits on me?" I laugh again.

"Well, then just fucking roll with it. It'll probably work out better anyway." She giggles.

"You're probably right."

I wake up sometime in the middle of the night still in Casey's bed. Surprisingly, we had a pretty good night. We gossiped, watched TV, and just let our guard down with each other. I hadn't ever felt that comfortable with Casey in my entire life. It made me feel so much better knowing I had someone who could relate with what I was feeling, and that I had someone to go to for comfort.

I call Simon after breakfast and tell him to meet me at the coffee house. My dad's file is still my only hope and the sooner we get through the rest, the better.

"Jesus, Celia. How many days are you planning to stay up?" he asks, eyeing my quad shot caramel latté.

"Trust me, I need it." I yawn, taking a seat next to him. "You will, too."

He rolls his eyes dramatically at me. "What would you do without me?"

"Uh, drink my coffee in peace."

"You're so lucky I deal with your shit."

"I know." I smile weakly at him, secretly thanking him for it. "Now, last time you mentioned something about my dad's finances. I want to go through and see if there's any mention about a lock box, security box, or something like that. Anything that would connect to the note I found in my mom's room." He gives me a disapproving look as I sip my coffee. "What?"

"You're getting your hopes up."

"No, I'm not."

"Yes, you are." He shifts his chair closer to me."

"Don't you think if the police knew about any lock box, they'd be the first ones in it? And if they knew, your mom would have no reason to hide the code?"

I exhale and think about what he says. He has a point. "Okay, you're probably right. So you think he hid money in there? I mean since his accounts were never consistent."

"It's possible. But maybe your mom doesn't even know. If she did, she wouldn't keep the code. Or need to hide it. I doubt she even knows what's in there."

"So why would you keep a code of a secret lock box for seven years and never try to find it?" I question aloud.

"Maybe she's waiting for something. Like a certain time."

"It just doesn't make sense. Maybe she knew about it? Or maybe she found the paperwork for it and burned it but wrote down the code so she wouldn't forget?" I sit anxiously, tapping my foot. "Gah, this is so infuriating. Why can't she just freaking tell me? Why does she act like everything is so dangerous when I question her?"

"Maybe she's keeping it a secret for a reason, Celia. Maybe there's secrets she can't bare to tell you, and wants to protect you. Maybe you should just let her," he says sincerely, but cringes as he takes in my expression.

"I think I deserve to know. I almost died that day too, or well, I could've had a bullet hit me in the neck or something. And this person is just walking around the Earth as if he didn't kill my father. It's just not fair."

"Of course, it's not fair. Nothing about this is fair."

"If I could just find something that brings me closer to him, something that tells me my dad died as a good person, maybe I'd be satisfied enough. But right now, there are just too many unanswered questions. It drives me insane. Every day, Simon, every day. I wake up with a million questions. I wake up wondering why I didn't get to keep my dad, why I was chosen to lose him, why he was chosen to die. They're questions I can't get out of my head. How am I just supposed to walk away from that? How do you continue to live without trying to do anything possible to find the answers to those questions?" I ramble without looking him in the eyes. It's painful letting everything out, but I feel safe with Simon. I feel comfortable enough to cry in front of him.

Tears slowly fall down my face and roll off my cheeks, hitting the table below me. I wipe them off before Simon can see, but I know he notices.

"Celia...c'mon, let's read through the rest." He shifts his chair directly next to mine, opening up the file in front of us.

CHAPTER THREE
BENTLEY

I PACE my office until the darkness has consumed me. The cleaning crew has been in already and turned the lights off when I was pacing the hallway. Once I came back in, I never bothered to turn them back on.

What was the point?

A full week has gone by without seeing or talking to Ceci. Not that I had expected to see or talk to her, but part of me—a messed up part —was hoping she'd at least try to contact me via email or text message.

I never planned to call the cops. Even my father won't because the press would get a hold of that and run with it—it would be bad publicity on Leighton Enterprises. However, that doesn't stop my father from chewing my ass out every chance he has.

The city lights shine through the window giving me just enough light to walk the length of my office. I don't know what else to do or how I'm supposed to handle this. From the file alone, there isn't anything remotely intriguing enough to sell—if that were her intent. Something inside me knows it wasn't. She's just a little girl that lost her dad and wanted answers. Perhaps that is what's worse—knowing she came in with the intention of stealing information for her own gain. She already had the internship—she wouldn't need to sleep with me to get anything else, but that sure as shit doesn't simmer the anger. All the unknown, all the rage building up inside me—makes it impossible to let it go knowing she was willing to risk my company's reputation for her own gain.

I haven't slept since last weekend. And even when I did, it was her that I saw. Her face, her laughing, her perfect curves pressed up against mine—everything about her is ingrained into my brain.

I grab my keys and bolt out of the office. I need to keep myself busy. I need to be productive in *something*.

I decide to hit the gym and run off some steam. There just so happens to be a kickboxing class starting. *What the hell?* Might as well join. Maybe it'll be good for me.

That class is mixed with both guys and chicks. It's a beginners' class, but I'm pretty sure I can kick the shit out of the bag.

"Welcome, class. My name is Maya. I'm going to go through some basic moves and then we can get into a routine."

She runs through techniques and stances before we really get into it. It's actually fun, and I find myself enjoying it. I kick and punch with everything I have, taking everything out on the bag.

She begins clapping to gain our attention and says, "Great job, class! Y'all did wonderfully! If anyone is interested, I'm teaching two classes a week—this one and a more advanced one. Feel free to stop in if you're feeling brave." She winks and claps again, applauding us for how well we did.

I walk up to her once the crowd leaves and tell her thanks for a great class.

"You did great," she beams.

"What day is your other class? I might stop in."

"Wednesday nights." She looks me up and down. "You should stop in. You can stay in the back if you're not quite up to the level."

"Sure." I smile back. "Sounds great. Thanks." I wave as I leave, and for the first time all week, I feel as if I have something to look forward to doing. Working out during my modeling days was part of the job, but now it'd be for fun. Something to get my mind back on track.

"Well, you look like you're in a better mood finally," Erika comments as I walk in Monday morning.

"Don't let looks deceive you," I snap as I walk past her. I felt great Saturday night after boxing class—re-energized. But Sunday morning, after spending the morning with my parents at brunch just reminded me of my fuck up and of *her*.

I barely finish my coffee and get through my emails before Ryan pops his head in.

"Dude, Senator Montgomery, breaking news. Conference Room. Now."

I jump up from my chair and follow him down the hall. We've been following the story for weeks now with his wife's embezzlement scam.

"Who's on PR?" I ask as soon as I walk in.

Joe sits taller as he hears my voice. "I am. Waiting on a return comment."

"Who's getting ready to write the report?"

"I am, sir," Toby responds right away, already typing away on his laptop. "As soon as we get the press release comments, it's going live."

"Who's making sure we even get a comment?" I ask, taking a seat across from Toby. "We need to act fast. They are going to get hounded."

"Michelle is emailing me right back."

"What's Plan B when Plan A goes to shit?"

"When have we ever needed Plan B?" Ryan muses. "It's fine, Bentley. Chill."

"Trust me. You never know when you'll need a Plan B." I groan.

"Well, right now, everything is fine. We have insider information that the misses didn't work alone," Ryan reports as he continues to stare at the TV.

"My money's on the senator," Toby offers. 'There's no way she was smart enough to pull that off on her own."

"Humph. I wouldn't doubt women with an agenda," I retort. All their eyes are on me as I realize I've said it aloud. "Never mind. Can we just get the story, please?"

We work the rest of the afternoon, building our story and using insider resources for our investigation. If embezzlement is proven, Mrs. Montgomery will be facing jail time. Better yet, if *we* prove it, it'll get my dad off my back at least.

I attend the advanced kickboxing class Wednesday night and get my own ass kicked. It feels good putting my anger into something, using it to release the frustration and tension building up inside me.

I attend class twice a week for the next two weeks—feeling better and better each time.

"You probably don't need a beginner's class anymore," Maya says at the end of class. "You could probably teach it by now."

I smile back at her, taking in her petite, athletic body. She's naturally tan with dark brown hair and bright brown eyes. She's been very professional, which has made me feel the most comfortable coming to class each time.

"Thanks. I have a lot of issues to work through." I grin, grabbing my bag and tossing it over my shoulder.

"I see that a lot in here. A lot of ex-girlfriends and old jobs as their muse." She smirks.

I give her a small smile, not wanting to divulge into my personal life. "I bet. It's a good stress reliever."

"It sure is. See you next week."

I wave goodbye as I head out of class. Before I met Ceci, I might've tried to hook up with her. Offer to take her out for a drink: code for one-night stand, or since I'd see her in class again, it'd be multiple one-night stands. But I hadn't even felt the urge. Perhaps Ceci took more from me than I thought.

CHAPTER FOUR
CECILIA

IT'S BEEN two months since Bentley kicked me out of his office. I can still feel his hands on me, his lips and tongue licking up my neck, and the tightness of him inside of me. I feel the butterflies, the shivers, and the quivering my body convulsed into as he made me climax. I remember everything my body felt, everything I felt for him.

I know I owe him an explanation. He deserves one. But how do you tell someone you manipulated, lied to, and potentially caused him and his company's reputation damage that the feelings you have are real?

I haven't slept. Barely ate. I lay in my bed and listened to the same sad song over and over again, self-torturing myself into exactly what I deserve.

I finally graduated high school, but it didn't feel like it. It felt like I was leaving a part of my life behind. A part of my life I'd never get back.

I was no closer to finding information out on my dad as I was the day I left Leighton Enterprises.

Simon's still trying to help, but so far, nothing. The file tells me everything about that day that I hadn't remembered, so at least I was able to get that much out of it, but other than that, I feel defeated—a failure. I don't have closure about my dad's murder, or about the way Bentley and I ended things. Rather, how he ended things.

So when I find myself parked outside of Bentley's condo, I

contemplate walking up the steps to his door. I feel guilty about what I did, what I've caused him, but most importantly, I feel guilty he doesn't know the truth—the *whole* truth.

I wrap a sweater through my arms and take three deep breaths. The sky is pitch-black with only a few scattered stars lighting my way to the front of his condo.

I walk up the stairs to his door and stare at the "7" nailed on his door. Reluctantly, I bring my hand up and knock three solid times.

My heart is beating so hard that I can barely hear my own thoughts trying to talk me out of this, telling me to quickly run in the other direction.

I wait in anticipated silence, nervous to see Bentley again. I'm not exactly sure what to say or if he'll even let me say anything at all. In fact, I won't blame him if he slams the door in my face.

I hold my breath as Bentley opens the door. I study him carefully and immediately noticed how casual he's dressed—ripped, faded jeans and a tight, dark blue T-shirt. He looks so fucking good that I have to remind myself to exhale before speaking.

"Hi," I say softly. His eyes are burning a hole into mine—hard and unreadable. I chew my lip as I watch him—unmoving and silent. My eyes drop, not wanting to see the pain in his face. "I'm sorry to just show up like this, but…I had to see you one more time. You deserve an explanation." I pause. "The truth," I clarify.

"Who the hell are you to tell me what I deserve?" He crosses his arms, his feet part, hovering over my petite size. He's intimidating, but I can't let that scare me. I need to do this.

I swallow and briefly looked back up at him. "I'm nobody. You're right. I just wanted you to know one thing. Although the internship was a fake, and I lied about my background, my feelings were one hundred percent real. I never lied about the way I felt about you. I never expected to meet someone like you, and then when you started coming on to me—"

"Don't you dare put that on me, Ceci. Don't you dare blame me for that."

"I wasn't!" I shout louder than I mean to. "Sorry…I don't blame you for anything. I got in too deep and then my feelings for you grew stronger and I-I didn't know what to do."

"Did the truth ever come to mind?" He narrows his eyes at me.

"Yes…" I whisper. "I mean, I wanted to. I knew it was the right thing to do, but I couldn't. I needed that internship."

"You manipulated your way into my company. You stole and lied. You could've cost me *everything*." His voice is calm but stern. He still sounds as angry as the day he kicked me out of his office.

I shiver as the cold wind passes through me. My nerves intensify as our conversation heats.

His lips form a hard line, and I wonder if he'll give me the chance to explain.

"I know I don't deserve any time from you, but if you'll let me, I'd like to explain." I swallow and look up at him. "To explain the *whole* truth."

He hesitates, scratching the back of his neck and thinking before he replies. "Fine. You have five minutes to tell me something real."

I nod graciously. He backs up and gestures for me to come in. I quietly thank him as he takes my sweater off and hangs it up.

I follow him into the kitchen and sit on a barstool. I lean my elbows on the countertop where Bentley has kissed and licked my bare skin. It brings back memories—memories that I wish were still my reality.

"Do you want anything to drink?" he asks in a soft tone.

"Sure. Thank you."

I watch him intently as he grabs a bottle of water from his fridge and hands it to me.

He leans against the counter across from me, crossing his arms once again. He's looking at me with no emotion as he waits for me to talk.

I take a sip of my water and clear my throat nervously. "Well, you know that my real name is Cecilia West and that my father, Brock West was murdered seven years ago." It hurts to say it aloud, but good in a relieved kind of way. Like saying it to someone else will make the pain real. "I witnessed it and since then have been trying to figure out the events that took place and who killed him. I've been searching for anything that links anyone to him. Things I wouldn't have known at that age. I have limited information and even worse memory of that day. A bullet nicked me and left a scar on my shoulder." I caress it lightly out of habit, remembering how he used to kiss it so tenderly. "I used Leighton Enterprises as my chance to dig into his files, or any files that would give me information." I tightly close my eyes and exhale slowly. "I selfishly used you to get inside for my own personal gain. I needed closure…and at the time, I was willing to do anything to get it."

I pour my heart out to Bentley. I can only hope he'll sympathize with me enough not to take legal action. However, I assume he would've already if he planned to. But I have no idea where his head is at right now.

He shakes his head in disbelief, or shock. Either way, I see his body tense at my confession.

"There's nothing I can say to tell you how truly sorry I am, Bentley. It was all suppose to be a simple get-in, get-out type of job. Learn my way around, dig into files, and find what my mother won't tell me."

"Simple?" he half-laughs in amusement. "Nothing about that is simple. Do you have any idea what you were doing? The risk you were taking?"

"Yes...yeah. I thought I did."

He shakes his head again.

"You were never part of the lies, Bentley. Everything I felt for you—"

"It doesn't matter!" He cuts me off. "It was based on lies. It's no different. You could've cost me my job. My reputation."

"I know," I say quickly. I exhale slowly, needing to get my emotions back in check. "I know...it was a selfish move. One hundred percent selfish," I admit. "I've never felt more regret than I did these past few weeks, replaying every decision in my head over and over."

We both stay silent, neither of us knowing what to say. The electricity between us is palpable—the tension evident in every silent breath not spoken.

I stand up from the stool and brush both hands on my jeans. I hesitate before finally breaking the silence.

"Nothing I can say will change what already happened, and I know that, but just know that I really am sorry. Even if it's too late to apologize, I am." I smile weakly at him before turning toward the door. I grab my sweater off the coat rack and attempt to pull it on when I'm hit with Bentley's scent.

He's behind me, just barely touching my back. I can feel his hot breath on my neck, instantly sending goose bumps down both arms. It's evident the power he still has over my body, entirely consuming and intoxicating.

He grabs my sweater, signaling to let it go. He slowly and torturously pulls it on me and secures it tightly across my chest zipping it up slowly. My back is still facing him, but my body is fully aware of how close he is now.

"Thank you," I whisper softly.

Both hands are gripping my upper arms, securing me in place. I'm not sure if I should move, or if I even can. I'll do anything for him to let me stay, but I know I'm completely undeserving of it.

He brings his mouth to my ear, my eyes closing on contact as he whispers, "Let me help you. I can help find whatever you're looking for."

My heart races at his words, my chest rising. "Why would you do that?" I ask quietly.

He lets out a deep groan as he presses our bodies together. "Because I haven't stopped thinking about you, Ceci. Everything in me screams to hate you, push you away, and not give a shit about you—but I can't. As much as I try to convince myself it was only sex, I can't."

My breathing quickens at his confession. My body aches for his touch, to feel his tongue against mine again, to be held in his arms—anything. I'm begging for all of it.

I squeeze my eyes tighter, holding in the tears that are threatening to escape. Hearing his pained voice tells me just how much I've hurt him, how much I've betrayed his trust.

"Bentley," I whimper, relaxing into his hold. I'll give anything to feel his naked body against mine again.

"Unfortunately, the damage is beyond repairable," he growls in my ear, making me almost breathless. His words speak one thing, but the way his breath hitches tells me another. It's painful for him to even say those words.

"I understand. Thank you for allowing me to explain it to you, at least." I bow my head, enjoying his touch.

He pulls me in closer to his chest. I anticipated his touch, the feel of his lips—*anything* to signal that he isn't letting me go.

I feel his nose in my hair, inhaling the scent of my shampoo. My eyes close on contact, taking him all in. His arms wrap around my chest, closing me in.

Reality sets in, and I quickly open my eyes. "Bentley, please." I sound weak, pathetic. "Please let me go."

"I don't want to. As much as I should, I can't."

"You have to…" I don't need to further explain myself because I know he knows. The damage is done—I've hurt him and there's nothing I can do to change that. I'll only hurt him again.

I feel his body go limp against mine, but I don't turn around to face him. I can't bare it. Finally, he reluctantly lets me go.

"Good night, Bentley."

I open the door and walk out.

CHAPTER FIVE
BENTLEY

GODDAMMIT, why did I still want her? After everything she has put me through, I know I should stay the fuck away.

But I can't. Instead, I text her and tell her to tell me everything she knows about her dad's death. I had planned to dig into his case anyway, but perhaps the information she has can help me out.

Cecilia: I know there were issues with money. My sister remembers hearing them fight about it. According to their finances, their monthly income was not stable and was inconsistent. Do you think that could be the reason someone wanted him dead?

Bentley: It's a possibility. Just let me figure that out, Ceci. Just tell me anything you remember or any dreams you've had. Have you had any dreams?

Cecilia: Well, most recently I had one that was like a flashback. I was sleeping when I heard them arguing in the kitchen about how my dad had spent all this money they didn't have. My mom was worried about having to sell the house. My dad told her he'd find a way to get a Ramiro to give him more time. I also found a note with the name Samuel Anderson on it with a lock box code. When I told my mother about it, she freaked out

and said I was going to get us killed trying to figure it out. I know she knows something…or at least has suspicions.

Bentley: Okay, thanks. That's all really good to know. I'll let you know when I find more information out. It might take a few weeks.

Cecilia: All right.

Cecilia: Thank you, Bentley. You don't know what this means to me.

I swallow hard as I read her last text. I never expected to be getting information from the victim's child years later about a case. It's almost unheard of but at this point…what did I have to lose? Ceci wanted answers and finding out any kind of truth would make Leighton Enterprises look good. I just hope my father feels the same way after everything.

I don't text her back because I don't want her thinking we're now coordinating on this together. This is strictly a business relationship. Nothing more. It can't turn into anything anymore…

I focus all my attention on everything Ceci told me. I read over the file, looking into his finances. They are definitely inconsistent for at least two years, which is ironic for someone who worked a salary day job. Something definitely looked suspicious.

I follow the bank that he and his wife shared. Turns out he had several accounts in his name without his wife's name. Definitely suspicious.

There isn't a whole lot to go off the name Ramiro without a last name. I look into our database anyway, perhaps a drug lord or dealer that's been mentioned previously, but I find nothing.

For the next two weeks, I engross myself into Mr. West's file. I go to my kickboxing classes twice a week and do more research. After awhile, I'm no longer doing this just for the sake of the company. I want Ceci to have closure as well.

A soft knock interrupts my thoughts, and I tell whomever it is to enter. My head lifts up as I watch Ceci walk in. She flashes a small smile as she walks over to my desk, taking the chair in front of me.

"Hi."

"Hi." I smile back.

"Thanks for…um…helping me. Letting me come here." Her voice cracks and I can tell how nervous she is. It's been a month since we've last seen each other.

"You're welcome. I've been doing some digging based on what you've told me, and I might have a few answers for you."

Her body stiffens and I know this is something she's been waiting to hear for a long time.

"I did an extensive search for Samuel Anderson, nothing linked back that was tied to your father."

Her shoulders slump as she lets out a disappointing breath.

"However, I investigated the lock box number and code and was able to trace it back to a bank in Iowa. It's registered under your dad's name." She wrinkles her nose as her eyes narrow, confused. "He used a pseudo name for the lock box, actually."

She adjusts her hair and sits taller. "Wait…*he's* Samuel Anderson?"

"Yes. He has a bank account set up through them that pays the monthly cost directly. When I spoke with the manager, he told me it was set up before he died. He has just enough money in that account to pay for it for ten years."

She gasps. "Ten years?"

"No one's allowed to open it until then."

"What? Why?"

I shrug. "Those were the orders."

She leans back in the chair, defeated. "That makes no sense."

I clear my throat to grab her attention. "I also checked into his financials again, getting the history on all his accounts. He had a joint account with your mom as well as his individual accounts."

"Okay?"

"They were all unstable. One month they'd be broke, the next he deposited thousands. A few months later, the same thing. It went on like that for a couple of years."

"But I thought we already knew that?" she questions.

"Well, yes. But he was taking out large chunks at once. As if he had been paying something off. One month there would be a lot, and the next completely broke."

I watch as she chews her lip and shifts her eyes from me to the floor several times before she speaks again. "I don't understand."

I shift uncomfortably in my chair, not wanting to tell her the bad news. "It's speculated, Ceci, that he was into gambling." I watch her breath hitch. "He was an addict," I clarify.

"No...that can't be right." She shakes her head. "We live in one of the nicest neighborhoods. My mom was a stay-at-home mom."

"The deposits were thousands of dollars, suggesting that he borrowed the cash to feed his addiction. He probably felt he could win it back and pay his debt. When addicts lose, they don't stop at anything. They will borrow as much money as they can to keep gambling. So he'd win a large amount and then gamble it all away. That was why the deposits were always inconsistent."

She continues shaking her head in disbelief, her eyes glazing over.

"I had a hunch, Ceci, and I ran with it. I contacted the nearest Casino and was able to confirm old records of his winnings. I know it's not what you want to hear—"

I stop when I see tears falling down her cheeks. Her head is lowered to her chest, but I can see her eyes tightly sealed.

I round my desk and kneel down in front of her. "Ceci...I'm so sorry. The last thing I wanted to do was deliver bad news about your dad. I swear. I'm extremely thorough. I wouldn't pass on information I wasn't absolutely certain of."

Her body begins trembling as she tries to conceal the cries that are escaping. I rub both thumbs under her eyes and wipe away her tears.

Her head falls deeper into her lap. Her hands catch her face as she sobs heavily. Her body shakes as she finally releases the horror that she's been living all these years.

I dig my face into her hair, trying to comfort her. I rub my hands up and down her legs in a consoling gesture, trying to get her to stop shaking.

"Shh...I'm here, Ceci."

She lifts her head up just enough to grab my shirt and dig her face into my chest. She sobs uncontrollably, not concealing her emotions any longer. My heart sinks at how badly she's hurting—reliving the event and the years she's had to live without him.

Being able to touch and comfort her when she needs it most sends a chill down my spine. As much as she hurt me, it can't be in any comparison as to how she's feeling finding the truth out about her dad—*her hero.*

While texting back and forth about her dad, it was easy to see how important he was to her, which makes it that much harder having to tell her this.

"Sweetheart, please don't cry." It's breaking everything inside me to see her like this. Knowing the strong, confident Ceci and watching her break down like this was breaking *me* down. I cup her face and force her to look up at me. Her eyes close on contact as I wipe her tears again with the pads of my thumbs.

I'll do anything to take this pain away from her. I'm desperate to hold her and kiss her—anything to console her, but I restrict myself, not wanting to take advantage of her situation.

Her tears finally start to fade away, and she sits back up, wiping her cheeks. She chokes out a laugh as she takes in my shirt. "I'm sorry. I ruined your shirt."

I cock my head and laugh with her. "You really think I care about my fucking shirt?"

She sniffs and composes herself before replying, "I can't believe I cried that hard. I haven't done that in years."

"Well, then maybe it's a good thing. Something needed to trigger those emotions to come out finally."

She nods in agreement. "I guess so." She swallows back the tears. "I was such a naïve kid. I thought we were the perfect family—apparently we weren't."

I lean in slowly and cup her face with one hand. "We're all naïve as children. You were supposed to think everything was perfect. That was their jobs as parents to protect you. And it sounds like they did a good job." I smile weakly, hoping to give her some clarity.

I look into her sad eyes and hesitate at first, but finally close the gap and softly kiss her lips. She matches my rhythm, soft and slow. My body is pressed in between her legs, making our faces align just perfectly. I feel her body heat up as I intensify the kiss, but realize I need to slow down.

I break the tender kiss, leaning my forehead against hers not ready to let go of her just yet.

I hear her swallow deeply, almost moaning from the sudden loss. I know I can't lead her on to think anymore can happen, or perhaps it's so I don't think this can go any further.

"Thank you," she whispers. "Thank you for everything. I still have a lot of questions, but at least I have some answers. It's better than being completely left in the dark..."

I rock back on my feet and kiss her forehead before standing up. I grab her hands and pull her up with me so we are standing chest to chest. Her eyes are still red and blotchy from sobbing, but I can tell she's feeling better since letting it all out.

"You're welcome, Cecilia."

She looks up at me with pain in her eyes. It's the first time I've called her by her real name since I kicked her out of my office, but I need to set boundaries. The truth remains—she lied to me.

"I know I don't deserve any of your kindness or your help, but I hope someday you can forgive me." She looks down before stepping around the chair and walking toward the door.

I'm living in a constant battle between wanting her and hating her. No...I could never hate her, but I was shattered when the truth came out. That much I know is true. However, it doesn't make my feelings for her any less real.

"Cecilia," I call out. She quickly turns around, her eyes pleading for me to not let her go. "Glad to help. I'll let you know if I find anything else."

She nods appreciatively and grabs the door handle. She stops just before stepping out and turns toward me. "Goodbye, Bentley."

PART II

CHAPTER SIX
CECILIA

THERE'S a reason your past is supposed to stay in the past. There's a reason you want to forget. There's a reason the past hurts.

Isn't time supposed to heal all wounds?

Well...twelve months hasn't done shit.

Forgetting about Bentley Leighton is next to impossible. No matter what I did to distract myself, no matter who I befriended, or how many 'dates' I went out on—it's his face I see every day.

No, literally.

Six months after leaving his office for the last time, his perfect square-jaw, and his intense eyes surrounded by his golden, messy locks were plastered everywhere. Billboards, magazine ads, E! News, T.V. Commercials.

Every-fucking-where.

Back to his roots, America's sexy-as-sin bad boy was back in full force—the press's words, not mine—doing international shoots, exclusive interviews, and promoting all the newest and high-end products such as underwear, expensive clothing, men's hair products, and even foreign cars. If it cost more than my tuition, he's promoting it.

At first, I was happy for him. I was happy he went after what truly made him happy. I could always tell he was meant for that lifestyle. He was meant to be in the spotlight.

After reading the first dozen tabloid magazines about his exclusive lifestyle of partying, girls, and wild drinking, I was done reading them.

I couldn't without crying. I kept thinking about who he was taking to bed, who he was giving himself to, if he were missing me, or even thinking of me…

Of course not.

I didn't deserve to be on his radar, and I've accepted that. We were supposed to move on. However, it's next to impossible when your biggest mistake, biggest regret is constantly around taunting you.

As long as he's happy.

As long as he is with someone who makes him happy.

As long as he's moved on from the damage I caused…I'm happy for him.

Or so I keep telling myself.

I was no more than just a shell, living on autopilot to get through my first year of college. A shell filled with regret and heartbreak.

I've adjusted to my new lifestyle—college classes, working part-time on campus, studying, and hanging with friends. I look like your average college student, doing average college things, but I'm anything but average.

I was able to fool my roommate for the past year, but now I was packing up and heading back home for the summer. Casey graduated college last year and moved to California to pursue her sudden dream of acting. Threw Mom for a loop, but who was she to hold her back…so she gave Casey her blessing and helped pack her bags. So now, it'll just be Nathan, Mom, and me. Oh joy.

"Can you believe we survived our first year? Holy shit. I can't believe how fast it went," my roommate, Katelynn gushes as she tapes up her last box. "I'm going to miss this place."

I turn to scowl at her. "You're going to miss this?" I wave my hands around. "This ten by ten prison cell?"

"Okay, so it's a little small…but that just made us closer." She smiles genuinely. She's the polar opposite of me, which is how I made it through my first year of college in the first place. Even when I tried to push her away, she never let me get too far.

"Perhaps a little too close, Kate." I grin at her as I nod my head toward her bed.

"You're never going to let me live that down, are you?" She narrows her eyebrows at me.

"Probably not." I laugh. "Hey, I'm all for self-pleasure. You want to use a vibrator to get your cookies off, more power to you. Just warn me next time so I can put my headphones in." I smirk at her, making her cheeks blush.

"I'm so glad we're going to be hundreds of miles apart." She turns and plops a suitcase on her bed.

"No, you're not. Stop lying."

"All right, fine. I'll miss you having my coffee ready for me every morning," she mocks, turning around to face me.

"And I will miss all your Internet stalkers."

She wrinkles her nose at me. "There was only two."

"I don't know why you sent them away. I mean, panty-sniffer is probably my favorite." I cock my head to the side as if I'm really thinking about it. "Or rather, I don't know. It's a close tie."

She makes a gagging noise and turns around, hiding her embarrassment. "I'm never online dating again," she confesses.

I laugh at how easily it is to make her blush. "Sure, sure. This time next year you'll be married and pregnant with your second child."

"That's hardly possible, Cecilia," she groans. "I'm going to become an old cat lady instead."

"Well, hope you'll have a spare bedroom for me. Most likely we'll be growing old together with all our damn cats."

We laugh together at all the bad luck we've had in the dating department this year. Not that I've really tried or even really wanted to date, but I went on double dates for her sake. Let's just say I won't be doing that again.

"I'll miss you," I say softly. I spin around and face her. "You've been a good friend to me."

She faces me with her arms spread wide. "No getting emotional," she teases. "C'mon, let's hug it out."

I laugh. "Hug it out? We don't hug it out. Or get emotional."

She shrugs, not giving up. "I know. But you can't be a brick wall forever."

"I'm not a brick wall," I counter as she swoops in anyway and squeezes me tightly.

"I'm gonna miss you, too, Cecilia. You're pretty awesome when you wanna be."

"Thanks." I laugh, knowing she's completely honest. I wasn't exactly the nicest roommate in the beginning. Still reeling from losing Bentley and the news of my dad followed me to college just weeks after

I last saw him. But she never gave up on me—she made sure I opened up.

"North Dakota isn't that far. We could meet up half way, if you wanted," she offers. "I could take a weekend off."

"Sounds good." I smile. "I'm going to look for a job just to get out of the house, so a weekend away already sounds perfect.

What the hell is so significant about ten years?

Ten years.

It explains why my mother kept the note hidden, but was she ever planning to tell us? Was she ever going to let us see what was in the lock box?

It didn't matter anymore.

Everyone important in my life has left or *walked away.* I have Simon and Cora, but after high school, we all went in different directions. I went to the University of Nebraska—*for real this time*—Cora went to South Florida, and Simon got a full scholarship for some study abroad thing in London. We kept in touch through emails and texts, but it wasn't the same as being together. I missed my best friends.

I drive home in a haze. I haven't seen my mother since Christmas. I didn't bother to come home for Easter since Katelynn wasn't leaving either. She begged me to stay with her since most of the campus was going to be closed for spring break.

She didn't have to beg very hard.

My mother and mine's relationship hasn't gotten any better, nor have I tried. She holds information about my dad and refuses to tell me—she's lucky I'm even coming home at all.

The house is empty when I arrive. Go figure. She didn't even take off the day I was coming home from my first year of college. Not that I should've expected her to.

I wheel my suitcases in and look around. Nothing's changed in the five months since I've been here. Everything is always in its proper spot, not a dish out of place.

I decide to take a shower and unpack a few of my things. I put all my clothes in the basket, mentally reminding myself to do laundry later. I walk around my old room, feeling out of place for the first time in my entire life. It was still my room, but why didn't it feel like mine anymore?

I sit on my bed and reflect over the past year. So much has changed that I'm not even sure I've mentally caught up yet.

What a difference twelve months make.

New school. New friends.

New everything.

CHAPTER SEVEN
BENTLEY

WATCHING Cecilia walk out of my office twelve months ago shot a dagger through my heart. As much as I wanted to hate her for what she did, I couldn't.

I was no longer *falling* for her.

I had fallen.

But none of that mattered anymore. We went our separate ways, living our separate lives. I haven't seen or heard from her since. And why would I? There was no way to repair what had been broken...

Or so I had reminded myself for the last three hundred and sixty-five plus days.

At first, I wanted to scream at myself for how stupid I was to ever let Ceci get that close to me. I should've known better—should've held my guard, but it was inevitable. My body had noticed her before my mind had a chance to catch up.

Looking back over those weeks, I should've seen it. The signs were there. The last name, the recommendation letter, her hiding in my office. *God.* So fucking stupid.

I resigned shortly after that. I knew I was letting my father down, so what was the point? My father didn't trust me after I told him about Ceci—fucking up twice in two years will do that to you. I had failed him, and better yet, I had failed myself. I wasn't there for the right reasons, and it was time I do what I really was meant to do.

I had to start living my life for *me*.

When fall arrived, I'd wake up before the sunset. It would be freezing out, but I didn't care. It cleared my head, giving me validation that I was alive—that I could feel even after all the damage that's been done.

I thought about her every morning as I ran. I thought about the first time I saw her, the first time I fucked her, the first time I woke up and she was in my arms. *All the shit that was built on lies and deception.* All the reasons I needed to clear her out of my head for good.

With my headphones in and hoodie up, I sit back and look out the window. We're flying to Brazil now—another photo shoot by some famous photographer that my agent, Angie set up. It's good for PR, she always said. It's good for your image, she'd continue.

Sure. Whatever.

No matter how far away I am, or how many miles I put between her and me, it doesn't matter. I still feel her. And worse, I miss her.

I thought this would help me get over her. Get over what happened —the lies, the betrayal, the fucking heartbreak. If anything, it's made me numb. Completely numb.

My phone beeps through my headphones and I see it's a text from Angie. *Landing in 20.*

Finally.

I've been living on planes and in hotel rooms for the past six months. It's made it easier at least. Easier to keep her off my mind, but with the long flights, my mind tends to wander.

Feeling the plane prepare for it's landing, I think of her. I think of the times we spent together, the times we snuck around in my office, the times we skipped dinner and went right for dessert. I think of all the times that I thought of telling her how I really felt about her—how I had fallen for her. However, *I* wasn't even sure I grasped it then. Once the truth came out, all those feelings turned to ice, making the rest of me frozen and unable to feel anything at all.

Although modeling has its perks, it's insanely isolating. It's numbing—which is perfect.

As a model, the media and press want every inch of you, every secret, and every intimate detail. The best part of being in the spotlight is having agents and representatives do all the talking for you. I sign autographs, wave, and do as I'm told—without having to attach to anyone.

The partying used to be something I wanted. It was the main reason

I hadn't wanted to work for my father just yet, but now it was a chore. Now it was *business*. Or networking, as Angie reminded me.

"Let's go."

We walk off the private plane and toward the stretch limo. It's past midnight, so luckily, it's dark out, and no paparazzi will be around.

Angie follows me into the limo and hands me my schedule. It's packed solid for the next week—shoots and interviews. Being off the modeling grid for two years was almost 'career suicide' as what I've been reminded of for the past six months. Luckily, my agency was eager to have me back and to represent me. It's not something that's common in this field. Once you leave, you're usually out for good.

We arrive at the hotel, which is more of a palace. I follow Angie's lead and make sure to keep my head down as we walk in. After check in, she hands me my key and leaves me alone for the rest of the night.

This is basically my life. Flying from country to country, living in hotels, being alone. Rinse, wash, and repeat.

But I can't say I regret it. I'm doing something I love, something I'm good at doing. I just wish I could feel happier about it…and stop thinking about the *what if's* and *if only*.

I work relentlessly the entire week in Brazil. Angie keeps my schedule packed enough that it doesn't take much for me to pass right out each night. Some of the events last until two or three in the morning, meaning I only get five or six hours of sleep before doing it all over again.

I'm relieved when we finally arrive back in the states. I plan to hibernate in my condo for at least a week until I get over this jet-lag.

By the fourth day in a row of eating Chinese take-out, I finally drag my ass to the shower. The hot water pours over my skin, burning the flesh until it's bright red. But I don't care. My thoughts take me back to the times Ceci joined me in the shower. The way her body would press up against me while goose bumps would appear over her skin. The way she'd bend over in front of me and spread her delicious legs just for me. No matter how much I try to erase those memories, they fly right back in.

My cock stands at attention as I visualize her on her knees, mouth wide open for me. God, she looked perfect like that. So damn beautiful. So anxious to please me. And so fucking good at it, too.

I firmly wrap my hand around my cock. I stroke it as I think about her, her lips wrapped around me, her perfect wet mouth. Her tongue would slide from my shaft to the tip. She'd repeat the motion several times over before I could no longer take it and she'd finally push it into her mouth.

My hands would flock to her head as I yanked her hair in my fists. She'd release the sexiest moans I've ever heard as she swallowed every drop of me.

My hand strokes my cock harder as I think about the way she'd look up at me. She loved watching what she did to me, the control she had over me at that moment.

I pump my fist more aggressively until the skin is raw. I envision her face as I release into my palm. My body shakes as the water streams down my body and washes away all the evidence—the memories I should be letting fade down the drain.

———

I grab my bottle of whiskey and shot glass and walk to the kitchen. It needs some serious TLC with all of the take out boxes and silverware scattered everywhere. But, as usual, it reminds me of Ceci.

A year later and she still consumes my life.

I lean up against the counter and tilt my head back as I take a shot. As the liquid burns its way down my throat, I relive the moments Ceci and I have had in this kitchen.

The naked moments.

The fun, playing around moments.

The moments we were just Bentley and Ceci.

Those moments were now gone.

After my fourth shot, I still can't stop thinking about her. Her scent. Her laugh. The adorable way she woke me up already riding me.

"Fuck!" I slam my shot glass down and tilt my body against the counter, my hands the only thing keeping me up as I feel like crumbling to the ground.

She may have lied like Hannah. Deceived me like Hannah. Hell, she even fed me the same bullshit as Hannah—but she *wasn't* Hannah.

I didn't feel this way.

I didn't break.

I didn't want her back after finding out what she did.

No matter how much I try to distract myself with kickboxing and modeling, it's never enough. She's always on my mind—since the last time I saw her.

I push myself off the counter and grab my keys and head out my front door.

It's lightly sprinkling out, but I can tell it's going to start pouring soon. I brush a hand through my hair, shaking it out as I get in my car and start the engine.

The nerves catch up to me before I realize what I'm even doing. I find myself parked on the opposite side of her street. She might not even live here anymore for all I know. It's an impulsive move, but that doesn't stop me.

The moment I see another car pull up, my body instantly reacts— my heart races faster and my skin feels as if it's on fire. It's far enough out of view that I can't see the driver, but the anticipation of seeing her is strong enough to kill me.

I grip the door handle about to step out when I see her exit the front door of her house. I look back to the car and see a guy exiting the car. Shit. She runs full speed toward him, screaming something, and wrapping her entire body around him—her arms clamp around his neck and her legs wrap around his hips. She's laughing and screaming as he spins her around like you see in some cliché, cheesy chick film.

She's stunning. Her hair is longer, but she looks exactly the same. Her eyes light up and her lips form into a wide smile as she eyes him. She's obviously excited to see whoever the hell this fucker is.

I let go of the handle and ball my hands into fists. Son-of-a-bitch. I should've known. It's been over a year, she isn't still thinking of me. Why would she?

Cue the anger, insecurity, self-pity, and heartbreak—it all comes at the same time my heart cracks even more—parallel to the regret that's building up inside.

Clearly, I'm dreaming this.

Or drunker than I thought.

As I jerk the car back into drive, I watch as the guy puts her down and lays a kiss on her mouth. Bastard. I race down the street needing to get out of there as soon as possible. What was I thinking? Why after all this time was she still on my mind? Why couldn't I fuck any girl after her? The realization frustrated me. I slam my hand against the steering wheel wondering when I allowed myself to become this person.

New strategy—focus on work. Find a hook up. Get a fucking clue.

CHAPTER EIGHT
CECILIA

"OH MY GOD! You're finally back!" I scream as Simon swings me around like a child. "God, I missed you!"

"I missed you, too!" he yells back. "But I'm pretty sure you just blew my eardrum out."

He sets me down and lays a kiss on my lips.

"Sorry." I smile up at him. "I just...you have no idea how excited I am to see you! Living here with my mother every day has been a fucking nightmare."

We walk into the house, slightly wet from the rain, and we immediately go up to my room to chat. "That bad, huh?" he asks, sitting on my bed.

"Our conversation consists of 'hellos,' 'goodbyes,' and 'Don't forget it's your turn to take out the trash.'" I mock my mother's tone, flashing my best fake smile. "It's been hell."

"She still won't talk to you about your dad?"

"Nope. She's pretty much set that in concrete with 'never ever go digging into your dad's case again or else!' lecture."

"You think she's going let you go to the lock box in two years when it's time?" He shuffles himself comfortably against the headboard.

"Whether or not she lets me, I'm going. I don't care what it takes. It's my right just as much as it's hers." He nods, agreeing. "I've thought about it so much that I've now convinced myself my dad was in the mob, he was their gambling dealer, and when he started losing, they called for a mob hit," I say in all seriousness. "I might've let my mind wander a bit," I say after Simon gives me a wide-eyed expression.

"I think you've been watching too much HBO."

"It's likely." I laugh in agreement.

I wake up in the middle of the night, pressed firmly against Bentley's rock hard body. I can feel his chest pumping calmly with each slow breath. It feels natural—like home—being with Bentley.

He stirs behind me and nuzzles his nose into my neck and hair, moaning. His hand runs down my body and reaches inside my pants. It doesn't take long for me to realize what he's after.

I shimmy my ass against his growing erection, feeling it expand through his briefs as he rubs it harder into me. "Mm…" I moan as my head falls back and he begins kissing my neck, which is now covered in goose bumps as my body anticipates his touch.

"Tell me what you need, sweetheart," he growls softly in my ear, his hand making its way to my pussy. He curls a finger inside making me jump at the intrusion. I moan out in desperation, wanting—*needing*— more. "Is this what you want? Tell me," he demands.

"Yes. God, yes."

He inserts a second finger, and then a third, stretching my walls to the brim. He works his fingers in and out, harder and deeper, making me dripping wet as he teasingly tortures me.

My hips match his rhythm, moving in sync as he drives into me faster. I whimper and moan as he drives me into an orgasm, my hips jerking with his powerful movements. His mouth covers mine as he wraps a leg over holding me still. His bodyweight feels amazing as I ride out the intensity.

He breaks the kiss as he climbs on top of me, flashing a mysterious grin as he lowers his body. He pulls my shirt up slightly and begins feathering kisses down my stomach. The softness of his lips is driving me insane as he makes his way toward my already aching pussy.

"Bentley," I whimper. "Lower."

I feel him smile against my stomach, but he doesn't give in. Instead, his lips make a path up my stomach and land on my breast.

"God, Bentley."

His lips wrap around my nipple, sucking hard as my body frenzies underneath him. He's torturing me and he knows it, too. His hand cups my other breast as he works my nipple, slowly and playfully teasing me.

"Pants..." I gasp.

"Yes?" he asks, amused.

"Off."

"I'm not wearing pants," he muses, laughing at how worked up he's gotten me.

"Asshole," I groan as I shift underneath him, pulling his mouth off me. "Take. Off. *My*. Pants." I clarify.

His lips form into a devilish grin as his hands make their way to my waistband, pulling them down my legs and throwing them to the floor.

"Better?" He cocks an eyebrow.

"Yes," I breathe out, pulling him back toward me. "Much better."

I pull him out, hard and ready. I stroke his shaft firmly as his tongue licks from my collarbone to my neck, and then makes its way to my mouth, sucking on my tongue before letting his dance with mine.

"Ceci..." he moans as I pump him harder.

"Hm?"

"Oh, God..." he breathes out, unable to keep up with our greedy kiss. "God, I love you."

My head pops up to his eye level and my hand freezes the second I hear his words—*those words.*

"W-What?"

...why the hell is my phone ringing?

"Bentley...what did you just say?"

"Answer your damn phone!" a voice in the distant screams.

Bang, bang, bang.

I gasp loudly at the sound of my door about to fall down. I look around and notice the sun shining into my room—it's morning.

I look around anxiously and finally realize my phone's ringing.

"Cecilia!" Nathan screams again on the outside of the door.

"Sorry! Chill out," I yell back in a daze from my dream. *Just a dream...*

Never fucking fails. At least once a week, Bentley enters my dreams, torturing and taunting me of what I had. What we had. What I screwed up.

You'd think I'd be used to it by now, that it's been long enough and that I should be over him after all this time, but if it were even possible, it's only been worse. Since Bentley is always in the spotlight or featured on some magazine, it makes it impossible to forget my feelings for him.

I grab my cell from the dresser and pick it up. "Someone better be dying," I answer without looking at the caller ID.

"Are you sleeping?" It's Cora.

"What gave it away?" I groan, sleepily rolling over and closing my eyes.

"Sorry, but I have news. Big news!" she gushes. I can tell she's ready to burst at the seams. I decide to sit up and prepare for whatever it is she's going to tell me.

"Okay, I'm ready. Tell me."

She squeals all giddy, making me pull the phone away from my ear. "I need you to pick me up from the airport today!"

"What are you talking about?"

"I'm flying in. I'll be there in four hours."

"WHAT?" I scream my eyes going wide. "You're coming home finally?"

"Yup. Oh, God, I can't wait to see you!"

"Yes! I'm so excited! Simon just got here, too. I'll finally stop being a hermit by myself and the three of us will be back together for the summer," I say happily, the smile reaching my eyes. I'm so happy.

"Ugh," she groans. "I haven't seen Simon since last summer. Not sure I really want to."

I roll my eyes even though she can't see me. "Seriously, you two are going to get along—whatever weird liking, not liking each other thing you have going on."

"Fine," she moans. "As long as I can pretend he doesn't exist, they'll be no arguing."

"Whatever works, I guess." I laugh. "So, what terminal are you coming in?"

We finish our conversation, and I immediately shower and get dressed. Cora didn't even come home for holidays, so it's been ten long months since we've seen each other.

Being with Simon and Cora again feels like home. It's comforting to be with my two best friends again, but also painful. So much is changing so fast and there's nothing I can do about it except embrace it and enjoy our time together.

I end up getting a job that summer as a cocktail waitress. I take whatever position I can find that gets me out of the house most nights. Cora takes a hostess position so we can spend more time together, and Simon visits us just to annoy us. But it was perfect, nonetheless—I get to be with the two people that really ground me.

Not knowing answers to my dad's case still haunt me. I anticipate being able to open my dad's lock box in two years. It feels like forever, yet I know it's not. It's sooner than never knowing at all, and I can wait since I know that I'll find out his secrets soon—hopefully.

Simon and Cora hookup once at the end of summer—kind of their way of saying goodbye, I guess. I try to not question it, but my mind spins at all the times they've taunted each other all summer. But then again, it makes complete sense.

Saying goodbye was the worst part of the summer. Simon transferred to a school in Florida after his study abroad. The romantic in me thinks it's so he is close to Cora, but both of them deny it.

Casey comes home for the Fourth of July and looks completely different. Her hair is short and dyed bleach blonde with pink underneath. She's lost a good twenty pounds and wears sunglasses as big as her face. She's gone complete diva. But I love her and spending that short amount of time with her was amazing.

Mom and I still don't talk much. She continues working a ridiculous amount of hours, and when she is home, we rarely make eye contact. A part of me knows she's nervous being around me since I know some of dad's secrets. Soon they'll all be out, and she won't be able to deny anything. Until then, our relationship will continue the way it is.

I look around my room that I spent the last three months in. It looks the exact same as when I came home from college. I didn't put up any new pictures or even change the color of my sheets. It still doesn't feel like my room anymore.

I load my car with my luggage and a couple boxes packed with my things. I had a feeling I wouldn't be coming home anytime soon, or at all, once my second year was completed. I'd probably look into an off-campus apartment or something.

"I love you," my mom says quietly as she stands by my car. "I'm glad you came home."

I swallow as I stare expressionless at her. "I love you, too, Mom."

She leans in and we awkwardly hug goodbye. I wish I could say what I really want to say, but it's not the way I want to leave things with her. For now, it's just awkward silence and glances, which is better than fighting with each other.

"Drive safe. Text me when you arrive, okay?"

"Sure." I flash a weak smile at her. I open the driver's side door and get in. I sit down and look back at my childhood home that's filled with secrets and tainted memories.

PART III

CHAPTER NINE
BENTLEY

I WALK OUT of the gym, dripping wet with sweat. I chug my bottle of water before getting into my car and throwing the empty container on the passenger seat.

Working out four to five times a week has made for an isolated, structured routine. It's definitely different from my corporate job I worked two years ago—working relentlessly ten hours a day.

I spent my first-year and a half of my modeling career traveling worldwide for exclusive photo shoots and magazine interviews. It was an amazing experience, but I needed to stabilize my life more. I've opted to traveling out of the country once every month or two now instead, leaving a lot more time for working out and more national shoots.

However, I was taking the majority of the summer off. She was able to move my press appearances for early fall.

Kickboxing has become a constant in my life. Maya helped train me by using my emotions into my workouts. She helped relieve all the pent up stress and misery I was feeling. In fact, she's been a complete life changer.

After a good six months of showing up for classes twice a week, she asked if I'd be interested in training others. My traveling schedule had slowed down, and I was game for anything she was offering. I had hoped helping someone the way she'd helped me would be fulfilling. And it is.

Now I train and instruct classes three times a week, plus working out one to two days on my own. It's definitely a different lifestyle than I'm used to before, but it's been the one thing that's kept me happy, and my mind free from wandering—thinking about her.

Cecilia West.

I couldn't help myself and looked her up a while back. She was attending the University of Nebraska and living on campus. Since I hardly left the gym or my house, and she lived on campus an hour away, our chances of running into each became slim—and I wasn't sure if I was happy or sad about that.

"Maya!" I call out as I walk into the gym with all the lights already on. I open up on Mondays usually, so no one should be here yet. "Maya, you here?"

"Bentley? I'm in the office," she calls back.

I round the door and step into her frantically clicking away on her keyboard in front of the computer.

"What's going on? You look like shit."

She slumps her shoulders as she scowls at me. "Will just bailed on me. He was taking over the intro classes this summer. Now I'm short staffed and have no extras to cover the class."

I think for a moment before responding. "That one is Monday evenings, right? I can teach it," I offer.

Her eyebrows rise as she finally stops slamming her fingers down. "You already teach the morning and afternoon classes on Mondays. Plus, you train in between."

"So?"

"That means you'll be here like all day."

I cross my arms as I lean up against the doorframe, cocking a smile. "Are you doubting my ability to work a full day or something? You're aware of who you're talking to, right?"

She rolls her eyes up at me. "Oh, yes. The all-powerful, all-too-perfect Bentley Leighton," she mocks. "I almost forgot."

"Well, I don't know about powerful, but I'll take perfect."

"You're so egotistical."

"And you love it," I fire back.

"Guys like you are the exact reason I don't date them."

"Oh, come on. Not all guys are like me." I grin. "I mean, it takes a lot of time and determination."

"You're annoying."

"And *your* life saver."

She groans and slouches before giving in. "Fine, you can take the class. But you had better bring your A-game. No slacking because you can't handle a nine-hour day."

"Maya, please. Give me a little credit."

She laughs at my confidence. "You start today. Hope you had your Wheaties."

I smirk as I push off the doorframe. "Always do."

June is the first month of summer classes. They only last through August, which means they are longer and more intense. I have my ten a.m. Kwando kickboxing class, which is a combination of techniques of boxing, Taekwondo, and karate. It's the most intense but pumps me up for the entire day.

My three p.m. class is Cardio Kickboxing, which is a medium-level based kickboxing class. It's a step above intro and a step below the combined class.

And starting tonight at six p.m. is my new women's intro class. Intro classes are twice a week, whereas the other two classes are three times a week.

I go to the studio where my first class is held and begin setting up. I crank the music and get myself pumped up for the first day of summer session classes.

By five p.m., I'm ready to die. Spring session ended two weeks ago meaning I had only trained on my own, but now I was getting my ass kicked working out back to back.

"You going to make it?" Maya pops into the studio and questions.

"Yeah…" I nod. "I'll be fine."

"Make sure you get something to eat. I don't need my best instructor passing out."

I curl my lips into a smirk. "I'm your best instructor?"

She sighs and begins walking away. "This is *exactly* why I don't date guys!"

I laugh and crank the music back up. If I'm going to make it through another class, I need to stay awake.

I eat a protein bar and drink another bottle of water before setting up for my last class. I can already feel my body burning and know I'll be sitting in an ice bath later.

At quarter to six, people begin piling into the room. Most are younger—between twenty and thirty—and once they notice me, they smile wide and take the closest spots in the front of the room. *Great.*

Some recognize me and ask for my autograph. I try to kindly reject, but I can't say no to a fan, so I sign whatever they have for me to sign and tell them that in this class, I'm their instructor. It's not always easy setting those boundaries right away.

At exactly six p.m., I welcome the class and introduce myself. It's packed to the max, and I can barely see everyone that's here with all the kickboxing bags.

I begin going through some basic things such as stance. I show them the proper way to stand, part their feet, and hold their upper bodies up. It's all very introduction-like, and probably the most boring part of the whole session, but if they don't nail it down right away, everything else will be a complete mess.

I walk around the room, and as they all work on their stances, I guide some of the ladies with my hands on their hips to make sure they can feel the difference in between what they were doing and what they need to be doing. Some of them giggle and shimmy their asses in front of me as if I'm going to be impressed. I'm not.

I should've known teaching a woman's intro class meant a handful of girls who were only there to gawk. Will was definitely a ladies' man. He's been the intro instructor since before I started here, which meant people were definitely familiar with him.

"Ladies, is something funny?" I scowl, backing away.

"No, not at all," one replies in a serious tone, but her face is anything but serious. She thinks she's flirting.

"Carry on then." I walk away annoyed and back to the front of the class where a few more are completely on the wrong side of their bag.

Just as I'm assisting another student, I hear the door open and slam shut. All heads turn toward it, but I'm on the opposite side of the room, so I can't see what all the commotion is about.

"Shit, sorry," a young girl's voice echoes through the room. "C'mon, let's go in the back." I hear her say to her friend next to her.

The disruption has interrupted my class and it ticks me off. I walk back to the front of the room and clear my throat to get their attention.

"Ladies, please make sure you are on time. Tardiness isn't something I take lightly. Next time, the door will be locked," I say sternly. I need to make sure they are all aware of how inconsiderate it is to show up late to my class.

"Sorry!" One yells from the back. "It won't happen again." I angle my body so I can get a glimpse at who I'm talking to, but they're all the way in the back, and I can't see between all the bodies and bags.

"All right, I'm going to demonstrate stance one more time—girls in the back, please pay attention so you can keep up."

Everything runs smoothly as I transition to the different types of punches—jab, cross, hook, and uppercut. I go slow, making sure they can all keep up and walk around as they practice the different punches once with their bags.

"You need to angle your body more to the right. And part your feet," I instruct to one girl. "That's it. Keep your chin up." She demonstrates for me once again. "Good."

I notice I'm running out of time, so I walk back toward the front of the class and go over basic kicks—front, side, and roundhouse. I demonstrate several times and tell them all to practice with me.

After a few minutes, I have them rotate between punching and kicking. I remind them to focus on keeping their stance while working on both.

I look around and notice many unbalanced girls. I chuckle to myself as I see them all try really hard. I make my way to the back since I haven't been there yet. I notice a few girls stumbling as they try to switch between punching and kicking.

"Steady." I grab her hips and angle her body the right way. "Balance your hips and keep your feet apart. Flex your arms and focus on keeping everything tight." I align my body with hers, showing her exactly what I mean.

"Like this?" Her voice is laced with seduction and I know exactly what she's doing.

"Yes. Great." I back away and brush a hand through my hair. This is definitely going to be a long eight weeks.

I walk behind the last row and watch as they all try to mimic my moves. There are a couple of girls on the way end whom I presume are the ones that stumbled in late.

I rub the back of my neck as I watch the one on the end. She has legs for days, all tan and solid. It's not hard to notice them, but her stance is all wrong as she pushes her ass out and bobs her feet back and forth.

Oh, God.

"There's a reason being late to my class is not something I usually allow," I growl, gripping her hips with both hands. I immediately feel her body tense from my fingers. I push myself closer to her and she shivers.

She's clearly nervous around me, so I take the opportunity and adjust her body to what her stance should be. I place my foot in between her feet and push her foot farther to the right, opening her legs wider.

"Make sure your legs are parted. Bend your knees slightly." I hear her swallow. Hard. She doesn't speak. She only nods at my demands. I can feel the heat radiating off her skin the longer I touch her. "Relax. You're too tense," I say against her ear. Her long blonde hair is pulled up in a high ponytail, exposing the goose bumps on her neck and shoulders.

Her body eases into mine as she straightens her back and perfects her stance. My foot is still in between her legs along with my hands on her hips. She trembles, her body giving her away completely. She's obviously affected by me and from the way that I'm touching her. I haven't even seen this girl's face, but I know there's something about her that makes me eager to spin her around.

"Perfect," I whisper.

At that moment, it's just her and me. I feel her steady breaths as I stand against her. *Back away*, I tell myself.

Hell no.

I notice the rest of the room is silent as everyone stares at us. *Shit*. I rub both hands up her arms and land on her shoulders, placing a quick, easy pat. "Good job," I say casually as the class watches me intently. I hear her breath hitch, as I feel something rough against my thumb on her right shoulder.

I glance down and notice a scar underneath her thin tank top strap. My own breath hitches as I recognize that very fucking scar.

CHAPTER TEN
CECILIA

I CAN'T BELIEVE I made it through another year of college. It ended up being better than my first—much better. I was finally able to open up more and even make friends besides my roommate, Katelynn.

I met Brandon spring semester in World History. He sat behind me, and we were matched up to be partners on an assignment. He's smart, funny, and so sweet. The very opposite of Bentley's domineering behavior.

We had spent six weeks together researching and planning our presentation. We'd meet at the same café every Tuesday and Thursday, and he'd always buy me a latté and a croissant, without even asking me. He always insisted that I needed my caffeine and food. After a while, we'd hang out outside of class and study sessions. I found myself really opening up to him and feeling comfortable in my own skin. He made me feel again. He had become a really good friend, and I was truly grateful for that.

On the day of our presentation, we both stood up and spoke as the slides displayed pictures and graphs. It really went perfect because he was the perfect partner.

The last slide was our 'credits,' which was really just our names and references we used in making the presentation—or so I *thought* was our last slide.

The class applauded lightly, and I began shuffling the papers on the podium together so I could go back and take my seat. However, Brandon clicked one more time to a slide I hadn't seen before.

Counting Stars by One Republic begins playing through the speakerphones as I read over the slides.

Cecilia West…I'm crazy about you.

Crazy about your face.

Crazy about the way you tap your feet when you've had too much caffeine.

Crazy about how you scrunch your face up when you're thinking too hard.

Crazy about the way you snort when you laugh too hard.

Like I said…crazy.

My eyes widened as I read over the words. The class was stunned silent as he clicked for another slide.

Cecilia West…Please, tell me you're crazy about me, too.

Otherwise, I'm just plain crazy.

I stood frozen in place. The entire classroom was quiet, looking eager for my answer. Even the damn professor was smiling like a hormonal teenage boy about to see tits for the first time. Fuck…I bet he was in on it.

God, this is so embarrassing.

I turned and looked at Brandon. A hundred feelings rushed in that I hadn't ever felt before. He was one of my best friends. How had I missed this? Had he always had feelings for me? Suddenly, I was seeing him for the first time. His charm, his looks, his wall-of-steel body. How had I missed it?

Bentley. Oh, right.

Jackass. He ruined me for all men. It was hard not comparing every other guy to him. My feelings for Bentley were raw and real, and came out of nowhere. Those feelings needed to be bottled up and put away. I had to move on.

I told him yes and we've been together ever since. The room filled with gasps and applauses, embarrassing me completely, but I felt lighter somehow. Like I had finally decided to let someone else in.

Cora begged me for two weeks to go to this new intro to kickboxing class with her, so finally, I agreed. I was sick of her begging me, so I caved.

"This better not leave any bruises on me," I groan as she drives us to the gym. "I haven't worked out in like...forever. I'll probably fall and hurt myself."

"Stop whining. It'll be fun. Plus, we can impress all the guys with our new moves." She wiggles her eyebrows as if that should sell me on the idea.

"What guys? You mean the old, drunk ones that come into the bar every night?"

Cora and I both got our summer jobs back. She and Simon spent another school year in Florida while I stayed in Nebraska with Katelynn.

"School just ended. Trust me. College guys will be coming in."

"And why does that even matter? Are you talking about *Simon* coming in every night?"

Simon and Cora are still pretending they aren't anything, but I'm not stupid. Once I called Cora and she answered the phone half-asleep. She quickly brushed me off saying her guy friend was out grabbing donuts and that she had to go. Curious, I called Simon right after and he told me he was out running to the bakery. When I asked what he bought, he said *donuts.*

Ever since then, I've tried to catch them in their lies, but they've made it pretty hard. In person, they pretend to hate each other, but behind closed doors...well, that's a completely different story happening.

"I don't care about Simon. But yeah, I'm sure him and his stupid friends will come and bother us."

I grin as I watch her cheeks blush as she talks about Simon. She'll never admit it though. I'll have to physically catch them in the act—which won't be something I willingly want to see.

We end up stuck in traffic and end up being fifteen minutes late. "Shit, I hate being late."

"Let's just not go in," I offer. "I'm sure we're not allowed to come in late anyway."

"Fuck that. I paid for us to join this class." She shuts the engine off and grabs her bag. "We're going. Let's go."

I reluctantly follow her inside. She slowly opens the door to the studio, but I don't catch it in time and it slams shut.

I close my eyes, embarrassed. *Shit.*

Cora announces our apologies and grabs my hand to lead me to the back row. "C'mon, we can hide back here."

I take the very end spot in the last row, hoping to keep eyes off me. I have no idea what I'm doing and am still pissed Cora dragged me here.

I don't notice him right away. In fact, it's not until I hear his voice that I instantly recognize him. I angle my head toward the front where he's standing and see him—all six feet plus, messy golden locks of him. He's barely changed in two years, yet he looks different. He's definitely more buff, which seems hardly possible considering how built he was back then. However, he's obviously been working out more and paying more attention to his physique for his modeling career. And the eighteen-year-old girl from two years ago is still very affected by him. My body responds to him the same, my heart—still shattered and ashamed.

I try my best to stay out of his view until I can successfully bail and never return. I can't tell Cora because if I tell her now, she'll definitely make a scene. I finally broke down last summer and told her the whole truth about Bentley and Leighton Enterprises. I told her everything I knew about my dad and the lock box that I'll be allowed to open next year. But she doesn't need to know that our new kickboxing instructor is *the Bentley.*

About midway through the class, my nerves get the best of me, and I almost tell Cora we need to leave. Instead, she leans over and whispers, "He looks really familiar."

Shit. Of course. Bentley's face is fucking everywhere. Now do I tell her? Or just suffer through the class until it's over and never return?

I'm almost in the clear with ten minutes left of class before he begins walking toward the back. I turn my body away from him in hopes he doesn't come this way. I pretend to be working on my punches and kicks when I *feel* him behind me.

His voice. God, his voice fucking ruins me. I immediately tense up at the sound of his coarse tone. It's the same tone he's used many times when we were in bed together—his domineering tone. It's sexy as hell, and it use to soak my panties every time I'd hear it, and, unfortunately, this time is no different.

My body tenses the moment I feel his hand against me. Does he know it's me? Did he recognize me and was now slowly torturing me?

My breath hitches for the hundredth time when I feel his thumb rub against my scar. Oh, God.

I expect him to make a scene or even yell at me to get out of his gym, but he doesn't. I soon realize the entire class is staring at us. His thumb rubs against my shoulder once more before he backs away and begins walking to the front of the class again. My body screams at the loss of his touch.

Fuck me.

"Uh, great session, everyone. I'll see you all Thursday." His voice is anxious, and I know I have to get the hell out of there—*fast.*

Everyone begins packing their things and swinging their bags over their shoulders. Cora is immediately to my side with her mouth agape.

"Holy fucking hotness! What the hell was that?" she asks half-shocked and half-amused. "I wonder if he has a twin." She cocks her head as she continues staring at him. He's surrounded by girls who are all chatting him up, flirting I'm sure, with the infamous Bentley Leighton.

"He doesn't," I answer without thinking. "I mean, he's an only child."

"I knew you knew him!"

I eye her, signaling her to keep her voice down. "That's Bentley... Leighton," I whisper.

"Shit," she whispers back, getting another look at him. "I should've known." She smiles wide. "What are the fucking chances?"

"Yeah, what are the fucking chances," I groan. "What the hell is a model doing teaching kickboxing classes anyway?"

She doesn't get to answer because both our heads snap up to the front of the room where another instructor waltzes in, shooing off his own personal fan club.

"Let's go," I say firmly. "I have to get out of here."

The other instructor places a hand on his upper arm and a tinge of jealousy flutters through me. She's laughing up at him, and then he leans down and kisses her cheek.

Goddammit. I *need* to get out of here now. Being around him brings feelings to the surface that I'm not allowed to have anymore. Feelings I left behind long ago. Or tried to anyway.

Feelings that make me feel guilty for having.

"I'll walk behind you. Lead the way." She grabs her bag and begins walking behind me as I walk along the wall, as far away from him as possible. I secretly thank the other instructor for distracting him as we make our way through the door and out of the gym.

"You better start talking the second we get in that car." She points a finger and scowls at me.

"There's nothing to say. I've told you everything," I remind her. She throws the bag across the car roof just before getting in.

I shake my head at her as I walk to the trunk and wait for her to pop it open. I shove the bag in and shut it, relieved to be leaving.

I think too soon.

The second I shut the trunk, I see him.

He's staring at me as if I'm his last meal, and I'm not sure what to think when he begins walking toward me.

"Ceci," he growls as we come face to face.

"Bentley," I say formally. He steps closer to me, instinctively making me take a step backward. "I didn't know you worked here," I blurt out. I swallow hard at his intensive stare. "Just so you know."

He brushes a hand through his hair, roughly. I can tell his mind is spinning just like mine is.

"What are you doing here?" he asks, taking me off guard.

"Well," I begin hesitantly. "Cora actually signed us up, and well, she made me come."

"No," he says roughly. "What are you doing *here*...in Omaha?"

I swallow, confused by his words. "I live here. What are *you* doing in Omaha? Aren't you like a world-renowned model or something? Why are you teaching an intro kickboxing class?" I ask more defensively. Who the hell is he to ask what I'm doing here?

"I thought you'd be off living at college," he admits. "And I'm taking some time off, didn't want to travel as much. I teach a few classes here in my spare time."

"I'm on summer break," I explain. "I live back with my mom until fall semester."

"Oh, right. I hadn't thought of that."

I cross my arms and take another step back, needing to keep a safe distance between us. "Sorry to have interrupted your class." I walk around him and head toward the passenger door. "Don't worry. I won't be returning."

I grab for the door handle, but he firmly takes my elbow and spins me around to face him. "No, you should come back." He stares intently into my eyes, and I can't find any words to say back to him. Hell, I can hardly find my own air to breathe. "Just don't be late next time." He releases my arm but keeps his stare.

"I'll think about it." I turn and open the door, getting in and slamming it behind me.

"Drive," I tell Cora.

"Well, that was intense," she finally says half way back to my house.

"No, that was awkward. I haven't seen him in two years. Holy shit."

"He's hot on camera, but damn, he's fucking gorgeous in person," she gushes.

I tilt my head toward her and scowl. "Don't even."

"A girl's allowed to appreciate a nice piece of man-meat, thank you. And appreciate I will…Mondays and Thursdays for the next eight weeks." She laughs.

"Then you're going alone. I am *not* coming back."

"Oh, yes you are. It's our only nights off from the bar. You have to come."

"I don't know," I mumble just before we arrive at my house.

"Just think about it. Ignore the fact that Bentley Leighton is your incredibly sinful, hot model that you used to sleep with and just come to class to learn kickboxing." She smiles as if she's just made this whole thing easier on me.

"I hate you right now." I grip the door and open it, letting myself out.

"No, you don't. You love me!" she yells just before I slam the car door in her face. I smirk to myself because I really do love her, dammit.

I walk into the kitchen to my mom making dinner, stirring something in a huge pot.

"What are you doing?" I ask suspiciously. It's past seven and there's no way she's making an actual home-cooked meal.

"Making a late dinner. I'm glad you could join, because I want you to meet someone." I raise an eyebrow at her.

"Who?"

She stops stirring and turns fully toward me. "A guy I'm dating."

"What? You're dating? Since when?" I nearly shout at her. When the hell did this happen?

"Cecilia, calm down. I've been seeing him a couple months now and it's becoming serious, so I wanted you and Nathan to officially meet."

"Oh, God. A couple months? You never said anything," I say softer this time.

"I know. I wasn't sure it would turn into anything, so I was waiting," she replies, turning back to the stove.

"Waiting for what?" Her body stiffens, and she doesn't have to answer for me to know what she's referring to. "Do I really have to meet him? I'd like to just go up to my room."

"It would mean a lot to me, Cecilia if you would." She looks at me pleadingly. "Please."

I groan because I don't know why it matters anyway. "It's not like he's going to be my new daddy," I snap. I never thought of my mother dating again. I don't know why, but it never occurred to me. She never brought guy's home before. Even if she had dated in the past, I never knew about it.

"Cecilia," she says sternly. "I didn't raise you to be a cold-hearted snot. You can be pleasant for one evening. It won't kill you."

"Humph. You didn't raise me at all," I fire back, turning on my heel and walking upstairs to my room.

Brandon: I miss you, baby.

A calm smile flashes over my face as I read his text.

Cecilia: I miss you, too. This is going to be the longest summer ever. :-(

Brandon: Don't think like that. It's going to fly by.

Cecilia: I hope so. I'm already dreading being here with my mom. I'm meeting her new "boyfriend" tonight. Yay…

Brandon: Be nice.

I can hear his teasing tone in my mind as I read his last text. He knows my mother and I don't get along the greatest, but I hadn't told him why.

Cecilia: I'm always nice. :-) I'll call you later, babe. Time for the meet-and-greet.

Brandon's originally from Wisconsin, so he went back home for the summer. It feels weird to be away from him after all this time as if a part of me is missing.

I sit next to Nathan whose eyes are glowing wide at the guy across from him. *Tony.* What the fuck kind of grown up name is that anyway? Tony?

He looks a couple of years older than my mother with short, brown hair. He's fairly built with a decent smile, but something about him doesn't sit right with me. Perhaps it's because there's another man in my house, but either way, I don't like him.

"So, *Tony*, what do you do for a living?" I ask, stabbing the chicken on my plate.

"I'm a college professor. I teach economics."

Hmm…impressive.

"Have you been married before?"

He swallows uncomfortably. *Good.*

"Yes. She passed away a few years ago."

Oh, shit.

I look down and apologize for bringing it up.

"It's all right." His voice is calm, light even. I look back up at him with a pained expression. "She had cancer."

"Oh."

I know I'm acting like a selfish brat considering Tony hasn't done anything to warrant my nasty behavior, but I just don't want another man in my house—my dad's house.

I mainly stay quiet for the rest of dinner. He asks about college and my major before Nathan talks his ear off. Nathan was too young to really remember Dad. He's never had a father figure in his life before, and from the way his face is lighting up, I can tell he needs one.

I'm anxious to leave, but I promised Mom I'd be 'pleasant.' I think I'm in the clear after dinner is over, but then she announces there's dessert.

Dessert?

We haven't had dessert in years.

I tap my foot anxiously as I wait for my mom to return from the kitchen. Nathan is talking sports and who's going to be drafted in some sport this fall. I don't pay much attention, but I notice how well they seem to get along.

I lay in bed, unable to sleep. I have way too much on my mind.

Bentley.

And Mom's new 'boyfriend.'

And seeing Bentley again in three days.

Did I want to see him again? *Yes.*

No. *Yes.*

Fuck, I don't know.

It's been two years. I was just getting to the point where I wouldn't see his picture and cry myself to sleep. I was just starting to move on from him.

Perhaps we could be friends.

Could we do that? Did I want to do that?

Perhaps it's too soon.

CHAPTER ELEVEN
BENTLEY

GOD, what was I doing?

I shouldn't have followed her out. But I did. I didn't even have a chance to talk myself out of it before I was standing in front of her.

And now my emotions were all over the place—remembering her scent, her delicate facial features, the way her body would tremble underneath me—memories that were impossible to forget and now they were all slapping me back in the face.

One second I wanted to hate her for all the agony she's made me feel over the last couple of years, and another second I wanted to get in between her legs.

Make up your fucking mind!

It's impossible when I spent the last year trying to forget her completely and then to have her show up in my class—a class I wasn't even supposed to be teaching.

Was it fate?

Or just a coincidence?

There are plenty of other gyms in the city that offer kickboxing classes. There are plenty of instructors. But she showed up in mine.

That has to mean something.

My mind isn't anymore made up by the time Thursday arrives. All I know is that I want to see her. Even if we can't talk, I just want to watch her. I want to get a glimpse of who she is now. I can still remember all the intimate details about her. The way she eats. The way she nervously rubs her shoulder. The way she bites down on her lower lip. I can't help but wonder if she's the same girl with all those traits.

"What's up with you today?" Maya asks as I walk into her office. "You're...cheerful."

I slap a hand to my chest as if I'm offended. "I'm always cheerful."

"You got laid, didn't you?" She raises an eyebrow in suspicion.

"No." *Not yet.* "Have any friends looking for company?" I tease.

"Not that'd be interested in you," she taunts.

I flash her a pained expression and she laughs. Maya has become a really good friend to me this past year, and I value her friendship more than anything. She's the one person I've really been able to open up to since leaving my father's company. I lost all my 'friends,' or rather acquaintances, and I haven't had the urge to find more.

She deals with my crazy traveling schedule when I get booked up, and always gives it to me straight—no bullshitting around.

"Excited for your intro class tonight?" she asks as I sink into the chair across from her.

"You could say that."

"You have quite the fan base."

"They're not fans. They're admirers."

"And the difference is...?"

"You'll see." I wink, teasing her because it's just too easy sometimes. "I can't help what God gave me, Maya. Sometimes it's a curse."

"Oh, shut up. You're so annoying sometimes."

"And you love me."

"You're an arrogant asshole, you know that?"

I push myself up and bend over the desk to where she's sitting. "I know." I smirk at her, knowing it always gets me out of trouble. "Wish me luck. I'm heading to vulture city now."

"I hope they eat you alive!" she calls out as I walk out of her office.

"Trust me, they will."

But I'm only *slightly* interested in one right now.

I walk into the studio at quarter to six, a few girls already sitting on the floor and waiting for class. Their eyes instantly light up as they see me. I flash a small smile at them, hoping they stay put.

No such luck.

"Bentley, we are like huge fans of yours!"

"Like totally! Such huge fans!"

"Can we have your autograph?"

They're looking up at me like lost puppy dogs. Fucking great.

"Sure. What do you want me to sign?"

"Oh...um..." one girl stumbles, looking back at her friend. My eyebrows rise in suspicion, as they have no paper or pens in their hands.

"Actually, can you sign *us*?" the other asks. It's a pathetic plea, but I go with it anyway.

"Um, sure." I step back to my stereo cabinet and grab a marker that's sitting next to it. "Where do you want me to sign?"

The both giggle as they push their shirts down, revealing their sports bras.

This is so unprofessional in so many ways. If Maya catches me, she'll chew my ass out. Instead of arguing, I quickly scribble my name on one of the girls' unimpressive chest.

"Oh my God! Thank you!" she squeals.

"Me next! Do me next!"

Oh, God. Someone please make her shut up.

This is the exact reason I stopped traveling and shooting as much as I was before. I just want to live a normal life while doing something I enjoy. But I know that's nearly impossible.

I sigh and turn to sign the other girl's chest. I hear the door open and glance over to watch Ceci and her friend walk in. She grimaces and turns her eyes away from me as she walks to the back of the room.

Fuck.

More people start piling in, so I quickly sign my name and shoo the girls back to their spots. I ignore the others that say hello to me as I make my way to where Ceci is.

"You're not going to stay back here the whole time, are you?" I cross my arms over my chest, smiling down on her. "You won't get a very good view."

She's on the floor changing her shoes and tying them as she replies, "I think the view is fine. I'll just follow bimbo one and bimbo two's leads." She mocks, standing up finally.

I cock a grin, leaning my body in toward her. "Jealous? I can make a spot up there for you."

She jokingly laughs in my face as if being jealous is not even on her radar. "No, we're good back here."

It's six o'clock, and I know I have to start class now. "Well, don't think hiding back here is going to keep you from participating in my class."

"Of course not, sir," she replies in a professional tone. She grins as she steps in front of her bag.

I can't help the stupid grin that forms on my face as I make my way to the front of the room. I laugh to myself as I think of her calling me sir. Shit, that brings back some memories.

I start with a refresher from last class. Having them show me their stances and punches. After watching most of them successfully nail it down, I demonstrate kicks again. We didn't have much time last class, so that's where I begin again. I show them a routine that I want them to learn.

"Keep doing it and soon we can add in some music to match the pace and rhythm," I call out as I walk around. I'm dying to rush to the back right away and get a chance to touch her again, but I'm not so sure she'd let me this time.

I finally make my way back toward her and her friend. Her friend is stumbling around like a spider on a hot plate. I re-position her body, pressing my hands against her hips and tilting her body to the right angle.

"Damn, Celia. You were right about his hands," she says right to Ceci as if I'm not here listening.

"Oh my God." Her cheeks blush instantly. "Ignore Cora. She has no filter."

I laugh, amused. I walk toward Ceci and watch her, nodding my approval.

"Celia, huh? How many names *do* you have?" I mock, walking away and heading back up to the front.

It's a rude comment, especially since we ended things on *okay* terms. We aren't friends, but I still care about her. I have so many questions I want to ask her—what she's been doing the past couple years, if her mom ever came clean, if she plans to go to her dad's lock box next year. But I'm not sure I deserve answers to those questions. The moment I let her walk out of my office was the moment I let her walk out of my life.

I see her scowling at me as I stand up in front of the class. She moved, angling her body and giving me a direct view of her now. Her body's matured some since the last time I've seen her. Either she's been working out or she's on the 'college diet' she use to pretend she was on before—ramen noodles if I remember correctly. God, she sure played that well.

Everything in me is fighting against each other. What she did versus who she is. Knowing why she did it helped give me closure, but it doesn't change the fact that she lied and manipulated me. It also didn't change the way I felt about her, but that was something I had to let go of the moment I found out.

I blast the stereo and tell them to do some freestyle moves. I tell them it's good to get to know the bag well, to know their strength, and to have fun. It's only the second class, and I like letting the students enjoy their time, especially in an intro class.

I use the opportunity to walk around, watching them punch and kick the bag with all their strength. It's humorous as I see girls the size of my pinkie beat the living shit out of a punching bag.

I step behind Ceci and watch her in amusement as she kicks the bags' ass. I can hear her laughing with her friend as I move in closer to her.

"Looks like you're really enjoying that," I say in a deep tone. Being this close to her again is putting every one of my senses on alert. I can practically feel the shiver that ripples through her.

"I am," she replies without looking back, giving the bag another hook. "Using your face as a target really helps my game," she spits out quickly.

I hold in a laugh at her serious tone because, fuck, she's so goddamn adorable when she's pretending to be pissed off.

"I guess I deserved that." I step around her and plant my feet next to the punching bag, crossing my arms. "Show me what you've got."

She eyes me curiously before curling her lip up into a suspicious grin. She cracks her knuckles and swings her arms around. She gets into the stance position I taught her and gets her arms up before kicking and punching the bag. She then swings around and back kicks it before one last jab.

She then stands upright with her feet together and puts her hands flat together, bowing down in front of me, like you would in the Japanese culture.

I try to hold in a laugh, but once our eyes lock and she bursts out in a laugh, I can no longer hold it in.

"What was that?"

"I don't know." She shrugs lightly. "Practicing."

"It's a part of her major," Cora interrupts, breaking our connection.
My brows raise in question.

"I'm studying Sports Management," she clarifies quickly.

My lips curl up in a hasty grin. "Looking for an internship?"

Her eyes narrow, obviously not amused by my joke.

"You're an asshole," she spits out, annoyance laced in her voice.

"I see you still have the same attitude as before." I smirk, unable to
stop myself from spewing the words out. Her body remains still, the
chemistry building between us doesn't go unnoticed.

I step toward her and place a hand against her cheek. I don't even
realize I'm doing it until she leans her face into it, making me forget
we're in a room of thirty other people.

"Good work." I nod, frazzled from the way two years of suppressed
feelings rush back in. I step back, needing to put space in between us.
She watches me with wide eyes as I back up and walk toward the front.

Once I'm in front of the class again, she doesn't make eye contact
with me, and I avoid her for the rest of the class.

This is a bad idea.

A really fucking bad idea.

But then again, nothing involving her has ever really been a good
idea...and that never stopped me in the past.

CHAPTER TWELVE
CECILIA

I DON'T KNOW why Bentley flirting with me evokes emotions inside me —anger and lust—both fighting with each other as to which one I should be feeling.

The first year after Bentley was so fucking hard. I isolated myself and stayed distant until Katelynn peeled back all those heartbreaking layers, still it took her a long time to break my shell and finally move on with my life.

So why the hell am I doing this? Why am I putting myself in a position to see Bentley twice a week and letting my blood boil every time he's near me?

Because you still love him.

Shut up, heart.

Cora makes me continue going for the next four weeks until Fourth of July week. Classes are suspended the entire week, and I can finally breathe without the anticipation of seeing him.

We haven't talked since the last time he cradled my face with his hand. There's something so familiar in his touch. Something that makes it impossible to forget him, or how he made me feel.

I call Simon and beg him to take me out somewhere. I don't care where. I just need to get out of my house.

"Thanks," I say softly as I get into his truck. It's already dark out so he can't see how bloodshot my eyes are from crying.

"Where to?" he asks enthusiastically.

"I don't care."

"Hey, what's wrong?" He turns and forces my face to look at him. "Why're you crying?"

I sniff once and reply, "Because I'm an idiot, Simon."

"You're going to have to be a bit more specific," he mocks. "What happened?"

"Bentley," I say quickly. "He's my kickboxing instructor."

"No shit!" he yelps. "No wonder you're enjoying that class so much," he teases.

I cock my head at him and tell him that's not it.

"Then what is it?"

"It's as if two years never even passed. My body still craves him, wants his touch. My minds a damn clusterfuck, and I don't know how to control these feelings lingering inside me. It's as if we could pick right back up where we left off. You know—before everything blew up in my face and I never saw him again."

"So what's the matter? Have you talked to him?"

"No, not really. We spoke the first week of class, barely, but he hasn't said a word to me since. He watches me and that's it. And I think that's what's pissing me off. He's treating me like any other student."

"Perhaps it's what helps him see you after all this time, Celia. Maybe he's struggling with seeing you just as much as you are. Maybe he's confused considering he probably didn't expect to see you again."

I know Simon's right, but I hate that he is. But I'm *not* like every other student in that room. He's had me in positions I've only ever read about. He's kissed me with such passion and aggression that my insides felt it. We had so much between us before it was ripped apart.

"I just hate that I'm having these feelings toward him. I thought I was over him, Simon! Over. And now? Fuck, I don't know."

"Have you tried speaking to him?"

"No. He always has like a hundred girls waiting for him. And one of the other instructors always comes in right after class and is like all over him. I can live with the idea of him moving on, but I don't think I can just sit there and watch it. That hurts even worse."

"Damn." I see Simon's pained expression, and I know he feels for me, but isn't sure what else to say. There really isn't much else to say. I put this all on myself. "Well, I know where I'm taking you." His lips curl into a wide grin. "Time to get you drunk."

I laugh as he pulls out into the street. "Why is that always your answer to everything?"

"Booze heals the weak and brokenhearted, my love. Trust me."

I narrow my eyebrows at him, confused at his words. "Who are you longing after?"

He tilts his head at me, but doesn't say anything because it's too obvious.

"I knew it!" I squeal. "I always knew, Simon."

"I know," he says softly. "I just wish she did."

"Cora knows. You just need to grow some balls and tell her. Tell her you want her exclusively, not just one-night sleepovers. Tell her how you *really* feel."

"I will when you do," he mocks. "You tell Bentley that your panties are still wet over him, and I'll tell Cora."

"Oh my God." I blush. "Such a romantic."

We end up at a bar where his friend works and gets us in since we aren't twenty-one yet. Simon keeps feeding me drinks until I finally loosen up and play pool with him.

I bend over the pool table and line my stick up with the red-stripped ball. I pull my stick back twice before finally smacking the white ball. It flies over the table and begins rolling down the floor.

"Shit!" I screech. I put the stick down and run after it. It rolls under a high-top bar table, so I bend down to grab it. I've had way more than I remember. I stand up, forgetting I'm under the table, and smack my head against it. "Dammit!"

I stumble backward into something else and immediately regret those last three drinks. "Son-of-a-bitch." I brace myself for the pain to come, but it never does. Two large hands wrap around my arms, securing me in place.

His scent consumes me immediately, and I know exactly who those hands belong to.

"Are you all right?" he asks, his voice raspy and deep.

"I'm fine. You can let me go," I plead. I don't want to see his face. I just want him to let me go so I can walk back to Simon.

"You're stumbling all over the fucking place. What are you even doing in here?" His tone is angry, and I feel myself getting brave as the alcohol floods through my veins.

"I was playing pool with a friend. Is that okay?"

"No," he responds curtly. "You need to go home and sleep it off."

I pull my arms out of his grip and turn around to see a pissed off Bentley.

"Who the fuck are you to tell me what I need to do? You aren't my boss anymore, *Mr. Leighton*."

He grabs my upper arm and pulls me closer to him, lowering his mouth to my ear so only I hear him. "Either I'll take you home or the police can take you home. Decide," he growls.

"God, you're an asshole. You haven't changed a bit, Bentley Leighton."

"Say goodnight to your friend. We're leaving."

The alcohol pulses through me and part of me is thankful he's here. I tell Simon I'm leaving with Bentley, and he gives me a wink before I walk away.

"Well, let's go," I mock, walking past him with my hoodie in hand.

He casually follows behind me, not hurrying along as I walk in front of him.

I make my way to his Range Rover that brings back memories of our time together and how every time I saw one afterward, my heart immediately squeezed at the memory of us.

"Oh, the good times we had in this thing," I say, an octave higher than necessary. "Do you remember?" I smile playfully as I lean up against the passenger door.

"I remember," he replies roughly. He stands in front of me, his chest rising and falling heavily as we stare intently at each other. He leans in, our eyes not breaking, until he grabs the door handle behind me, and motions for me to move. I swallow, wishing I was sober enough to keep myself from acting like a damn fool. "Get in."

The ride is awkward, but I'm too drunk to care at the moment. He keeps a firm grip on the steering wheel with his eyes focused on the road as rain begins to pour down all around us.

"I'm glad you decided to go back into modeling," I say, breaking the silence. "I mean, I'm glad you went back to something you loved."

His body relaxes a bit before responding. "It was inevitable, eventually, that I wouldn't stay working for my dad. It just took a couple fuck ups to make that clear to him."

I swallow deeply, feeling guilty. "I'm sorry. I'm sure that was my fault."

"It didn't help my case, but no it wasn't all your fault. I knew better," he says harshly. I knew it. He regrets being with me. *He knew better.* He knew better than to hook up with an intern. To be with someone that he worked with.

"Even so."

"We don't have to do this, Ceci. I know you're sorry. I've moved on from it."

"Good. Me, too."

"I know."

I snap my head in his direction. "You know?"

He ignores my question and says, "We're here."

He gets out and comes to my door. He opens it and puts his hand out for me. I don't take it as I stumble out of the car myself.

"I'm fine," I snap. "Thanks for the ride."

I clench my hoodie and begin walking toward my house. I can walk my damn self to the door.

"Ceci, wait!" he calls out. I hear his shoes hitting the wet cement as he comes up behind me. "I don't want you to fall," he says genuinely, placing a hand on my lower back.

"Don't touch me."

"I'm just guiding you. It's wet and you're drunk."

I laugh at his words.

"You don't get to talk about being wet, Mister." God, I'm a fucking lush. I wish I could freaking talk normal to him, but now my body is ready for a fight.

"What are you talking about?" He spins me around, making me face him. My hair is getting soaked, but I don't care. His golden locks are molding to his face as he looks down at me. "I'm trying to be nice, Ceci." He grips both of his hands on my upper arms, stabilizing me.

"Well, stop it. Stop being nice to me. You don't get to be nice to me!" I scream, breaking the hold his hands have on me.

"You think I *want* to be nice to you? You think I like caring about you after all this time?"

"Well...I'm sorry to be such a damn burden! I'll stop ruining your life and stay as far away from you as I can. Happy?"

"No, I'm not happy," he says softer. "I've been fucking miserable for two goddamn years, Ceci. Why do you think I've worked relentlessly after I got back into modeling? I needed to be away from here. Everything reminded me of you. I needed to keep my mind busy just so I wouldn't think of you!"

"I'm sure all your hot model friends helped you plenty with

forgetting me. Don't even pretend you haven't moved on. Stop being a hypocrite," I fight back.

"I never moved on," he says softly. "Don't believe everything you read."

"Then why couldn't you forgive me? Why didn't you come back for me?" I scream over the rain, tears flowing down my cheeks. His words have completely sobered me up now that we're finally having the fight we needed to have all this time.

He firmly grabs my arms again, pulling me closer to him. "I did! I came back for you last summer. You'd already moved on. I wasn't going to interfere with your happiness."

"What?" I gasp. "I wasn't with anyone last year. You think I could move on from you that easy, Bentley?"

"I saw you," he admits, releasing his hands. "You ran to him when he pulled up. You wrapped your hands around him and he kissed you. That's when I knew…" he stalls, pushing his wet locks off his face. "That's when I knew it was too late. *I* was too late."

I push him back forcefully with all the anger and regret building up inside me. "You were here?" I scream and push against his chest again, although he barely flinches. "You were here and never said anything?" I continue screaming, angrily.

He grabs my fists and holds them to his chest, stopping me. "And say what?" he asks softly. "I wasn't going to interrupt your reunion with your boyfriend. I knew I hadn't earned that."

"You weren't too late," I sob. I lift my head up and meet his dark eyes. "You weren't too late!" I repeat louder. "That wasn't my boyfriend. He never was. Simon's my best friend, and he had just returned from London," I explain.

"Shit," he curses, dropping his eyes. "I don't know why I drove here that day. I shouldn't have."

"Why didn't you call?" I ask. His hands are still wrapped around my fists. "I haven't stopped thinking about you, Bentley. I know I fucked up. I *know* that. But if you were thinking of me, why didn't you call?"

"Because I didn't know what to feel, Ceci. You royally fucked me over, yet I wanted you. I wanted every fucking piece of you! You know how messed up that made me feel?"

"I have an idea," I breathe out. "I became a tortured soul that didn't let anyone in because I was so damn regretful for what I did. I was angry and broken, and I didn't even want to live a life without you, yet I had to learn how because it was my only option."

His hands grip around my face so fast, I don't even see him leaning in. His mouth is on mine before I even have time to register it. My palms lay flat against his chest as he holds me, cupping my cheeks with his strong hands.

I moan and pant against his mouth as he strokes his tongue with mine—thirst and desire taking complete control. His mouth consumes me, holding me tightly against him as he takes me. I inhale his scent as one of his hands grip the back of my neck and the other hand slides down to my hip, holding me firmly in place.

It's just as I remembered. His lips are fucking heaven and nothing ever compares to the way he kisses me. Feelings rush through me harder than the rain pouring down on us, and I realize I need to make him stop.

I push against his chest, breaking the heated kiss. He looks down at me curiously, and then his eyes widen as he realizes what we just did.

"God, I'm sorry." He releases me and brushes a hand through his soaked hair. "I shouldn't have done that."

I don't know if it's because he regrets kissing me, or the way he's looking at me right now that hurts the most. It guts me completely as I see the mixed emotions in his eyes.

"I should've called," he says, taking me off guard. "But I was a coward. I wanted to forget, but I was a fool because I could never forget, Ceci. I can't forget."

A sob reluctantly releases deep within my chest. The last thing I want to do is cry in front of him, but what's it matter anymore. This whole situation is fucked up.

I look up at him and we lock eyes when I finally say, "You're too late."

"What?" he gasps, training his eyes on me still.

"You weren't late back then," I clarify. "But you're too late *now*."

I spin around and begin walking toward the house. I'm soaking wet and freezing, but I don't even care. I just want to feel numb.

CHAPTER THIRTEEN
BENTLEY

GODDAMMIT. I'm an idiot.

Why did I fucking tell her all that? She's drunk, and I'm a damn fool for thinking I had any claim on her.

"You weren't late back then. But you're too late now."

Did that mean she had moved on and was with someone else or that she didn't want me at all? From the way that her body reacted to me—the same way it did two years ago—I refuse to think she can easily ignore that. There's no way she can deny it.

I've been battling my feelings for two years. It's exhausting, and no matter how much I tell myself to move on—*to forget her*—I can't. I never will.

Watching her in class for the past month has been pure torture. Not talking to her and barely making eye contact with her has been worse than trying to forget her. At least then, I didn't have to look at her and watch her perfect little body moving and bouncing around during class. I could at least pretend my feelings were non-existent and that I was just a pussy for not being able to get over her.

But I'm tired of being that person. I'm going to make her see that giving in is much easier than fighting the inevitable. Giving in *is* what we both want.

My mind is made up, and I'm not going to take no for an answer. Unless she's sporting a diamond ring, nothing's going to stop me from making sure she knows exactly what I want and how I feel.

I watch her walk in Monday evening with Cora. She keeps her eyes down as she makes her way to the back of the room. I grin selfishly as I walk toward her.

"Where is everyone?" Cora asks, looking up at me as I step in front of Ceci. They're sitting on the floor, changing their shoes out and realizing the room is completely empty except for the three of us.

"Class got pushed back to six-thirty," I state. Ceci finally jerks her head up, staring at me suspiciously. "I sent an email out."

Cora looks at her phone, checking her email for the message she won't find. "I didn't get one." She narrows her eyebrows before looking back up at me. She smirks, obviously understanding the silent plea I'm sending her.

I never sent her an email.

"Well, since we have a half hour, I'm gonna grab a protein shake." She uncrosses her legs and stands up to walk out.

Ceci goes to stand up and blurts out, "I'll come with you."

"No, stay and watch our stuff," she blurts, rushing away before Ceci can protest.

She stands up and faces me chest-to-chest. She crosses her arms, scowling up at me. "What are you doing?"

I flash a confused expression. "As in general?" I raise brow, making her steam even more.

"As in *this*." She waves her hands in between us.

"I just wanted a few minutes alone to talk to you," I admit. "I want to apologize," I clarify. "I'm sorry for how I acted last weekend. It was inappropriate." She continues staring at me, not saying a word. Her expression reads that she doesn't believe me. She *shouldn't*...but that doesn't mean I'm not going to try to convince her of it. "We can be friends, right? I mean, I'm going to be your instructor for another two months."

"Friends?" She furrows her brows, still scowling at me.

"Yeah, it's when two people talk casually. Maybe hang out. Strictly platonic."

"I know what being friends is, asshole. But I don't think that's a good idea."

I slap a hand to my chest as if I'm offended by her dismissal. "All right. Have it your way." I smirk. "You always did prefer the subordinate role."

"Excuse me? What did you just say to me, Bentley?"

"It's actually, Mr. Leighton," I taunt. I wink at her, causing her anger to fuel even more.

Oh, yes, this will be fun. If she doesn't want to admit that she wants to be more than friends, I'll just have to make her realize it on her own.

I purposely avoid eye contact with her as I go over more lessons. I walk around the classroom like normal, but don't step in to help her. Instead, I yell at her for slacking and tell her to try again.

She glares at me, dropping her arms to her sides. "If you need extra help, Miss West, you're welcome to come to the front of the room. It's a much better view." I smirk at her.

She bites her lip, stopping herself from making a scene before she finally releases it and responds. "I'm just fine back here. Thank you, Mr. Leighton."

"My pleasure." I grin wide. "Keep your arms tight. You're falling out of your stance. Flex your muscles as you drive into the bag," I instruct and walk away, but I can feel her eyes daggering into the back of my head. She hates the fact that I know her so well. Even after all this time, I know her better than she realizes.

After a great class, I dismiss everyone and begin packing up. Maya walks in as usual after class and grabs a hold of my arm. I lean down so she can whisper in my ear. I laugh at her comments about bimbo one and two in the front row, and grin as I look up to find Ceci staring at me. She's scowling and shaking her head at me. *Shit.* She's going to think I'm playing her.

Good.

She's jealous.

I'll take it. Anything to make her realize she has feelings for me.

"Dude, that girl was close to lighting you on fire with her eyes. What'd you do to piss her off?"

"Oh…that story could take a while. Let's just say, we know each other well. Very well."

"What about her friend?" She watches them walk out of the studio and exit out of the gym. There are windows surrounding the building, so it's easy to see everything outside. The windows are tinted from the outside so you can't see in.

"Pretty sure her friend is straight. Sorry, Maya," I say, teasingly. "There might be a few in the front that are your type."

"You're such a bastard," she spats. "I can find my own dates."

I stroke a hand down my shirt, smoothing it as I walk up to Ceci's door. I know she's home because I recognize her car in the driveway. I'm prepared for a pissed off Ceci, so this'll be interesting.

I ring the doorbell and impatiently wait for her to answer.

She whips the door open with a toothbrush in her mouth, her hair up in some kind of rat's nest bun. She looks fucking adorable.

"Vhat arr you doiin herr?" she says with a mouthful of spit. I try not to laugh, but I can't help it.

"Uhh, bad time?" I lean in, hoping she lets me in.

She brings a finger up, motioning for me to wait as she runs and disposes of her toothbrush. She walks back with a bottle of water, chugging it before responding.

"Why are you here?" she asks again, popping her hip out to one side.

"I came to hang out," I say matter-of-factly.

"Hang out? We don't hang out."

"Friends hang out."

"We're not friends."

"We could be friends."

She narrows her eyes at me, clearly confused by my sudden intrusion.

"C'mon. Friends catch up. We have a lot to catch up on."

"I'm not exactly ready to *catch up*." She waves a hand down her outfit. She's in stretchy, black pants and a purple tank top.

"I'm not taking you to the opera. You look fine."

She sighs, dropping her shoulders as she stares me down questioning my motives. I'm here to prove to her that we belong together, even if I have to play the friend-zone card.

"We can watch a movie. I still have 50 First Dates recorded on my DVR."

Her face lights up. "You do? I thought you hated that movie."

"Nah, I grew to like it." I shrug casually. After watching it for three weeks straight, I grew to fucking hate it because it reminded me of her.

She knows every damn word and every time the penguin scene came on, she'd flap her arms out pretending to wobble like one. Seriously, adorable.

She inhales deeply as she thinks about it for a moment. "Fine. Let me change. Or at least brush my hair."

"I can wait." I grin.

Ceci meets me back at the door in less than ten minutes. She's brushed her hair out and put it up in a high ponytail. She's wearing black skinny jeans and a casual pink top. Just looking at her makes my dick swell in my jeans. This is going to be more challenging than I thought.

CHAPTER FOURTEEN
CECILIA

WHAT THE HELL am I thinking? It's as if he has this invisible pull on me. He could say, "Come with me…" and my arms would spread out in front of me as I followed behind him like a zombie. I'm worse than a damn groupie.

"What if I had plans tonight?" I ask, buckling myself in. "What was your backup plan?" I mock.

He tilts his head toward me, flashing a cocky expression. "Have I ever had to have a backup plan?"

"Well, I see your arrogant attitude hasn't changed." I smirk. "Same old Bentley."

"That's not true," he bites. "I only act like that to amuse you." He grins.

"Now who's living a double life?"

"Ha! Not even close. Although, traveling around the world can sure make you feel that way."

I look up at him curiously. "Why's that? I thought you'd love the traveling—modeling, hot dates, sunny beaches, walks along the market's that sell fruits and vegetables right out of their car.

He narrows his eyebrows at me before bursting into laughter. "Where exactly do you think I'm traveling?"

I laugh shyly. "I don't know. Just seems very world-*traveley*."

How was it that one moment his mouth was on mine, his body consuming me entirely and now I'm in his car 'hanging out.' It's as if that moment never happened as if we're just pretending it didn't mean anything.

Could Bentley really be my friend? Was it possible to be friends with someone you shared yourself with?

A part of me is screaming *No!* while the other part is ignoring it. I could do this. We could be friends. He knows we aren't hooking back up, so perhaps it was that simple.

We arrive at his condo and everything inside is exactly same. It's like walking into a time machine, and it's two years ago. Everything's familiar and feels comfortable…like home.

"Wow…I love what you've done with the place," I tease, walking through to the living room.

He laughs lightly. "Yeah, well that's what happens when you aren't home often enough to do anything to it."

I nod, agreeing. I take a seat on his couch, on the far end, and get comfortable. He grabs the remote and sits on the opposite end as he flips through his DVR.

"Can I get you anything to drink before we start?" he asks.

"Sure, thanks." I smile weakly back at him. This is a whole new Bentley. This isn't possessive, eat-me-alive Bentley. This is genuine Bentley with maybe a bit of brokenness. I'm really fond of both sides of Bentley—knowing he can be this person as well plays with my emotions even more.

I should've known coming here would pull at my heartstrings, but part of me just couldn't say no. We used to have a lot of fun together cooped up in this condo. We had a lot of fun basically anywhere.

"Hope this is okay. My fridge isn't stocked." He hands me a can of diet Pepsi, and I nod graciously.

"It's perfect, thanks."

He sits back down and turns the movie on. Soon, Adam Sandler is trying to hit on Drew Barrymore and her house made of waffles. Of course, she turns him down, and the whole scene is hilarious because she doesn't remember past one day.

We sit comfortably with a bowl of popcorn in between us, laughing in between bites. It's so easy. No pressure, no unsaid words—just two friends hanging out.

We continue casually hanging out for the next few weeks. Each time, Bentley picks me up and we talk about everything and anything on the ride to his house or restaurant. Sometimes we stay in and watch movies and cook, or he takes us out for pizza and wings. It's honestly nothing like I pictured being friends with Bentley would be. We were growing closer, but without all the sexual tension lingering between us.

"What are you doing?" Cora asks, accusingly from behind me as I look over myself in the mirror.

"Just making sure this shirt matches these shorts," I answer casually, rubbing my hands down the fabric to smooth it out.

"Not that, dumbass. What are you doing *with* Bentley?"

I spin around, narrowing my eyes at her. "We're just hanging out."

She tilts her head, disapprovingly. "Celia, I love you, but you, my friend are living in delusional-land."

"Am not," I say, defensively. "Why would you say that?"

"He's taking you out to meals and you watch movies at his house. Alone. It doesn't take a genius to figure out."

"Well, you're wrong. We're friends. There's no touching, kissing, nothing. Strictly platonic." I nod my head affirmatively. "Plus, he knows I have a boyfriend."

"Do you?" she snaps.

I glare at her as I grab my purse off the bed. "Yes. We're not breaking any rules."

"Does Brandon know you two are hanging out?" she fires again. "Have you even bothered to tell him?"

"He knows I have friends here, Cora. I don't see the big deal."

She snorts and stands up. "Okay. You keep telling yourself that. When shit blows up, don't say I didn't warn you." She begins to walk out of my room, but a fiery anger ripples through my veins.

"Why are you acting like such a bitch?" She halts and spins around, aggressively eyeing me.

"Now I'm acting like a bitch? Celia, take a look around. Look at what you're doing. I'm just telling you what you're apparently too blind to see."

"I'm only home for the summer, Cora. Can we not fight, please?" I beg softly. The last thing I want is to get into a fight over Bentley.

"He loves you, Celia. He's *still* in love with you. This act, or whatever he's doing, is in hopes you'll fall back in love with him."

I shake my head feverishly. "No, he wasn't in love with me. He's just wasting time while he's not modeling this summer. It's nothing. I promise."

240

She walks over to me and grabs my hands in hers, locking eyes with me intently. "Well, for your heart's sake, I hope you're right. After hearing how you dealt with it and knowing how long it took you to move on, I just don't want you to go through that again. I don't want you to get hurt."

"I won't. I'm fine. Honest." I smile back at her. She leans in and hugs me goodbye before leaving. I glance in the mirror once more before heading downstairs and waiting for him to pick me up.

"I thought we could see a movie tonight," he says as soon as he pulls out into the street.

"You're going to make me watch one of those gory-guts-everywhere-type movies, aren't you?" I cringe, wrinkling my face at him.

He laughs, gripping the steering wheel slyly as he weaves us in and out of traffic. "No, actually. I thought we could watch one of your sappy, romance movies."

I cock a brow in disbelief. "Well, this new side of Bentley is very refreshing. A gentleman and a chick flick. It's like you've turned into my gay bestie," I tease.

His hands tense and I see his eyes darken. Apparently, that was the *wrong* thing to say.

We arrive at the theatre and Bentley completely surprises me when he buys two tickets for The Fault in Our Stars.

"Are you fucking with me right now?"

His eyes widen, taken back. "Um, no. We don't have to see it if you don't want, I just figured—"

"Yes! I've been dying to see this movie! Oh my God. Please tell me you brought like ten boxes of tissues."

I nearly skip to the theatre, the anticipation of finally seeing this tearjerker is almost too much. I read the book last year during my Freshman year when I was in my self-torturous phase and putting myself through emotional pain.

"How'd you know I'd want to see this?" I ask, bumping my shoulder with his as we sit down.

He winks at me as he looks around the theatre, obviously taking in a large female audience number. "I had a hunch."

The theatre is packed by the time the movie begins. We both end up shoulder to shoulder—the people sitting next to each of us smothering us together.

"No crying." He leans down and whispers against my ear. I look up at the grin he's sporting. He so did this on purpose.

"That goes for you, too."

"That won't be a problem." His face is firm, not giving anything away. It's the first time I've seen this particular expression. I couldn't tell what it was—remorse, maybe? His jaw is tense and his eyes are locked on mine.

The buzzing of my phone breaks me from his stare. I grab it from my pocket and see it's a text from Brandon.

Brandon: 45 days until school starts...45 days too long.

Cecilia: You're counting?

Brandon: Counting the days until I see my beautiful girlfriend again, yes. I can't wait, baby. I miss you so much.

My heart aches at his words. God, what am I doing? Is Cora right? Should I tell him I've been hanging out with Bentley? Knowing Brandon he'd be totally trustworthy.

Forty-five days. Was that it? How had this summer flown by so fast without me realizing it?

I glance up at Bentley who's watching the screen. I've let myself get completely distracted between our kickboxing classes and hanging out *as friends*. But were we? Friends?

It was like a switch. Once Bentley kissed me and confessed everything to me, I had turned that part of my heart off. But now it was definitely back on. He's the one it's beating for. He's the one I've let back into my life when I have a boyfriend waiting for me.

The realization of what I've done and how I'm feeling hits me right in the gut. After last year, I had tried really hard to get over Bentley. I *needed* to get over Bentley. But now, here he was. Next to me.

I sink down in my seat, having no choice but to curl up next to him. The heat radiating off his chest burns into me. I know I've been ignoring my attraction to him. My feelings are still there and I know I've been lying to myself every moment I've allowed myself to spend time with him.

I swallow roughly as I think about the position I've put myself in.

Why the hell did I let myself go along with his little 'friends only' charade? Had I secretly wished for more this whole time?

I think about Brandon and how he's the perfect guy for me. He's sweet, caring, smart—he's the boy next door any girl would be lucky to have.

And then there's Bentley.

The forbidden fruit.

Brandon is the obvious choice—the safe choice. He'd take my heart and guard it for the rest of his life, never causing me any heartbreak or pain.

Bentley was like a rollercoaster. One minute my hands would be up in the air, enjoying the high, and the next I'd be curled over hurling my guts out at the nausea my stomach was feeling. Bentley was the dangerous choice—*the tempting choice.*

Bentley wraps his arm around my shoulders, leaning closer to me. My heart quickens at the small gesture, but my entire body feels it. God, how does he have this affect on me? *Still.*

I try to convince myself it's natural. Bentley was my first...*love.* I never told him that though. Perhaps I should've, but what good would it have done? It would've only hurt worse when everything blew up.

I try to focus on the movie and soon tears are streaming down my cheeks. They come forcefully and without notice, but I continue watching because I don't want Bentley to see me like this. I can't even tell which tears these are—for Hazel and Augustus, or for Bentley.

"Hey," he whispers, so close to my ear I feel his lips vibrate against my skin. "You all right?" I hear the sincerity in his voice, so smooth, so soothing.

I look up at him, tears evident as they mark my cheeks on their way down my face. How did I miss it this entire time? I had built my Bentley towers up, hoping to avoid feeling like this ever again, yet here I was completely smitten and uncontrollably in love with him.

I smile weakly at him and nod. "Yeah...I just know what's coming."

He presses his palm to my cheek, wiping away the tears with his thumb. He lets it linger there as our eyes lock, lust and desperation potent in his touch. Bentley's the reason I have any answers about my father at all, the reason I get to open his lock box in a year. He was always much more than a friend to me, and I don't know why I refused to see it before.

Brandon.

I curse under my breath as I remind myself what I'm doing and who I'm with. Brandon is amazing, and I could really see myself with him for a long time, perhaps even a lifetime, but I'm not sure I could live with the *what if's*…the unknown if I just gave in and went for it.

I sink into his touch, telling him everything with my eyes. I'm not this person, or at least I'm not now. I had worked on becoming a better person, not one that lied and manipulated people for their own personal gain. But looking back, I know I wouldn't do it any different. I was determined to find information about my dad and it brought me here. It brought me some closure and that's more than I could have ever asked for.

"Bentley." It comes out as a whimper and I know he feels it, too. I bite my lip to keep myself from melting completely under him. "I'm fine now." I nod my head so he knows he can take his hand off me.

I wipe my hand under my other eye, needing to compose myself. I'm pretty certain our 'platonic friendship' just went out the window.

The drive back to my house is quiet. Neither one of us knows what to say. I cried my eyes out at the end—uncontrollable, breathless sobbing. I'm sure Bentley thought it was due to the movie, but some of it wasn't. I had decided to let Bentley go. This *friendship* couldn't exist anymore.

He opens my door for me, and I let him take my hand as he escorts me out. Usually, we'd be laughing and joking around, but something had shifted tonight. I can feel every movement he makes deep within me. My heart thumping rapidly against my chest—rising and falling with every gesture Bentley makes. My body is fully aware of him and how he's making me feel. And I can't…I just can't. I'm too conflicted. Letting him wedge his way back into my life is one thing, but giving up everything I worked so hard for the past two years could do me more damage than before.

"Thanks for the movie. It was amazingly heartbreaking." I grin shyly up at him. I need to say goodbye. For good this time.

"It was my pleasure, Ceci. Surprisingly, I enjoyed the movie."

I laugh lightly. "I bet that hurt to admit."

"Yeah, I've kind of lost my man card. But oh, well. It was worth it." His eyes are intense as they burn into mine. I blink and shift them away, unable to directly look at him.

I stand there, stumbling over my own thoughts. I can't let him think anything's wrong with me, so I go for the casual routine before bailing —a quick kiss on the cheek and a friendly goodbye hug. I can do this.

"Well, good night," I say breathy, feeling like my brain is running out of oxygen as I take him in. The wind picks up and blows my hair up, sending his scent directly into me. God. He smells so fucking good. Mixed with his perfectly snug jeans and dark blue shirt, he could convince the blind to jump him like a wild tiger.

"Goodnight, Ceci." His smirk forms into a devilish grin before he leans into me, giving me my chance to kiss his cheek and hopefully, walk away without melting into a hysterical round of sobbing fits.

Before my body reaches his, he has me pinned against his Range Rover. Each one of his hands is gripping my wrist, holding them up against my head. His mouth is on me before I can protest, his tongue licking inside my lips demanding entrance.

My mind doesn't fully wrap around what's happening before it's too late. My mouth invites him in, our tongues reuniting and fighting for control. His lips move around mine desperate and eager as if it would physically pain him to let them go. His hands release my wrist as one grips the back of my neck, pulling me closer to him. The other hand wraps around me, his palm flat against the small of my back. His fingers press into the flesh, pleading with me to say the words he's secretly begging me to say.

Bentley is a man who likes to hold control, but he wants to know it's exactly what I want.

My hands lay flat against his chest, not sure if it's to push him away or to grip his shirt and pull him closer. I can't think when his mouth is on me. My mind is spinning at what I want and what I should want.

Perhaps I need to just stop thinking altogether.

"Take me to your place."

CHAPTER FIFTEEN
BENTLEY

I CAN'T GET my keys out of the door fast enough. Stumbling, I finally jerk the door open and press Ceci to my chest. I kick the door shut and throw my keys to the ground. I crash my mouth to hers, feeling the heat, and electricity spiral between us. I've craved her taste for over two years—her palpable desire—that belong only to me.

I lead her down the dark hallway to my room, lips and body parts fighting to touch every surface. She whimpers against my mouth, earning a moan from deep within my throat. God. I've been dreaming about this for too fucking long. It doesn't seem real right now, but I'm going to take my time with her—reunite with every inch of her body.

I grab the hem of her shirt and break away just long enough to pull it over her head. My lips find hers again as I grab the bottom of her ass and pull her up, legs wrapping around my waist. I place her on the edge of my bed, my body pressing on top of hers. I feel her crumbling underneath me, soaking up everything I'm giving her.

"You know I'm not doing this without hearing you say it first," I growl against her ear, my left hand gripping her breast through her bra. She arches her back as my mouth kisses her neck, marking exactly where I've been and where I always want to be. "You need to say it," I repeat, squeezing her breast harder.

"Bentley. Mm...God." Her voice is pleading, but it's not good enough.

I bend in between her legs and slowly unzip her jeans. I let my finger play with the button, finally popping it and exposing her barely-there panties.

I drop my mouth just above the panty-line and suck her skin hard. She moans as her body arches off the bed to meet my greedy lips.

"I need to know you want this, Ceci. If you want it, you're going to have to beg for it."

"I-I thought we were *just* friends…" she whimpers weakly as I begin ripping my own shirt off. She's delusional if she thought we were *just* friends.

My lips continue grazing her skin, slowly brushing her panties down so my mouth can explore lower. I feel goose bumps rise as she shudders underneath me.

"We weren't friends, Ceci," I growl, roughly. I lower to my knees, yanking her pants down with me. I loop a finger in her panties and pull them to the side. As soon as I see her perfect, taut pink pussy, my mouth is on her. A moan rumbles up my throat as I inhale her scent and taste the deliciousness that is she. "We were never just friends."

Her hands fist in my hair, squeezing with every lick my tongue drives into her. God, she tastes so fucking good. Better than I remember —if that's even possible.

I press my hands into her hips, forcing her to arch them up deeper into my mouth. She screams out at the intensity my mouth is causing her.

"Sweetheart," I say, slowly licking my tongue up her stomach. "I need to hear you say it."

"Say what?" she asks, breathy.

I smile, amused, because I know she fucking knows. "Say it, Ceci," I demand, my tongue making its way to her bra, yanking it down to cover her nipple with my lips. I suck hard, getting a mumbled moan out of her. My hand reaches down to her swollen clit, rubbing my thumb in circles as she convulses. Her body jerks as she gets closer to release, but I slow down before she can.

And then, just before I pick the pace back up, her entire body jerks, moving out from under me.

"Stop," she pleads. She pushes her hands roughly against my chest as she rolls away from me. She swings her legs off the bed, frantically looking for her clothes.

I'm off the bed and in front of her before she can put any clothing on. "What happened?" My voice is eager and worried I'm going to lose her.

"I-I can't do this." She shakes her head, but I'm not sure if she's shaking it at herself or me. Her eyes are blinking more than normal, and I can tell she's having an inner battle, one I'm sure I won't be winning this time.

"Talk to me." I grab her chin and force her to look up at me, her eyes swelling with tears.

"I don't want to be *this* person, Bentley. I have a boyfriend." Her breathing is rapid, her chest falling and rising quickly. *Fuck.*

"I'm sorry," I whisper, but I'm not apologizing for that.

"Please, take me home." She pulls out of my grip and leans down to grab her shirt off the floor.

"You don't have to go home, Ceci. We can talk," I say sincerely. I don't want us to leave on bad terms. This is the last fucking thing I intended.

"I don't want to talk. I just...I need to think."

"What's there to think about? You know how I feel about you."

She spins around, her face tense and bright red. "You broke me!" she screams. She shakes her head, defeated. "I loved you and you broke me. You let me walk away and you never told me how you really felt. If you loved me, you would've fought for me," she declares, anger boiling over. "And now it's too late! I gave my heart away to someone else."

Insert a hundred daggers into my fucking heart.

She gave it away to someone else?

I'm firing with rage. She has this all wrong.

"I broke you?" I question, loudly. "Well, you *destroyed* me! You were the only one I've ever loved, Ceci, and letting you walk away was the only thing I could do to make sense of how I felt about you."

She freezes in place, the blood drains from her face as she responds. "You loved me?"

I close the gap between us and grab her arms, jerking her body toward me. "Yes," I growl. "I *still* love you."

Tears begin falling down her cheeks, her eyes staring up at me in shock. "Do you have any idea how long I've waited to hear that?" she sobs. "Why didn't you ever tell me?"

"I was scared," I admit. "Hannah fucked me over so bad. I didn't want to get close to another person. I didn't think I wanted to love."

Her tears come faster as she chokes on sobs. I brush her tears away and lay a gentle kiss on her lips.

"I need some time."

I swallow hard. That's probably the worst fucking thing a girl can say. "How much?"

"I don't know. Everything we do now will be tainted. It's not fair to Brandon."

Motherfucker. I didn't need to know his goddamn name. My hands ball into fists imagining her being with someone else. The thought puts me into a blinding rage, my body fiery with jealousy and anger.

"Let's go."

I walk past her, scooping my shirt off the floor and pulling it over my head. I find my keys on the floor and dart out the door, Ceci not far behind me.

I don't know what to feel once I drop her off at her house with neither of us knowing what to say.

I tell her to call me when she's ready right before she walks out—for God knows how long.

I can't blame her really. I should never have let it get that far, knowing she has a fucking boyfriend. One that apparently doesn't live here, because she's been spending her free nights with me. *With me.*

I can't go home. Not with the scent of her still lingering in my place, reminding me that I can't have her and that she isn't *mine.*

I drive to the gym—the only place I can go when I feel like this. I let myself in and lock it back up. Maya doesn't usually mind as long as I remember to shut everything down when I'm done.

I hit the bag hard, working on kicks and punches as the music blasts through the stereo system. When I've had enough, I move to the treadmill and run five miles. Before I got into kickboxing, I began working out a lot and really got into running. It was soothing and helped clear my head, however now, my head was anything but clear.

I drink some water and recharge, not yet done. My body is buzzing as the pain intensifies, but I don't care. It's not enough. I go to the weight room and work on my arms, legs, and abs. My blood is pumping fiercely through my veins, my body burning with pain.

I finally collapse on the floor, panting for air as my chest rises and falls rapidly. It's the most intense workout I've ever had, and I still can't get the taste of her out of my mouth.

That was ten days ago.

And not one fucking word.

CHAPTER SIXTEEN
CECILIA

W<small>HEN THE HELL</small> *did he fall in love with me?* Why did he never tell me?

God, this was such a damn mess!

I collapse on my bed, my eyes sore and bloodshot. I don't want to cry anymore. I hate crying. I just want to crawl into a ball and have my dad make everything better.

He's been on my mind more and more as the 'date' gets closer. For two years, since Bentley's told me about his gambling addiction and opening the lock box after ten years, my life's been in limbo—just waiting for the day until I get all the answers that I've been begging for. At least, I hope that's what I'll get. There has to be something in that box that puts all the pieces together.

I wake up the next morning not feeling any better. I'm not even sure I slept.

I grab my phone off the dresser and see three text messages. All from Brandon. *Crap.*

Brandon: I was thinking of making a road trip down to see you. I have a few days off work. What do you think? Could you get a day or two off?

Brandon: Baby? You there?

Brandon: You must be at work, or asleep. Either way, I miss

you. I can't stop thinking about you. I hope to see you soon. Xoxo

Fuck. Me.

Brandon's the last person that deserves to have his heart broken. Not only is he a complete sweetheart, he's damn hot, too. He's one of those real clean cut guys, wears nice, form-fitting clothes, and don't even get me started on his gorgeous blue eyes. I couldn't even believe he was single, nevertheless that he wanted to date me. And now I was going to have to break his heart. His perfect, sweet, and sensitive heart.

When the school year ended, we agreed to not be overly clingy. Brandon was always good about that, never smothering me. He knew I was kind of shy and timid when it came to dating, so he never pressured me into anything. He didn't know much about my past, but he never drilled me for any information I didn't want to share.

Brandon worked at his dad's company and would be working twelve-hour days. We both knew there wouldn't be a lot of time to talk between the both of us working, especially opposite hours—him eight a.m. to eight p.m., and I usually worked bar hours from seven p.m. to two a.m.

But now he was thinking of coming here. I have to tell him the truth.

"Cecilia? Good morning, darling." His smooth voice stings my heart even more.

"Hi, morning. Sorry for missing your texts last night. It was on silent from being at the movie theatre."

"Oh, no problem. I passed out early anyway. So what do you think?" His voice sounds hopeful, eager to hear me say the words.

"About you coming here?"

"Yeah, I figure if I leave tomorrow morning and make only a few stops, I can get there in about nine hours."

I swallow at how happy he sounds. He hasn't a fucking clue, and I'm about to rip his damn heart out.

"I don't think that's a good idea, Brandon," I say softly.

"Oh. Do you have to work?"

"That's not it." I exhale deeply, bracing myself for the storm I'm about to walk through.

"Oh, what's wrong?"

"We need to talk first," I explain. I can hear his breathing starting to pick up, his nerves obviously sensing that something is wrong. "I'm not who I portray myself to be."

"What are you talking about? You're fucking scaring me." Brandon hardly ever swore unless it was in light fun. He was usually so gentle and sweet, but I could feel the rage building up in his words.

"I screwed up two years ago, and I've been paying for it ever since. You don't know this about me, but my dad was murdered when I was eleven years old. Ever since, I've been selfishly trying to put the pieces together and have hurt some people along the way." I finally exhale, pain rippling through me as I talk about my father again.

"Cecilia, I'm so sorry." His voice cracks, sympathizing with me, but I hate that he is. He shouldn't.

"I'm in love with someone else," I blurt out. I close my eyes as I imagine his face, pain etched all over his perfect features. "I always have been."

He stays silent, but I can hear his unsteady breaths. "I'm so sorry, Brandon." I pause, giving him a moment, but I need to get this out. He should know the truth. "It was a messy, forbidden, hungry love that before I had a chance to fix what I had done, it was too late. And so I went to college and tried to start fresh, and that was when I met you." I slowly exhale, lifting my eyes upward so I don't cry with him on the phone. "And you…are so great. You were exactly what I needed, and I'm so happy we found each other. But I'd be lying to myself if I said I could stay with you while being in love with someone else. You deserve so much more, and I wish I could give you that. But I can't."

"Wow…" he finally breathes out. "Talk about a messy kind of love." I can imagine him pacing, his breaths blowing through the phone. "I want to come tell you in person, Cecilia."

"God, no. Please don't, Brandon. I—"

"But since I can't…" he pauses briefly. "I love you."

I close my eyes, but it's too late. The tears escape, streaking down my cheeks. They grow heavier, pouring out of me like a leaky sink.

"I needed to say it," he explains. "Even if you don't feel the same way, I love you. And it's hard to be mad at someone just because they can't love you back."

"You have no idea how much I wish I could. You're an absolutely amazing guy. But I can't be that person for you. I'd never be good enough for you."

"You are good enough, Cecilia." He pauses, clearing his throat. "Just not the *right* one."

I grin, shaking my head at how he's always so damn nice even when someone is ripping his heart out.

"I'm sorry," I whisper. "God, I'm so sorry."

I'm an awful, awful person. I'd do anything to take back what I'm doing to Brandon. Even though he's being strong, I know his heart is breaking. But that's just how he is. He never wants to make anyone hurt or feel bad. He's always a light in someone else's darkness.

I tell Cora all the details and she flashes me her mischievous grin, silently telling me an 'I told ya so,' but she doesn't rub it in my face. She knows I'm torn, hurting for two men right now.

Bentley—not knowing what my decision is and if I can let him back in.

Brandon—for breaking a perfectly kind heart in two.

How can I be with Bentley right after breaking up with someone? Wasn't that a rebound? Tearing someone else apart just to be happy with someone else was making me sick to my stomach.

"Just take a few days to yourself. If Bentley really loves you, he'll wait. He'll wait until you're ready," she says, hanging my shirts up in my closet.

"What if I'm never ready?" I lay back on my bed, staring up at the blank ceiling. "What if I forever live with remorse and guilt?"

"You won't. You just need some time to adjust and to really think about what's going to make *you* happy. No distractions." She grabs another handful of my clothes, swinging it over her shoulder and walking back to the closet.

"What are you doing?" I finally ask, leaning up on my elbows.

"They're going to get wrinkles, Celia. That's why they invented this thing called a hanger." She smiles at me as if I'm a moron. Who knows? Maybe I am.

"Celia, you're in love with him. He's in love with you. Why not just make it that simple?"

"Before Bentley, I never even thought I could love someone. I didn't feel any of those emotions with Jason, and we slept together numerous times. When he moved away, it barely fazed me. So why did he have such an impact on me? Why is he different?"

"You don't always get to chose who you love. Sometimes love

chooses you and you just roll with it. Don't question love, or fate butts his ugly ass in and messes everything up."

I narrow my eyes at her, wondering if she's ever going to take her own advice with Simon, but I know this isn't the time to bring it up.

Could it really be that simple? Could I just say yes to Bentley and we'd be...happy?

I take her advice and take some time to myself. Not speaking to Brandon or Bentley allows me to clear my head—just focusing on what I want and on me. I need to stop feeling guilty and just let it all go. I didn't sleep with Bentley...Brandon doesn't hate me...perhaps I wasn't completely tainted.

I wake up refreshed and decide today's going to be the day. I'm going to go to Bentley and tell him I chose him. That I've been in love with him, and I've never stopped. I'm going to tell him I want everything he has to offer—whatever that may be.

My nerves are making me shaky and anxious as I drive into the gym parking lot. It's been ten days since I've last seen him, and I can't help the giddy feeling that overcomes me with seeing him again.

I haven't been back to my kickboxing class in weeks, but I know he teaches some others today. And this is something I need to say to his face, not over the phone.

I swing the front door open and scan the place for any sighting of Bentley. There are fewer cars in the parking lot than usual, so I know there aren't any classes going on right now.

I walk past the studio and some of the workout rooms thinking he must be in his office if he's not out on the floor. I haven't been back here before, but there're three different offices leading to the back.

I hear a woman's laughter—one I've heard before—coming from the first office. The other gym instructor. I could recognize her laugh for miles—nasally and loud. She always found something so freaking funny as she was clawing her nails into Bentley's bicep.

I jump at the sound of the door opening, but before I can quickly walk away without being noticed, it's Bentley's face that makes me freeze.

His left arm is wrapped around her as he's looking down at her, smiling. She's perfectly tucked into his arm, her right arm wrapped around his waist. Oh, how fucking cute.

His face finally tilts up, and when he notices me, his smile drops.

"Ceci…" I hear the shock in his voice, but it does nothing for the ache that's brewing in my chest.

Her eyes flash between us as a grin forms on her face. She releases Bentley's hold as she pushes her hand out in front of me.

"You're Ceci? Hi, I'm Maya!" I look at her hand like it's a dead rodent, refusing to touch it. "I've heard so much about you."

My eyebrows rise, wondering why the hell Bentley told his new fling of the month about me.

I finally take her hand aggressively and shake it. "Hi, *Maya*. Sorry I haven't heard anything about you. But it's clear it hasn't taken Bentley long to move on." I release her hand and look up at Bentley, my eyes narrowing at him. "It's been what…ten days?"

"Ceci…" he begins, but I cut him off.

"Ten days!" I yell, unable to control the fire that's building inside me. "You couldn't even wait ten days! Or was she before, during, and now after?" I snap. They were always touchy-feely. I should've known.

"That's enough," he bites, his mouth forming into a firm line. I look and see a knowing grin on Maya's face. *Bitch*.

"Go ahead. Have him. He's good at ruining lives." I cannot even believe I considered this.

I scowl at both of them not even hiding the anger and hurt I'm feeling. I spin around to walk out the door.

I feel Bentley directly behind me, but I continuing stalking out. I feel him grip my elbow, grabbing me and turning me to face him.

"Let me go."

His lips curl up into an angry scowl, his eyes hooded and a bit amused.

"I'm not letting you go, Ceci. Not now, not *ever*."

"Sorry, but I'm not into the whole ménage à trois thing. Plus, I don't share." I try to yank my arm out, but he grips it firmer, pulling me closer to his chest.

He leans in close to my ear as he growls, "She'd be more interested in you, than me. Maya is just a friend."

"What?" I ask, confused. "I saw her hanging all over you. I saw her hanging all over after each class. I'm not blind."

He pulls back, grabbing my hand in his as he walks us into an empty studio. He slams the door and presses me into it, his body weight firmly against mine.

"You're either blind or ignorant." He presses both of his hands flat against the door right above my shoulders, towering over me.

"And you're an asshole." I try to ignore the rush of feelings that are consuming me from having Bentley this close to me, but it's hard considering I can feel his arousal against my hips.

"Maya's gay," he says with amusement. "Even if I *were* interested, she'd be much more interested in *you*. I've known her for over a year, so yes, I've spoken some about you." He smirks at me as if he's just won the fucking Super Bowl. Smug bastard.

He presses himself into me harder, telling me exactly what's on his mind. This whole time…I thought he was a manwhore, flaunting Maya around like some prized possession just to piss me off.

"Are you done accusing me of being a dirty player now?"

I look up at him, not really sure what I should be feeling right now. "I never called you a dirty player," I retort.

"It was well implied." His voice is no longer filled with anger, rather he sounds amused by the fact that I thought Maya was after him this whole time. He smiles wide, leaning in closer toward me. "I've missed you."

He nuzzles his nose into my neck, my body staying frozen as Bentley consumes me—his scent, his touch, his body fully reminding me of everything I've been missing the past two years.

"Did you come back for me?" His mouth lands below my earlobe, his lips making a path down my neck. "Otherwise, this may get awkward." I smile wide as I feel him smirk against my flushed skin. Goose bumps appear, butterflies take over my stomach, and soon, I'm holding the door just to keep my balance.

"Yes…" I whimper. "Of course, I came back." My eyes close as his lips suck on my collarbone, heat rushing in between my thighs as I think about how fucking amazing his lips are.

"I can't wait any longer," he protests, gripping the crotch of my jeans with his palm. "Do you have a full bladder?"

My eyes pop open at his awkward question. "What?"

"You heard me. Do you?" His lips make their way back up my neck, sucking on my earlobe. He presses his other palm against my stomach and forcefully applies pressure.

"Oh my God," I squeal in shock. The pressure against my stomach intensifies my arousal growing down below.

"I'll take that as a yes," he says, amused. "Come on."

I whimper the moment his body is off mine. He grabs my hand and leads me to the other side of the studio, pulling me into a back stretching room.

"What are we doing?" I ask, his hand gripping mine. Our fingers are intertwined, firmly holding each other as if our lives depend on it. My emotions are all over the place, but one thing I know for sure is that Bentley is the only one that makes me feel this way—the control he holds over my body, the intense ache I feel when I'm around him, the disappointing loss when we aren't together—I've never felt these things with anyone before.

"We needed some privacy. I wasn't about to give every guy out there a free show." He shuts and locks the door behind him. "And we need to talk."

I stand anxiously, wanting to get this awkward conversation out of the way so I can finally tell him what I need to say.

He cups my face, leaning in, but he doesn't kiss me. "Ten days." I hear his pained tone deep within his voice. I made him wait ten painful days without knowing what was going on...

"I'm sorry. I just...needed time to deal with things. And to think."

"And?" His brows rise in anticipation. One of his hands lowers to my hip, forcing our bodies closer together.

"And I realized that you're it for me." I look up at him, watching the expression in his face. "No matter how much time has passed or how much hurt we've felt—it's always been you. And I woke up this morning not wanting to spend another day apart from you." He smiles so wide it practically reaches his eyes. "I love you, Bentley. I always have."

CHAPTER SEVENTEEN
BENTLEY

I'VE BEEN DYING to hear those three fucking words for what feels like a lifetime. God, even the way her voice cracks is sexy. She's looking up at me pleadingly, begging for me to take control.

I press our bodies together, cupping her face so she looks directly into my eyes when I repeat those very words back to her.

"Cecilia…I love you. I love you so fucking much, it's pained me to not to say those words every single day to you. I knew I did, but I didn't know how to handle it.

"Once I found out the truth, it freaked me out, and no matter how hard I tried to push thoughts of you out, I couldn't completely. I never could. And I never will."

CECILIA

I sniff back the tears that are threatening to flow over. Who knew Bentley could be so tender and sweet, yet domineering and hot. He's a triple threat that holds all the qualities that I love and want. He's my perfect other half and that's something I'm not willing to let go of again.

"We are so fucked up," I mutter, hardly believing the rollercoaster ride it has taken to bring us here. "I hate that I hurt you so badly. I hate that I made you wait, that I left, and that I ever thought you were someone you aren't."

"Stop." He places a finger over my mouth, not letting me continue. He leans down and brushes his lips gently against mine. "Never regret what brought us right here, right now. We had to struggle to get to where we are, and I'm quite enjoying where we are right now." He grins smugly, pressing his hips into me, his cock rock hard against the fabric of his shorts. God, I've waited too long to feel him inside of me again.

It's been too long.

I don't want to wait a second longer.

I wrap a hand around his neck, pushing his mouth against mine finally. His hands hold me firmly on my hips, molding us together. I moan and pant against his lips, not wanting to ever break this kiss. His taste consumes me, heating every part of my body that begs him to touch me.

His thumbs are pressing deep into my lower stomach again, my bladder feeling full and uncomfortable the more he does that.

"Stop." I laugh against his mouth. "You're going to make me pee my pants."

He grins slyly, unbuttoning my jeans and lowering the zipper. "Good…get ready."

I look up into his eyes to see if he's serious. His eyes darken with hunger, showing me that he is. He lowers my jeans off my hips and motions for me to step out of them.

"Come here." He guides me to the middle of the mat where a large yoga ball is set. "Sit down."

I do as he says and the ball bounces lightly as I sit.

"Lean back slightly," he demands. "Hold yourself up with your hands." Oh, God. I watch as he kneels in between my legs, separating them with his greedy hands. He brushes his lips up one leg, the feather-light touch shooting shivers up my entire body and back down the other leg. Damn, how does he do that?

He pulls my panties to the side and inserts a finger, stretching my walls out gradually. It's been too long since I've felt him inside me. It's a feeling I could never be tired of—could never have enough of.

My body rocks with the ball, but he tells me to let go. He's holding on to me and won't let me fall.

"Oh…God, yes." My eyes close on their own accord as my pussy devours his perfectly skilled finger. He adds to the pressure by inserting another finger and speeding up the pace. I can barely control my movements because I have nothing to grip. My palms lay sweaty against the yoga ball, my body jerking at every thrust as his fingers drive into me. The ball moves quickly underneath me, making for an entirely new sensation that I've never felt before.

And if that isn't enough to set me off, he lays a flat palm against my stomach adding pressure as he curls his two fingers deeper inside me, searching for pleasure.

"Bentley...oh my God!" The combined pressures are intensifying the climax that's about to erupt through me.

"Come on, sweetheart. I need to feel you tighten around me," he growls so effortlessly, pressing down harder on my lower abdomen.

I swear he's going to put my body into an orgasmic a coma the second he adds his tongue and licks up my juicy slit, twirling his tongue directly on my clit.

The sensation is almost indescribable—the fullness that my stomach feels mixed with the building orgasm is almost too much to handle.

"Yes, oh, God, yes..." I purr, unable to hold in the screams and moans anymore. I hope the whole fucking gym hears for all I care. "Bentley!"

My body rips in half as I scream and moan through my orgasm. His fingers continue driving my release, jerking harder and curling deeper inside until I've completely covered his fingers with my arousal.

"Oh, God, sweetheart." He licks up my pussy, sucking one last time before releasing me. "That was fucking hot." He pulls his fingers inside of his mouth, slowing licking up my juices. The act itself is so erotic, I'm about to beg him to fuck me right here.

"Holy shit," I breathe out, panting and dropping my hands off the ball. My body lays limp, needing to recover from the hardest orgasm I've ever had. "I don't think I've ever come that hard before. That was... so intense," I breathe out.

He grabs my hands, pulling me up so we can lock eyes. "Well, I hope I haven't worn you out. We have about two years worth of making up to do." He smirks knowingly.

BENTLEY

By the time I get her back to my house, I've run out of patience. I need her like the air I breathe and I wasn't about to wait any longer.

I slam Ceci into my bedroom wall as one hand grips the back of her neck, holding her securely to me—I don't plan on letting her go this time.

Our mouths collide, tongues dancing together as we find our rhythm again. The heat between us is palpable as we pull and tug clothes off one another. I can't stand having a barrier between us a second longer.

"I'm not going to be gentle, sweetheart. It's been too fucking long," I growl against her ear, picking her up and wrapping her legs around me.

"Good. Don't be," she whimpers against me. I kiss up her chin and land on her lips. She's quivering underneath me, growing deeper with anticipation.

"Did you think of me when you touched yourself?" Her body shudders underneath me as I tease my cock against her opening. God, I don't know how much longer I can wait. I feel her swallow, but she doesn't speak. "Sweetheart, answer me. I need to know."

"Mm hmm," she barely whimpers out, biting down on her lip. "Yes, every time."

I push my cock inside her, but I don't move just yet. She's dripping wet, barely able to keep herself up. "God, Ceci. I'm begging to drive my cock so fucking deep inside you."

"Yes, please," she begs, moving her hips around to angle our bodies together. Her head falls back as she bites her lip, unable to wait much longer.

I grin down at her, grabbing her face in one of my hands. "Show me. Show me how you touched yourself thinking about me."

She rests a hand on my shoulder as the other hand slowly slides down her stomach landing on her clit. She licks her lips as she circles her finger, moaning and aching for release. Her eyes close as her head falls back, her finger moving faster and faster as she works her way to orgasm.

Watching her is one of the sexiest things I've seen. I push my cock all the way in and drive deep inside her as she continues to work her clit harder and faster. She gasps, digging her nails into my shoulder as I continue the pace.

I pull out and drive into her again, stretching out her walls for me, taking her arousal, and multiplying it by a hundred.

"Bentley! Oh, God…" she pants, hanging on to me for support as her body stays pinned against the wall. "Yes, harder…don't stop." I feel her hand work faster, her breaths uneven as her body's about to rip in two.

I crush my mouth to hers as I drive my cock deep inside her, giving her exactly what she's begging for. I release my hand and grab her leg. I place it on my shoulder, getting a better angle to thrust inside her deeper and harder.

I feel her pussy tightening around me as I continue driving into her forcefully, harder and harder as she screams out in pleasurable pain.

"God, sweetheart…" I moan, holding her leg straight up as the other one continues to clench tightly around my waist. "You're body is fucking perfection."

"Oh, God, yes, yes…don't stop. Please don't stop," she chants over and over, as I bring her over the edge, her nails clawing into my skin, drawing blood.

I release her leg and carry her over to the bed and bend her over the mattress. "Lay out for me," I demand. "Let me see all of you."

She bends perfectly over the bed, her back arched and her ass straight up in the air for me. I soothingly rub a hand down her back, causing her body to shiver underneath me.

I bend my body over hers and lick slowly up her spine, causing goose bumps to form. I feel her quiver, her body aching for me to be back inside her.

I kneel down in between her legs and push them apart, spreading her wider for me. I grab her ass cheeks with both hands and lick a trail from her clit all the way down. She moans against me, pushing her ass out more, giving me better access.

I insert two fingers as I drive my tongue deeper inside her. "Mm… yes, sweetheart," I purr against her, her body shaking as she tries to hold herself up. "God, I'm addicted to that flavor."

She hums eagerly as I devour her, licking up her arousal again, wanting to keep her thoroughly pleasured.

"Baby, let me…" she pleads. "I want to taste you."

I stand up and flip her over so I can see every perfect part of her. Her chest is rising rapidly as she licks her lips in anticipation. I crawl over her body, making sure to keep my weight on my knees. I bend over her face, and she eagerly takes me in her mouth. She wraps her hands around me and grips my ass, clawing it as she pushes me deeper into her perfect, round mouth.

"Fuck! Holy shit, Ceci…" I growl as she deep throats all of me. I wasn't going to come in her mouth, so I needed to stop her soon. She makes the sexiest little sounds as she enjoys fucking my cock with her mouth. But I need her to stop. "Stop…I want inside you."

She reluctantly releases me, licking her lips seductively. I crawl down her body and gently place a kiss on her nose. She smiles back up at me just as I grab both of her legs and urgently place them on top of my shoulders, bending her in half as I drive back inside her.

"God, sweetheart. You could destroy me with this…if I never get to feel this again, I don't know what I'd do. Life wouldn't be worth living."

"Don't say that," she whispers.

I gradually slow the pace down, no longer eager to drive hard inside her. I can see the sincerity in her face and the last thing I want to do is rush this. I want to devour every part of her for as long as I can.

"I missed this," I say softly, locking my eyes with her. "I've missed you."

"I've missed you for over two years, Bentley. It's always been you." She looks at me knowingly, genuinely, as I read into what she's really saying. She hasn't slept with anyone since me, and knowing that makes being with her again that much more special. She's always been mine…

She pushes me in deeper, hitting just the spot that causes her to erupt, screaming out her orgasm as it floods through her. Her back arches as her body shakes, her slick walls tightening around my cock and making me release with her.

"God, baby…it's like we've never been a day apart. So fucking amazing," I say into her ear as I ride out my own orgasm. I slowly kiss down her neck, making sure to thoroughly claim every part of her. "You taste incredible…*everywhere.*"

"I'll never get sick of feeling you inside me."

"Good…because I plan to be there like it's my air to breathe."

I bend down and kiss her. Gentle. Our tongues slicking over each others, gliding into blissful heaven as our bodies rediscover each other. I release her legs so I can touch every part of her, feathering a finger up her arm and back down the other. I lightly kiss the trail my tongue makes, making sure to touch and taste every inch.

I kneel down on the floor in between her legs as I grab her hands and pull her body up so our eyes connect. She smiles weakly up at me.

"I love you, Ceci. I want to love you and love on you the rest of my life. Whatever it takes, I'll make it work. I'll drive to you every week while you finish school, I'll be there when you walk that stage at graduation, I'll hold your hair as your throw up on your twenty-first birthday." She chuckles lightly. "Please let me. I want to be here for all of it. I want all of you."

She smiles wide, cupping my cheek with one hand. "Yes." She leans in and gently brushes my lips with hers. "I want all of that. All of you. Every day. No more obstacle courses. No more barriers. If we're going to do this, we have to be all in." I nod in agreement, placing my hand on top of hers. "No more secrets," she promises.

CHAPTER EIGHTEEN
CECILIA

Seeing Bentley naked again instantly sends arousal down my body, landing directly in between my thighs. I couldn't get him deeper or fast enough, I needed more.

His tattoos are something that I've had embedded to memory since the first time I saw them in person. He's stunning, but the tattoos add so much more—perfection. The way each detailed line curves into his body makes my heart flutter ever faster.

I outline his tattoos with my finger as I lay next to him as he sleeps. He looks so peaceful, so content. I wish I could bottle that Bentley up forever.

"Good morning." Oh God, his morning voice.

"Morning," I reply sweetly. "I've missed your tattoos." I continue outlining them as he stirs awake. "I've been thinking about getting one."

He shifts to his side facing me. He traces a finger down my face, pulling a piece of hair behind my ear.

"Really?"

"Mm hmm. On my right shoulder."

His finger slides down my chin and neck, landing directly over my scar. He traces the outline several times before leaning over and pressing a light kiss over it.

"That's a perfect spot." He smiles. "What did you have in mind?"

I close my eyes briefly, thoughts of my dad consuming me.

"I'm going to have the words *Let it be* written across my shoulder and a princess crown on my shoulder blade. It was his nickname for me, and I think it'll help bring me closure, no matter the outcome. I don't want to keep holding onto hope that the lock box will give me answers, so I want to remind myself to let it be—that I can't let it be the reason I stop living my life."

He soothingly rubs my face, his thumb circling over my jaw. "I love it. But don't give up so easily. The Ceci I know is prepared to break into anything she has to get what she wants." He cracks a smile, amused.

"Well, perhaps I'm turning a new leaf. I want to move forward. I can't do that if I'm constantly hung up on the past. I want us to move forward *together*. And I can't do that if I'm hung up on the past—something I can't control."

He leans in and brushes his lips against mine again, putting his body weight on top of mine so I'm forced to roll over on my back. He brushes his hands through my hair, lightly tugging as he moans in my mouth.

"Just promise me one thing," he says, breaking the kiss.

"What's that?"

"Wait to get the tattoo until after you get to open it."

"That's almost a year away," I protest.

"You're not a very patient person." He smirks.

I lower my hand in between us, gripping his erection with my fingers. "No..." I smile wide. "No, I'm not."

He slides into me with ease, already wet with anticipation. "How impatient are you, sweetheart?"

"Right now..." I gasp as he drives deeper inside me. "Not patient at all..." I moan, begging him for more as he slowly eases in and out of me. "That's torture," I plead.

"How do you want me, Ceci?" he whispers into my ear, stroking his tongue underneath the lobe as my body shivers against him. "Fast and rough?" He pulls out briefly and thrusts back inside me, making my head fall all the way back. "Or gentle and slow?" He pulls out slowly, leaving the tip in and sliding back in ever so gently. The desire to feel him builds up inside me, my need for him growing stronger and stronger.

"Both—give me both."

He grins against my neck, sucking lightly on my shoulder. "I love when my girl is greedy for me. So needy."

I scratch my fingers down both arms as my body arches up to greet him. "More…" I beg.

He releases me, leaning back on his heels. I groan weakly as I feel him leave my body. He kisses my leg and smiles back up at me. "Roll over."

He helps me lay on my stomach, my legs flat in between his legs. He grips my thighs and parts them slightly as he places a knee on each side of me. He leans over me, pushing back inside me from behind. The sensation is thrilling—tight and so intimate. He thrusts into me slowly, but deep. The way our bodies lay together gives him all control as he drives into me, claiming my body as his.

"You feel that, sweetheart? That's our bodies becoming one. Our bodies recognize each other. They don't ever want to be a part."

"I can't be a part from you, Bentley. My body can't handle it."

"Our bodies were meant to stay together—just like this." He brings a hand around and rubs my clit as he thrusts deeper inside me. His hand works my clit as his cock drives into me over and over again—bringing me over the edge.

"God, yes. Oh…yes," I scream into the pillow as his finger and cock work me into an overloaded frenzy.

"Christ, Ceci…." he growls deeply, feeling my pussy tighten even more around him. He pulls his body back, gripping my hips with both hands as he releases his own orgasm into me. "*Jesus.*"

"Do we ever have to get out of bed?" I whine playfully as Bentley's and my legs are intertwined together, sheets and blankets lay messily on the edge of the bed.

"If it were up to me, hell no."

I lean up on one elbow and face him. "What's going to happen when I go back to college? And you go back to modeling? How are we going to make this work?" I hate being a mood killer, but I need to know.

He brushes my hair off my face, stroking his finger gently. "I'll do anything to be with you, Ceci. Just tell me what you need."

I sigh because honestly, I don't know. "Can you make it so I've already graduated and can travel with you across the world as you model?" I smile jokingly at him, but he doesn't bite.

"You need to finish college, sweetheart. Imagine what a degree like yours could get you."

"A lot of sweaty, nasty guys," I deadpan.

He laughs lightly. "Do what will make *you* happy. I'll be right there with you."

"What about your career?"

He shrugs nonchalantly. "It'll be there when I'm ready."

"You're kind of an arrogant ass," I mock his overconfidence.

"*Your* arrogant ass," he counters.

"Good. I'll take it." I bite my lip, hiding the giddy smile that's threatening to display. God, how does he make me this person?

"I'll buy a house in Lincoln so I can be close to you. That way you could still focus on school, and I'll get to see you after class," he says as if he's just solved all our issues.

"Lincoln is only an hour from Omaha. Why would you go through all the trouble of finding another place? We can make it work. I'll drive to your place, or you can visit me…" I offer.

"No…" he whispers into my hair, pulling me closer into him, "I'm not wasting an hour when I could be with you. Plus, I'll make sure to buy a very comfortable, large bed. That way I know you won't be able to say no."

I tilt my head, giving him better access as he begins brushing his lips against my flushed skin, shooting shivers down my body. "You can't just tempt me with a good bed…that's not fair."

"It's plenty fair…for me." I feel him grin, and no longer want to fight about it. I want him close just as much as he does, so I give in.

"Okay, fine…don't forget a nice, big shower, as well," I offer. "Because if not, that *could* be the deal breaker," I tease.

"Mm…" He kisses the lobe, biting gently. "A shower sounds nice… perfect actually."

He scoops me off the bed, dangling my legs over his buff arms. I link my arms around his neck as he carries me into the bathroom and sets me gently on the countertop.

"Ah, that's cold," I wince, my bare ass pressed against it.

"Don't worry, sweetheart. I'm about to warm you right up."

He kneels in between my legs, spreading them wide as his mouth finds my swollen lips. My whole body is aching for him, craving him—I can never get enough.

He devours me, leaving me gasping and moaning as his tongue

proves his talent over and over again. I come on his tongue hard. He swipes his tongue up my slit, sucking gently on my clit as I fist his hair, pulling his locks in between my fingers.

"Oh, yes…" My body crumbles against him as another wave of pleasure hits me. "Bentley!"

He stands up grinning at me as he purposely licks his lips. "You were dirty…" His voice is thick with amusement. "I had to clean you up."

I put a finger to his chest and run it down to his cock, hard at attention. "I guess that means I should clean you up next."

He arches his hips, allowing me to grip him harder. I begin stroking him gently, teasing as he bucks his hips into my grasp.

He leans into me and whispers, "I'm *very* dirty. Make sure you clean me thoroughly."

I push against him and hop off the counter. I turn the water on and step into the shower, leaving the door open for him.

He follows suit and steps in the shower after me. His eyes widen as he sees me already on my knees waiting for him.

"Christ, Ceci…" He shuts the door behind him and looks at me with hunger in his eyes. "You look so fucking sexy like that—waiting for me. Only me."

I bite my lip in anticipation. I open my mouth wide for him, letting him angle himself inside me. I close my lips tightly around him and stroke him with my mouth.

The water cascades over us, making his body slick and defined. His hard muscles never seize to amaze me, but the way he looks is breathtaking.

He leans back, giving me all of him. His cock touches the back of my throat, pulsating against me as I suck him hard. I work my hands on his shaft, rotating my hands up and down as I work the tip. He groans, grabbing a fistful of my hair as I pick up the pace. I release him, licking a path from his shaft to the tip, and pulling him inside me once more before he releases. I love that Bentley gives every part of him to me— every perfect inch of his body.

"Jesus, sweetheart," he growls, lifting me up by my arms. "Your mouth is fucking heaven."

He grips the back of my neck and crushes our mouths together— desperation and love consuming us both.

We each take our time washing each other's bodies, slowly

exploring one another again. I can never get enough of the sight of him, the way he makes me feel, and the way he craves me just as much as I crave him. I didn't want it to end—this moment or us.

Bentley and I stay mostly in hiding through what remained of the summer. Cora and I finish his kickboxing class and I continue working at the bar, except I only work two nights a week so I can spend more time with Bentley before my classes start back up.

As summer comes to an end, I make sure to spend some time with Cora and Simon since I won't see them for another nine months. Although they make it impossible for all three of us to hang out, I finally tell them to suck it up so I can spend time with both of them.

Since this will be my junior year, I don't have to live on campus anymore. Bentley insists I stay with him to 'save tuition money' so I can hardly argue with him.

I text Katelynn a few days before school. We haven't spoken much all summer, but I still plan to hang out with her once she moves back.

Cecilia: Any new creepers we get to discuss when we get back?

Katelynn: Don't even get me started. I'm starting to think being the crazy cat lady is more suitable for me anyway.

Cecilia: Oh, stop it. There are plenty of good guys right on campus. You just have to come out of our dorm room long enough to meet them.

Katelynn: You know I'm shy. It's hard for me.

I love Katelynn, and I think she's gorgeous, so it's really saddening that she can't find a decent guy.

I make a mental note to get her out of her apartment at least few times this semester.

CHAPTER NINETEEN
CECILIA

It's surreal to see Bentley's new place or as he's calling it 'our new place.' It feels like after all the struggle to be together and time apart—this is it. We're finally happy and moving forward together.

Bentley helped me pack, and I finally introduced him to my mom. It went surprisingly well. She's pretty much smitten by him. But that doesn't change the fact that she continues to hide our past from me. Soon enough though—I'll know all I need to know, and then I can finally move on from what happened that day.

Tony moved in after I left. I know it makes Nathan really happy to have a guy around finally after being stuck with girls all his life. I've warmed up to him some, but the thought of him in my dad's house still makes me cringe.

Bentley told his agent that he needs a few more months off, although I told him to stop putting it off. I'll miss him when he travels, but I have plenty here to keep me busy. However, he insists on staying around—not that I'm complaining. I think he's waiting for when I can finally go to my dad's lock box. He's worried that whatever is in there will crush me.

"Go on. Go out," Bentley insists, wrapping his arms around me. "You're in college. You're supposed to go party." He kisses me quickly on the nose.

"It feels weird though. Leaving you here while I go have fun." I pout against him. "You could come with?" I offer.

He shakes his head with a weak smile. "Sorry, sweetheart. I'll be here when you get back. Or call me if you need me to pick you up."

"The reality of being with an older man," I sigh, teasingly. "You could re-live your college days. I'm sure you were bad."

He laughs, pulling me in tighter. "No, thanks. I'm content right here." He presses his body into mine, my arms not wanting to release him.

"Fine," I sigh again. "I'm going to go pick up Katelynn."

Although Katelynn has a bubbly personality, she can be awkward around guys. I find it humorous how she helped me so much my first year of college, yet she can't find a decent guy that isn't going to come on overly strong.

Simon calls me on my way out, so I pick it up quick. "Hello?"

"I have less than a minute. Cora's going to call you and be freaking out...act like you know nothing."

And then he hangs up.

Well, that was weird.

I look at my phone, stunned, but wait for her call anyway. It comes two minutes later.

"Hello?"

"Oh, thank God, Celia." She breathes heavily.

"What's going on?

She's silent at first and then finally blurts out, "I'm in love with Simon."

A knowing smile curls up on my face as she finally confesses what I've known all along.

"Um..." I'm not sure what to say. Simon knew I knew, but she didn't. "What exactly do you mean?"

"Stop playing stupid, Celia. I knew you knew." Her tone is laced with stern amusement.

I laugh relieved. "Oh, thank God. Can I just say...it's about fucking time?"

"I know." She laughs.

"So...tell me. What made this confession come to light?"

She stays quiet before softly answering. "He proposed. He said he was sick of pretending we weren't together and that he's always loved me. I cried. And you know I never cry." She laughs through light tears. I gasp, picturing Simon down on one knee with an engagement ring.

"That asshole didn't tell me he was going to propose!"

"That's because he knew you'd snitch!" Simon's voice echoes through the phone.

I laugh because he's absolutely right. I probably would have.

"Ignore him," Cora says, giggling. I can hear her pushing him away.

"All right, you lovebirds. Call me later. I want to know all the details," I pause as I pull up to the dorms, "well, perhaps not all the details. Just the part where he proposes," I tease.

We say our goodbyes and I text Katelynn that I'm outside waiting for her. She skips giddily to my car, a smile plastered on her face.

"Someone's excited."

"I'm actually really nervous," she admits.

"Don't be. It's going to be fun. Just like a back to school party. Plenty of opportunities to meet new guys."

"You mean plenty of wackos to ask how many children of theirs I wish to bear."

I burst out in laughter at her concerned expression. "I swear, you attract the crazies."

"I actually did meet someone online from campus," she admits, biting her lower lip.

"You did? Who?" I ask excitedly.

She clasps her hands tightly on her lap, not looking directly at me. "I-I'm not really sure. We've been chatting for the last few weeks. We both figured out we go to the same campus. We're supposed to meet tonight actually. He's going to be there."

"Oh my God!" I screech. "What's his name? What does he look like?"

"I don't know."

I turn and face her, narrowing my eyes. "You don't know? You didn't think to ask those questions or what?"

"Well…I know his username. I stopped giving out my real name because there were so many psychos. Once he told me he'd be coming tonight, I told him to wear a red shirt so that if I went I could spot him."

"Katelynn…what if ten different guys are wearing red tonight?"

"That's also why I'm wearing red." She points to her own shirt, raising a brow.

"How's that going to help?"

"Just trust me. I'll know when I see him," she replies confidently.

"Hmm…a hopeless romantic? I like it." I grin.

The party is in full force by the time we arrive. There's a ton of people we know, so we stay amongst them most of the night. Later on, I spot Brandon and decide I should apologize to him in person.

I tap him on the shoulder nervously, not wanting there to be any tension between us. We're bound to run into each other on campus this year.

"Hi," I say weakly as our eyes connect.

"Cecilia! Hi!" He engulfs me in a hug I wasn't expecting. I wrap my arms around him as he squeezes me. "How're you?"

He releases me and I stare at him stunned. He looks great, and I'm beyond ecstatic he's not upset with me. But he's almost too excited.

"Hey, Brandon. It's great to see you."

"You look great, Cecilia."

"Thanks, you too."

Awkward silence.

"So look—"

"You don't have to explain anything to me, Cecilia. It's okay," he says genuinely.

"I just feel like I owe you something...I feel horrible that I hurt you. Like I deserve for you to be really mad at me. Yell at me. Tell me what a slut I am. Anything."

"You're anything but a slut, Cecilia. And really, yes, I was upset, but the more I thought about it, I was really okay. I don't want someone to be with me if they don't want to be with me."

I swallow, pained that I couldn't love him the way he loved me. "Wow, Brandon. You're really too nice to me."

"I'm glad you're happy." He smiles wide. "You look really happy and you deserve it."

"So do you." I smile back.

"Yeah..." He brushes his hands down his shirt, teasingly. "Being dumped looks really good on me, don't ya think?"

He's laughing and the next thing, I'm laughing with him. It's such a relief to know we can continue the school year without any hard feelings.

One second he's looking at me, the next his eyes flash to something behind me. His jaw tenses, his eyes freeze in place, and his body stiffens.

I turn around to see what's behind me when I notice Brandon staring directly at Katelynn. I look back at him to notice he's wearing a red shirt.

I gasp softly, putting the pieces together. I look again and see Katelynn's eyes linking with Brandon's.

Holy shit.

I can't help the stupid smile that appears over my face. What are the fucking odds?

Katelynn nervously walks over, unsure of where she should look—at me or at Brandon. From their stunned faces, neither of them expected it to be them.

"Shit…" Katelynn finally says.

"Yeah…" Brandon says, brushing a tense hand through his hair.

"I-I really had no idea, Cecilia. If I had—"

"Stop it, you guys." I smirk, looking back and forth between them. Their chemistry is palpable—obvious attraction between them. "I can't think of two better people for each other. So don't stop on my account," I assure them both. "My ex-boyfriend and my old roommate. Who would've thought?" I smirk wide. They both relax, smiling back at each other.

Brandon hung out in our dorm room countless times during our sophomore year. Before Brandon and I were dating, he'd wait for me in my room with Katelynn until I got out of class so we could go study and work on our project. Now that I think back, they always got along great back then, too.

I excuse myself and reassure them both that I'm perfectly fine with whatever they decide to do. I chat with a few other friends, giving them their privacy, and then Katelynn texts me and says she's hitching a ride home with Brandon.

Cecilia: I want details later. Unless he ends up asking what paint color you want your master bedroom.

Katelynn: I always share the good deats with you.

I smile, thinking how happy I am that I know she's found a good one.

Katelynn: Red.

Cecilia: Huh?

Katelynn: Bedroom color ;-)

Cecilia: Oh God. Of freaking course…

I shake my head and smile. Red.

Katelynn: Lol. Love you, Cecilia.

Cecilia: Love you, too.

I was going to tell her not to hurt him because he's already been hurt. But I don't want him to hurt her either. So they just better make it work so I don't have to hurt either of them.

I leave the party and head back to Bentley's—or rather, my house. It's still early, so I plan to surprise him with a little special surprise.

After I park in the garage, I strip off all my clothes before entering the house. I lay my clothes on the floor and tiptoe down the foyer to find Bentley.

He's passed out on the couch, the remote still lingering in his hand. He looks stunning the way he's laid out in his half un-buttoned shirt and dark, ripped jeans. His hair lays loosely on the pillow in a messy kind of way.

I slowly peel the remote out of his hand and set it on the floor. I brush a finger along his jaw, so strong and chiseled. I push his hair back off his face and admire all of him.

I lay next to him, wrapping my arm around his waist. I lean up and kiss his lips softly, not wanting to startle him. He stirs briefly before recognizing my lips and begins kissing me back. He brings a hand to my arm, pulling me on top of him. His hands brush down my body, his eyes popping open as he realizes I'm completely naked on top of him.

"Well, that's the best fucking wake up call ever," he growls.

I wiggle my hips against his growing erection. His hips buck to press into mine. I giggle against his mouth as he tries to keep me firm against him.

"Shh, baby. Let me take care of you." I lower my body and torturously unbutton and unzip his jeans. I pull him out, hard and ready. I grip my fingers around him and stroke his long length.

"Mm…God, sweetheart," he growls, digging his fingers into my hair. I love feeling his arousal grow deep inside me. I love knowing what I do to him. I love everything about this man.

I work effortlessly, sucking and licking every solid inch of him. I wrap my hand around his cock, stroking over his thick vein. My mouth and hand work him hard, faster until he can no longer take it.

"Fuck! Ceci...God, your mouth..." I accept everything he gives me, letting the heat shoot down my throat as he clenches his fists in my hair.

I continue licking him until he's perfectly clean again. I tuck him neatly in his jeans, zipping up and buttoning him back up.

"I could get addicted to that wake up call," he taunts as I crawl back under his arm.

"I'd be happy to feed your fix," I say smoothly, looking back up at him.

He smirks his eyes gazing down at me. "I think that's called being an enabler."

CHAPTER TWENTY
BENTLEY

LIFE WITH CECI IS NATURAL. She brings out the youthful and playful side of me. Better yet, she brings out the loving side of me.

She's helped me in so many ways. Learning how to forgive. Learning how to love unconditionally. Learning how to accept the things I can't control.

Kickboxing first became an outlet for me to help me forget. I didn't want to let go, I wanted to forget. Forget what Hannah did. Forget how badly I loved Ceci. Forget the career I so thoroughly fucked up.

But nothing could prepare me for this. Not today. Today is all about Ceci.

July 16th.

The day of her father's death.

I can barely contain the emotions that are flooding through me. I can hardly imagine what's going through Ceci's mind. She's strong though.

"Sweetheart, it's all right to not be okay today," I remind her for the fourth time. She's putting a façade on, but I can see right through her.

"I don't want to be sad."

I grab the room key off the dresser and close the gap in between us.

"I know. But if you need to cry, you can. Let it go…if you need to."

We stayed at a hotel last night since we had to travel to Iowa. She was up half the night tossing and turning.

"Thank you," she says, looking up at me with a straight face.

I smile weakly down at her, brushing a piece of hair behind her ear. "You don't have to thank me. I wouldn't miss this for anything."

"Not for that," she says softly. "Thank you for everything—investigating it even when I had hurt you, supporting me when I let it consume me, coming with me. Always understanding. I know I come with a lot of baggage."

"Sweetheart…" I lean down and brush her lips gently, closing a soft kiss on her mouth.

It's been exactly ten years since her dad was shot down and murdered in front of her childhood home. It's been ten years since she last saw her father. It's been ten years that she's been searching for answers, and now today, she'll be getting them.

Hopefully.

My biggest fear is this won't give her answers. I fear it'll add more questions. Worse, I fear it won't give her the closure she needs to move on.

Spending the last year with Ceci has been perfect. We've loved. We've fought. We've tested one another. We've grown closer. Everything about being with Ceci is a life lesson. I never did the relationship thing, but for her, I wanted to.

But now…I want much more.

I don't want this date to be tainted with the death of her dad. I don't want this date to come every year and her to be sad. I want to make this date a date she remembers because it makes her happy.

CECILIA

I rub my sweaty palms down my shorts as we walk into the bank. We called ahead of time and they know we're coming. Casey couldn't fly home from California because of some audition and Mom said she couldn't bear to see what's in there.

Part of me thinks she knows, or at least suspects what's in there. It's a very legit reason why she hid the code in the first place. Whatever it is, I'm ready. I've waited ten years for this.

"Miss West, I'll need to see your license, social security card, and birth certificate before I can give you access."

I nod, handing everything over to her. I already knew what was expected. I wasn't going to let anything get in my way of getting inside that box.

"Thank you," she says, handing me back all my documents.

My body trembles as she leads us into the back. I anticipate what I'm about to find. I just want closure. Anything to give me a piece of my father back.

"It's been set up for you already on the desk." She gestures her hands behind her where the metal box is laying. "Take as long as you need." She smiles genuinely just before walking away and giving us privacy.

Bentley presses a hand on the small of my back, leading me in. I swallow deeply as I stand in front of the box I've thought of relentlessly for the past three years. This is it.

This is really it.

I rub my fingers together, hesitating momentarily before entering the code from the post-it note. I hear it unlock and I stop breathing.

I bow my head, unable to open it just yet. My body is shaking at just the thought of touching something my father had once touched. But I've come too far now to back away.

"I'm ready," I say, more to myself than to Bentley, but he nods anyway encouraging me to open it.

The first thing I notice is a manila envelope. There are three of them —one with each of our names—Casey, Nathan, and mine—written on them. There's another envelope, but it's much thicker. I grab it and feel pictures inside. I flip it open and am immediately hit with a flashback from my childhood. I flip a few over and realize my father has written something on the back of every picture—over two hundred of them.

"What are those?" Bentley asks.

I laugh lightly, scanning through all the silly ones. "Pictures of my dad and us."

"You were pretty cute as a child." I look up and see his grin.

"I wonder why he has these in here."

I flip through some more and land on a picture of my dad and me. It was the last birthday I had with him—my eleventh birthday party. He was standing behind me as I was blowing out the candles of my birthday cake. I laugh lightly to myself as I take in my face—my cheeks pudgy from holding air in just before I go to blow it all out. My dad's standing behind me smiling, his arm wrapped around my shoulder. God, he looked happy. I had no clue that deep inside he was hurting.

I quickly wipe away the tear that falls down my cheek. I don't want to cry. At least not yet.

I decide to open the envelope that's labeled with my name. My hands begin sweating again as I hold the couple of pieces of paper in my hand. I set the envelope down and slowly unfold the paper.

To my Princess,

I hope you're reading this on good terms. I have my reasons for making you wait ten years, baby girl. I don't know if your mother told you about the safe box or not, but I sure hope you get to it soon.

First, I know you have a lot of questions. I know you were too young to understand. But please know that what I did was to protect you. You, Casey, Nathan, and your mom are my world and I promised your mom I'd do anything to keep you all safe.

I had to keep that promise, princess.

I planned my own murder.

Damn, that hurts to write down on paper. But it's only fair that after all this time you know the truth.

I did this to protect you, sweetheart. Please understand that. Please know I'm so upset I won't be around to watch you grow up, to watch you enter high school, go to prom, get your first car, your first job, your high school graduation, your college graduation, your wedding, and all the babies I know you'll have. This is my deepest regret, but I made a big mistake. And you didn't deserve to be in the middle of it. Only I could fix it. The only way was to be out of the picture for good.

There are some bad men after me, and I know they'd come for you, Casey, and Nathan if I didn't disappear. Except they wouldn't stop until they got their money. Money I didn't have.

I told your mom to use the life insurance money to pay them off for good. I also told her to burn the note.

It was the only way, baby girl. Please believe me when I say I tried everything to fix this and make this right.

Please know I love you. I love you so much that I'd rather be dead than let anyone harm you.

I love you, Princess.

And remember… don't let one mistake keep you from taking on the world.

Love,

Dad

My knees haven't stopped shaking since I read the first paragraph. They gave out completely when he confessed he had himself killed. Bentley caught me just in time, but he kneeled down with me as I sobbed through the rest of the letter. I'm not even sure how I finished reading it, but I couldn't stop. I kept waiting for some punchline, or something else, but it ended and it never came.

How could he do this to me? How could he plan this and let his own family suffer?

It didn't make sense.

And my mother knew. Or she knew enough.

I try to put the pieces together, but the sobs continue. My face is covered in my uncontrollable sobs. Bentley continues to hold me as I shake and cry on the floor with him, my fingers gripping the letter.

"Shh…sweetheart," he soothes, brushing his hand through my hair. "Talk to me, Ceci," he pleads.

My chest rises rapidly as I try to get the words out, but every time I try, a sob releases instead.

He rubs my back as he keeps me pressed against him, holding me tight. I'm not sure how long we sit there, but he doesn't release me until the tears have dried up.

He runs the pads of his thumb under each eye, wiping away the tears so I can at least see clearly.

"He was in trouble," I blurt out, knowing he'll understand considering he already found out about his gambling addiction. "He owed money and didn't have it," I continue, trying to remain strong so I can keep it together long enough to tell him. I look into his pleading eyes and say it aloud. "He planned it. He had to die in order to protect us and pay off whomever he owed. He planned everything." I get the words out, but the tears are right behind them. I bury my head in his chest as he holds me tighter and my body continues to tremble.

"I don't understand!" I yell into his shirt. "How could he leave us? How could he leave me when I needed him the most?"

It feels good to scream. Although deep down I understand why my dad did what he did, but it doesn't make it any easier. I'm relieved to know the truth, but now I wish my mom and Casey were here with me.

"Sweetheart, let's go." He tilts my head up, concern laced in his tone and face. I nod, agreeing that I need to get out of here. I grab everything out of the box and lock it back up.

BENTLEY

Nothing could have prepared me for what would be in that lock box. I had hoped closure, but now I'm not so sure she'll ever have that.

Not having her mom here wasn't helpful because she knew much more than Ceci and I ever did, but I also think it was good she did this on her own. She had so many questions, now she finally has her answers—even if they are devastating.

"I wonder why he waited ten years. Why not five? Or fifteen? Or twenty?" she rambles as we drive back to the hotel. I squeeze her hand, knowing that I can't give her any of those answers.

"He had a reason, sweetheart. You just have to trust him."

"Trust him?" she squeals, turning her head toward me. "He left me!"

I don't argue with her because I know it won't do any good. She's upset. She has every right to be. I know she needs some time before she can calm down.

Once we get to the hotel, she collapses on the bed and sobs. I grab her and make her lay next to me. She pushes away, making it impossible to comfort her, but I don't care.

"Sweetheart, stop fighting me. Let me hold you," I growl. Her body finally relaxes as my arms wrap around her. She cries into my chest until her body goes limp and she falls asleep.

I run my fingers together, debating whether or not I should still propose to her today. I wasn't prepared, and now I'm starting to think I'm a major asshole for wanting to take this day away from her.

She stirs awake, but she doesn't let go of the grip she has on my shirt. She wiggles in close to me and tilts her head up at me.

I brush a finger over her cheek and smile down at her. "Feeling better?"

"Yeah." She nods. "I dreamt about him. I haven't dreamt about him in awhile, so I don't think it's a coincidence."

I lean in and kiss her forehead, relieved she's feeling better.

"It scares me to think of what my dad must've been feeling that day —knowing that was the day. He was so happy that morning. He made us all pancakes. I wanted ham, but Casey wanted bacon so he made both." She laughs lightly. "Nathan was too young to care, so he ate anything we gave him." She smiles at the memory. "Mom slept in that day. Knowing what I know now, I guess she probably hadn't been sleeping too well. If they were fighting, she was probably stressing."

"Your dad loved you," I tell her. "It's evident in the way he wanted to protect you."

She sinks into me deeper and sighs. "I know. That's what hurts the most, I think. Knowing the amount of love our family had and having it be ripped away from us seems so unfair."

"Addiction is an awful disease. It tears people apart. He was apparently involved with some pretty influential people."

"Do you think my mom knew?" she asks, her eyelashes flickering up at me. "That he planned it?"

I shrug. "I'm sure once she read the note it was easy to speculate, knowing the money troubles he got himself involved in. She had to know who to give the money to." She nods, agreeing. "She wanted to protect you too, Ceci. That's why she didn't want to tell you too much —keep the memories you had and let them be the ones you remember of your dad."

She nods again, tears streaming down her flushed cheeks. I can tell her emotions are all over the place. And so today, I'm just going to hold her.

CHAPTER TWENTY-ONE
CECILIA

"Is it going to hurt?" I ask as the tattoo artist turns the gun on.

Bentley grins at me, pointing to his ears to signal that I've yelled that a bit too loudly. I'm lying sidewise with my headphones on listening to music to distract myself of any pain that's about to come my way.

Bentley holds my hand and mouths *close your eyes* just before I feel the first sting on my right shoulder.

I inhale and exhale slowly as I concentrate on the music. I squeeze Bentley's hand every time I feel a tinge of pain, which is basically the entire time. It ends up not being as bad as I thought, but I'm relieved when it's finally over.

I open my eyes and watch as Bentley takes my headphones off.

"You did it." He smiles wide. He helps me sit up and hands me a mirror. "Well, take a look."

He took me to the same tattoo artist he's gone to, so I fully trust him, but I've wanted this tattoo for the past year.

Don't let one mistake keep you from taking on the world

It's perfect. What's even more perfect is that he was able to sketch it from my dad's own handwriting. The final words from my dad are now inked over my right shoulder just above the scar that will forever connect me to his death.

"I love it," I say, holding back the tears. "It's perfect." I look back at

Bentley's friend and thank him. He gives a half grunted head nod back before Bentley grabs my hand and helps me stand up.

"It's fucking sexy as hell," he whispers in my ear.

"Bentley, you know the rules," his friend warns. "Hands off."

"Dude, you're the worst cock blocker." They both laugh as his friend bandages me up.

Casey finally flew home and all four of us looked through the pictures together and sobbed. She had no idea what was in the lock box, but she said she always had an idea of what happened that day and why. She had been trying to protect me this whole time from feeling this way, which now I completely understood.

If the people my dad worked for ever found out we knew the truth, they could come back for us. It was too much of a risk for my mom to ever say anything, so she's kept her mouth shut for ten years.

Experiencing this with Bentley has made it all worth it. I finally feel closure from my dad's death. I feel complete.

Having part of him on me somehow helps. It's as if he's not really gone, but still with me.

"How's the shoulder?" Bentley asks concerned. He's been gentle with me ever since and I'm getting very sick of him being gentle.

"It's been a week. I'm fine," I bite out. He closes the gap between us and lays a sweet kiss on my shoulder, his lips trailing the words and ending on my neck.

"Good…because I need to touch you." I arch my neck, giving him the access we both need. "Mm, sweetheart. You smell so fucking good. Delicious." His nose nuzzles my neck, sending shivers down my body as he presses our bodies closer together.

I reach down his body until I feel his firm cock in my hand. I grip it from the outside of his pants, eager to touch and please him. He grabs my hips and pushes me into his erection. I moan as his mouth grows eager, sucking me harder and releasing a hard shiver over my body.

His hands brush under my shirt, gripping my hips hard. He presses his thumbs into my stomach, making me feel the pressure that's building up there.

I jerk in response. His lips make their way up my jaw and to my mouth. He coaxes his tongue with mine feeding the hunger we're both after.

"I need to taste you," he whispers in my ear, licking up the lobe teasingly as goose bumps appear over my entire body. Even after all this time, a single lick can still consume me.

He pushes me back until my ass hits the couch behind me. He begins nipping and licking my skin as he makes his way down my body, moving my clothes with his mouth. He undoes my pants and eagerly lets them drop the floor. I step out of them and kick it to the side. His mouth moves rapidly down my stomach and against my lace panties. I cross my arms and rip my shirt off, letting it fall next to my jeans.

He pushes my panties to the side, teasing his finger against me. I jerk my hips telling him what I need, but it only encourages him to taunt me.

"Sweetheart, God, you're beautiful," he moans as he continues kissing around my panties.

"Bentley," I whimper.

"What do you want, sweetheart? Tell me."

"I need you. Please." I lean back on the couch, arching my hips out for him. "I want your mouth on me."

I feel him grin against my thigh as his tongue licks over my panties, still torturing me.

Fuck this. I pout angrily, grab the thin straps, and yank them apart, ripping them in half.

He smirks up at me, amused by my determination. "I hope those weren't important."

"No, from an ex-boyfriend," I taunt, remembering how upset he got the first time I told him that. His jaw tenses knowingly, but before I can tell him to relax, his mouth is on me forcefully.

"Oh, God!" I shriek, gripping the couch tighter as he holds my thighs apart. I hear him devouring me. The aggressive moans rumble from deep within his throat, making me coat his tongue with arousal. "Bentley! Oh, my God…more." I close my eyes, unable to take the sensation any longer. His tongue is relentless as he moans into my pussy, licking and sucking. My body is trembling against him as he brings me close to climax. Just when I think I'm close to release, he backs outs and quickly turns me around.

He stands up behind me and rubs his erection against me. Fuck, why is he still wearing pants?

"Baby…" I whimper as he cups my breast.

"Hold tight, sweetheart."

I hear him unzip his pants and pull them down. His shirt goes next.

"Bend over," he demands. I do as he says and bend over the couch. It's pressing directly over my stomach, adding pressure to my already built-up need. "Spread those perfect little legs, baby. Let me see all of you."

God, I love the deep tone of his voice. It's an octave deeper, harsher than usual, but I'm instantly aroused.

I'm bent over, spread wide and ready for him. He slowly, and so fucking torturously, licks a trail up my spine. I shiver underneath him, dripping wet with desire. He pushes our hips together, letting me feel how hard he is for me.

"You feel that, sweetheart?" I nod, desperately. "Only you do that. Only you."

"God, Bentley…" I moan. "Fuck me…I need you," I beg.

"Show me. How badly do you want it?"

My hand covers my pussy and begins rubbing my clit as he pushes his cock behind me. He's teasing me and it's fucking torture. I'm tired of waiting.

I rub myself harder, finally getting some relief. I moan out in pleasure, letting my head fall back and sink into his chest.

"Christ, Ceci…you're fucking killing me," he growls in my ear. He bends us over and pushes inside me finally, feeding the need I begged for.

"Yes, Bentley…God!" I scream as he holds us in place, his cock driving deep inside me.

"So fucking tight, sweetheart. So fucking good." My legs are just wide enough for him to enter me, but he's pressing firm against the walls that are gripping him tight. The sensation is consuming. Every thrust rips through me.

"Yes. That's perfect, sweetheart. I love when you touch yourself." I work my clit harder, moaning and panting as an orgasm builds inside me. He drives deeper inside me making me explode at the double sensation.

"Oh, God! Yes! Bentley…yes…" He pumps into me once more as he milks his own release within my tight walls. I'm bent almost all the way over the couch, my ass up in the air. But I don't care. I love giving myself to Bentley.

Meeting Bentley has changed my life, and I'd never take back the journey we've been on to get where we are right now.

Because right now is perfect.

CHAPTER TWENTY-TWO
BENTLEY

Ceci lays her head on my shoulder as we fly over the Atlantic Ocean, heading to Europe for an exclusive modeling shoot. She's been traveling with me since she graduated college, insisting on being with me even though I know she hates flying.

It's the twelfth anniversary week of her father's death and she has yet to bring it up. Either she doesn't realize it's mid-July or she wants to move on from it—either way, I plan to change the meaning of that day for her—make it a reason to celebrate July 16th.

We land in France and take the next day to adjust to the time difference, sleeping and ordering room service before I have to work for the next four days. I've arranged a shoot on the anniversary date for us to do together. It's not for a magazine like I told her it was for, rather it would capture every moment of my proposal.

I don't think she'll be expecting it. I've been planning the shoot for months, wanting to give her something she'll absolutely love.

I've had her ring for two years, but the timing never seemed appropriate. I knew she needed time to digest her dad's letter and to accept everything the way it was. The year after she graduated college, she insisted she wanted to travel with me. I figured one more year and then I'd propose. One more year to make sure she could handle the high demands of being with a professional model.

"I feel like I could sleep for a week," she groans, grabbing the covers and curling up into a ball in the middle of the king size bed. She looks gorgeous—her long blonde hair spiraled out beneath her and face completely makeup free.

"C'mon, sweetheart." I lift her off the bed and she whines. I carry her into the shower and turn on the water. She screams as the cold water hits her first before it transitions to warm water. "Don't make me fuck you against this very luxurious shower or we may never make the shoot in time."

She eyes me, challenging my words. She rubs her breasts together, the water hitting over them just perfectly. My cock twitches as I watch her. Her taut nipples hard at attention, taunting me to suck them.

Fuck. Me.

My jaw ticks as she lowers one hand and begins rubbing her clit. She lets out a moan as she pleasures herself—torturing me—knowing very well that I'm fully dressed. Instead, I decide to play along with her little game.

"Put your finger inside," I demand. "Feel how wet you are for me, sweetheart." She fingers herself slowly, but deep. "God, you're going to fucking kill me," I groan harshly.

"Mm, Bentley…I wish it was your cock buried deep inside of me." She licks her lips as her hips buck from the sensation.

My head falls back in a deep howl. Jesus. How does she do this to me every time? No matter what, I always want her, always crave her.

We'll be so damn late, but right now, I can hardly think about that. I wanted today to be perfect—to surprise her with the proposal of a lifetime—but Ceci doesn't need that. She just wants me, and I just want her.

"Fuck the shoot," I growl, throwing my shirt off and undoing my pants. I'm naked in under thirty seconds, joining her in the shower.

I lower my body, grab her finger out of her and pull it into my mouth. "Mm…so fucking delicious, sweetheart." I lick a trail up her slit, landing on her clit and suck hard. "You taste like heaven."

She pants against the pressure, her body aching with need, begging for release. Her hands are in my hair, guiding my mouth as I torturously devour her—her scent, her taste—it's all too consuming and I need to be inside her.

I stand up and grab her neck as she leans into me. She grabs my cock with one hand, stroking it as my hips buck toward her entrance.

"Mm…so full and heavy for me," she purrs against my lips. Her other hand cups my balls, massaging and stroking so roughly.

"Fuck, baby," I growl, pushing her against the ceramic wall. She slows her movements down as my body tenses, desperate to explode inside her. "Turn around. Let me see that sweet, perfect ass."

She spins around and grabs the wall, opening her legs wide for me. I slide inside her effortlessly, her body on fire as I thrust against her. I guide her body as I grip her hips, pounding into her roughly and uncontrollably.

"Yes, more...just like that," she pleads. I wrap a hand around her waist and begin rubbing her clit. It's not long before I feel her pussy tighten around my cock, her body letting go around me. I continue my fast pace, grinding against her, needing to feel her come on me once more.

"Do you have one more for me, sweetheart? Let me feel you again," I hiss.

She arches her ass out, letting me slide in deeper. I lay my palm flat on her back as I drive deeper and harder into her. Her hand works her clit as I grab a handful of her hair and pull.

"YES! Holy shit," she pants, my cock still hard and deep inside her. "Oh, God..." Her body shakes in a frenzy as I take another orgasm from her.

"Good girl..." I whisper against her, the water cascading over my back still. "Don't move, baby." I pump into her once more before giving her all of me, coming inside her as if I'm claiming her—marking her body with my seed.

We spend the rest of the shower cleaning each other. Thoroughly washing each other. I can't control the smile that spreads across my face any time Ceci traces her finger along my tattoos.

"Have you thought about getting more?" I ask, drying her off.

She shrugs lightly. "I don't know, they're so permanent. It has to really mean something special."

"Is permanent bad?"

"No. As long as it's something I can live with forever." I smile at her, ready to ask her the most important question of my life.

I wrap a towel around my waist as she tucks hers under her arms. Her hair is messy and wet, but God, she's so stunning. This right here. This is perfection.

I grab her hands and kiss them softly as she looks at me. "You know how much I love you," I say, gripping her left hand in mine.

"As much as I love you," she says back, smirking.

"You've distracted me from what I had planned for today, but I'm okay with that. I want to have those distractions for the rest of my life. I want to make this date a new memory for you. I don't want it to feel tainted. It'll be a day we can both celebrate."

Her eyebrows narrow, the smile slipping from her face at the thought of her dad. I lean over and grab my pants that are holding that blue box I've had for two years now.

I kneel down, her eyes widening as she sees the box in my hand. She stills and all the air leaves her lungs as I continue.

"Cecilia West, sweetheart. I love you." I smile, gripping her hand in mine tighter. "I've loved you long before I even knew I did, but my heart knew. My body knew. I've been waiting two years to ask you this question…"

Her breath hitches and I hear her swallow deeply.

"Ceci, sweetheart," I continue, "will you spend a lifetime of love, adventures, and sometimes crazy with me? There's no one else I can imagine spending my life with. I want that with you. Forever." I open the box in front of her, showing off the ring I've had personally crafted just for her. "Will you marry me?"

CALL YOU MINE

INTERN TRILOGY #3

CHAPTER ONE
CECILIA

I could've never imagined how drastic my life would change the moment I said *yes* to Bentley's question. We lived a simple life in Omaha and traveled around the world for Bentley's career. We kept to ourselves mostly with the exception of traveling to L.A. for events and interviews.

I was now slowly getting use to Bentley's lifestyle. I learned quickly that every move you make was documented by paparazzi. It only happened when we traveled thankfully, but ever since the press captured my engagement ring, they've been relentless.

The summer I graduated college, we moved back to Omaha and bought a house together. *Well, Bentley bought a house.* I had yet to find a job, and being fresh out of college, left me limited options as a sports management major.

Once we settled in, Bentley's agent and assistant, Angie said it was now or never. I urged him to do it and that I'd be fine here searching for a job while he traveled. I knew the modeling industry wasn't a nice one and, if he had the opportunity, he better take it or I'd forever regret setting him back.

He didn't accept that very well. He said he'd only go back into it if I went with him, knowing how often it'd keep him away from me.

I tried to tell him that I'd be okay and that we'd be okay, but Bentley Leighton doesn't take no for an answer.

Deep down, I was thrilled he wanted to take me with him. I knew I didn't want to be without him, but I also didn't want to be the one to get in the way of his dreams. Traveling with him from state to state and country to country has been surreal—I never imagined, in my entire life, I'd be able to see the world with the man I loved.

After opening my dad's lock box previously, something in me changed. Not only did I finally have closure, but I also felt this eagerness to live life. Not everything had to be structured or planned out. Not everything had to be perfect, but things *were* perfect.

Bentley had given me more opportunities than I could ever imagine. I never wanted to take that for granted, so when he knelt down on one knee, there was no way I'd ever want to spend my life without him. I knew I'd marry him. I knew he was my forever. I knew it was only ever Bentley.

Growing up in the sheltered lifestyle that I had could never prepare me for what was to come. The press dug everything up about me as soon as word of the famous model, Bentley Leighton, was officially being taken off the market. They dug up my father's case. They dug up how Bentley and I met. They dug up the stories that were once reported on my dad's cold case murder. To the officials and society, it was still a cold case to them, and that was how it was going to stay.

I tried to ignore it, turn off the TV when I saw it, and stopped reading all the magazines. I avoided the internet like the plague and tried to focus on the next step in our lives.

Our marriage.

CHAPTER TWO
CECILIA

"I swear to God, Celia. You make me try on one more goddamn dress—"

"Please, Cora," I beg, blinking my best doe eyes at her. "Just one more store."

Katelynn laughs next to her and rolls her eyes. "You said that two stores ago."

I turn and scowl at her. I've been dragging these two around all day, but I had yet to find the right dress.

"This is the exact reason I eloped. You didn't see me dragging you to a million stores," Cora huffs.

I sigh and narrow my eyes at her. "You also didn't have a future monster-in-law breathing down your neck."

"Reason number two Simon and I eloped," she says proudly.

Shortly after their engagement, Cora called me from Vegas and announced her and Simon had gotten married. I about strangled her through the phone, but I was beyond excited for them. My first reaction was to ask if she was pregnant, but once she put that to rest, they both started looking for jobs. Once they had saved enough money, they bought a house in a small town outside of Omaha. I'm actually very impressed with how put together they are. They work perfectly as a couple.

We walk into another store, and I immediately scan for the bridesmaid dresses. We have less than an hour before we have to leave.

If Bentley's mom finds out we're shopping without her, I'll never hear the end of it.

I've explained to Bentley's mom—Mrs. Leighton—what kind of wedding Bentley and I want. All I get in return is a mumbled response —usually something about how awful my ideas are and how this wedding needs to be 'elegant' and 'charming'—aka Leighton's signature over-the-top society-approved event. Basically, she wants to show it off for the press.

She *insists* on helping and even wants to hire a wedding planner, but I don't want that. I don't need that. I can plan my own damn wedding.

She's lived the prestigious life much longer than I have. I'm still getting use to everything—if I can ever get used to it.

Ever since our engagement was broadcasted, the paparazzi have been actively trying to dig out the details of our wedding. They weren't bad at the beginning of our relationship since we were good at keeping out of the public, but now, with a ring on my finger, they think it's fair game. We were fortunate in keeping most of our personal lives a secret while we lived in Lincoln, and since he took a break the first year we were back together, there were no issues at all.

However, now that we were living back in Omaha, and Bentley was back to modeling fulltime, the media went crazy with our story.

"Oh, I love that one!" I gush as I take a good look at Cora in the mirror. She's wearing a strapless, light purple dress that sits mid-thigh in the front. The back flows longer, just past her knees. The fabric is light and flowy—perfect for our summer wedding.

"That is definitely the winner," Katelynn agrees. "The color works, the fabric isn't heavy, and it'll definitely push my boobs up."

I laugh at her remark. She's been so great throughout all of this, knowing how Mrs. Leighton has been on my back about certain details and how she would like her son's wedding to be planned.

Katelynn tries on the same dress in her size, and before we leave, I quickly put a down payment on both before Mrs. Leighton can get her greedy hands on them and switch them out.

Bentley's been traveling lately, and I opted to stay home while I worked on wedding details. It was a short trip this time and he should be arriving home any moment.

We say our goodbyes before I head back out to my car. I keep waiting for a text from Bentley to let me know his plane arrived safely, but I haven't heard from him yet.

I start driving back home when my phone rings and assuming it's him, I pick up without looking.

"Hey!" The smile on my face widens but quickly turns into a frown when I hear a female voice on the other end.

"Cecilia, darling." *Mrs. Leighton.* I cringe at the sweetness of her voice, but I know there's discontent underlining in her tone. "Bentley is on his way home, and I think we should get together for dinner tonight. Smooth out some details that I've put together."

I bite my lip, really wishing I could tell her where to put those details of hers, but for the sake of being polite to my future mother-in-law, I hold back.

"Sure. I'll let Bentley know as soon as he gets home." I force a smile even though she can't see. "What time?"

"Eight p.m. will suffice, dear. See you then."

Before I can agree or say goodbye, she hangs up. Just great.

I park in the garage, noticing Bentley's car is already parked.

I begin searching around the house, calling out his name, but there's no response. I turn the corner to the kitchen when a hand grabs me from behind, pulling me to their chest.

"Oh my God!" I squeal. Once I'm hit with his scent, I know it's Bentley, and given the smirk I feel against my neck, he enjoyed scaring the living shit out of me. "What the hell? You didn't call," I groan as his hands find my hips and his lips coast under my ear.

"I wanted to surprise you," he whispers, amusement laced in his tone. "I believe I have succeeded."

My heart races as I melt my body against his chest, closing my eyes as his breath vibrates over my flushed skin. God, I missed him.

He rubs his hands loosely over my hips and to my lower stomach —my body tensing at how close his hands are to where I really want him.

"Sweetheart, you're so stressed," he says calmly. My eyes pop open as a shiver runs roughly down my body.

"No, I'm not," I lie while I allow the warmth of his body to consume me. His hands palm my breasts from the outside of my shirt, making my nipples fully erect for him.

He leans in closer and whispers, "You're a liar." His lips lazily linger over my ear. My head falls to the side as his tongue darts out, licking just below my earlobe.

"It's just…I want certain things…and your mother…" Words fail me as I feel his erection pushing against my back and his mouth continues his delicious torture.

"Let me help you de-stress. You're so tense." His voice is low and laced with seduction. He pushes our bodies closer together—if possible —letting me feel his hard and firm erection.

I moan at his words—his mouth assaulting my neck—as both of his hands wonder down beneath my panty line. My eyes blink closed as my head falls back just as I feel a swipe of his finger against my wet and needy slit.

"Mm...sweetheart. Your body is so ready. Always craving my touch," he growls into my ear, his finger sinking deeper. "I love how wet you are for me. Did you miss me?"

I feel his chest rising and falling, my own heartbeat racing at his words and touch.

"Yes," I pant. "God," I moan, sinking my body into his. "I love how you do that to me."

"What's that, sweetheart?" he asks softly but with authority. "This?" He rubs the pad of his finger over my sensitive clit, rubbing it in circles. I moan louder. "How about this?" He inserts his index finger as his thumb continues its circular pleasure.

"Yes..." I pant. "All of that."

My back is completely pressed up against his chest, his erection jabbing into the dip of my back. He deepens his finger, making me jolt at the intense intrusion.

One of his hands roughly skids under my shirt and up my stomach, landing over my breast. He moans deeply into my ear as he palms it, owning it.

"Mm...Bentley, yes." I breathe heavily as I accept everything he's giving me. My body responds immediately to him, soaking his fingers in my arousal.

"Relax, Ceci," he demands. I'm trying, but it's nearly impossible. He twists his hand, grinding his fingers deeper and harder against my aching pussy. God, I need him inside of me right now.

My eyes flutter, blinking closed again as he picks up the pace. He's guiding my hips into his hand, forming a rhythm that's soon building up inside me—pleasure and need close to ripping me apart.

"Bentley...yes. God, yes. I'm so close," I pant, hardly able to control myself anymore. I reach down and circle my clit as his fingers work me harder. I reach up with my free hand and squeeze my other breast, desire hitting straight through my core.

"C'mon, sweetheart. Let me hear you," he coaxes, his lips vibrating against my ear. My entire body trembles as the orgasm builds stronger, my body tensing as it rips through me, shaking the pleasure right into me. "Good girl." I feel him smile. "You have another one for me? I bet you do."

"Bentley," I breathe out heavily, hardly recovered at all. "I-I…"

"Shh, baby. I want to hear you this time. Scream my name," he commands.

"I can't," I plead, needing to catch my breath. My body goes limp into his chest, needing a moment to come down from the pleasure high I've just been sent on.

He spins me around aggressively, my face completely flushed. He smirks suggestively as he bends to his knees. My eyes follow him as my brows rise in concern.

"Bentley, wait—" I begin to plead, but he interrupts me with a harsh tug on my jeans. He yanks them all the way down, panties included. I grip the counter behind me, stabilizing my weight against the palms of my hands.

"Spread your legs, sweetheart. Let me see you." I do as he says, knowing I can't argue with him. He rubs his hand up one leg spreading me wider as his the other hand works my clit. I'm completely distracted, unable to fight him when he's in between my legs like this. "God, baby. You're so gorgeous. So ready and greedy for me. I can see you dripping down your thigh already."

I blush crimson as he mentions how wet I am. It shouldn't after all this time, but his words still have that effect on me.

I respond in an achy and needy groan, craving his tongue on me. His perfect, smooth, fuckable tongue.

"Taste me," I beg. "I need you to."

"I know you do, sweetheart." His voice remains calm as his fingers jerk inside me, twisting his wrist as he grinds deeper and harder against my G-spot.

"Oh, God." My hips buck at the tight sensation. His fingers work me into a frenzy, relentless in their need to please me. "Jesus, Bentley," I pant. I'm not sure how much longer I'll be able to stand.

He nuzzles his nose into the crease between my pussy and thigh, licking a trail around my swollen lips. Damn him, he's fucking torturing me and pleasing me all at the same time.

"Christ, Ceci…sweetheart, you're so greedy for me. You want me to lick you, don't you?" His voice is laced with amused seduction. He loves getting me worked up, begging and pleading him until he gives me exactly what I need.

"YES!" I scream. He knows I do, dammit.

"Say it again."

"Yes. Yes. God, please. *Yes!*" I buck my hips toward him, leaning farther away from the counter and closer to his perfect, delicious mouth. "I want your mouth to fuck me, Bentley. God, I need it." I'm ready to take control and drive his head in between my legs just as he dips his head and swipes his tongue once up my slit. I quiver at the way he teases me, his tongue taking all control from my body.

"Mm…you're so fucking good. So fucking delicious, sweetheart. Always." His voice is rough, growly, as he grasps my thighs in his hands, keeping my legs parted and giving him full access to my aching pussy.

He laps my slit again, dipping his tongue in deeper this time, but still leaving me sexually frustrated.

"I'm about to fuck your mouth with my pussy if you don't stop that," I bite out.

I feel his lips curl up in a grin against my skin. Of course, he's amused.

"Never mind, you'd enjoy that," I groan.

He nods lazily, lapping my pussy again, this time with a deeper and harder force. God, finally.

"Don't stop," I plead. "Please don't fucking stop."

He finally gives me exactly what I'm asking for. His hands spread me wider as his face drives deeper, his lips and tongue tasting, licking, and sucking me so damn hard I can barely hold the grip on the counter that is supposed to be holding me up.

"Yes. God, yes. So good." I rock my hips, matching his rhythm. His pace is aggressive and needy as he drives harder and faster, driving to the built-up orgasm that's ready to explode inside me.

"Mm…that's my girl." I hear him, but my eyes are sealed shut as I fight for control. "So delicious." He stands up and braces our bodies against the counter. "I love when it's dessert for dinner night." I open my eyes and look right into his. He's clearly amused, cocking a smirk on his too-perfect face.

I smile wildly. "Speaking of dinner…" I lick my lips, wishing I could return the favor and bend down in front of him. "Your mother is going to be here at eight."

He checks the time and grins. "We have an hour."

He picks me up and lifts me over his shoulder, guiding us out of the kitchen and upstairs to our bedroom. I laugh playfully as he continues to take control, showing just how much he's missed me.

CHAPTER THREE
BENTLEY

I LAY with Ceci cradled into my chest. Her breaths rapid and heavy. God, I missed her. I miss her every time I leave, but lately, it's become harder and harder to leave her behind.

I enjoy taking her with me, but I knew she had a lot to do yet before the wedding. I knew my busy schedule wasn't allowing us to have a lot of one-on-one time, and it especially didn't allow for me to help out with wedding details.

"Your mother's going to be here in fifteen minutes," she says, clenching onto me tighter. "I don't have anything made." I look at her as she bites her lip, worried she's going to let my mother down or something.

My mother can definitely be intimidating, but she's harmless. I'm her only child, and she isn't accepting the fact that I'll be a married man soon.

However, I know Ceci is struggling to make a connection with her even after all this time. I've encouraged them to spend time together to ease both of them into this new chapter of our lives, but my mother has been quite insistent on not accepting change.

"I'll take care of it." I lean over and kiss her softly on the cheek. "Get ready and meet me downstairs."

I quickly get dressed and brush my hands through my hair, trying to tame it down. I grab my cell and call in an order of Thai food, my mother's favorite.

"Well, hello, dear." She smiles as I answer the door.

"Come in, Mom." I smile back at her, moving away from the door to allow her inside. I'm hoping the food will warm her up so she doesn't make Ceci feel uneasy. However, by her strong stance, I'm not so sure she's even breakable at this point.

Ceci meets us both downstairs, grabbing us all drinks as we casually stand by the bar. Ceci's body is rigid as my mother talks about the guest list.

"I'm thinking three, three-fifty at most. Keep it just to family and friends." She smiles wide, gripping her glass of wine.

"Three hundred and fifty guests?" Ceci gasps as her eyes widen in shock. I'm sure, between the two of us, we don't even know that many people. They'd be a mixture of my parent's high-end 'friends.'

"Mother, that's a bit much. Don't you think? We were thinking something small, a bit more *intimate*," I say exactly what I know Ceci is thinking.

I watch as my mother ponders for about five seconds before she retorts, "It will be, dear. Don't you worry." She smiles sweetly at the both of us. I know she loves party planning and anything to draw in the Leighton name. "Most of them just send gifts anyway. It's not like they'll all show up," she reassures.

Ceci swallows as her body tenses. The last thing I want to do on my first night back is get in an argument with either of them.

The doorbell rings with our food, and it immediately breaks the tension. We all sit around the table as my mother discusses her centerpiece ideas. Ceci stays quiet, sweetly nodding at everything my mother says. I can tell she's checked out of the conversation, and I know she's unhappy with everything my mother's suggesting.

"Bye, dear." She pats my cheek as if I'm a child. "We'll speak later, all right?" She smiles at me and turns her head toward Ceci. "We can talk bridesmaid dresses later this week."

Before Ceci can respond, she grips the door handle and escorts herself out. I slowly shut the door behind her, bracing myself for what's to come.

The following morning, Ceci wakes me up eagerly with her body pressed against mine. We didn't discuss my mother or any wedding details last night. I know she won't talk about it, but I want her to be happy with all the details, as well. I wish I could be around more so I could help, but I'll be happy with anything she chooses.

"Good morning," I say roughly, barely opening my eyes.

"Morning." She kisses my neck softly as her hands roam free in my hair. "I thought we could grab some breakfast at that one coffee house downtown. I've been craving a bagel."

"Mm, breakfast sounds wonderful," I say as her lips move down my stomach. I brush the hair off her face as she inches down my body, seductively kissing and licking on her way down south.

"I've missed waking up to you," she pouts playfully, kneeling back on her heels as she rips my briefs down. I spring free, my back arching as she grips my cock firmly in her hands.

"God, sweetheart." I pant heavily as her lips swirl around the tip. My hands fist her hair as she slowly—and torturously—licks up my shaft before putting it fully into her mouth. "Jesus Christ."

She moans as she switches from sucking and stroking, working me hard until I release in her mouth. I watch as she licks up my shaft again, cleaning every messy inch.

She sits up and smirks at me as she licks her lips and pulls my briefs back up. "Ready?"

I sit up and grab her by the shoulders, pulling her flat to the bed and covering her body with mine. "Not quite." I grin.

I make sure to return the favor as I devour her pussy. She fists the sheets as her toes curl around my neck, releasing hard around my tongue.

"Now, I'm ready." I grin wide, placing a gentle kiss on the inside of her thigh. "I'm getting in the shower, join me."

We make it to The Grind Café shortly before lunch. Ceci and I are both in line looking over the menu when someone calls out her name.

"Cecilia?" We both turn toward a guy who's already seated. I look him over quickly before Ceci releases her hold on me and walks toward him.

"Jason? Oh my God," she squeals. He stands up and embraces her into a hug. The instinct to break both of his arms comes to mind, but I stand down as soon as he releases her.

"Wow, Cecilia." He noticeably eyes her up and down—making me want to gouge his eyes out instead. He's clearly checking her out while I'm standing right behind her. "You look amazing."

"Thank you," she responds sweetly. "I haven't seen you in what—five, six years?"

"Yeah, it's been a while." He crosses his arms, sticking his chest out.

I wasn't getting a good vibe from him before, but now—now I was ready to intervene.

"I'm Bentley," I interrupt, shoving my hand in his face. "Ceci's fiancé."

He shakes my hand with a shocked expression. "Fiancé? Congratulations. I'm Jason. I went to school with Cecilia. Or I guess you go by Ceci now." He turns and looks at her for clarification.

"Either one is fine," she explains. "I'm actually surprised you haven't heard. It's only plastered all over the local newspapers," Ceci informs, rolling her eyes.

"Oh, I actually just got back a few days ago." He pulls a chain of dog tags out from under his shirt. *Shit.* "I was overseas for eighteen months."

"Oh my God!" Ceci about screams. "I had no idea. Good for you!" She smiles genuinely.

"Thanks," he responds softly. Now I feel like a complete douche, but that didn't mean I was happy he was checking her out. "Well, listen, I'll let you guys get back to ordering. Call me if you ever want to hang and catch up. My phone number's the same."

"Awesome, I will. It was great seeing you." I guide her back to the checkout line, my arm securing her to me.

"So Jason…was a good friend?" I begin, hoping she'll fill in all the blanks.

"Yeah, I mean, he was kind of an ex, fling, er—friend fling. I don't know. We were together, but it wasn't really official."

"So he's an ex-boyfriend?"

"Not really. We didn't date, we just—" She stops herself, knowing how uncomfortable this is.

"You just fucked?" I whispered so only she could hear, but needing to know the truth. I wasn't about to let her hang out with some guy she used to sleep with.

"God, Bentley," she scowls, blushing. "Yes, okay. We were fuck buddies, happy?"

"Not particularly." I deadpan. It's our turn to order, so I drop it. For now.

We both order multigrain bagels with fat-free vegetable cream cheese and caramel lattés. We end up sitting outside since it's a surprisingly warm winter day in Omaha.

After a couple bites, I have to speak up, or it'll weigh on me the entire day.

"You aren't really going to meet up with him, are you?

"Who, Jason? Why not?" she asks, finishing the rest of her bite.

"Well, because it's kind of awkward letting my fiancée spend time with a guy she used to sleep with. Doesn't make me very happy to know he was checking you out, probably imagining your naked body."

She cocks her head and scowls. "You don't trust me?"

I grab her hand forcefully, knowing she knows the answer to that. "Of course, I do. However, I don't trust him for a second. He's been overseas for months with no sexual outlet. The second he saw you, his entire face lit up. He wanted you. He didn't even care that I was right behind you."

"That's not true. I haven't seen him since my junior year of high school. There's nothing between us, Bentley. And even if he did, I'd turn him down."

"Men can be quite persistent." I cock a smile, knowing I was more than persistent with her.

"So I've heard."

CHAPTER FOUR
CECILIA

BENTLEY and I enjoy another week together before he's shipped back to L.A. He and Angie are flying somewhere to Europe within the next day or two. She's booked him solid for two weeks, but I'm hoping to be able to fly out there at the end of the week for the last five days of his visit.

Bentley: I miss you already, sweetheart.

Cecilia: I miss you, too. Be safe. Call me when you land.

Bentley: It's going to be like 3 a.m. your time.

Cecilia: I don't care. I won't be able to sleep, anyway.

Bentley: All right. I love you.

Cecilia: I love you, too.

His traveling schedule has been more hectic this past year. The more exposure he's had, the more in demand he's been. He signed a contract with a worldwide company, and they have over fifty different name brands. About a month ago, his agent brought up the idea of him shooting commercials, not just doing shoots. That'll definitely add to his already busy schedule.

"I have an appointment to pick out flowers today. I'll pick you up at eleven. And then we can grab lunch at the country club," Mrs. Leighton says, giving me no choice, but to agree to everything she says.

"All right."

"Great, see you soon, darling." She hangs up before I can say goodbye. Not that I really want to spend the day with her, but perhaps it could be a good time to let her know what I want.

I dress in a simple outfit with black leggings and a teal shirt. I'm not quite sure what one wears to a country club, but I'm sure I'll be out of place anyway.

We arrive at a high-end flower shop. It's the most popular in town with its elegant and pricey showcases. Definitely one I know would be way out of my budget if Bentley and I didn't have a joint account. Once I graduated college and traveled with Bentley, I never looked for a job. I wanted to, but with his schedule, it was near impossible. He's reassured me that I should enjoy planning the wedding now and that I can go back on tour with him, but some days, I wished I had something to look forward to besides picking out flowers and lunches at the country club with his mother.

"Wow, this place is gorgeous," I say as soon as we walk in. "So stunning."

"They do the best work in the state. Juan is a family friend, Ceci. He's eager to help. You'll love him," she reassures.

I fake a smile in return, knowing I'm already uncomfortable with this whole situation. I would've been happy with something simple, but I know that isn't in Mrs. Leighton's vocabulary.

Soon, I'm surrounded by Mrs. Leighton and Juan as they discuss centerpieces 'we must have' and everything for the bouquets and boutonnieres. It's really over the top and extravagant to have a bridal bouquet cost more than our monthly mortgage.

"These are a lovely color," Mrs. Leighton says, turning toward me.

"Oh, are you speaking to me?" I ask unsurely since she's hardly said a word to me as she and Juan had been discussing every detail. She nods, ignoring the resentment in my tone. "I don't think it matches," I say.

"Off white is a perfect accent color to blue," Juan clarifies. *Blue?*

"Blue what?" My eyes widen. My wedding colors are not white and blue.

"The tuxedo vests and ties are blue, darling. Didn't Bentley tell you that?" She turns, fluffing another bouquet that is surely to cost more than my car payment.

"No…no, he did not. They're purple…to match the bridesmaid dresses."

"Oh, don't be silly. Blue is powerful. It'll be beautiful for a summer wedding." She smiles wide, ignoring everything I'm saying. It's useless to even argue with her at this point.

What she really means is that blue means *royalty*, because that's what she thinks she is.

I clench my mouth tight for the rest of the appointment, wishing I could tell her where to put those white flowers, but for the sake of Bentley and keeping the peace, I don't. I'll be sure to bring it up to him later. He can tell his mother the bad news instead.

I break away during our lunch to use the restroom and to quickly email Bentley. I know the plane has WI-FI but no phone service, so I'll get to him faster this way.

Please tell me you didn't agree on blue for our wedding color. Your mother took me flower shopping today. She has picked out bouquets that cost more than my entire car. The bridesmaid dresses are purple. I thought that's what you and I agreed on. You need to tell her because she won't listen to me.

He responds almost immediately.

I haven't agreed to anything, sweetheart, but blue is nice, too. I'm sure she hasn't ordered the tuxes yet. I'll tell her as soon as I get back.

That's two weeks from now. Who knows how much damage she can cause in two weeks.

No, you have to right away. She'll have the whole thing planned and picked out before you even get back.

All right. I'll call her tomorrow.

I sigh in relief and quickly email back before I sit back down with his mother.

Thank you. I love you. Call me when you land.

I nod and pretend to be invested in the conversation with Mrs. Leighton. I wish I could connect on a different level with her, but right now, it's like two cats fighting for the same territory, and she's pissing all over mine.

I thank her for lunch before she drops me off. I pass out on the bed ready for this day to be over already. I just want to hear Bentley's voice.

My phone rings at three-thirty a.m., waking me out of my sleep coma. I'm eager to talk to Bentley, so I shuffle around searching for it.

"Baby?"

"Hi, sweetheart." His voice instantly soothes me. "We made it. We're at the hotel now."

"Oh, God. That makes me so happy. That was a long flight."

"Yeah, I'm beat. I'm going to be jet legged for a week now."

"I wish I could fly out sooner. I miss you already."

"I know, sweetheart. But it's always so busy the first few days. You'll be here soon."

"I can't wait. I need a break. Your mother is stressing me out."

"I'll set my alarm and call her in the morning," he reassures me.

"Wait…no. You need to sleep. I don't want you to have to wake up just to call her." Shit, now I feel bad. The time difference means he'll be sleeping while we're awake and vice versa.

"Okay, I'll call her in a few days when my sleep schedule is not as messed up. I'm not sure how much longer I can stay awake." He yawns.

"I can't wait to see you."

"Me, too. I'll have off the day you arrive, so I'm sure we can find something fun to do."

"I don't think we need to leave the room in order to find something to do," I tease. "I can think of plenty of *fun* things to do."

"You're so bad." He laughs. "I love it."

"I'll let you get to bed, babe. I love you."

"I love you too, sweetheart. Sweet dreams."

We hang up and I'm immediately on a high from hearing his sleepy voice. I hate sleeping alone. I need a dog or something.

I call Cora in the morning, pleading with her to do something with me so my mind didn't consist of Bentley or his mother. She had plans with Simon already but invited me to come with them.

"Never mind. I don't need to be a third wheel," I whined.

"You're never a third wheel, Celia. Come with us."

"Nah. It's fine. You guys enjoy your day off. I'll call Katelynn to see if she's busy."

The downfalls of not having a job to go to or a fiancé around. I'm starting to lose my mind when Katelynn says her and Brandon are out of town for the day.

Just great.

I decide to shower and get ready anyway. I'll find *something* to do.

I end up back at The Grind Café with my eReader. I order my usual latté and bagel and find a comfortable spot in the corner.

I'm halfway into my new book when a male voice interrupts me.

"Well, hey stranger." I look up and see Jason sitting across from me. He's smiling wide holding a cup of coffee.

"Hi!" I smile back. "Your new favorite spot?"

"It is now," he mocks. "I work across the street." He nods behind me.

I turn around and see an old vintage bookstore. "You work at a bookstore?"

"Well, kinda. A friend owns it and is on vacation for a couple weeks. He asked me to watch over it while he's gone. And since I don't really have a job—and apparently nothing better to do—" He laughs at the irony. "I said I would."

"I've never been in that one. I read mostly eBooks now." I hold up my Kindle. "I wouldn't peg you for a bookstore type of guy," I tease, remembering what a slacker he was in high school.

He looks down and scratches the back of his neck. "Yeah, I was a dumb kid. What can I say?" He laughs lightly. "But I graduated, joined the army, and really got my shit together now."

"I can tell." I smile genuinely. "You've definitely changed."

"So what about you? Engaged to a professional model and planning 'the wedding of the year?'" He smirks, doing air quotes as if he's read it in a magazine.

"I see you've done some research now." I sigh, wishing it wasn't so easy to know intimate details about my personal life.

"Well, I had to once I saw you again. I felt like I had to catch up on civilization." He laughs lightheartedly. I end up laughing with him because he really had been out of the loop while he was gone.

"I guess I don't blame you. But—" I warn, pointing a finger at him. "Just don't believe everything you hear. Bentley isn't cheating on me with French models, and I'm not secretly pregnant with another man's baby," I retort, quoting an article for a gossip magazine.

"Wow, your life is way more interesting than mine." He smirks.

I shake my head at him. "I doubt it. I'm in a coffee house in the middle of the day. How interesting can it really be?"

"Well, you're welcome to come keep me company at the store. I get about three customers a day."

I think it over, wondering if there'd be any harm in doing so. He knows I'm engaged, so I'm not leading him on, and my afternoon is wide open with nothing else to do.

"Sure, I can stay for a little bit."

We walk over, and as soon as he unlocks the door, the scent of old paperbacks hits my nose.

"Wow...that smell," I gush.

"Yeah, it's a little strong." He closes the door behind me.

"No, I love it. I haven't been in a bookstore or library in ages." I close my eyes as I inhale deeply. "God, I could spend all day in here."

I run my fingers along a shelf of books. Most of them are old, unknown authors. I pick one up and ruffle through the pages, letting the smell overcome me.

"You're welcome in here anytime, Cecilia. I'll be here all week, unfortunately." He laughs weakly. "I could use the company," he says genuinely. I look at him and a feeling of warmth hits me. I feel bad he's all alone because I know that feeling all too well sometimes. He's come back from overseas after a year and a half and probably hasn't settled back into civilization yet.

"Sure, I'd love to. I don't know if I'll be good company, though. I plan to dive into as many books as I can," I say sweetly.

"Fine with me." He stands with his arms crossed, staring intently at me. I can tell he's genuine. He needs a friend, and if I'm honest, I could use a friend, too.

I ended up stopping at the store every day for the rest of the week. We would walk over to grab something to eat and coffee every afternoon. It's become a nice tradition.

Bentley and I email since it's easier with the time difference. I'm so excited to see him soon. I leave tomorrow morning for a very long twelve-hour flight.

"I'm going to miss the smell," I say, breaking the silence as we eat. "I wish I could bottle it up."

"When will you be back?" he asks.

"A week from tomorrow. Bentley and I will fly back together."

"Does it bother you? The traveling and crazy schedule," he asks, genuinely. We've had plenty of time to talk all week, but mostly, I've talked because I didn't want to pressure him in telling me anything he wasn't comfortable discussing.

"Yes, sometimes. But I know it's important for him. Once the wedding is over though, I'll travel with him more again. It's just now that it's less than six months away, I'm staying behind to finish planning the wedding. Or rather, watching his mother plan it." I roll my eyes.

"Why don't you say something?"

"She doesn't listen. It's really no use. Bentley's supposed to talk to her when we get back. Every time he tries to talk to her on the phone, she changes the conversation." Sipping my latté, I say, "She's good like that."

"What do *you* want for your wedding?" he asks sincerely, locking eye contact with me.

"I want something simple, small. I want purple bridesmaid dresses and white flowers. If I hadn't already agreed to the venue, I'd want a beach wedding or something outside at least overlooking the water. In fact, I wouldn't mind flying somewhere just to have an Ocean-side wedding. But I know Mrs. Leighton would never go for it. She'd have a *royal* fit."

"So let her," he retorts bluntly.

"What?" I cock my head at him. He can't be serious.

He shrugs unapologetically. "Let her. It's your wedding. You deserve to have exactly what you want."

"I wish I could, but then I'd be putting Bentley in a tough spot. He doesn't want to upset her either. She's not easy to please, but she's ten times worse unsatisfied."

"Why can't he just tell her what he wants?"

I swallow hard, because I know exactly why. It's because of me. It's because of what I did at the internship that caused bad blood in his family.

"It's complicated." I shrug. "He's trying to keep the peace. His family isn't exactly easy to deal with and his parents love being in the spotlight. It's hard to make them happy."

"But isn't your happiness more important?" he counters. "If it were me, I'd make sure you had everything you imagined. I wouldn't care about the cost or who didn't agree. I'd let you have anything you wanted."

I freeze at his confession. I couldn't tell exactly what he'd meant by that. It was the first time all week he's crossed *that* line. I shift uncomfortably, needing to change the subject.

I stand up and grab my empty coffee cup. I throw it out and brush fake lint off my clothes.

"I really appreciate you letting me come all week. It's kept me busy. Most importantly, kept my mind busy." I smile.

"Anytime, Cecilia. I'll be bored now for another week, but I hope you have a great time."

"Thank you," I say sincerely. I wish he didn't have to be alone. He looks so depressed with no one around to keep him company. "There's a big time difference, but you can text me if you'd like. I'll try to text you back."

"You don't have to do that. I know you'll be busy." He grabs his own garbage and throws it out.

"It's fine. I feel bad you'll be alone."

"Don't feel bad for me, Cecilia. I've been alone a lot longer than you can imagine."

I cringe at his confession. I can't help but wonder what he's been through over there.

I bite my cheek in hesitation. "You can talk about it if you want. If you need to, I mean." I pause. "When you're ready," I clarify.

"Thanks." He smiles weakly.

We say our goodbyes—a part of me sad to be saying goodbye to him —before I have to rush home and pack for a long flight. Jason's a good person, a friend. I wanted him to be able to tell me things if he felt ready to. I knew it couldn't be healthy to leave it all bottled up inside.

CHAPTER FIVE
BENTLEY

"I CAN'T WAIT to see you, sweetheart," I say softly, trying to stay awake. I'd set my alarm so I could talk to her before her flight left in the morning.

"I'm so excited," she gushes. "I plan to read and sleep on the flight." Her voice sounds like heaven when she's this excited about something.

"Oh yeah? Which book are you reading on your Kindle?" I ask.

"Oh, it's actually a paperback." I hear her shuffling some things around. "It's an old book I got from a vintage bookstore. It's really neat."

I adjust the phone so it lies in between my ear and shoulder. Hearing her voice awakens a part of me that's needy to feel her.

"Mm, that's cool. You'll have to show me," I say, only half-interested because right now, all I'm capable of thinking about is the growing erection under my sheets.

"What are you doing?" she asks accusingly. "I know that moan," she teases.

"Mm…I can't help it. You have a sexy phone voice."

"A sexy phone voice? That almost sounds like a compliment."

I grin although she can't see me. "It is, sweetheart." I grip my cock in one hand and begin stroking it. "In fact, it's fucking turning me on right now."

"Oh, really?" she asks in a higher octave. "I think I can help with that."

"I wish I was inside of you right now. God, I can't wait to just spend a whole day in bed with you." I begin panting as I work myself harder while thinking of Ceci's perfect body.

"That sounds like heaven," she says softly, her words slowly seducing me. "I can't wait. Until then—" she lingers, shuffling more things around. I hear her luggage hit the floor as she shifts herself comfortably on top of the bed. "Let me help you. You have me dripping wet now. I can't focus on packing anymore."

"Packing is overrated, anyway…it's not like you'll need many outfits. I plan to have you naked ninety percent of the time," I growl, working my cock harder at the image of her.

"Mm…good point. I hope the hotel is stocked with extra sheets then. And towels. I only plan to shower, sleep, and fuck you."

"Jesus, Ceci…" I hiss, loving every naughty thing she's telling me. "Feel how wet you are for me, sweetheart."

"Soaking wet," she pants. "It feels like it's been forever." I grip my shaft, stroking up and down at her words. God, I love when she does this to me. Having to travel without her has made her an expert at phone sex.

"Good. Now insert your finger. Push it in real deep for me."

"Mm…it feels so good. I wish it was your cock buried deep inside."

"Imagine it's me, baby. Insert another finger and fuck yourself hard and deep."

"Oh, yes…" she moans. "Is your cock hard and ready for me?" She breathes heavily. I imagine rocking inside her, bringing her over the edge soon.

"So fucking hard." I stroke it faster. "I'm ready for you, sweetheart. I'm so close."

"Yes. God, yes," she continues, moaning and panting as her fingers work her deep and hard. "I'm almost there…I can feel it."

My body arches off the bed as my release comes close, but I wait in anticipation to hear Ceci come first.

"Let me hear you, sweetheart. Scream my name," I demand. I'm so close. I can barely control my breathing. "Imagine your legs wrapped around my waist as I drive deep inside you. I wouldn't be gentle."

"Good, I don't want gentle," she pants. "God, I'm so wet. I—" Her words are interrupted with incoherent screams and moans as she erupts roughly around her fingers.

I'm not far behind her. As soon as I hear her scream my name, I release fiercely around my hand, pumping everything I have.

"Jesus Christ…" I growl and then I lay motionless on the bed. "I can't wait to get you back here."

It feels like forever until Ceci's flight arrives. We were able to email a few times back and forth so I could check in on her, but I was getting restless—I couldn't wait to see her.

I wait anxiously until I see her walking toward me. She looks exhausted but so fucking adorable. I run to her and scoop her up, wrapping my arms around her tightly.

"God, I missed you!" She wraps her arms around me, but soon, her body stills and arms drop to her sides. "What's wrong?" I pull back and watch as she cringes.

The flash of cameras behind us is a dead giveaway that the paparazzi have found me here. They are relentless in capturing every second without even caring how rude and intruding they are.

"When is the wedding?"

"Have you set a date?"

"Are you here to get married? Is it this weekend?"

"Is Ceci pregnant?"

I see her scowl as they all ramble off questions at the same time. I wrap my arm around her, keeping our heads down as I lead her to baggage claim.

I'm used to this every time I travel, but it's been a while since Ceci has traveled with me. She's adapted well to my crazy lifestyle, but I know it still bothers her.

"Just ignore them," I remind her, whispering closely to her ear. "We'll be back to the hotel suite in no time." I smile, kissing her cheek.

My driver, Antonio, is outside waiting for us as we make our way outside. Antonio grabs her luggage as we make a beeline for the car.

"Ugh, I forgot how annoying they are." She frowns, shifting her body to the other side of the car. Fortunately, the windows are tinted and the paparazzi have finally given up when they can no longer see us.

"Don't worry. They're gone now. Angie made sure none were allowed in the hotel, so they can't bother us once we get there." I smile and grab her hand to place a soft kiss. "I'm so happy you're finally here."

She turns toward me and smiles back. "Me, too. But all I can think about is getting something to eat—besides airport food—and a bed. I'm so tired."

I wrap my arm around her so she can rest her head on my shoulder. "I'm pretty sure that's all we're going to do tomorrow. Eat and lay in bed naked," I confirm.

She giggles lightly. "I never said naked…"

"You didn't have to because I already know."

"You really are a cocky son-of-a-bitch." She laughs, wrapping her arms around my waist as she sinks into my chest.

I ended up carrying her up to our suite. She passed out before we even arrived, so I didn't want to disturb her. I lay her as quietly as I can down on the bed, making sure to cover her up so she stays warm. I look at her and think how fucking beautiful she is and how lucky I am that, after everything we've been through, it's lead us to right here.

CHAPTER SIX
CECILIA

I WAKE up to the breathtaking smell of breakfast—crepes, bacon, and fresh fruit. Bentley's even ordered my favorite—homemade pure maple syrup.

"This smells delicious." I inhale dramatically, smiling up at Bentley who's only wearing his briefs. "And looks delicious."

"How do you know? I haven't uncovered them yet." He gives me a sly smirk.

"I wasn't talking about the food that time…"

"I see you've recovered from your jet leg," he teases.

I yawn, stretching my hands over my head. "Not really. I woke up to eat, and then I plan to pass back out."

He uncovers our breakfast and serves everything to me while I'm still in bed. He sets everything on a tray and sets it on the white, plush comforter. I take a moment to just look around—Bentley's serving me breakfast in bed in a gorgeous five-star hotel in a luxury suite. The patio doors are slightly open, letting the fresh breeze in. Everything is covered in white, and the sun is shining perfectly outside. It looks like a dream. However, fortunately for me, this is my reality.

"You all right?" he asks, handing me a glass of orange juice.

I smile at him and nod. "Yes, perfect. Just soaking in the moment."

After I finish, he sets everything back on the room service cart and crawls on top of the bed next to me. He sits adjacent, rubbing a hand over my cheek. "It's a perfect moment," I say, leaning my head into his embrace. "Like paradise."

"All the moments with you are perfect. No matter what we're doing, what country we're in, or what the weather is like—they're all perfect." He lovingly rubs the pad of his thumb under my eye.

"A girl could definitely get use to this."

"You're plenty use to it," he mocks.

"I don't mean just the materialistic things. I mean—you. Just being with you. The downtime is nice, but even when things are crazy around us."

He shifts and grabs my hips so I'm now straddling him. He brushes my hair back, cupping my face. He presses our foreheads together like a sealed bond that can't be broken before taking my mouth in his. The kiss is filled with passion and love, deep and tender. His tongue mixes with mine while heat and desire brew between us as I rock my hips against his.

He grabs my thighs, rocking us harder together. I feel his thick cock hard against me, begging for attention. He pulls my shirt down, revealing my shoulder. His lips trail down my neck, landing right over my tattoo and scar, kissing fiercely as we rock back and forth together.

"Mm, Ceci. God—" he pants against my blistering skin, desperately wishing to rip all the cotton that's keeping our bodies from connecting. "It's amazing what this body does to me."

I arch my body, giving him better access to my shoulder and chest. He palms my breast, massaging it firmly in his hand, as he continues his trail of kisses.

"Let me touch you," I plead. "I need to feel you."

He palms my breast harder, trailing his lips down to my nipple. He sucks—hard. I gasp at the sensation, my chest heaving as he continues his pleasurable torture. I lean back, giving him complete access to my body, begging him to take it.

"Bentley…" I whimper. "Please."

His tongue makes a path from my chest to my neck, tilting my body backward as his lips suck and nip at my skin.

"God, you're beautiful," he whispers. His mouth wraps around my earlobe, making my entire body quiver.

I'm completely wrapped up in him, loving how he devours me and loves me all at the same time. He always makes me feel so cherished and needed.

A firm knock at the front interrupts our bliss, but Bentley is hell bent on not stopping. "Just ignore it. It's probably just housekeeping."

I smile as his mouth continues to lick up my body's arousal. "That's why there's a 'do not disturb' sign available."

I feel him smile before replying, "There was no time."

The knocking continues. Someone is definitely eager, but that doesn't stop Bentley. In fact, it urges him on.

He lays me flat on my back and wraps his legs around mine, securing them to him.

I moan as his lips make their way down my stomach, slowly making their way to where I really want him. I arch my back, leaning back on my elbows as I close my eyes—surrendering to his touch.

I gasp as his tongue begins lick down my stomach, slowly making its way under my panties.

"Mm…" I moan softly, urging him to go lower.

"What do you need, sweetheart? Tell me."

"I need to not be wearing clothes," I mock.

"Oh my God!" a woman's voice squeals. My eyes pop open to Angie standing in the doorway with a frightened expression. I push Bentley off and cover myself up immediately, my cheeks blushing from embarrassment.

"God, Angie," Bentley growls. "What are you doing in here?"

"I'm sorry, I-I thought you were still sleeping. I knocked for like ten minutes."

"And yet, you didn't get the hint." He adjusts himself, sitting on the edge of the bed to hide my body.

"Well, when my most important client doesn't answer his phone or his door, I go to extreme measures." Her tone is firm as is her stance. She's pissed.

"I'm off today. I told you that. Ceci just got in and she needed a day to rest."

"Yeah, I saw the *resting* that was happening." She smirks slyly, crossing her arms. Bentley's body tenses as she continues. "Well, she can rest all she wants. I need you to meet me in the lobby in twenty minutes. You need to meet with the photographer to discuss wardrobe."

She leaves before Bentley can argue his way out of it. And just like that—paradise over.

I spend most of the day in bed, switching between reading and watching TV. Bentley had to leave almost immediately to avoid getting his head chewed off—and not in a good way.

I've almost fully recovered from jet lag when a waiter brings in a tray of food. I tighten my robe as I rub my eyes, trying to remember if I had ordered food.

"I didn't order room service," I say politely.

"Mr. Leighton ordered it for you, Miss." He stands firmly, waiting for me to allow him into the room.

"Oh…all right. You can bring it in here." I wave my hand to the living room, not wanting him in my room any longer than necessary. "Thank you."

He nods and walks toward the door, leaving me with the massive tray of food. I lift one silver platter to find spaghetti and meatballs, and the other of chocolate cheesecake.

I grin widely as I grab the small card that's printed with my name.

I'm sorry I can't be there to eat your favorite meal with you. Enjoy.
I love you,
Bentley

I laugh silently to myself. *Favorite meal.* The only meal we can successfully make together without overcooking. I sit down and begin devouring both plates when my phone goes off with a text message. Expecting to see Bentley's name, my eyes widen when I realize it's not him.

Katelynn: OMG…guess who's getting married??

Cecilia: OMG…is it a Kardashian sister? Is it Kourtney?

Katelynn: No, you reality TV junkie. ME!

I gasp aloud, almost dropping my phone.

Cecilia: WHAT? Omg! I'm missing it? I missed it!

Tears begin streaming down my cheeks as I imagine Brandon on one knee confessing his love to her. They've been together for over two years now and are beyond perfect for each other, so I knew it was coming. However, now I'm so depressed that I'm not home to celebrate with them.

Katelynn: God, Celia. It was so romantic. He's so perfect. I'll tell you all about it when you get back.

Cecilia: You better! I so can't wait! Send me a picture of the ring at least.

I smile as I look at her perfect engagement ring. Reality sets in how traveling with Bentley has made me miss these kinds of things back home. I want to be here for him, but I feel like I'm missing so much of my life back in the states. I feel like I need a purpose besides keeping his hotel room occupied.

Cecilia: It's gorgeous, babe! I can't wait to see you!

I lay back on the couch and wonder when this became my life. Bentley chasing after his dream is exactly what I wanted, but at what cost if it's only going to jeopardize our relationship and alter our once-dreamed of perfect future?

CHAPTER SEVEN
BENTLEY

GOD, what a fucking horrible day. It started out amazing, and then all went to hell the second Angie walked in our room.

She nit-picked every single outfit I wore. She said it didn't go with 'my image' and I needed to look the part. Whatever the hell that meant. I didn't care as long as it got me out of there faster—which it didn't. Twelve long, dreadful hours later, I was finally back at the hotel.

I tiptoe inside, the room completely silent. I curse under my breath as I see Ceci lying on the couch by herself, sleeping. I feel like the world's biggest jackass. I bring her all the way out here just to leave her in here with nothing to do.

She's lying on her side with a book pressed up against her chest. She's wearing a white, plush robe—her hair lying wildly across the pillow.

I softly brush her hair back and kiss her temple. I grab the book and set it gently on the table before pushing my arms underneath her. I slowly pick her up, her arms wrapping around my neck as I carry her into the bedroom.

"Mm…" she moans softly into my ear. I smile as I lay her down gently, pulling back the covers. "You're back." Her eyes are still sealed shut, but she continues to mumble. "I missed you."

I cover her up and kiss her cheek. "I'm sorry I took so long. I missed you too, sweetheart. Get some sleep. I'm going to quickly take a shower."

"Mmkay."

I wash the smell of the stale studio off me, along with the cheap perfume that surrounded me. The constant retouching, primping, and grooming sometimes becomes too much. All I thought about was Ceci today and how much I was letting her down.

I crawl into bed next to her and pull her firmly to my chest. Her body relaxes against mine, something she's done countless times over the past two years. This—*this* is my heaven. I can't wait until we're married, traveling across the globe as husband and wife, and experiencing everything together.

"Sweetheart, it's time. We need to eat and get ready."

She curls her body into a ball, mumbling something as she closes her delicate eyes again.

I walk to her side of the bed and catch her smiling, pretending she doesn't hear me.

"You think you're clever, don't you?"

"Come back to bed," she whines. "I promise it's nice and warm." She wiggles her body deeper into the mattress as she folds her hands underneath her face.

"I don't think so, Ceci…" I whip the covers back as she gasps and crunches her body tighter together. I pick her up and lift her over my shoulder, squealing and laughing as I carry her into the bathroom.

"Bentley!" she screams. "Put me down!"

"You know the drill, sweetheart."

"No, please, no!" She's screaming and laughing at the same time, punching my back with no success.

I grin as I set her down on the bathroom counter, pulling her robe open and exposing every perfect inch of her skin. "Jesus, babe."

"You know this is like assault or something. You can't just take me out of bed and throw me around like a ragdoll." She pretends to sound serious, but I hear the sarcasm laced in her voice.

I pull her robe open more, letting it drop over her shoulders. Her hair is a wild mess, completely matted. Her eyes have dark circles around them, indicating she's still exhausted from her long flight. Her skin is flushed, goose bumps appearing just from feeling my harsh breath against it.

I stand in between her legs; she wraps them around my waist eagerly. I bring my knuckles to her cheek, rubbing softly over the pink tint that's covering her cheeks.

"You're so beautiful in the morning. So raw, real, and completely you." I lean down and kiss her lips softly. She moans in anticipation, but I don't give her more just yet. "I really am sorry I had to leave you here yesterday." She frowns as her eyes look into mine, showing me she understands. "Will you forgive me?"

Her frown turns into a breathtaking smile as she nods. "Of course. I know work is important."

I lean down again and crush my lips to hers, eager to be inside of her, but I don't just yet. She wraps her arms around my neck, pulling me in deeper.

I brush my hands on her thighs, her skin soft to the touch. Her body quivers against me, letting me know she's fully aroused and greedy.

"Sweetheart," I groan, not wanting to let her go. "We're going to be late…"

"Then you better be quick." I feel her lips curve into a smirk.

In one quick movement, I flip her over and tear her robe the rest of the way off. I bend her over the counter, her arms spread out as she grasps the sink. "Hold on, sweetheart," I growl. I run my hands down her back, smoothing her skin against my fingertips until I land on the small of her back. I press a firm palm down on her, angling her body lower. I rub my palms over her ass, spreading her cheeks a part. I bring my hand up and slap her hard against one cheek, making her yelp in surprise. Before she can scold me, I rub my hard length up and down her cheeks. She moans in response, dipping her head lower and giving me access right where I need.

I firmly rub my cock, pumping up and down the length, before entering inside her. She moans loudly as I take every inch of her, deep and roughly before setting the pace.

"God, baby…" I growl as I thrust inside faster. I grasp her hips and pound into her hard, greedily. She dips her back, raising her ass against me higher, which makes me slide in deeper. "Jesus Christ," I cry out as I feel her walls tightly consuming me.

"Faster…" she pants. "Don't stop until I come," she demands.

I do as she asks, squeezing her hips harder as I pick up the pace. The only sounds are our muffled breaths and the slapping of our bodies. I look up and see her looking at me through the mirror. It's an intimate gesture I hadn't expected, but being able to look at her as she comes in this position almost makes me come on the spot. Damn, she's gorgeous. Beautiful. Striking. She's everything. The way she gives her body to me, trusts me, and loves me—reminds me of everything we've been through to get to where we are now.

Our eyes remain locked as her body shakes, unraveling underneath me as an orgasm takes over. "Oh my God, Bentley..." she moans, her head falling back as I take her over the edge. She brings her face back down, meeting my eyes again as I pump forcefully—releasing deep inside her. I continue eye contact with her as my body comes down, relaxing against her. The way she's looking at me is so intense that I can barely take it. I pull out of her and flip her over to face me as I grab her neck, pulling her mouth to mine. The kiss is deep and greedy, and I can't find it in myself to let go, even though we're going to be extremely late now—I don't give a fuck.

I pull her up, wrapping a hand behind her back and one behind her neck. Heavy breaths and silent pleas linger in the air as I carry her back into the bedroom.

"I thought you said we're going to be late," she says breathily as I lay her on the bed.

"Who fucking cares? You need me and I need you. The rest doesn't matter."

She's exposed so flawlessly, brushing her hand up her stomach and resting over her breasts. She's teasing me, eyeing me hard to see what I'm going to do next with her.

"Jesus, Ceci...you drive me so fucking insane, I can't stand it." I lay over her, resting my palms on both sides of her face. "So. Fucking. Insane."

She wraps her arms around my neck, pulling me to her. Her lips cover mine, consuming me before I can protest. Her kiss is needy and urgent as if she hasn't tasted me in months. The way she pants in my mouth let me know how much she wants me.

I break the kiss and run my lips down her jawline, her body arches as I kiss down her neck and below her collarbone.

"Grab the bed and hold on."

She fists the sheets, gasping as my tongue runs a line down her stomach. I bend down, kneeling on the floor as I take her pussy into my mouth. I push her legs wider as my mouth and tongue lap her clit, her body shaking underneath.

"God, Bentley...that's fucking incredible," she pants, barely audible. I pull her clit into my mouth, sucking hard as she jerks her hips. She releases the most delicious sounds, a mixture of pleasure and torture, as her body battles between wanting more and needing her release. Her voice is raspy, almost a growl as she cries out.

I lick up her slit, twirling her clit around with my tongue as I insert two fingers. I drive deep and hard as my mouth continues working her. I lap her pussy over and over until her body trembles and her sweet flavor fills my mouth. I groan as I taste her—our mixed juices captivating me on a temporary high.

I finally come up for air as her body slowly comes down. I kiss her thigh gently before crawling over her body and applying sweet kisses to her heated skin.

"Christ, I can't believe I get to experience that for the rest...of...my...life." I dramatically drag out, letting each word linger on my breath as I smile down at her.

"You're going to kill me with that perfect mouth of yours, so I'm not sure how long I'll actually have." She keeps her smirky pout in place as I lay over her.

"That'd be one interesting tombstone—Death by orgasm."

"Orgasm-overload would be more like it." Her face heats as my breath brushes against her ear.

"That'd be one hell of a way to die." I grin against her neck. "However, I'm going to be dead if we don't leave soon."

We finally get ready for the day, two hours behind schedule. Angie's called my cell thirteen times, left me four voicemails, and texted me eight times. I am so fucked.

Angie surprisingly didn't chew my ass out. At least not in front of everyone. I wouldn't be surprised if she did later, though.

Ceci came with me today. She patiently waited and watched as people dressed me, posed me, and ordered me around. On days I have shoots, this is what my days consisted of. Not all days were constructed this way. Some shoots were on location or with other models. Sometimes I was able to take her out and enjoy the scenery in between shoots. This week would be similar to that—each day bringing something new.

The rest of the week was perfect. Ceci and I started and ended the day as we always do—naked and out of breath. I made sure to take a break every couple of hours in between interviews and shoots to kiss her and remind her that I'm hers. Some of the shoots were with other models, specifically women. Ceci has never said anything to me about it, but I know it makes her a bit uncomfortable. She knows it means nothing, but I know I'd feel the same way if the roles were reversed. In fact, I know I wouldn't take it as well as she does. I'm sure I'd be right next to her, making sure his hands didn't unnecessarily touch her somehow. It's probably for the best the roles are, in fact, not reversed.

I watch as she yawns, her eyes heavy as she sits in the seat next to me. We were in for a long flight, but knowing we'd spend a good two days in bed when we arrived home got me through it. Those were always the best days.

"I can't wait to get you home," I whisper softly. "Once we leave LA, we get two uninterrupted days—phones off, food delivered and a whole lot of steamy sex. Forty-eight perfect hours."

She giggles lightly, shaking her head at me. "I don't know...that sounds like that could be my death sentence."

"I promise to be gentle...at first, anyway."

"I wouldn't be surprised if your mother comes pounding on the door looking for me." She sighs. "I don't know why I even bother pretending to plan this wedding anymore."

"Sweetheart." I lift her chin so she'll look at me. "I want you to have exactly what you want. My mother's just trying to stick with her image. She thinks if her son has this extravagant wedding, it'll somehow push her farther up the social ladder. Just remind her and tell her what we what."

She scowls, lifting her upper lip at me. "That's way easier said than done. She's a bull. She doesn't listen."

"Then make her listen," I suggest. "It's the only way you'll get through to her. I'll talk to her, but it won't do any good until you stand up to her."

"You want my future mother-in-law to hate me?"

"She won't hate you. I promise."

"You know I don't do well with mothers. Look how long it took to build a relationship with my own mother," she scoffs.

"All right. I'll talk to her."

"Let's just ditch the whole thing and elope like Cora and Simon," she suggests playfully, but suddenly, that doesn't sound like a bad idea.

CHAPTER EIGHT
CECILIA

WE FIRST LAND in L.A. for Bentley's conference with his agency. We usually spend a day or two here in some nice luxury suite before heading back to Omaha.

"I wish Omaha was this warm in winter," I whine, unpacking a few t-shirts from my suitcase.

"And then you'd complain about it being too hot and not having a white Christmas and all that." I can feel him smiling against my neck as he wraps his arms around me from behind.

"You're probably right, but after a long winter already, I'm happy to soak up the sun here for now."

I zip up my suitcase and turn to wrap my arms around his neck. "I think I need a vacation from our vacation." We spent half the day on the plane, and I was beat just from following Bentley to his shoots all week. I was ready for some major R&R.

"I'm glad it was a vacation for you…I, on the other hand, was working," he says in amusement.

I glare at him, trying to hide a smile. "Yes, I saw how hard you were working. Dressing in designer clothes, free food, and girls all over you. You really have it bad." I roll my eyes dramatically, keeping a serious face.

He begins tickling me, making my body convulse into spasms as I try to pull myself out of his grip. "You think you're funny, do you?" he taunts, chasing me around the bed.

"Stop!" I laugh, falling down on the bed. He's laughing at me as I squirm for freedom, his greedy hands continuing their evil torture.

"Take it back," he says, trying to look serious, "and I'll stop." He cocks a smile.

"Fine, fine!" I surrender. "I take it back..." *But not really.* His hands finally stop, locking my wrists in his palms. "Now let me go," I beg, trying to sound serious, but the devilish grin he's displaying makes it hard not to smile back at him.

"I don't think so." He pins me against the bed, keeping my wrists locked. "We aren't quite even yet."

He bows his head and puts the cloth of my shirt in his mouth, moving it upward and exposing my skin. He begins lightly kissing my lower stomach, sending chills down my spine as the roughness of his beard rubs against my flesh. I know exactly what he's doing—thinking he can get me all worked up—but it's not going to work.

"Nice try...I'm not falling for the bait," I warn him, lying completely still. I feel him smiling, not giving up on his plan.

He maneuvers his lips lower by my panty line. I try to concentrate on anything but his mouth, but it's nearly impossible. Instead of moving the fabric down, as I expect him to, he continues lowering his mouth right over my pussy. He mouths it, biting the lips right through the fabric of my shorts.

His hands never leave my wrists, his upper arms pinning my hips down. I could get out of his grip if I tried, but I know he'd put up a fight—that'd I'd end up losing.

"Mm..." I hear him moan, his mouth continuing its blissful torture. The sensation feels incredible considering his mouth isn't even touching my bare skin. The fabric rubbing against my clit as he moves his lips is intoxicating and has me close to convulsing.

"Ahh, oh, God..." My back arches, putting his mouth on me deeper. "Mm, yes." It's too late before I realize I'm giving into what he's doing to me. *Dammit.*

"That a girl," he encourages. His mouth moves to the top of my shorts, his chin pushing them down. He grips the top of my panties with his teeth and pulls them down half past my thighs.

Sweet Jesus...*he just pulled my panties down without even using his hands.*

I'm fully exposed to him now as his mouth captures my pussy

again. His tongue runs up my slit twice before pulling my clit into his mouth, sucking hard until I come in his mouth. "God, Bentley…"

My body relaxes against the mattress, surrendering to him. Okay, he wins. *For now.*

By morning, I feel so much better. I must've gotten over twelve hours of sleep. Bentley's side of the bed is empty, but I know he has to be near. I walk around the bed and out of our room to find him and Angie sitting in the TV room.

"Morning," I say softly, not wanting to startle them. "Or rather, afternoon." I smile as I make my way to them.

They both turn around and face me. Instead of seeing Bentley's bright expression, I see panic, fear, and anger.

"Ceci…" Bentley whimpers out. His jaw ticks as his eyes flash a wave of concern.

I walk closer and get a glimpse of the TV. It's then I realize what they are both watching—CTV News—*Celebrity TV News.*

"What is it?" I ask. His expression is firm and tense.

"I'm so sorry, sweetheart." He bows his head as he continuously shakes it back and forth, fisting his hands in his hair. "God, I'm sorry."

"Bentley, you're scaring me. Please tell me what's wrong." I kneel in between his legs, forcing him to look at me. "What happened?"

He brushes his hand over his face, obviously stressed and overwhelmed. He doesn't say anything, which scares me even further.

Angie grabs the remote and turns the volume up. The sound of a reporter jerks my attention away from Bentley and to the screen where a collage of Bentley's pictures parade over the screen.

The reporter is talking about his career and how this exclusive interview could shamble it into pieces.

"What's she talking about?" I ask to anyone who'll give me the answers. "What interview?"

"It's Hannah." Bentley finally speaks up, disbelief written all over his face.

"What about her? I thought that was taken care of years ago," I say, needing more clarification.

"She...she went to the press. She exposed herself as being involved with me years ago—leaving out what she did of course—and revealed that we were intimate together. She did a full interview with pictures and descriptions of our nights together. The tabloids ran with it, magazines claiming I'm still hooking up with her, and that our engagement is now in jeopardy." I swallow hard as I take in everything he's saying. "They took everything she said in the interview and dramatically twisted it online." He rubs his hands forcefully over his face, showing just how much stress he's under. "She's only doing it to further her career. That has to be the only logical explanation why, after all this time, she's talking now."

"What career?" I ask softly since the tears that are threatening to take over are making it nearly impossible to speak. "I thought she was a journalist or something."

"Yeah, she was. She's been trying to get into acting, I guess—trying to nail an audition. Apparently, she hasn't been successful and is now using me to get herself there."

I breathe deeply, trying to remain cool. This is about Bentley. It's his name on the line. "What can we do? Can you sue for slander? Or get the articles down? Or rebuttal?"

He shakes his head. "Not sure."

Angie finally speaks up. "I'm working on doing damage control—making sure to handle the press. They're going to do anything to get a comment from him or even you—anything they can use as a story or comment." She sighs. "It's a fucking mess."

"Bentley..." I grab his face and kiss his lips lightly to distract him from the TV. "It'll be fine. I mean, it's old news. You were together years ago."

"It doesn't matter," Angie intervenes. "It's juicy gossip with a high-profile model, and they'll run with anything they can get."

"But how do they even know it's true? I mean, couldn't anyone make shit up?" I question, sitting on the edge of the coffee table.

"She has proof," Bentley interrupts.

"Proof? What proof?" I ask hurriedly, panicking that Bentley has some crazy sex video that she released or something.

"Pictures," Angie answers. "Pictures of them together, looking like a couple, going to charity events," she rambles on. "It's enough proof to take what she's saying as true."

"Shit," I whisper, panic rippling through me as I take in how bad this can be for Bentley's career. "Can something like this blow over?" I ask, hoping she tells me it'll be old news by next week.

"Not likely." She deadpans.

Bentley begins rubbing his palms over thighs; his telling sign when he's stressed out.

"Maybe it's not as bad as it seems," I say, trying to comfort him.

"She...told them *everything*," he responds, his tone flat. I give a puzzled look and he continues. "What Hannah...what she said is pretty detailed and explicit. She went into our sex life. She told them intimate details about us. I don't want you reading that shit. It's awful."

I gasp unintentionally. I hadn't thought about that, but now it makes perfect sense. Of course, she would. After what she did before, it shouldn't surprise me she'd use him again.

"God, Bentley..." He must feel so humiliated. I hardly know what to say.

It stays awkwardly silent for a few moments

"You're going to need to stay low for a while," Angie finally says. "The paparazzi will try to get a glimpse of you or to goad you into saying something. They'll use whatever you give them and run with it."

"I wouldn't say anything," I confirm.

Once Angie leaves, we just sit silently, neither of us knowing what to say. I sit at the edge of the couch, wishing I could get the reporter's voice out of my head. They've basically pegged Bentley as a 'typical man-whore model, who can't keep it in his pants,' which is complete bogus considering how long we've been together. But as Angie explains it, tabloids will use anything to make a buck. Considering Hannah was more than willing to spill, they were more than anxious to broadcast the story.

Bentley stands up and begins pacing. I anxiously rub my hands together before standing up to speak.

"Bentley? Are you all—"

Before I can finish, he grabs my neck and pulls me to him. His grip is firm, needy. I feel him before I see him, his mouth on mine before I have a chance to protest. He slams me against the wall, his body pressing hard into mine. One of his hands is firm on my hip while the other grasps my neck. He's aggressive and needy in his touch, completely taking me off guard.

"Bentley..." I whimper, unable to keep up with his demanding lips.

"Not now, Ceci. I need you," he pants, slamming us against the wall, holding me hostage. He pulls me up, forcing my legs to wrap around him. He pushes back against the wall and walks us to the dining room table. He gasps in my mouth, our lips never parting as his tongue fights for control. I try to stable the pace.

"Wait…" I plead. I push my hands on his chest, barely breaking away. "We can talk," I offer.

"Don't push me away," he breathes, crushing our lips back together. "I don't want to talk. I just want *you*," he moans, desperation in his tone. I finally give in and allow him to devour my lips.

I pull back slightly and pull my shirt off over my head. I ring my hands around his neck and pull him down to my mouth, my legs tightening around his waist. His hand moves to my back, unhooking my bra and pulling the straps down and off me. I can feel the urgency in which he needs me, so I let him take full advantage. Whatever he needs for whatever reason, I let him take it.

CHAPTER NINE
BENTLEY

CECI GIVES me just what I need—clarification. I need to have her, be inside her deep, and fuck her hard. We weren't making love this time, no—this was desperate and needy.

I lay her back gently on my table, scooting her legs to the edge so they hang down. I finger her panties and slide them down her legs where they pool to the floor. I pull my own briefs down, stroking my cock in my hand as I take in her gorgeous body in front of me.

Our eyes lock, no words need to be said. She knows why I need this.

I stand in between her legs, putting one of them on my shoulder. I stroke my cock up and down her slit, preparing her for what's to come. She grips the outside of her thigh as I slam inside. Her body automatically arches as she gasps at the intrusion.

"Jesus Christ," I spit out, my own body shuddering. I pull out and drive back into her, harder and deeper. She screams out, grabbing and clawing the skin on my arms. Her body accepts mine and takes everything I'm giving her.

"God...you're so good..." she pants.

"If you're able to talk while I'm fucking you, apparently, it's not good enough," I growl, bending lower, almost touching her chest as I thrust harder into her. She's flat on her back with one leg over my shoulder, her body almost bent in half, but God, she's stunning.

I crush my lips to her mouth as I drive into her harder, faster—

barely giving her room to breathe. I just want to feel her—her to feel me. If this is the last time I have her, I want it to be all of her.

"Bentley and I were more than friends. He'd take me anywhere and everywhere he could. He was aggressive and needy, and I ached for it every time."

Her words cut through me as I imagine the damage that'll do to my career. I can't react. I can't give my own interview. Anything I say would be a 'he said/she said' scenario anyway. The press wouldn't put me on a pedestal or take my side—they'd take the side that brought in the most drama, and unless they knew about the deception and lies Hannah told years ago—the ones that almost ruined my family's company—my side won't even make them blink. I have no power in this one-sided betrayal. I can't even imagine what my parents are going to do to me now. Another Leighton scandal that I won't be able to fix. This time, it's too public to even try to fight it.

I pull back from her lips and look at Ceci as her eyes roll to the back of her head as my cock is buried deep inside her, filling her. We're both panting and sweating as our bodies heat up, both close to release.

"Bentley..." she barely whimpers. I drive into her faster, feeling her pussy clench tight around my cock. "Ah, God...yes, yes..." She comes hard around me, her fingers drawing blood into my forearms.

I follow behind, jerking and releasing fiercely inside her. My cock is so deep inside her delicious body that I can't control the hot liquid that fills her completely.

I wait for our breathing to slow and return to normal before pulling out of her and readjusting myself.

I slide my briefs up and grab her panties that landed on the floor. She sits up and grabs them, her eyes filled with questions. She doesn't speak, and I don't offer answers. I know it's only a matter of time before everything is ruined.

She doesn't deserve everything that's about to come her way. The aftermath of my past haunting our future—our lives—could potentially be her breaking point. I know she loves me, and she thinks it's unconditional. However, I know she'll walk away when it becomes too much being with someone that's in the spotlight.

"Bentley..." she whispers. I feel her eyes burning into me. I don't look up, I can't. I don't want to see her look of pity. "We can talk," she offers. "I don't plan to read the interview if that's what you're worried about."

I swallow hard. She'll want to believe everything Hannah says is bogus, but the truth is that some of it's real. My past. The way I chased after women, let them use me for my name *and* cock, was something I became accustomed to, and I welcomed it after a while. But it's the way Hannah's using my past to further her future...

> "Bentley was a lost soul before I came around. He was still living the luxurious model's life when he started working at his father's company. He didn't want to settle down. He didn't tame his wild ways, but I had changed that. Or so I had thought. After a while, he became loyal only to me, even after the dozens of women that had a taste of him before me. He made me feel special—cherished. I was the only girl who was able to get Bentley for more than a weekend fling. He ditched the one-night stands and partying. That's when I knew it wouldn't last long. That's when I knew he'd eventually run. Bentley doesn't do serious."

Her words echo in my mind over and over, as I imagine the fake frown on her pathetic face. She wants the world to feel sorry for her and envious for her all at the same time. She wants them to feel sorry for her and love her for being able to claim the infamous 'Bentley Leighton.' It's all an act, but, unfortunately, some of her words are true. I wasn't tame when I first met Hannah. I had more flings than I had suits. I woke up next to chicks I couldn't remember the names. I partied harder than I ever did before...simply because I could. No one told me I couldn't. In fact, it was accepted in the modeling industry. It was part of the job—networking, as I recall. I never did drugs or ended up on the cover of magazines as a drug addict, but I definitely had a rep as a playboy. Something I regret wholeheartedly as I think of what it's going to do to my career and Ceci.

I shake my head as I try to rid the words from my mind, but it's no use. I can hear her wretched voice in my head as I imagine her telling the reporter all about our sex life.

"Whatever she said, I don't care. I knew your background

beforehand, but I know who you are now. That's all that matters," Ceci says soothingly. Her words should calm me, but they only put me more in a panic.

"Ceci, there's more than just that. She's...detailed. She talks about things you should never know about. She talks about our sex life, places we had sex, and...well, other things. If it were you and some douchebag was talking about—God, I don't even want to know what I'd do. But I know I wouldn't be able to handle it. I know if some guy talked publicly about you like that, I'd be a mess."

"I'm not you, Bentley," she says calmly. "I have no doubt what she said would infuriate me, but it's best if we ignore it. I know who you are now, and to me, that's all the matters. Why can't you accept that?"

"Because it's not going to stay quiet forever. You'll hear it whether you want to or not. People will start harassing you for comments, or you'll start to hear quotes here and there on the news or on the radio. It's inevitable."

She silently walks toward me. My eyes find hers, her lips forming in the sweetest, sympathetic smile. She shrugs as she begins, "This is the life of being with a professional model. It's not always perfect or even fair at times. I have to share you with dozens of people every time we travel. I get looks every time we go to the store or even the damn coffee house. I mean, we're anything but normal. But I think, after two years of this, I've adjusted well, and you just need to trust me that we can get through this. I highly doubt this is the last time someone will try to mess with you. It's all part of the job, right?"

I pull her toward me, wrapping my arms around her. I clench tightly, embedding the feeling of her warmth into my brain, molding it to memory. I don't want the love we feel for each other right now to change...I want it to stay just the way it is. I don't want the media, press, or public to get in the way of what we have. Still, I feel so helpless now that I know I can't do a fucking thing to change what's already happened.

The damage has been done.

CHAPTER TEN
CECILIA

I KNOW Bentley well enough to see when he's panicking. I try to give him the reassurance I know he needs, even if part of me is scared to death of what's to come.

Bentley and I haven't spoken much about anything else. He's so worked up about what this is going to do to his career—booking shoots and jobs don't come easy to those with bad raps. Most photographers don't want to work with them—it gives them a bad name, as well.

A couple days pass and all Bentley's been concerned about is clearing his name. I can understand his concern, but at the same time, he's not the only celeb to get a story exposed about them. Even though he won't listen, I keep trying to convince him it'll be okay.

Traveling with Bentley over the past year has been an incredible experience. We've been able to do things I only could've dreamed of doing.

However, now it was my time to build a career—to make something of myself aside from the girl that's on Bentley Leighton's arm.

I told Bentley this morning that I wanted to start looking for a job. I need something to do besides sit around and 'plan' our wedding. Traveling with him was causing him to be late for his shoots and that was the last thing he needed to be known for doing. I enjoyed traveling with him, but I know he needs to remain focused. Competition in his industry was too fierce to be slacking off now.

Once I checked my phone, I noticed I have a voicemail from Jason—

the last person I expected to hear from. He had seen the article online and was checking up on me to make sure I was all right.

My heart squeezes at the way he's concerned about me. It reminds me I have to text Cora, Katelynn, Casey, and my mom to give them a heads-up. They're used to stories of Bentley being twisted in the media, but I know this one will shock them a lot more.

I decided to fly back to Omaha by myself, giving Bentley the time he needed to sort things out. I felt invisible anyway just waiting around for Bentley to let me be there for him. He wasn't taking any of this too well.

The following day after I arrive back home, I head to The Grind Café and begin my job search. I order my caramel latté and find a corner booth to sit in. I pull out my iPad and start searching for jobs online— anything related to sports management or perhaps something in fitness. I knew it'd have to be something flexible with the wedding coming up and Bentley's demanding schedule. I knew I still wanted to be around to support him and travel with him occasionally, but I also knew I had to start building my own career.

I'm half way through my latté, emailing my resume for the third time, when I'm interrupted by a familiar voice.

"Cecilia?" I look up and see Jason staring down at me. "I was hoping I'd run into you."

"Jason? Hi!" My eyes light up at seeing a friendly face. "How are you?"

"I'm doing great, now." He smiles wide. "Do you mind if I sit with you?"

I shift in my seat, move my iPad over, and wave my hand. "Oh, of course."

"What are you doing here? I'm surprised you've even left your house." His tone is sincere, but I hear the concern laced in his voice.

I frown, hating that everyone in this city probably knows my business by now, especially Jason.

"I'm not going to let the assholes keep me from living my life. Plus, as soon as a famous celeb goes into rehab, everyone will forget." I shrug, trying to play it off. "Thank you for checking up on me before. I really appreciate it."

"You're welcome." He keeps his eyes on me as he brings his coffee up to his lips. He looks like he wants to say something else, but instead, shifts his eyes to the iPad in front of me.

"So what are you doing? Writing a rebuttal story?" He smirks.

"No..." I laugh lightly. "Job searching. Every college graduate's —*with zero job experience*—dream."

"*You?*" His brows rise. "You're searching for a job?"

"I'm offended!" I jokingly put a hand to my chest. "I am very capable of working, thank you."

"Well, I'm sure you are, but..."

"Just because my fiancé is a model, doesn't mean I want to just sit at home and knit."

His lips form into a devilish grin. "Um, I don't think anyone does that anymore. Unless you're living in a nursing home, which in that case...I'd be out looking for new friends."

"You're an ass," I scowl playfully, punching him in the arm. "I'm probably your only friend."

"My only *hot* friend, yes. Otherwise, the rest are covered in tats with shaved heads."

His confession hits me off guard, but I choose to ignore it anyway.

"Well, *friend*, I need to get back to job searching. Minimum wage isn't gonna find itself."

He laughs, but suddenly his face goes serious. "Wait. What kind of job are you looking for? I might have a few connections, depending on what you can do."

"Well, I'd love to do something with sports and fitness. I did an internship at my college with the hockey team, but that's basically my only experience. I'd probably even get denied being the water girl." I frown.

"I don't think that's even a paid position." He laughs.

I scowl at him, and then begin laughing. "Oh my God. I'm never going to find a job. My experience is laughable."

His face turns genuine. "I have an uncle who works at the university. He's one of the men's baseball coaches. I could...ask him if he has an opening available. I mean...if you're interested." He grins as he watches my expression.

"Seriously? You aren't just messing with me?" My eyes light up as my heart speeds up at the thought of getting my dream job.

"Yes, for real. When I came back, I moved in with him, and he just mentioned an opening—"

"Oh my God!" I squeal, jumping up and hugging him. "That'd be so amazing!"

He wraps his arms around my waist, making me highly aware that we're touching. I didn't mean to—it just sort of happened when I got so excited about the job opening.

I push back slightly, taking a step backward to avoid any awkwardness. I think he feels it too, his hand brushing roughly through his hair as we avoid eye contact.

"I'll give him your number, I mean if that's okay?" He smirks.

"Yeah, absolutely! I can email him my resume or whatever," I stumble, too excited to slow down. "Let me know what he says." I smile back.

"Will do. Well, I'm going to head out. I'll let you know what he says." He nods, and I thank him for his help. I can hardly believe it, but for a moment, it helps me forget the mass chaos that my life is in right now.

I sit back down and scroll through my iPad and groan over the hundreds of emails I have yet to go through. Most of it is spam, but the rest is Mrs. Leighton emailing me details of 'my wedding' and reminding me of appointments and fittings. I'm so over her taking charge that I decide to email her back—with a piece of my mind.

I drive back home with peace and happiness finally overwhelming me, instead of anxiety and stress. I've let Mrs. Leighton know exactly how I feel about her taking over my wedding and that from now on, I'll be handling all the details. I expect a phone call or threatening email to come any time now.

I walk in with a ginormous smile on my face when my cell rings with Bentley's name on it.

"Hey, I'm just getting in—"

"What the fuck did you do?" he growls, his voice deep and demanding.

I stop dead in my tracks when I hear his words.

"Wait, what?" I throw my purse on the table, standing in the middle of the dining room. "You told me to stand up to your mother, that's—"

"This isn't about my mother, Ceci."

"What the hell are you talking about then? What's wrong?" I ask hurriedly.

I hear something slam against a wall through the phone, an object sitting in the hotel, I assume.

"I just got a call from Angie. Apparently, you've been spotted hugging and *flirting* with a guy at the coffee house. Not only that, there are pictures to prove it, and not *only* that, they're headlining them as *'Trouble in Paradise? Bentley Leighton's fiancée moves on already.'*"

I gasp as my heart sinks at his words. I have no clue what he's talking about.

"H-How is that possible? I was literally *just* there." I wave my hand in back of me although he can't see me. I'd only been gone a few hours.

"The Internet, Ceci. Someone recognized you, took your picture, and tweeted it."

"But...it's not true!" I shout, defending myself. I shouldn't have to, though. Bentley knows me better than that. "It was Jason. It was not some random guy or a hookup. And we weren't *flirting*. I was there looking for jobs just like I told you I'd be."

"Well, you left out the meeting up with Jason part. However, now everyone thinks my fiancée has moved on since Hannah's story. It's exactly what they wanted."

"Exactly! They're just spiraling the story out of control to make money. It's not true."

I hear him moving around as he speaks. "Well, even to me it looks true." His voice is low, defeated.

I rush to his office and immediately get on his computer. I Google my name, the article popping up right away. I examine the pictures displayed online. There are a dozen of them. Me laughing. Jason laughing. Me gasping when he told me about his uncle's job opening. Jason looking at me in pure lust. Us hugging. Shit, shit, shit. It was all innocent. But, of course, they could pull any story out of their asses without actually knowing what was really going on.

"You're a moron," I spit out, chucking the mouse across the room.

"Excuse me? I'm a moron?" His voice is higher now, obviously taken back by my response.

"Yes." I throw my hand up in frustration. "I wasn't even doing anything. You of all people should know how the tabloids twist shit around and form fake stories."

"Ceci, I know that. It's the fact that they have *pictures*. It's hard to deny something that's clearly obvious."

My blood boils as I hear the accusation in his tone. "Obvious of what? That I was hanging out with a friend who happens to be a guy? That I was thanking him for helping me and for being there when I needed someone?" I question loudly, but I continue without letting him speak. "I stand by your side when your ex-whatever-she-is goes public with your sex lives and even your horrendous playboy ways. I stand by you in your career—putting *mine* on hold—while we travel, and I sit by awkwardly watching as girls throw themselves at you. And the one time—*one* time—I go and actually do something for myself, I get it thrown back in my face. I wasn't there to meet Jason. He was there grabbing coffee. And if you must know—because it's not like you've asked—once I told him I was looking for a job, he offered to help me. His uncle is a coach for the baseball team at the university. There's an opening, and he offered to give my information to his uncle. So, yes, I was overly excited and hugged him for helping me. Excuse me for showing *any* excitement that isn't about you and your career."

The words spew out of my mouth before I realize what I'm saying, and then, once I start, it continues to spill out of me. But part of me feels relief that I did.

The line stays silent on the other end. I'm practically panting, waiting for him to say something—*anything*. Nothing between us has ever been easy. We've always had to fight to be together and this is no different.

"Sorry...I don't mean to yell at you, it's just...this is really unfair," I speak up again. "You know I support you in your career. I just want something I can feel proud of for myself. I didn't go through all the trouble of finding out about my dad and finishing college to just sit around and plan a wedding or following you around to watch you make your dreams come true. I have dreams and goals, too, and I want to do them with you. But I need your support, as well." I finally hear him breathing on the other end.

"God, I'm sorry. I...didn't mean to take it out on you." His voice is weak, defeated. "I'm just so over this bullshit. It's been days and still the press and media are all over this damn Hannah story, and now they'll be all over it with you. I just...I don't want to lose you over this, and you know that's my biggest fear. The media is good at pulling people apart. And with Hannah's interview and your pictures, they'll really make up some bullshit story."

I sniff back the tears. I love strong, determined Bentley, but I fall in love with him even more when he's vulnerable Bentley. It reminds us that throughout everything—his career and how we met—that we're still just two people who want to maintain a normal, healthy relationship.

"We're going to get through this," I tell him. "We can't let the press get in between us. We need to stay strong and lean on one another. We can't turn on each other."

I hear him exhale deeply. "You're right. I just...hate this. Being in different states makes them think it's true. I hate letting anything get in between us, and I fucking hate the fact that they think you're with that guy."

"He's just a friend," I remind him calmly.

"Friend or not, he looks at you like he wants more. It was quite obvious to me and the person who snapped the pic."

"Well, it's not my fault he looks at me like that. I don't give him any advances to think we're more. When I hung out at the bookstore, it was strictly friend-zone. I mean, there was nothing electric between us."

"Wait." He pauses. "What bookstore?"

"Across the street from the coffee house," I clarify.

"You're going to have to fill me in." His voice is rough, demanding.

Shit, I was sure I told him about this.

"Jason was watching his friend's store for a couple weeks while he was on vacation or something. While you were gone that first week, I went and kept him company. We just hung out while I looked through books."

He's silent for a split second before rushing out, "Are you fucking kidding me? You...you spent *days* with this guy? You hung out with him while your fiancé was out of the country? Do you know how wrong that fucking sounds?"

My heart begins racing again. "What the hell are you talking about? I can't go to a bookstore now? How many times do I have to tell you...HE'S JUST A FRIEND!" I wave my hand in the air to emphasize it although he can't see it. I continue ranting, "We haven't hooked up since I was seventeen years old, and oh, yeah...I'm engaged now," I mock, upset that we're *still* arguing about this.

"Well, you could've fooled me." He deadpans. Before I can respond, the phone goes dead. I pull the phone away from my ear. He hung up on me.

When it rains, it fucking pours.

"AH!" I scream out in frustration, not knowing what else to do. One minute we're fine and the next...it fucking goes to hell.

My cell interrupts, beeping with a message.

Jason: Shit, Cecilia. I'm so sorry. I just saw. Anything I can do to help?

I sigh to myself. Jason has only been kind to me and it's the last thing he deserves to be in the middle of.

Cecilia: Not unless you have a time machine?

If it can go wrong, it will go wrong.
Murphy's Law.

CHAPTER ELEVEN
BENTLEY

DEALING with the bullshit of the press is becoming too much. I'd always been able to handle them. I'd ignore their absurd comments and move on, but now it was different. Now it was affecting Ceci and I, and I wasn't about to let that happen.

I decide to seek Hannah out. She's living in Hollywood right now with about five roommates. Angie contacted her agent and told her she's been struggling to get auditions. I wasn't about to let her damage my name to get ahead and get away with it.

Angie told me to let it go—for now—but I brushed her off anyway. I was going to handle this my way.

It wasn't hard to find out her address, especially when you know the right people. She lives in a crappy part of the city, but I drive there anyway. Unsure if she'll be home, I'm determined to find her somehow.

I stand outside my rental car in front of her apartment complex—if you can even call it that. The siding is falling off, the front covered in weeds, and the metal mailbox is smashed to the ground.

I hesitantly walk up to the front door and hit the buzzer. I already know which apartment number she is, but I buzz anyway.

Before anyone can buzz me in, the door opens. "Oh, hey, man. Buzzer is broken. Just walk in."

I nod my thanks, not surprised to hear that too is busted.

I walk up the steps to apartment number nine and knock. I look completely out of place in my three-piece suit and designer shoes. I wanted her to see the Bentley she last knew.

The door flies open and smoke immediately blows out into my face. "Yeah?" A girl asks. I take notice of her messy appearance. She's sickly petite, her hair a nest on top of her head and her eyes are bloodshot.

"Um, yeah, is Hannah here?" I ask, disbelief running through my mind as I get a full look into Hannah's new lifestyle. She opens the door wider for me, allowing me to step in.

"She's in the room down the hall," is all she says, walking out and disappearing into the hallway.

"Thanks," I mumble. I immediately look around and can't believe more than one person even lives here. It's a complete disaster—garbage and cat shit littering the carpet.

"Hannah?" I call out, not exactly sure which room I'm looking for. "Are you back there?" I hear movement in the next room and slowly push the door open. "Hello?"

Nothing in my time of knowing Hannah could've prepared me for what I was seeing. That wasn't Hannah. There's no way. Hannah was a well-put together woman with a highly-competitive journalist position. The story she wrote about the Leighton's skyrocketed her career to the top. This woman lying on the bed in front of me couldn't be her.

She was mere skin and bones, her long hair now short and ratted. Her arms were scrawny and filled with bruises.

"Jesus Christ," I mutter as I walk toward her. "Hannah?"

She slowly raises, her eyes only half open, as she looks me up and down. "Well, well, well. If it isn't the infamous perfection of a man, Bentley Leighton. Long time no see." She smirks, sitting all the way up now.

"Shit, Hannah." I brush both hands through my hair in complete disbelief that this is actually her. "Are you all right?"

She scowls at me. "Don't come waltzing into my apartment, into *my life* and mother me. I'm just fine." She parades to what is acting as a table and grabs a cigarette. As she lights it, I get a better look at her. She's a fucking junkie.

"Screw you, Hannah. You might've ruined your career and life all on your own, but you didn't have to take mine down with you. Considering you were the one that fucked *me* over."

"Oh, Bentley. Are you still upset over that?" She wraps her lips around the end, inhaling and holding it in briefly before exhaling. "I should be the one upset, after all. Once your mother clawed her teeth into my career, what did I have left?"

"Don't you dare blame this on my family. You brought that all on yourself." I stand up, ready for a fight, but there's no use. She's pathetic.

"So what do you want anyway?" she asks, as she leans down to snort a line of what I presume is cocaine.

"Don't be doing that shit around me," I growl, grabbing her arm and pushing her away from the table.

"Let go of me," she hisses. I release her immediately, regretting this whole thing.

"You're a fucking bitch, you know that? You deserve everything that happened to you after you pulled that shit on me." She sits on the bed, her back facing me. I can tell she wants to speak, but she doesn't, so I just continue. "I'll help you, Hannah," I say softly. "You retract your interview, and I'll get you into rehab. I'll pay for it."

Hannah doesn't deserve my help, but I can't just walk away knowing she's slowly killing herself. She was better than that at one point. She was a shark and to see her defeated is just sad.

She turns around slowly, her expression filled with amusement. "You think I need your help, Leighton?" She laughs coldly, taking a hit of her cigarette. "That's rich."

"Fine...have it your way. I'll make sure your junkie ass never sees the inside of a studio. Have a nice life." I walk out of the bedroom, rage and regret consuming me almost immediately. Fuck. I fight with myself before I even get to the front door.

"Bentley, wait!" she calls out after me. I turn around and see her weak body rushing toward me. "Wait, just a fucking second." She begins panting as if walking ten feet is too much for her.

I sigh, annoyed that it's come to this. "What?"

"I'll do it. I'll do it, okay?"

"What's it gonna cost?" I ask expressionless.

She shakes her head. "No, nothing."

I stand silent. I'm stunned that she's agreed to what I'd asked. "Come on," I plead. "Let me get you some help. You're a damn mess, Hannah."

She's hesitant at first but then slowly nods her head. "All right."

I fly back home the following day, wanting to get back to Ceci and some kind of *normal*.

I'm sitting back in my office chair when I hear Ceci walking in. "My interview is the same day you fly out." She looks defeated and worn out.

I fly out in a few days for another shoot—hopefully, one of my last ones for a while.

"Do you want me to reschedule my flight?" I've been attached to my desk for the past two days. Between emails and phone calls, I'm still dealing with the press as well as keeping in contact with Hannah's rehab clinic.

"No, of course not. I was going to ask if you wanted me to reschedule my interview so I could come with you to the airport." Her voice is soft, weak. She slowly walks closer, her hands crossed in the front.

Ceci's been busy preparing for her interview so we haven't talked much. Ever since the pictures of her and Jason went live, it's been one of those things we're trying to get through. They fueled the fire that Hannah's interview already set off.

"No, I'll only be gone a few days this time. I told Angie I wanted to fly in, do the interview and shoot, and get back home."

She nods, fidgeting with her fingers that are placed in front of her.

I push myself off the chair and walk toward her. She angles herself so we're facing each other, chest to chest.

I press a hand to her cheek, her face leaning in as her eyes close on contact. "I'll miss you," I say softly. Her lips curl up into a small smile.

"I'll miss you, too." Her eyes open. "I have a catering appointment with your mother...so I will *really* miss you."

I smirk, removing my hand and leaning in to graze her lips lightly. "I'm so bummed I'll be missing that."

She scowls playfully. "I bet."

"We'll figure this out, okay? I know it hasn't been easy on you." I watch as her eyes stay locked on mine. "I trust you," I clarify. I want her to know that I do wholeheartedly. I've had Ceci to myself for a long time while we traveled, and we always stayed low in Omaha. Now things are spiraling out of control and rumors are being spread that it's making me feel so out of control—something I definitely don't accept willingly.

"You have nothing to worry about," she says sincerely. "I mean, it's only like twenty or so college guys stretching in really tight uniforms. No biggie." She shrugs, knowing damn well that definitely doesn't make me feel any better.

I play her game, knowing she'll be just as uncomfortable as I am. "All right. Good to know. I'm only shooting with four other girls in bikinis. I'm glad we can be mature adults and comfortable with being around hot people."

"I never said hot!" she mocks, pushing me playfully in the chest. "Not to mention, half-naked!" I step back, pretending she actually has enough power to push me backward. I laugh as her face heats up, obviously on to my little game.

"What?" I ask jokingly. "You aren't insecure, are you?"

She pushes me again, scowling. "You don't play fair." She tries to hide the smile that's forming.

I wrap my arms around her, bending at the waist as she tries and gets out. "Sweetheart, you know you're the only girl I ever look at," I say sincerely. She stops fighting me and finally looks me in the eyes. "You're the most beautiful person I know—inside and out. You have nothing to worry about."

She bites her lip, taking in every word I'm telling her. She should know this by now anyway, but I know it isn't easy seeing each other around other men and women.

"I hope *they* know that." She grins, throwing my words back at me.

"They know, don't worry." I kiss her lips, slow and soft. "*I* know... and that's all that matters anyway."

"Does this mean you won't be following me around if I get this job to make sure guys don't hit on me?"

"Of course not," I say seriously. "I'd hire someone for that. I couldn't possibly do that all day and work."

"You're such an ass." She laughs. "Okay, but for real." Her face turns serious, both of us standing straight up now. "We need to trust each other fully. We can't let the media get to us and tear us apart. It's ruining us and I hate it."

I stroke her cheek, slowly brushing her hair back behind her ear. "You're absolutely right. We can't pay them any attention. We're happily engaged and that's all that matters."

"Good to hear, Mr. Leighton. We'll prove to them how wrong they all are." She wraps her arms around my waist, tilting her head all the way up to lock eyes with me.

I wrap my arms around her. "Sounds perfect to me."

Half way through my flight, Ceci emails me and tells me she was offered the position right on the spot. I could sense her giddiness so I respond with how proud I am of her. I know she was really excited about the position. She spent hours doing research about the campus and learning about their baseball team. She was always good at making sure to cross her T's and dot her I's.

Luckily, I would only be gone for three days, but most of it will be spent adjusting to the time difference and being told where to stand and what to wear.

It sucks being away from Ceci, but it makes it easier during shooting knowing she isn't bored or uncomfortable watching me pose with the other models.

This shoot is for a swimsuit company that wants couple and group shots. Unfortunately, it's freezing cold out and we have to shoot outside for the summer issue.

By the end of the day, I'm exhausted and frozen, happy to be flying out the next morning. Ceci and I email a couple more times before I pass out for the night, preparing for a long flight home.

It's when I'm sitting in first class during the sixth hour that it hits me. Is this career really worth it if it's constantly tearing us apart? Is a career that sends me thousands of miles away really worth jeopardizing everything I fought so hard for?

I'm not so sure anymore.

CHAPTER TWELVE
CECILIA

I can't breathe. I'm losing more oxygen by the second, and I can't get my lungs to open up.

I gasp, clawing my neck. *Breathe, dammit.*

I sit up in my bed, clenching my chest and throat. I inhale deeply, finally feeling relief from the oxygen that I wasn't receiving. It's only a dream.

Just a dream, I remind myself.

I claw the sheets, rubbing them over my forehead and face to wipe off the sweat. That was one of the worst dreams I've ever had.

I lay back, relieved. My heart is still racing as I think what I had just dreamt.

I lied to Bentley about reading the interview. I lied to him about looking at the pictures. I lied about all of it. And now I was paying for it.

My mind spins as I recall the dream—rather, nightmare. One moment it's Bentley and I—him making love to me. The next—Hannah and Bentley.

Hannah and Bentley.

The thought of them together makes me jump out of bed and head straight for the bathroom. I throw up last night's dinner of shrimp and pasta. Katelynn and I had gotten together to discuss wedding details for her and Brandon's Winter Wonderland wedding at the end of the year.

Thinking of her and Brandon instead of my dream soothes me for a few moments. I rinse my mouth and wash my face before heading back into bed. My stomach feels queasy and I'm completely nauseous just thinking of the images in my mind.

Hannah on top of Bentley.

Bentley bending Hannah over.

Bentley driving deep inside her.

Hannah moaning and screaming his name as he continues pumping forcefully from behind.

His nails digging into her hips as he bucks into her, harder and deeper.

Oh, God.

I run back to the bathroom for a second round. The dream felt so real—looked so real. It was as if I were watching them from above as if I had a front row viewing.

Nothing like this has ever happened before. I've never imagined Bentley with other women. We both had past lovers, and I knew that going in he was clearly not a virgin, but this was different. Now I had read her words *and* had a visual.

I make a pot of coffee, no use in trying to get back to sleep anytime soon. Every time I close my eyes, the images of them pop back into my mind.

I decide to tackle my email, something I've been avoiding for days.

Half way through my cup of coffee, I come across an email that's addressed to me, but I don't recognize the email.

Dear Cecilia West:

You don't know me, but I know you.

I met you when you were only five years old. I've known your dad for many years. I know it's been years since his death, but if you're interested, I'd love to see you again. If so, email me back. We can meet somewhere public if you wish. I know this is a random message, but you can trust me.

Sincerely,

Ava

Ava? A woman is emailing me about my father? I always suspected he worked for a mob-type of guy. No one outside of my family and Bentley know that we know the truth…we never made it public. So who was she? Was she his mistress? His gambling partner? Nothing ever came up with an Ava.

I scroll down and notice she sent me another one just a couple days ago.

Dear Cecilia West:
I don't blame you for being hesitant to email me back. I know your fiancé is in the spotlight right now, and I promise it has nothing to do with that. But…I'd like to see you again before it's too late. Please message me back.
Sincerely,
Ava West

Oh my God.
Ava West.
My heart races as I read the last email she sent me. I read it over twice just to make sure I read it correctly.

I do a quick Google search for an Ava West, but nothing comes up. Not even a Facebook page. *What the hell?*

I slam my laptop shut before deciding I must still be dreaming and go back to bed.

I wake up to the sound of shuffling coming from the hallway. It's just after five in the morning, and I'm convinced someone's broken into my house.

I quickly reach over and click the lamp on. I open my eyes just in time to see Bentley walking in with his luggage.

"Bentley?" I gasp, holding a hand to my chest. I wasn't expecting him back until this afternoon.

"Morning, sweetheart," he says in a soft tone, his face lighting up. "Sorry, I woke you up. I wanted to surprise you."

A hundred thoughts start rushing in—the dream, the images, and the email from Ava. Jesus...it's too much.

I feel the blood draining from my face. Seeing him after those vivid dreams is making it hard not to burst into tears and overreact.

"That's okay. I'm glad you arrived safely," I say weakly, not entirely awake yet. "I haven't slept well."

"I didn't either. I hate sleeping without you." He bends down next to the bed so our eyes are level. He cups my face as he softly kisses my lips. I inhale his scent, reminding myself that he's *mine*.

"I hate it, too. I think I need a companion," I offer lightly. "Perhaps a dog. One that won't mind my cuddling with it while you aren't home." I smile hopefully.

"A dog, huh? Well, I might not be gone as much anymore."

"What do you mean? Angie had you booked for practically the rest of the year."

He rubs his knuckles up and down my cheek, looking deep into my eyes. I have no idea what he's talking about, but I can tell he's definitely up to something.

"We'll talk about it later, okay? Let's get some sleep."

By the time I wake up again, it's well past noon. Bentley looks to be unconscious, so I don't wake him. I know he's always beat when he gets home from long flights.

After making coffee and breakfast, I decide to open my laptop and read Ava's emails again. I contemplate telling her to leave me the hell alone, and that I'm content with the closure I have, but the nagging part of me is eager to hear what she has to say.

With shaky and sweaty palms, I begin to write her back. I ask her when is the soonest she can meet me. I tell her I'll be bringing my fiancé with me because I don't trust her. At least she'll know that much.

Once I click send, my body shivers with nerves and anticipation. I can't believe my father's death has resurfaced again. His death has always hovered over me—the questions and never-ending obsession to know what happened. Once I knew—once I read his letter—I finally felt at peace.

Now this could change everything—*again*.

I tell Bentley about the email as soon as he's capable of retaining information. He's still groggy from traveling, but he's just as surprised as I was.

"It just seems odd, right? Like all these years later and now, she's contacting me. Do you think it has anything to do with the recent…rumors?"

"Ceci…a lot of people will suddenly appear in your life when fame or some kind of celebrity status hits you. The fact that you're engaged to me—that brings no surprise that you'd get an email from a family member or something—if it's even legit that is. Just…don't get your hopes up. She could definitely be a fraud, but it doesn't hurt to know for sure.

I bite my lip as I take in his words. He's absolutely right. It's like when someone wins the lottery or suddenly has an overnight success—long lost cousins and siblings surface looking for a hand out.

"Well, my hopes aren't up, but I just need you to go with me. Please," I plead with my eyes. He's sitting across the table from me going over emails in his phone.

"Of course, sweetheart. If she's not legit, I'll be able to tell. I can call in a favor as well if I have to." He takes a sip of his coffee that has been sitting untouched for the last twenty minutes. "The guys from the firm could do a more thorough search," he clarifies.

"Perfect." I smile back weakly. I notice how busy he is and hate interrupting him when he's catching up on work stuff. "Well, I'm going to go shower and get ready for the day. I'm sure there's something I'm supposed to be doing. An appointment, fitting, or something." I sigh.

I notice my phone flashing before I get undressed.

Cora: 9-1-1. Call me.

Shit.

"What's wrong?" I ask as soon as she picks up.

"I'm…oh, God…" She's breathing heavily. "I think…I'm…shit."

"Cora? Speak English. What happened?"

"I missed my period," she finally blurts out. I stifle a laugh as I put two-and-two together.

"Cora…breathe. Is Simon home?"

"No! The bastard left for his dad's cabin this morning." I know she's overreacting, but for Cora, she's panicking.

"Okay, I'm getting in the shower now. I'm coming over with a test, chocolate, and tums."

"Tums?" she asks.

"If you're pregnant, you should be feeling heartburn any day now," I reply with a smile although she can't see me.

"Don't say the P word. I'm not. I can't be."

I laugh. "I'm sorry. I wasn't aware it suddenly became a swear word."

"Shut up. I hate you right now. This isn't funny. Oh my God. My life is over," she spits out dramatically.

Yup…she's pregnant.

I fill Bentley in as soon as I finish getting dressed. He looks disappointed that I'm leaving just as he got back, but once I fill him in, he soon understands. He's used to *Cora 9-1-1 dilemmas.*

"We'll talk about what you wanted to discuss when I get back, okay?" I wrap my arms around his neck, showing him how desperate I am to have alone time with him.

"All right. Don't be too long. Tell Cora I want my fiancée back home soon. Preferably in one piece."

"I'll be fine." I kiss him softly. "Love you."

By the time I arrive at Cora's, she's hovering over the toilet. She doesn't look too well, so I put a cold washcloth over her forehead.

"You look like shit."

"And you look like the fucking Queen."

"That's the Cora I know and love."

"This sucks ass, Celia. Seriously. I'm on the pill. This isn't supposed to happen."

"You're aware the pill is only ninety-seven percent effective, right?"

"I thought that was just something they had to print on the box? You know…to avoid lawsuits and shit."

I purse my lips. "No…it's on there to actually tell you there's always a three percent chance you'll get pregnant."

"Son-of-a-bitch."

I walk to the kitchen, grab a bottle of water, and hand it to her. "Drink this, mama. You need to stay hydrated."

"Don't call me that. Seriously, Simon is going to freak."

I narrow my brows at her. "Why? You guys are married. You both have jobs. You have a home, two cars, and life together. Most people would die for the stability you guys have created. This is actually a perfect time to have a baby." I try to calm her, but Cora is anything but calm.

"Exactly. It was perfect. Now I'm going to get what…cramps. Fat.

Ginormous boobs. Gas. Oh, God." She sinks to the floor, covering her face up.

"Your child will definitely have a career in drama."

"I hate you," she mumbles.

"All right, get up. Time to pee."

She groans, finally getting off the floor. I hand her the test and smile. "Do you know how to use this?"

"I've taken a few tests in my day, thank you," she snarls.

"Well, then, stop being a pussy and take it already."

She rolls her eyes as she starts unbuttoning her jeans. "God, I can't wait until you're knocked up."

"Let's hope you don't have to drag me off the bathroom floor."

She chuckles lightly as she angles herself and aims for the stick. I try not to laugh, but the way she's sitting has me bursting out unintentionally.

"Stop laughing at me. I'm going to end up peeing on myself." She laughs with me, unable to control it anymore.

"Well, at least I got you off the floor and laughing." I smirk.

She's finally successful on aiming for the stick. She covers it and sets it on the counter. I start my phone timer for three minutes, anxiously waiting to see that little plus line.

"You'll make a good mom," I say sincerely. "You know you have me. And Katelynn. And hopefully, Simon." I laugh. "You'll have us all."

Her lips curve into a small smile, her head nodding. "I know. I'm just scared. Simon and I are just getting our careers off the ground. I don't want to mess up what we have."

"It's normal to be scared, Cora. But it won't mess anything up. You guys are going to be the most adorable family," I gush.

She closes the gap between us and wraps her arms around me. "Thanks, Celia. I love you."

I hug her back, telling her I love her, too. The moment feels surreal. We've been through almost everything together. Since we were kids, we've experienced so much together and now here we were about to find out whether or not she is expecting. It feels good knowing I have someone solid like her in my life.

My phone beeps, alerting us it's time.

"Ready?" I ask, smiling.

She nods. "You look for me."

"You sure?"

"Yes. Just tell me."

"All right." I turn around and grab the stick. I can't stop the smile that spreads wildly across my face. Cora's about to become a mom.

"Well?" she asks anxiously from behind me. "Don't leave me hanging!" I feel her bouncing back and forth between her feet.

I spin around, trying to cover up the stupid grin on my face. "It's…" She raises her brows, waiting for me to finally tell her, and then I smile and laugh lightly as I continue, "positive!"

Her expression drops as her eyes widen in fear. "No…really?" she asks, almost giddy. "Don't fuck with me, Celia."

I laugh at her bluntness. "I'm not. Swear to God. See?" I show her the dark, pink plus sign that proves it all. "Congrats! I'm so happy for you!" I wrap her in a hug as I feel her body convulsing with tears. I know she's worried, but she has nothing to worry about, because she and Simon are going to make wonderful parents.

CHAPTER THIRTEEN
BENTLEY

OUR LIVES WEREN'T ALWAYS this confusing. There was a time when Ceci was going to college and I was driving to Omaha twice a week to teach kickboxing classes. Moving to Lincoln to be close to her was the best decision of my life. It gave us the time to just be together without any of the drama or spotlight. We became isolated in our little bubble, only coming up for air when necessary. At times, it was near perfect.

Now our lives are a breathing nightmare. I don't feel secure anymore. It feels as if our safe little bubble has been popped, and there's no way to get back in. Our security blanket has been ripped from underneath us, and the only way to surface is to go through the agony and pain of what's to come.

Ceci's happy at her new job. It's been two weeks since her interview and she started almost immediately. Every night she comes home with a bright smile on her face, telling me everything she learned. Her boss, Coach Tanner, is the one training her. He's an older guy in his fifties, so I feel a bit more comfortable with her spending time with him all day. Although she has a degree in sports management, she needs some on-the-job training. College baseball season just started, so it's fortunate she's a fast learner.

We talked briefly a couple weeks ago about my decision to step back from modeling, but knowing I have contracts, I can't just quit. Now that she's working, she's much more understanding of my demanding schedule. So far, I've been able to get Angie to postpone some of the stuff she had booked. She always preferred I did face-to-face interviews, but I told her she's going to have to accept phone-only interviews for a while. I also told her shoots needed to be national from now on. All the overseas traveling is starting to become too much, especially when the wedding is only three months away.

"Hey, babe!" Ceci calls as she walks in the door. She heads right for me at the breakfast bar and gives me a quick kiss on the cheek. "How was your day?"

"Fine, how was yours?" I fold the newspaper up that I was reading.

"Great. I think I'm finally getting the hang of it. They moved me into my own office today and even started giving me a schedule. I start working one-on-one with the players at the end of the week."

"Awesome." I smile and spin around, facing her as she sets her things on the kitchen table. "Any chance you get off early tomorrow night?"

She wrinkles her forehead for a moment before answering. "I can ask. Why? What's tomorrow?"

I raise my brows at her. Clearly, she wouldn't forget. Girls don't forget their birthdays.

"Um…the fourteenth."

"Oh my God. Is it really?" she gasps. "Wow, I didn't even realize it was the middle of the month already. I've been so busy lately. Totally blew past the dates."

I sit awkwardly, wondering if she would've even realized it had I not mentioned it.

"So…" I step off the stool and walk toward her. "Any chance I can have my fiancée for one night?" I wrap my arms around her. "You use to go nuts over your birthday."

"I only went nuts because it meant I'd for sure have you all to myself."

"Well, I can do one better. You can have me to yourself as long as you want."

She smiles widely. "Then I will definitely get done early." I lean in and kiss her. The past two weeks have been a bit rocky with her starting the job, the emails from Ava, and the press still pushing for comments.

I have something romantic planned, as usual. The past couple of years we were traveling during her birthday. Since I never knew the area well, we'd stay locally around the hotel and find cool things to do. But this year, I wanted it to be extra special.

"We could always start the activities early," I suggest, cupping her face and leaning in to kiss her. "You know, just in case we don't have time to fit everything in." I smirk seductively against her mouth.

"Since when have you not been able to fit everything in?" she teases.

"Touché." I crush my lips to hers, desperate to feel her against me. I know she's been holding a lot in lately, not wanting to express how upset she is about everything. I know she's overwhelmed, so I want to help her relieve some of that stress. "Let's get these clothes off," I offer, pulling her jacket down her shoulders. She continues stroking her tongue with mine as we fight to get her shirt off next.

"Strip," she says, taking me off guard. She begins taking her shoes and jeans off. She points a finger up and down my body. "Strip, mister. I'm not going to be the only one naked."

A smile spreads widely across my face, as I happily oblige. "Someone's in a hurry."

I watch as she pulls her panties down to the floor and unhooks her bra. "My body's missed you. It's not in a very patient mood right now." Her voice is laced with seduction, grabbing my cock's attention instantly.

As soon as I'm finished tearing everything off, I grab her around the waist and immediately guide her body to mine.

"I like the way you think," I growl, setting her up on the kitchen table. "Patience was never a good quality of mine anyway."

She laughs, tilting her head back. "That's an understatement." My lips find her neck, immediately drawn to her blistering skin. Her body is on fire, her nails clawing at me to get inside her.

"So anxious…"

She begins stroking my cock as my lips surrender to the skin just below her collarbone. I moan against her flesh, loving the way her hands work me. She's aggressive in her touch, but not to the point where it's too much—it's fucking perfect.

"Mm…" I hear a throaty moan release from her lips.

"Lean back," I order, standing up. With her ass on the table and legs around my waist, I release one of her legs and push it back toward her face. "Let's see how stretched out for me you are." I grin widely, knowing she's *always* stretched out for me.

"Like you need to doubt me," she mocks, stretching her leg higher. I grip my cock in one hand as I hold her thigh up with the other. I rub against her slit torturously, making sure she's wet and ready.

"Fuck, you're wet." I push in slightly, just enough to make her back arch in anticipation. The tight sensation is almost too much, but God, it's amazing.

"Ah, God…" Her head falls back as she tries to reach anything to grip.

I push all the way in, letting her body get used to it before thrusting against her. She relaxes, taking everything in easily.

"Jesus Christ," I growl, clenching my eyes closed. My body heats—overwhelming love and anticipation taking over. I pull out before driving back in harder and deeper, nearly taking her over the edge. Her fingers claw at my arms, grasping for any kind of support. I lean down, allowing her to hold me as her body clenches around me. "Yes, baby… let go," I demand.

Her eyes pop open on command, but rather than overwhelming euphoria as expected, I see *fear*.

"Stop!" she shouts. "Please, stop." Her body goes rigid, pushing me away and finding her footing.

"W-What's wrong? Did I hurt you? Are you all right?" I spit out frantically. I have no idea what I did, but she's completely panicking. She climbs off the table and begins grabbing her clothes off the floor, covering herself up. "Ceci, talk to me." I grab my briefs and slip them on quick.

"I-I can't…I just need a moment, please." She begins sobbing, something I haven't seen her do in years.

"Ceci, you're killing me…" I try to grab her, but she races down the hallway, closing the bedroom door behind her.

Shit.

CHAPTER FOURTEEN
CECILIA

I DON'T EVEN KNOW what happened, or how. Bentley and I have been together several times in the past two weeks, but suddenly, tonight something changed.

I love when Bentley is spontaneous and just picks me up and sets me anywhere when he has that wanton need and desire to have me. I live for moments like that with him, so when flashes started spiraling into my mind of him and Hannah, I couldn't take it anymore. I felt physical pain as my mind replayed the dream, making me feel ill at the image.

I don't know why my mind is trying to kill me, but it feels like I'm at war. I love Bentley and want nothing more than to share my life with him, but it's starting to haunt me in a way I can't control anymore. I don't know how to move on from something I can't change.

"Ceci, please...talk to me." I hear his pleas from outside the door. God, I'm so embarrassed. I feel sick. I don't know how to explain to him what I feel—or rather see. This is such a disaster.

"I just need a moment," I say, hoping he can understand that I need to figure out my own feelings before I can even try to explain them to him.

"All right..." I hear the worry in his voice. "I'll be right here. I'm not going anywhere, sweetheart." He voice is sweet, tender. He's not demanding or impatient, but rather, I hear the heartbreak in his tone.

I take a few moments to compose myself, putting my clothes back on before facing him. I hardly know what to say, but I know I owe him something. I've never run out on him before like that.

I inhale. Then I take a deep breath before I exhale slowly. I grip the door handle and slowly open it. Bentley's standing against the wall, looking defeated and worried. As soon as he sees me, he pushes himself off and closes the gap between us.

"Are you okay? God, I…I'm sorry. Just tell me what happened, and I can fix it." His words are rushed, eager to do whatever it takes to make me feel better.

"Bentley, stop," I tell him before he starts freaking out. "It's nothing you did. And it's nothing you can fix."

"I don't understand." His face drops worried I'm about to give him bad news.

I turn around and walk to the bed, motioning for him to follow me. I sit down and wait for him to sit next to me, knowing I need to just spill it.

"I had a dream a couple of weeks ago…" I pause, needing to take a deep breath before continuing. "At first, it was you and me, and the next it was you and Hannah. I woke up, gasping for air and sweating. I ended up throwing up twice at the images alone, and then they kind of started haunting me randomly." I feel his body tense as I talk about Hannah. "Tonight, they came back. It was out of nowhere. One minute it was just you and I on the table, and the next I was above watching you with Hannah…" I bow my head, feeling embarrassed. "I started to feel sick the second the images came to mind and that's when I freaked out. It was the only way to stop them," I explain.

"Why didn't you tell me this before?"

I shrug. "Because it was only a dream. I felt better when you arrived home and things were fine. I mean, we've been intimate since then, so there was really no reason to say anything. I knew you were already stressing over her, and I didn't want to add to it."

He cups my face, tilting my chin up toward him. "You should always tell me these kinds of things, even if you think I'm too stressed. I want to be able to help."

"But that's just it—" My voice gets louder. "You *can't* help me. You can't do anything about it. I know she means nothing to you, yet my mind keeps torturing me. I just…I just need to wait it out. It'll go away, eventually."

"This is all my fault. Fuck…I shouldn't have freaked out over the interview. Had I just let it go, you wouldn't be stressing over it as much."

"If you weren't bothered by it, I'd probably be upset about that, too. It would've made me think you missed her or something, although deep inside I know that's not true."

"That's how I felt with the Jason pictures," he confesses. "You didn't seem bothered by it."

I shrug again. I hadn't even thought of it like that. I was upset over the pictures, because they upset Bentley, but in reality, they meant nothing. Those pictures captured two friends having coffee and an innocent conversation. However, now that he brings it up, I can see his side of it.

"I'm sorry," I apologize genuinely. "I hadn't thought of it like that before now. I guess I'm just insecure at times." I lower my head, ashamed I was feeling this way when he's given me no reason.

"Don't be sorry," he growls, taking me off guard. "I never want you to be sorry for something that we don't control. The media, tabloids, photographers—all of them are only after one thing. Money. They don't care how they get it, who they hurt, or what they ruin. But we can't let them anymore. I don't want that for us."

I nod, agreeing with everything he's saying. And now I know I have to tell him the truth.

"I read her interview," I say softly, unable to keep eye contact with him. "That's what triggered the dream, I think. You were gone still and I was beyond curious. Once I started it though, I wish I hadn't, but I couldn't stop. It was like some kind of self-torture." My face is expressionless as I recall the night I read her words about the length of Bentley's cock.

I see him brush both hands over his face in frustration. I swallow hard, waiting for the outburst he's about to lay on me.

"I saw Hannah," he states softly, looking down. "In L.A.," he clarifies.

"What do you mean? I thought Angie was handling all that." I turn and look at him.

"She was but it wasn't good enough. At first, I wanted to find her and chew her ass out. And then once I saw her—"

"What?" I urge him on.

"She's an addict, Ceci." He turns and faces me. "She's skin and bones. Her hair is falling out and she looked like absolute shit. Her apartment—"

"Oh my God! You went to her apartment?" I know I shouldn't get off task, but I can't help feeling uncomfortable with the fact that he was there.

"It was the only way to find her. She has no job to go to. Besides, it was barely an apartment. It was awful." I hear the pain in his voice and decide I need to stop overreacting. She's obviously in trouble.

"What did she say?"

He looks down, ashamed. "She blames my mother that her career tanked. Her job was everything to her. Once it was gone, she fell into drugs and just...wilted to nothing."

"Wow," I breathe out. "I wouldn't have expected that from her."

"Me, either."

"So what happened?"

"I asked her to retract her interview."

"Is she?" I ask hopeful.

"She's too sick to do anything, Ceci." He looks up at me again. "I put her in a rehab center. She needed help."

My eyes raise as my shoulders push back in surprise. "You what? You sent her to a rehab clinic?"

"She needed the help," he says simply. "She would've died had I just left her there."

"I can't believe you didn't tell me," I remark, my face expressionless as I debate with myself on being upset with him or not.

"I know. I'm sorry. I should've, but I just wasn't sure how much more you could take."

"So does that mean you're keeping in contact with her now?"

"Not her directly. I've been emailing and speaking to her counselors. Since I checked her in, and am paying to cover her time there, I told them I needed to stay updated."

"You're paying for it, too?" I squeal. "Bentley...do you know how messed up that sounds? The woman who's trying to sabotage your career and ruin our lives is the same woman you're now trying to save?" I stand up, needing to distance myself. The words come out harsher than I meant for them to, but I was pretty certain I had to still be dreaming.

"Ceci," he growls, his voice firm and his tone low. "It was the right thing to do."

I sit back down, needing a moment to think. If I'm upset, then I'm the bitch that wishes Hannah would've eventually overdosed, and she would've gotten what she deserved. Otherwise, I can be that girl that understands Bentley felt he had a responsibility to uphold. I'm still not sure which way I should feel.

Before I can apologize for the way I acted, I feel the bed shift as Bentley stands up and walks out of our room without a word.

I end up falling asleep on the bed by myself. I cried myself to sleep, harder than I have in a long time. I kept waiting for Bentley to walk in, but he never did.

I wake up to my panties being pulled down. My eyes blink open, but it's pitch black and I can't see a thing. I hear Bentley's pants as he towers over me.

"What are you—"

"Shh." He puts his mouth over me, slowly pushing his tongue inside, and massaging it with mine. "I want to make love to you," he says effortlessly. It's hard to argue with that, but I can't get past the fact that he just left me in here.

"No…" I say softly, pressed up against his lips. "You walked out on me," I pout. "You left me."

He rubs the pad of his thumb under my eye as a tear sneaks out. "I'd never leave you, Ceci." His tone is gentle, tender. "I always fear losing you. My lifestyle being too much and one day you deciding you can't handle it. I lost you once and it scares the shit out of me that I'll lose you again. So I called Angie and fired her. Then I called my agency and told them I was done and to shove their contracts up their asses. And then I called my travel agency and got us plane tickets to get the fuck out of here. So, no, I didn't leave you." I feel him grin against my mouth. "Now, can I make love to my future wife?"

I would've gasped and said a crap load of *oh my Gods* had Bentley let me. He covers my mouth again with his, giving me no room to speak or ask questions. He grazes my shirt up, slowly lifting it over my head before dropping it to the floor. I moan in his mouth—giving him my silent apology that he never gives me the chance to say—as my hands claw at his biceps while he enters me slowly.

"Good morning, sweetheart." He cups my face and kisses me tenderly on the lips. It's barely after three in the morning. "Happy birthday." He smiles down at me as we stand in the bedroom. "It's going to be a long day. We've got to get going soon."

I smile back. "You mind telling me where we're going?" I ask giddily, packing my suitcase. "I need to know what to pack," I whine.

He cocks a smile and shakes his head. "It really doesn't matter—you won't be wearing clothes."

I scowl, pretending to not be impressed with his answer. "You always say that and then I end up wearing the wrong thing," I pout. "At least give me a hint."

"Bikini weather," is all he says, backing out of our room, smirking at me. I pull my lower lip into my teeth, hiding the stupid grin that's formed on my face. I'm in complete awe that Bentley's planned something—something that gets us away from all the drama. "Oh…" He pops his head back in, only standing halfway into the doorway. "Pack your passport."

My jaw drops before I can get a word in. He backs out into the hallway before I can interrogate him. I have no idea what he's up to, but I know I can't wait.

Bentley gives me absolutely no hints on our way to the airport. The only thing he's told me is that we'll be spending seven days and six nights in 'paradise.' I was reluctant at first, because I just started working my new job. However, Bentley told me he spoke with my boss this morning and handled it all for me, which meant I could truly enjoy every minute of whatever Bentley was up to.

CHAPTER FIFTEEN
BENTLEY

I LOVE SURPRISING CECI any chance I can get, but this'll be the surprise of a lifetime. And I can't fucking wait, especially since it's her twenty-fourth birthday.

I've worked with my travel agent for years now. So when I decided we both needed out of here, she was the first one I called to make arrangements. She's always been good at getting last minute flights for me. Everything she has helped me plan is going to be beyond amazing.

The flight has one layover and overall, will take twenty-one hours before we arrive at St. George, Grenada in the Caribbean's. Although it's a long and grueling flight, it's one of the most beautiful places on Earth. I booked with one of the best resorts that I know will give Ceci everything she deserves.

"I hope I remembered to pack everything," she says, going through her mental checklist as she always does.

"Sweetheart," I interrupt her pretending to make checkmarks in the air. "If there's anything we forgot the staff will be more than accommodating."

She latches onto my arm, snuggling her body against mine as we sit in first class of the last plane.

"When do I get to know what we're doing?"

"When we arrive," I say flatly. She knows we're headed to the Caribbean now, but she has no idea exactly where or why.

"Just maybe a small hint?" She tilts her head up to look at me with pleading eyes. I let out a soft chuckle at the way she continues to be persistent.

"Okay, fine." I clear my throat. "We'll be doing something we've never done before."

"Hmm…" she thinks it over a moment. "Are we swimming with sharks? Please tell me we aren't. Ooh! Maybe dolphins? I'd love to swim with dolphins once." I raise my brows at her, trying to keep a straight face. "Am I warm?"

"Not even close." I laugh.

"You love this, don't you? You could be kidnapping me for all I know. My family and friends would have no idea where to even start looking for me." She huffs in a pretend pout. She hates not getting her way, and it's just too damn funny seeing her get all worked up.

I lean in, bringing my lips directly to her ear and whisper, "I promise you it's going to be incredible. Just enjoy yourself." I lightly kiss just below her ear, her body shivers in response.

She grins, looking back up at me. "All right, fine. I trust you." She leans her head against my shoulder and proceeds to sleep the rest of the way.

My body is all jacked up as we land and grab a cab to the resort that is only a few miles away. I'm beyond excited to see her reaction as she sees where we'll be staying the next week.

When I viewed the pictures online, I knew it was just right for her. The ocean is clear blue, the sand is white; the entire view bright and sunny and unlike anything I've ever seen. Once I saw the photos— that's when I knew—this was the perfect place to elope.

"Are you ready?" I whisper against her ear, my hands covering her eyes. I made sure she kept them closed as a driver brought us to the resort. Once we arrived, he unloaded our luggage as I helped Ceci out of the cab, her eyes remaining closed.

"Yes, I'm dying!" She giggles. "Please let me look."

With the time difference, it's only eleven pm here, making it still her birthday.

I kiss her neck lightly before whispering, "Happy Birthday, sweetheart," and uncover her eyes. My hands land on her hips as she lets out an audible gasp, her hands covering her mouth as she takes in the full view of where we are.

"Oh my God! Are you serious? Oh my God, it's gorgeous!" She

spins around and waits for me to confirm it. "Holy crap," she shrieks. Her arms lock around my neck, pulling me into her. "It's stunning."

"I'm glad you like it."

"I-I fucking love it. I can't believe this is where we're staying! This is like where A-celebs would stay or something," she continues rambling.

I narrow my brows at her, hiding the laughter that's eager to burst out. "Are you saying I'm not A-level type?" I pretend to sound offended, but it's ruined by the laughter that escapes her throat.

"Of course, you are, babe. Definitely." She gives a final nod before she can no longer conceal her laughter.

I grab her neck and pull her mouth on mine. I stroke her tongue with mine, filling her in a way that only I can do. She moans in my mouth, her hands flat against my chest as we give the other guests a show.

"I think we need to move this to the room," I suggest seductively.

"Twenty-one hours hasn't done anything to kill your drive," she teases as we lock hands and make our way through the entrance. I hadn't even noticed our driver had put our luggage on a cart and already hauled it into the hotel lobby.

"Nothing could ever kill it when I'm around you, sweetheart. Get ready." I smirk in her direction although I'm one-hundred percent serious.

"I can't wait for you to see the room. Took a lot of convincing to book this room. Apparently, it books months in advance."

I pull her against my chest before slamming us into a wall. "You always have a way of getting what you want, don't you?"

I dip my face into the nape of her neck, kissing a trail up to her jawline. "That's how I got you, isn't it? A little persuasion and sweet talk."

She bursts out in laughter, nodding in agreement. "I guess so."

We finally make it to our suite. I booked the South Seas Grande Butler Suite with a private pool. It allows us our privacy but is close enough to enjoy everything else the resort has to offer. It's like a beachside house that comes with room service and housekeeping.

"All right, gorgeous. Get ready." I open the door and guide her into the suite. The entire thing is stunning and even I'm in awe at the replica of the pictures.

"Ohh, my God, Bentley..." She starts spinning around, taking everything in as we walk through the open-floor concept. The bedroom is a part of the living space with TV and bar area and to the left of the bed is a dinette kitchen table. There are windows all around with long drapes to open or cover them.

I watch as she walks around, touching everything and taking it all in. She walks behind the wall that the bed is against and into the bathroom.

"Holy shit!" she shrieks. I follow in after her and notice that this is not a bathroom. No, this is a suite all on its own with a hot tub set in the middle and a huge walk-in shower and a countertop that goes for days. "I'm not sure I'll be leaving this bathroom."

I laugh, taking her hand and guiding her to the patio doors that are wide open, the perfect amount of breeze blowing in.

The doors lead right into the pool. There aren't any stairs or anything. You literally go from the house to the pool. It's incredible.

"Wow…this… oh, my God, this is perfect." She wraps her arms around me and secures herself to my chest.

"I wanted it to be perfect for you, sweetheart. The perfect getaway."

She leans back, wiping back a tear that's escaped. "It is. I can't believe you planned this in only a couple hours. You're insane." She lets out a half-throaty laugh. "In a good way, of course." She leans up on her tiptoes and crushes her lips to mine. "Thank you," she says softly. "Thank you for taking us somewhere safe and new and somewhere we can reconnect without all the added drama. I love you."

I pull her closer, wrapping my hands under her ass and grasping her thighs so they lock around my hips. Our lips find each other eagerly as we fight the need to have each other, but I'm not fighting. I'm giving into everything we want.

I walk back toward the bed, laying her gently on top. I crawl over her, keeping her mouth on mine as I wrestle with the button on her jeans.

"Did you super glue these or something?" I pout, too eager to give a damn. I sit up, straddling a leg on each side of her. I grip each side of the button and pull, popping the button and yanking the zipper down all at the same time. I smirk at her. "That's better."

"You could've just asked for help," she says, amused by my eagerness to get them off.

"Well, it's not like you'll need them anytime soon." I crawl off her body, freeing the jeans off her legs.

"Those were my favorite pair," she says seriously, as I toss them to the floor.

"I'll buy you ten more." I kneel in between her legs and spread them wide. "Now, stop talking." I grin slyly as I push her panties aside and immediately stroke a finger against her slit. I feel how wet she is for me, making my cock instantly aroused. I nuzzle my nose and lips against her pussy, inhaling her perfect scent.

She moans and fists both hands in my hair as I begin licking up her pussy, lapping my tongue in and out of her. Her body arches, tensing every time I drive my tongue in harder. I insert a finger as I suck on her clit, making her body shiver against me.

"Mm...God. Yes..." she pants hard as I continue eating her. Fuck, I can't control myself as I insert a second finger and begin sucking against her harder and faster. "Oh, shit. My God..." she moans out, her body trembling harder now against me. Her body tenses as she releases against my tongue, her delicious flavor filling my mouth.

"Good girl," I praise. I lick up her slit once more before pulling my fingers out. I crawl up the bed and lean in to kiss her. She surprises me by grabbing my hand and breaking the kiss.

She brings my hand to her mouth, closes her eyes, and devours my fingers. She wraps her lips around them as she sucks her juices off them.

"Jesus Christ," I growl. My cock is rock hard, but the sight of what she does about brings me over the edge.

"Mm..." she moans as she thoroughly sucks my fingers. "I can see why you spend so much time down there," she mocks.

I laugh at the way she's taunting me. "You're going to fucking kill me."

She releases my hand and scoots herself up, so we're both sitting up. She lowers both hands down to her shirt, pulling it up and over her head. I watch mesmerized as she unhooks her bra and dangles it off her finger before slowly releasing it to the floor.

My body is in overdrive now as heat and passion fueling my actions. I grip her jaw, pulling her toward me as I crush our mouths together. I pull her on top of me, her legs straddling my waist. I'm in full clothing and she's only in her panties. I'm ready to combust out of my jeans at any moment.

I lean up on one elbow and grip her body to me, her legs wrapping around my waist. I stand up and walk us to the bathroom. I set her down on the countertop as I back up and strip all my clothes off.

"That's better," she says amused.

"Almost." I grin. I hook my fingers in her panties and pull them down her legs, letting them pool to the floor. "Now *that's* better."

She's expecting me to take her right then and there—which I'm eager as fuck to do—but I know we are both sore and exhausted from the long flight.

I turn around and head toward the Jacuzzi that's at the center of the bathroom. I turn the hot water on and turn the timer on.

"Why must you torture me?" she asks as I walk back toward her. She links her arms around my neck and pulls me into her legs. My cock is right at her opening—just one more step and I'd be balls deep inside her.

"Sweetheart, right now you're the one torturing me." I smirk. "Stop." I try to take a step back, but she holds her grasp. She arches her body, letting her legs dangle off more. She pulls me once more, making the tip rub against her.

"Baby...I need it," she pleads. Her fingers claw at my shoulders. I try to hide the smirk of amusement as she whines. "Just a little bit..." she grins.

I laugh, holding her hips in place. "There's no such thing as just a little bit."

"Fine, go turn off the water and fuck me right here on this *very* expensive counter. I want it rough and hard, and I'm not taking no for an answer."

"So bossy," I mock, loosening my grip on her and walking backward to the tub. As requested, I turn the water off but continue standing there. I cross my arms over my chest and look directly into her desperate, greedy eyes. "Bend over," I demand.

I watch as she hesitates a moment, but soon, hops off and bends over the counter as I asked.

"Spread your legs and arch your back," I say, walking back toward the bedroom. "Don't move." I walk over to our luggage and grab a bottle of lube.

I walk back in and stand directly behind her. I press a hand to her back and push down, getting her to arch her back deeper for me.

"Perfect," I whisper. I grab my cock in one hand and begin stroking it up and down her ass cheeks. "Wider," I demand. She adjusts herself, pushing her feet farther apart. "That's my girl."

With my free hand, I squeeze the lube over my erection and rub it over my shaft with the other hand. I make sure to get the tip nice and wet for what I have planned for us.

I rub a hand up and down her back again, making sure she stays nice and low on the countertop. I lean down, gently kissing her shoulder and whisper, "Relax, sweetheart."

I stand back up and firmly grip her ass cheeks, spreading them apart. With one hand, I grab my shaft and begin pushing against her tight entrance. I slide in slowly, letting her body get used to the intrusion. I watch as she holds on firmly, relaxing against me. I push in again, her body widening as I continue going in further.

"Fuck, sweetheart. That's so good." Jesus, that's tight. It feels like a vice grip is holding my dick, but the second I begin thrusting against her, her body relaxes and opens up for me.

"Holy shit," she pants out. I haven't taken her this way in a long time, so the sensation was overwhelming.

"Jesus…" I growl as her body accepts all of me. I thrust against her, pulling in and out. "So fucking good."

"Mm…" Her fingers claw at the tile as I grip her hips and pound into her harder.

"God, baby." With one final thrust, she cries out in ecstasy the same time I release deep inside of her.

CHAPTER SIXTEEN
CECILIA

I LEAN my back against Bentley's chest as we sit in the hot tub together. The boiling water soothes every sore surface on my body and feels incredible. Bentley wraps his arms around me, securing me tightly against him.

"I think we've officially christened another piece of the world," he says against my ear, grinning.

I let out a whine. "I can't feel my legs."

"Lucky for you…" he pauses, letting his lips linger on my neck, "we get to hide out here for the next six nights. Room service and a pool less than twenty feet away."

"You really thought of everything," I remark. "I don't know how you do it. You always plan for it all."

"Oh, sweetheart." He pulls my earlobe into his mouth and sucks hard. "You have no idea," he whispers.

We end up soaking in the tub for at least two hours. The quiet time we spend together is perfect. It's such a relief after the past few weeks we've endured.

"Did Ava ever set up a time to meet you?" he asks as we sit together at the small table. It's two a.m., but we were both starving and there's 24/7 room service here.

"She was going to book a flight for a few weeks, I guess."

"Are you nervous?" he asks cautiously, shoving a forkful of pancake in his mouth.

"Yeah, but after a few emails, I feel she's being honest with me. I don't know what her intentions are, but I'm eager to hear what she has to say." We've been up for almost twenty-four hours now with the exception of napping on the plane here and there. "I'm exhausted. I'm pretty sure I'll be sleeping the next twelve hours." I yawn, setting my fork down in surrender. I don't even have the energy to feed myself.

He smirks at me before saying, "I'll give you eight hours. And then you're mine."

"I'm always yours." I smile back. "But I'm about to go belong to the bed." I point behind me, standing up and pushing my chair in. "Are you going to join me?" He raises his brows at me and begins chasing me toward the bed, catching me just in time as we fall against the mattress.

He grabs the covers and pulls them back for us to get in. I snuggle up next to him, tracing my finger along his tattoos as I fall into a solid, deep sleep.

The sun beaming on my face wakes me up. It's well after noon, but Bentley is nowhere to be seen. I swing my legs off the bed and stretch my arms over my head. My body is freaking sore...for many reasons.

I walk over to the table where I see a note in his handwriting.

Sweetheart,
You looked so gorgeous snuggled in bed that I didn't want to wake you.
I went to make some arrangements for us later. I'll be back soon.
Love,
Bentley
P.S. Check the fridge.

I set the note down and walk to the mini fridge that's next to the bar. I open the door and find a silver platter filled with chocolate covered strawberries.

I grab the platter with a stupid grin on my face. I love when he does things like this. It's always so unexpected and thoughtful. There's a tiny note folded on top.

Sweetheart,
Enjoy your delicious strawberries overlooking the beach. It's
gorgeous.
Love,
Bentley
P.S. Wear your suit.

I smile as I pop the first strawberry in my mouth, devouring the chocolate shell. I walk to my luggage and pull out my black and red swimsuit. I put a white sundress over it. I don't have a clue what he's planning, but I'm excited and eager to find out.

The warm breeze hits me, putting a smile on my face. I walk down the path that leads me to the luxurious beach. The sand is perfect, warm and soft. The water is so clear, I can almost see through it. The sky is a perfect shade of blue, almost mesmerizing. And the sun is shining directly above me warming my skin. The whole view is stunning—something you'd see in magazine.

I'm not sure what I should be looking for. Bentley could be up to anything at this point. I begin walking and looking for any clues or a trace of him when something catches my eye.

There's a cliff off the beach nearby. I see a white arch in the distance on top of the cliff. White flowers are intertwined in the vinyl of the arch and two strands of white tulle are tied to it. From where I'm standing, it looks like a wedding arch.

The curious side of me wants to walk closer and examine it, but as soon as I take a step, Bentley comes into view.

He's standing on top of the cliff next to the white arch. He looks adorable in khaki's and a purple button-up shirt. His hair is styled wildly and his eyes are glued on me.

He smiles down and waves his hand at me, motioning for me to follow him up there. A smirk creeps up on my lips, wondering what in the hell he's up to.

I climb up the cliff to where he's standing. He's directly under the arch, which is nearing the edge of the cliff and another man. Once the other guy comes into view, I flash him a look of confusion.

"What are you doing? Are you crazy?" I shout over the waves. The wind is faster up here, blowing my hair into my face.

"I am crazy," he admits, taking my hand and guiding us both under the arch. "Incredibly, madly, crazy in love with you. So insanely in love with you that I planned this for you. Something I knew you wanted all along. Something I knew I had to give you. Something I want to mark as our day on the calendar and celebrate it every year for the rest of our lives." His voice is low, but every word is genuine and serious. I continue staring into his eyes, wondering if this is really happening.

"I want to give you the wedding of a lifetime." He looks out into the water. "The wedding you would've wanted had you been able to plan it your way. I couldn't live with myself knowing you didn't get that. So, sweetheart…" he pauses, pulling me in closer to his chest, "marry me, today. Marry me and be my wife. Make me the fucking luckiest man on Earth."

I gasp at his words, my eyes widening as he confesses exactly what we're doing. "What? How? We don't have our marriage license. I don't have something blue or borrowed. Are you sure?" I ramble without thinking. My head is spinning at the absolutely perfect set-up Bentley has given me.

He smiles and replies, "Sweetheart, this isn't a marriage ceremony. This is a vows ceremony. I don't need a piece of paper to call you my wife. This day will forever be *our* day."

"Really?" I cry out, tears beginning to run down my cheeks. "You did all this for me?" The trip. The perfect suite. The incredible ceremony. It's too good to be true, but I know Bentley stops at nothing to make me happy.

"Really. So?" He lets go of my hand and digs into his pocket, revealing two wedding bands. "What do you say, sweetheart?"

I can hardly believe it, everything I wanted for our wedding—down to the purple color—is about to happen. I'm beside myself with emotions right now.

"I can't believe you did this!" I cry out again, covering my mouth with both hands. "Yes!" I drop my hands and lock them around his neck. "Yes, of course!" I crush my lips to his, soaking up this perfect moment.

It takes me a few seconds to remember we aren't alone. I back up slightly and eye the guy next to us.

"This is Miguel. He's going to do the readings."

I nod, surreal feelings of happiness overwhelming me. We stand across from each other, facing each other as we lock hands. Miguel begins with passages from the Bible, telling us everything we are vowing and committing to.

"Ceci, you may begin your vows." He nods toward me and my eyes bulge out of my head. I haven't written my damn vows yet. Shit. Bentley senses my panic and grabs my chin so I look up at him.

"Sweetheart, don't overthink it. Just speak from the heart."

I nod in understanding and clear my throat. "Everything about this feels like a dream. I keep waiting to wake up one day and find out I've fantasized the whole thing since I laid eyes on you in my *interview*." I grin at him, remember the exact moment. "From the moment you finally told me you loved me, I haven't been able to imagine my life without you. From the moment you asked me to be your wife, I knew it'd be the greatest pleasure of my life. And now here, committing myself to you, I can't think of anything that feels more right, more perfect, and more destined to happen." I quickly wipe the tears off my cheeks so I can continue. "I promise to give you every part of me. The love, the tears, and the good, bad, and crazy moments. I promise to love you with everything I have, to always be honest with you, and to tell you every day how much I love you." I swallow hard as the emotions become overwhelming. "I promise to always encourage you, support you, and stand by you. I promise you every day for the rest of my life."

I've never seen Bentley the way he's looking at me right now. He's staring at me with such raw and real emotion that I'm not sure how much longer I'm going to be able to hold it in.

BENTLEY

I'm captivated by every word she's saying. The way she expresses her love to me is almost too much to handle. I love Ceci more than anything in my entire life, but God, right now, I could explode with the love I feel for her at this very moment.

"Bentley, you can begin your vows now," Miguel directs.

I feel like I'm sweating and it's not from the heat.

I squeeze her hands in mine as I begin. "Wow, I'm not so sure I can compete with that. God, sweetheart. There are hardly words to express the way I feel for you. You came into my life like a tsunami—

unexpected all while leaving traces of you behind. You turned my life upside down. You made me feel for the first time in a long time, which scared me, but I was willing to risk it because I knew you were something special. I knew you were worth remembering when I never fully forgot you. As much as I tried to convince my mind, my heart knew otherwise. And once I decided to stop fighting it, I knew I had to have you forever—temporary would never be enough." I pause needing to exhale slowly as I watch her sweet expression. "Ceci, I can't promise I'll be the perfect husband, or even the perfect person sometimes. I can't promise I'll always know what to say or how to comfort you. I can't promise I'll know when to stop being overprotective of you, but if there's one thing I know I can promise— one thing I know without a single doubt in my mind—it's that I will love you unconditionally. I'll love you until my very last breath. I'll love you until my memory is so awful, you'll have to remind me who you are." I smile and she lets out a light laugh. I grip her hands firmer. "I promise to give you everything I can. I love you fiercely, Cecilia. I will love you until my heart beats its very last beat."

I didn't realize before, but my cheeks are soaked. I quickly wipe the tears away, but by the sly smirk on her face, I know she's caught me.

"Bentley, the rings?" Miguel asks, holding his hand out. I hand both of them to him before he continues. "With this exchange of rings, you are binding your lives together, vowing to love each other for eternity."

He hands me Ceci's wedding band. I motion to Ceci for her hand, gripping it firmly in mine. I push the wedding band over her left ring finger next to her engagement band and rub the pad of my thumb over it. It looks perfect.

Miguel gives Ceci my wedding band as she grasps my hand in hers. She smoothly pushes it over my ring finger, a part of me that's been bare for thirty-two years.

We hold each other's hands as Miguel finalizes the ceremony, announcing us as husband and wife and that we may now kiss.

Ceci smiles giddily up at me, almost laughing, as I cup her face and bring my lips down on hers. I kiss her slow, softly. I open her lips apart with my tongue, massaging mine with hers as our kiss intensifies and heats up. She wraps her arms around my waist holding us in as we kiss on top of the cliff, promising each other forever.

CHAPTER SEVENTEEN
CECILIA

"I WAS GOING to wait a few days into our trip but I just couldn't wait another day to call you my wife."

I bite my lip in response, hardly knowing what to say. Bentley can be intimidating and the stress can overcome him a lot of the time, but Jesus…when he's vulnerable and genuine, he melts the panties right off me.

"I can't believe you did that. How…how did you even plan that so fast?"

He shrugs, grinning. I know exactly how he did. *Money talks.*

I never question his ability to get what he wants because I already know—he's too dreamy to be denied.

"So what now? You're my husband…" I let the word roll off my tongue, it feeling completely out of place. "That sounds weird." I laugh, insecurely.

He wraps his arms around my hips, pulling me in closer. "A piece of paper is just for legal reasons, which we can easily get at the court house, but the vows, promises—those are what matter most." He leans in, brushing his lips against mine. I open up, giving him access as the emotions overwhelm me at the realization of being *Mrs. Bentley Leighton.*

I moan into his mouth, silently begging him to take all of me. After our ceremony, we walked down the beach and jumped into the ocean.

It's not exactly a traditional wedding, but to me, it was absolutely perfect—swimming, laughing, and kissing in the ocean was perfection. "Your mother is going to kill us," I deadpan. "Do we have to tell her?" I raise a brow, only half kidding.

"I won't if you don't." He winks, flashing me a devilish smile—the one that could get me to do practically anything.

I burst out in laughter. "Yeah, right. She'll continue dragging me to fittings and probably wax appointments soon. That woman is relentless, you know?" He smirks, letting go of my waist and grabbing my hand.

"Let's worry about that when we have to. Until then…" He lingers off, walking us to the hot tub that's next to our small, private pool.

I nod in agreement. Talking about your mother-in-law on your honeymoon is a mood killer.

He walks us into the Jacuzzi, the water boiling hot. It's perfect, soothing my still sore muscles from the flight.

I straddle his lap as he finds a corner to get comfortable in. "So, Mr. Leighton, what are you going to do with your wife the rest of the week?"

"Well, first, *Mrs.* Leighton is wearing far too much clothing." He reaches around my neck, pulling my bikini string, freeing my breasts.

"A triangle-shaped piece of cloth is barely too much clothing," I mock. "But if that's the game we're playing…" I lower my eyes to his groin. "I'm not the only one going commando."

"You aren't going commando," he corrects. "Yet."

He pulls the string of my bikini bottoms, releasing them completely from my body. He tosses both parts of my bikini on the cement next to us. *"Now* you're going commando." He winks, flashing his panty-dropping smile.

I bring my hands down to his swim trunks. I feel his erection against my palm through the fabric. I squeeze lightly, teasing and torturing him as I loosen my grip to pull them down his legs. They float to the top, and I quickly throw them out before he can grab them from me.

"Now we both are." I grin back at him.

He looks at me with pure wanton desire, no play left in his eyes. He cups my neck and pulls me toward him, slamming our mouths together. His kisses are greedy and fast, leaving no time to prepare me for what he's about to do.

He lowers both hands over my hips, lifting me up just long enough for my body to cover his cock. Our lips stay locked as he slowly pushes me down on him.

I moan eagerly into his mouth, the pressure of the water surrounding us and the rhythm of our bodies make for a whole new sensation I've never felt before.

Once we form a steady pace, his hands begin wandering up my body, landing on my breasts. He squeezes and massages them as I continue riding him, hard. I grip his shoulders as I balance myself, not wanting the flow of the water to slow us down.

"Jesus Christ, Ceci…" he pants out, releasing our lips. His head falls back against the edge of the hot tub as my body tightens around him, releasing a loud inaudible moan.

"Oh, God," I breathe out, keeping up the pace so he comes next.

"Yes, sweetheart. Just like that. Don't stop." He grips my hips, moving them rapidly as his body tenses. I watch him as he releases inside me, his eyes rolling to the back of his head.

I slow the motion of our bodies, the water continuing to bubble around us. We're both breathing heavily, beads of sweat layering over the both of us.

"I sure hope they clean these things regularly," I quip, realizing we're probably not the first to partake in hot tub sex.

"I think the hot water makes it an auto-cleaning tub."

I narrow my eyes at him, wondering if he's serious. He lets out a light laugh at the way I'm looking at him. "That's doubtful," I tease.

Bentley helps me out, wrapping me in a towel right away in case we have any onlookers. We both get dressed and decide to take a walk out on the beach.

As we walk across the white sand and linking hands, I ask, "Are you still sure you made the right decision?" He looks down at me, pulling his brows in. "About your job," I clarify.

He looks away a moment and nods before speaking. "Yes. I'm positive. As much as enjoyed it at first, it was becoming more of a job than something I was passionate about. When I first started, I loved every part of it. I was a single bachelor living in the modeling world, so really, there was nothing to hate about it. If my father would've just waited until I was ready to start working with him, I would've eventually gotten to that point where I would've wanted more. And that's where I am now. Although the past couple years have been great, it isn't something I see myself doing long-term. I hate that it takes me away from you and my family. I can still be involved in the modeling industry without modeling."

I tilt my head to the side in question. "Oh, like how?"

"Well…there's a lot of aspiring models with no direction on where to go or how to get noticed. A lot are looking for agents and small gigs until they make their way. I have a bunch of agent contacts as well as photographer contacts that would set me apart from the rest. I could be the middle person that matches models up with agents. It's not something that's done typically, but it'd allow me to weed out the prospective ones and seeing which agent would suit them best."

"But didn't you kind of burn all those contacts when you fired them all?"

He shrugs. "Yes, but that's business. It's not personal. They're always looking for new and hot models. And that's what I'd be doing. It'd mean less traveling, more steady hours, and I'd be my own boss."

"Have you been thinking about this for a while? Seems you have a lot of figured out." Our hands begin swinging in between us as the wind picks up.

He shrugs casually, but I can see the excitement in his body language as he continues to talk about it.

"Yes, sort of. I've been thinking the traveling is becoming too much." He stops and turns toward me, pulling me to his chest. "I don't want it getting in the way of us. I'm not going to risk that."

My heart sinks as I feel like I'm the reason he's throwing his dreams away. I know I'd do anything to be with him, even if it meant changing a major part of my life, but I can't help the feeling that overwhelms me.

"I hate that you are just quitting because you're scared we aren't strong enough to survive." I try not to sound weak, but I do. It sounds pathetic.

He grabs my chin and tilts my face up to look at him. His face is firm and serious. "I would never quit something I didn't want to quit, Ceci. You're the reason I wanted to go back. You're the one that inspired me to follow my dreams after we broke up. I admit, I wasn't always a saint. The career can really beat you down, and the pressure can be overwhelming, but it was always you I thought of. And the moment I got you back, I wanted to do anything to keep you. Once I went back again, it just didn't feel right unless you were there with me. And now that you can't be, I don't want to live that life anymore. You're it for me. You're all I want, and I don't care the price or consequences it comes with. You have every right to go after your dreams, and I'll be next to you the entire time."

He literally takes my breath away at his confession. I gasp for air as the tears threaten to pour out, but I don't even care. I let them flow down my cheeks at the beautiful man in front of me—both inside and out.

"If I hadn't already married you, I would do it all over again. I could never get tired of hearing you talk so passionately about us. It makes me want to stay here forever." I wrap my arms around him, pulling his mouth to mine. His hands firmly grip my neck, keeping the pace slow and sweet.

The rest of the week is just as magical. We ended up scuba diving, snorkeling, paddle boarding, and windsurfing before we left. When we weren't out on the water, we camped out in our suite enjoying the endless room service and hot tub. Before we left, Bentley scheduled us couple massages, ending the most relaxing and happiest week of my life.

CHAPTER EIGHTEEN
BENTLEY

"Do we have to go back?" she whines, sticking her bottom lip out like a child.

I tilt my head, trying to hide the grin forming on my face. "Sorry, sweetheart. Reality calls."

"Reality sucks."

We've been on the plane for over sixteen hours now with one layover already. We have five hours left, but I can't wait to get Ceci back home. I plan to announce the news to my family as soon as possible. I know my mom will probably shit a brick, but I don't care. We're happy.

We arrive back to Omaha around eleven p.m. the following day. All we plan to do is sleep and order in for the next twenty-four hours.

"I can't wait to hug our bed," she says in all seriousness as we get out of the car. "That and my pillow, of course."

"Okay, just don't forget your husband while you're in there." I smirk, grabbing the luggage from the trunk.

"That still sounds weird. Can't I call you something else?"

"Like?" I question.

"Slave boy. Hot stuff. Mine to please. Take your pick."

I burst out laughing as I begin walking up the walkway. "You need sleep."

"Yes, please. Lots and lots of sleep." She stumbles inside, flicking the lights on to an empty house. Memories flood in of the last time we were home—the Hannah interview, the Jason pictures, Ava's emails, the media—all the drama we left at home eight days ago.

We sleep for ten solid hours. We had an amazing time in St. George, but it feels amazing to be in our own environment again.

"Wake up, sweetheart," I softly whisper in her ear.

"I am," she insists, mumbling and turning over.

I roll her back over and begin kissing up her jawline to her ear. "I highly doubt that."

"Just five more minutes," she begs.

"We've already slept through breakfast and lunch. I think it's time we eat and get moving. Plus, we need to go apply for our marriage license," I say matter-of-factly.

She opens her eyes finally. "We're going to need witnesses."

"Yup." I shoot her a look of excitement. "Who do you want to ask?"

"Cora will kill me if she finds out I got married without her. Simon will, too."

"Cora and Simon it is. Give them a call and see if they're free this afternoon." I kiss her on the nose just as I'm about to get off the bed. "Oh, go hop in the shower. Our food will be here shortly."

I wink at her just before leaving our bedroom. I haven't even touched my email since before we left. I had turned my phone off and only used it to let my mother know we'd be out of the country for a while without actually telling her anything. I'm pretty sure I don't want to be anywhere near her when she finds out.

I have about three hundred emails to sift through. Angie has sent me thirteen messages, all threatening me to call her *or else*. I laugh as I imagine her petite body threatening me. Her voice is loud and proud though, I'll give her that.

I decide to call her since I just heard the shower start and knowing Ceci, she'll be in there a good half hour.

"It's about fucking time, you asshole!" she answers the phone in a bloody rage.

"Nice greeting. Is that for everyone or was that specially for me?"

"Asshole. I swear to God, Bentley. I'm going to kill you."

"Angie, pipe down. You really should work in theatre if you're going to be so damn dramatic."

"Dramatic? I'll tell you dramatic. Everyone from the media to photographers has been up my ass this entire week. You didn't answer my calls or emails. You could've been dead for all I fucking know." She sounds out of breath from yelling at me, so I take the opportunity to finally fill her in.

"All right, I'm sorry I left you hanging. You have every right to be pissed about that. But if you stop yelling, I could explain to you my new plan," I say calmly, hoping she'll give me the chance.

"Fine, Bentley. You have five minutes or I'm putting you on my shit list."

I laugh to myself at her being adamant on being pissed off at me, but she won't be once I tell her my plan.

"As much as I'm not happy to lose my best client, I do actually like your idea. It's gonna be a business adventure, that's for sure."

"Well, I was hoping to get my best agent on board," I say with a grin, which I know she can hear in my voice. She's used to my grinning pleads.

"You know I can't say no to you, asshole."

"That's the attitude I love."

We finish hashing out some details, but I don't want to get too much into right now. Not when I have more important plans. I schedule a business meeting with her for another time and hang up.

I walk down the hallway to find Ceci in the kitchen making a pot of coffee. She gracefully walks from the fridge to the counter and back again, putting the creamer away. I watch as she grabs a spoon and stirs the creamer in, her body so relaxed and flawless.

I walk quietly behind her and wrap my arms around her waist, resting my chin on her shoulder.

"Glad to see you finally got out of bed." I kiss under her ear, feeling a shiver run down her body.

"At least someone is," she teases. "I'm going to have to call my boss and see if I still have a job," she groans.

"Why wouldn't you have a job?"

"Because, after two weeks, I up and left. Doesn't make me look very good for an employee of the year award."

"I'd give you an employee of the year award…"

"Shut up." She laughs, spinning around to face me with her cup of coffee in hand. "I'm serious."

"All right, all right." I hold my hands up in protest. "I told you I called him and made arrangements. It's fine. He just said to have you call when you got back."

She narrows her brows at me, suspiciously. "How'd you get him to agree to giving me the time off anyway?"

"I told him the truth—that I was taking you for a surprise getaway." She puts a hand on her hip, not believing me. "And I might've promised him some promotional shoots." I begin walking backward, ready for her to come at me at any moment.

"Bentley!" she squeals. "I told you not to get involved in my work."

"Technically, I didn't. I asked him what it would take to get you some time off. And I wasn't about to say no when that's what he asked for."

Her scowl turns into a smirk as she fights to show that she's mad at me. "Fine," she breathes out. "Last time!" she warns, pointing a finger at me.

We eat our late lunch and finish drinking our coffee before we head out to the courthouse. In order to officially elope, we'll need to get our marriage license and plan a date with her friends to go down there to make it legal. I don't care what a piece of paper says—to me, she's my wife. But for legal reasons, I want to make sure it's official.

"Ready?" I ask, handing her the pen. She nods with a huge smile on her face.

"I think it's a little late to back out now, Mr. Leighton." She forcefully grabs the pen from me, ready to sign the document the woman prepared for us.

"Technically, you could back out," I tease. "But I wouldn't let you get very far."

She signs her name, dramatically signing 'West' for the last time. "I think that'd be an understatement," she mocks.

Since there isn't a waiting period for Nebraska, we can get married right away. Fortunately, when I called to make an appointment, they had one free timeslot this afternoon after someone apparently canceled.

"Cora knows it's at four, right? It's quarter till and she's not here," I ask, worried.

"Yeah, she knows. She likes being fashionably late."

"Should I be worried?" She turns and gives me a questioning look. "That she'll murder me for taking you to elope?" I clarify.

"No." She laughs. "Once I told her, she said it was very romantic." She smiles. "Plus, her and Simon eloped, so she's just glad she doesn't have to be a fat bridesmaid." I pull my brows together, wondering what the hell that means. "Oh, shit." She covers her mouth. "She was keeping that a secret." I pull back slightly, pretending to be upset she's keeping a secret from me. "Secrets from my best friend don't count as keeping secrets," she says matter-of-factly.

I let out a light laugh, not really minding she let that information slip. "Well, I'll expect a thank you from her then."

Cora comes barreling in, squealing and running with her arms wide open. It's one of those overly dramatic slow motion affects where two people run in toward each other.

"I can't believe you!" Cora wraps her arms around Ceci tightly, swinging her side to side. "God, I'm so excited."

"What about me?" I put a hand to my chest, pretending to be mad I'm being ignored.

"All right, fine. You did good—so I heard." She gives me a quick hug before releasing. "Plus, now I can scratch that diet." She grins in all seriousness.

Simon and I exchange quick hellos before we rush to the elevator and make it to the courtroom just in time.

The ceremony is quick and a lot less romantic than our first one, but I don't care. All I want is for everyone to know she's mine.

As soon as the judge announces us as husband and wife, I grab her face and pull her in for a long, passionate kiss.

"Hells yeah!" Cora cheers from behind, causing Ceci to laugh mid-kiss. I shake my head, giving her lips one last peck.

As soon as we get back to the car, I pull Ceci's hand to my chest. "Time to put those rumors to rest."

I grab my cell phone and take a selfie of us holding our hands up with our rings on full display. I upload it to my Instagram with the caption, "This happened!"

It takes my mother all of forty-two minutes before she calls and begins screaming at me. Apparently, I've ruined her life and I owe her the wedding she's planned.

The picture went viral in less than three hours. Tabloids captioned, "Our favorite couple finally wed!" and "Bentley Leighton, officially off the market!" First, they trash our relationship with speculated rumors and now, they were sending their congratulation wishes.

CHAPTER NINETEEN
CECILIA

ONCE NEWS GOES LIVE, both of our phones begin blowing up with calls and texts. My mom and Tony are actually very happy for us. She knew I was stressing out with the planning, so she's glad I won't have to worry about that. Katelynn was a bit jealous she wasn't there, but now she says I can put all my focus into helping plan hers instead. It was hard to argue with that so I agreed. Casey said she was taking the next flight out of L.A. to come yell at me, which I laughed it off at first until she showed up at my door.

"How could you not invite your big sister?" she yells at me, once again. She crosses her arms over her chest as she leans back in the office chair across from me. "I mean, I'm supposed to be there next to you, watching my baby sister give herself away and all that." She continues to ramble keeping me from working on my second day back.

I roll my eyes at her, not even sure how to explain my decision. It obviously wasn't planned, but I'm beyond grateful that Bentley knows me well enough to know that it was exactly what I wanted.

"I guess I have many reasons. First, I really wasn't even getting a say in the planning. It took a lot of the fun out of it. Second, I didn't want something big and over the top—yet again, I wasn't getting a say in that. And even if I had been able to do all that, imagine planning the perfect wedding, Casey," I pause briefly. "Imagine the flowers, the music, the bright, gorgeous colors. Imagine the perfect dress. The veil and shoes. I mean, it's stunning, right?" She nods, agreeing with everything I'm saying, but not understanding where I'm going with this. "Imagine that perfect scenario and having no one to walk you down the aisle," I breathe out. Thinking of my dad brings up emotions I've tried to push back so I'm not constantly dwelling on them. "I didn't bring it up to Bentley, but imagine that perfect moment until you realize your dad isn't there to give his little girl away. Imagine that moment and how you should feel happy but all you can feel is sadness because he's not there. Through all the planning and appointments, it was all I could think about. And then, when Bentley surprised me, it felt like a sign. I could be happy on my wedding day. I could enjoy saying my vows to the man standing in front of me without the feeling that something was missing, that I was empty. It allowed me to focus on just me and him."

I don't stop until I get it all out of my system. If anyone could understand, it should be her.

"Wow, sis," she breathes out. "I guess I didn't think about it that way. I just saw all the great advantages you were getting with Mrs. Leighton helping plan and thought you were just being a little brat." She giggles lightly.

"Trust me, that is *not* an advantage."

"All right, all right. I get it." She grins. "So are you having a reception or anything?"

I shrug because we haven't really talked about it. Bentley's been dodging his mother as much as possible, but I know we'll have to give her some answers soon.

"If we do, we'll plan it, but for another date. I want something small and intimate, not something big and extravagant, and that's the only thing Mrs. Leighton knows how to do."

"Well, will you *please* send me an invite to that one at least?" she mocks in all seriousness.

"Yes." I laugh. "Now leave. I'm supposed to be working."

"All right. But we should talk later."

My brows rise in curiosity. "Bad?"

"No, not bad. Just some changes I'm thinking of making," she says slyly.

I tilt my head to get a better look at her stomach, wondering if that's part of the *change* she's making.

"Stop it. I'm not pregnant." She scowls.

I put a hand up. "Just checking."

We make plans to meet up later that night over dinner so we can talk before she finally heads out. I make a check list of everything I need to get done. One including speaking to Mrs. Leighton and apologizing for the email I sent her—we still haven't spoken since then. And now, making her cancel all the plans she made for the wedding. Now that I think of it, she might not want to talk to me ever again.

It's almost lunch time when I hear Jason's voice out in the locker room. I'm catching up on training materials so I haven't done much of anything else. I was surprised to see that Coach Tanner had an office ready for me when I returned. As soon as I was done, I'd be back to working with the players in strengthening and conditioning in preparation for their upcoming games.

"Hey, Cecilia," Jason greets, popping his head in.

"Hey!" I smile wide. "What brings you here?"

"Just stopping in to see my uncle. He wanted to meet for lunch."

"Oh, that's nice," I say genuinely. "Any luck on the job hunt?"

"Yeah, I think my uncle's going to hire me as an assistant coach."

"Oh, awesome!"

"Yeah, it's not much, but I'll take it for now."

"Hey, it's something. Can't complain about that."

"Hey, sweetheart," I hear Bentley's voice from behind Jason suddenly. I do a double take as I he comes up directly behind him.

Jason turns around, intimidated by Bentley's size. "Hi, Jason, right?" Bentley asks, a tint of harshness in his tone.

"Right." Jason bows out, nodding at me. "Well, see ya later."

"Later," Bentley calls out, not letting me get a word in.

Bentley comes in and grabs my face, kissing me deeply. "I brought you lunch."

"You did?" I ask surprised.

"I thought you'd like the company. You know, lunch with your husband is what you do when you're married," he states matter-of-factly.

"Oh." I laugh. "If you say so." I grin. "What did you bring me?"

"Tuna fish on rye and a pickle."

"Ohh, thank you." I grab the bag from his hand and empty the contents on my desk. "Aren't you going to eat?" I ask, noticing he didn't bring anything for himself.

"No, I'm heading to the gym this afternoon. I'll have a protein shake afterward, instead."

I narrow my brows at him. "So, you came to watch me eat?"

He shrugs, grinning. "Yeah. I missed you."

"Aw, husband points."

"I don't need points, sweetheart. I already won the prize."

Our work lunches continue like this for a couple weeks. Jason and I end up sharing an office since there really wasn't an open position, but his uncle gave him one anyway. It really doesn't matter because I'm hardly in my office anymore unless one of the players has set up an appointment with me to discuss nutritional habits.

Bentley has been quite vocal on his feelings regarding Jason and me sharing an office. He has no reason to be concerned, but I understand his discomfort for it.

"Hey, Jason!" I call out, running up to meet him. "Wait up. I'll walk with you." I nudge him in the arm when I finally catch up to him. "Thanks for waiting, punk."

"Sorry." He laughs. "I've been training with the team lately, so I can't afford to slow down."

I give him a questioning look. "Training for what?"

"I want to run a marathon in the near future, but I needed some motivation. So coming in early helps."

"Oh, that's awesome. Good for you."

"So how are things with you? Any news?"

"News?" I narrow my brows. "I see you every day. If there were news, you'd know."

"Okay, just checking." He smiles.

"What?"

"Nothing."

"Just ask me, Jason. We're friends. You can ask me anything."

His shoulders relax as he finally comes clean. "Okay, fine. I wanted to ask about Casey, but without sounding like a creeper."

"Casey? My sister, Casey?" I squeal, giddily. She's been coming to visit me at work a few times ever since she dropped the bomb that she was moving back to Omaha. Apparently, she caught her boyfriend cheating on her with her roommate and her roommate is a guy. So that was quite the surprise.

"See? I knew I should've kept my mouth shut."

I step in front of him, making him stop. "No, tell me. I'm just surprised, that's all." He finally stops walking and starts talking.

"Okay, I think I might, well, she's pretty attractive," he stumbles.

I try to conceal my laughter, but I can't. It's just too cute seeing him all flustered.

"Shit, Jason. You like her, *a lot.*"

"I hate you." He pushes around me and starts walking again.

I chase after him, laughing. His cheeks are tinted pink as I've clearly embarrassed him.

"Okay, I'm done. I'm sorry. You want me to set you up? I can give her your number? Oh my God, you two would be the cutest couple."

"I don't do...girl, Cecilia," he pouts as we make our way to our office. "I don't girl talk, so just stop it."

I smirk, finding it entirely sweet he likes Casey. I was worried he wasn't taking the news of the sudden wedding well. After I returned to work and it got around, he began acting weird around me. Although I always said we were just friends, I truly never knew if he had different feelings than I did.

"Well, I'll invite her for lunch today. You can do the rest and I'll stay out of it." I lift my hands up in promise. He contemplated it for a moment before nodding his head in approval. "Great!" I clap my hands dramatically. "It's a date." I wink, making him shake his head at me.

BENTLEY

I've been networking with all my contacts since we got back from St. George. Ceci's been busy with work, and I've chosen to stay home and work back in my office again—for now. I have been setting up a team of agents, photographers, and designers before officially starting up my new project. It's going to take some time getting everything finalized and ready, but when it's finally time, it'll all be worth it.

I grab myself another cup of coffee from the kitchen when I realize Ceci forgot her purse. I could call her and ask if she needs it, but I decide I'll stop by Starbucks first and grab her favorite drink and bring it back to her. The break from sitting at my desk will be nice.

I'm walking in with her caramel latté in one hand and her purse hanging from my other hand when I spot Jason sitting on Ceci's desk leaning toward her and laughing. I don't know what it is about that guy, but now he's crossed the line.

I barge in, startling them both. I drop her purse on the floor and set her coffee on the table. Heat is steaming from my entire body as I eye in on Jason.

I point at him and say through seething teeth, "What the fuck are you doing?" I don't give him time to respond before I grab him by the collar and force him up against the wall.

CHAPTER TWENTY

BENTLEY

I SEE red the second I see him that close to her and my body instantly reacts, my mind not exactly catching up to what I'm doing. I pin him against the wall, his face filled with shock and horror.

Jason isn't a little guy. He could easily give me a run for my money, but in that moment, rage and adrenaline take over enough to take him off guard.

"What are you doing?" I hear Ceci yell behind me, but I don't answer her.

"I don't know what kind of sick fantasy you have about my wife, but you need to back the *fuck off*. You're constantly around her when she's clearly taken. Next time, I'll be doing a lot more than just slamming you against the wall. Are we clear?" I seethe, feeling the vein in my forehead popping with intensive anger.

"Bentley, put him down! He wasn't doing anything!" she pleads, concern laced in her voice.

"Yeah, man, it's not what you're thinking. I swear," he says calmly. Almost too calm.

"It better not be." I push my face closer to his, making sure there's no way he can misinterpret what I'm saying. "She's *mine*," I hiss through clenched teeth just before dropping him.

"Bentley." Ceci grabs my arm, forcing me to turn around and face her. Her face is crimson red and she's fiercely scowling at me. "Jason, give us a minute, please," she asks, clenching her lips tightly.

Jason adjusts his shirt and nods before walking out and closing the door behind him.

"What the hell is he doing on your desk?" I growl before she even gets a word in.

"Are you insane?" she yells, flailing her arms at me.

I close the gap between us. "You are *my* wife, Ceci. Excuse me for not wanting some guy—some ex you use to fuck—near my wife."

"God, you're such a moron sometimes." She pushes her hands against my chest with all the power she can muster up, but I barely flinch. "He's not interested in *me*! He was telling me about another girl he wants to ask out. Had you given more than two seconds for us to explain that, you wouldn't have made yourself look like such a jackass."

"That doesn't explain why he's always all over you and *sitting* on your desk. C'mon, Ceci. I'm a guy. And *not* a blind one."

"Go ask him for yourself then. Since he came back, we've only ever been friends." She waves her hands behind me, motioning for me to run after him.

My jaw ticks at the thought of having to speak to him one-on-one, especially since I already hate the guy.

"I have nothing to say to him."

"You could start with an apology." She crosses her arms, pushing my limits even further.

I adjust my shirt and give in anyway. "Fine."

She raises her brows at me as I walk out, guilt settling in my gut. Now that I know the situation, I know I crossed a line by grabbing him.

I walk through the locker room and find him in the hallway.

"Jason!" I call out, jogging toward him. He turns around and waits until I catch up to him. "Look, I'm sorry for overreacting. I shouldn't have laid my hands on you."

He shuffles his shirt, putting it back in place. "It's fine," he finally says. "I know how much you love her. But I'm telling you, it's not like that."

"Well, why don't you start by telling me how it is?"

I see him swallow before cracking his jaw and finally making eye contact with me.

"Cecilia…is someone I knew back in high school, as you know. She was someone very special to me even though we were never able to commit to each other in that way. She's still that special person to me, but in a different way. She's matured now. Ever since I've been back from overseas, she gives me a sense of…comfort. She's a piece of the old me that was from before I enrolled in the army. She's that piece that I want to remember because being over there really fucked me up. I became isolated after a while and stopped contacting my friends and family. Cecilia has a way of bringing out the old me, if that makes sense. She's the same stubborn, sassy-mouthed girl she was in high school." He grins to himself. "She's my security blanket. She's like home." I see the vulnerable way he's looking at me, letting me know he's telling the truth.

"I hadn't thought of it like that."

"I know…I should've made an effort to talk to you or at least let you know that getting into her pants wasn't my intention."

I smirk. "So whose pants are you trying to get into?" He raises his brows at me in surprise. "What? I thought we were doing that brother-bonding thing, or whatever."

That makes him laugh and blush.

"Casey. How weird is that?"

"Really?" I rub my finger and thumb over my jawline. "That…I could probably help you with. Casey's a spitfire just like her sister, so you have to have a plan going in. They aren't the type of girls you just go after. It's like a fucking maze."

CECILIA

I always knew Bentley was overprotective, but I've never seen him go at someone the way he went toward Jason. I'm sure the rumors of us had something to do with his speculation, but apparently, it took the two of them to finally talk to ease Bentley's mind.

"I feel like a dick," he says softly, standing in front of my desk. I see the vulnerability in his face.

"Good," I spit out. "At least that's one less thing I have to call you."

His lips curve up into a small grin. "Will you forgive me?" He pleads with his eyes and panty-dropping smile. I'm so doomed.

"Why do you do that? You know I'm a sucker for that look."

He laughs and comes around my desk, kneeling in front of me. "That's what I was counting on."

"I'll forgive you on one condition."

"Okay, spill." His hands grasp my hips.

"Get your mother to meet up with me for lunch. We need to settle everything in person. I hate that we have so much to get off our chests and that it's causing an awkward tension."

He raises his brows at me in surprise. "Wow, very mature of you."

I dramatically pull a hand to my chest. "Um, excuse me? I'm *very* mature, thank you," I say with certainty laced in my voice.

I follow his eyes to the bottom of my shirt as a smirk forms across his face. "Says the girl with *Hello Kitty* underwear."

I burst out in laughter and shake my head at him. "Well, if my husband would stop ripping all my good panties in half, I'd actually have something half decent to wear!" I defend.

"Well, if my wife would stop wearing underwear."

CHAPTER TWENTY-ONE
CECILIA

I CAN'T STOP FIDGETING in my seat as I wait for Ava. The only thing I know about her is that she's related to me somehow and that she's flying in from Florida.

I stand up the moment I see her red blazer. That's our code so I knew who I was looking for; however, she didn't look anything like I had expected.

She's wearing a head bandana where her hair should be, but you can clearly see she's bald. She's pasty white, which seems odd since she lives around sunny beaches.

"Cecilia?" she asks, the closer she approaches.

I nod and smile. "Yes. Ava?"

"It's so great meeting you!" She surprises me by swarming me in a big hug. "You look just like your father." She takes me off guard, but I just swallow and nod in return. We both take a seat, sitting across from each other.

"Are you going to tell me how you know my father? It's been weighing on me and I need to know," I ask cautiously, getting right to the point of this whole meeting.

"Of course." She smiles, adjusting herself in the chair until she's comfortable. "We only got to spend nine months together."

"Oh my God." My heart begins racing as I draw my own conclusions.

"Yes, nine months in the womb that is." She chuckles lightly.

"Wait, what?"

"I'm your dad's twin sister," she states matter-of-factly.

"I didn't know he had a twin sister," I exclaim, shocked that my mother never brought it up.

"Your mother doesn't exactly…approve of me."

"What, why?"

"When they first started dating, I got into some trouble. Okay, a lot of trouble." She laughs lightly to herself. "Your dad had to bail me out a few times financially. After they were engaged, your mother wouldn't let me borrow anymore money because it all had to go to their wedding. And when I wasn't invited to the wedding, that's when I knew I wasn't wanted. And the last thing I wanted was to get in the middle of their marriage, so I backed away."

"For over twenty years?" I blurt out. "I'm sure my mom would've gotten over it."

She shrugs. "No, she didn't. I wasn't exactly a good egg, Cecilia. I had a little rebellious side to me. Back in my younger years." She points to her head. "Obviously, I haven't been for a while now." She smiles, accepting her fate.

I swallow, nervous to even ask. "Are you sick?"

She nods simply. "Yes. I have been for a while."

I swallow as the realization of what that means. "Do you have a family in Florida?"

She smiles wide. "Yes, I have two sons. Jackson and Jamison."

"Two cousins," I remark, giddily. My mom's an only child and up to today, I thought my dad was an only child, as well. "Could I meet them sometime?"

"I don't see why not. They're a bit younger than you."

"Oh, both of them are?"

"Yes, they're twins."

"Wow. I had no idea twins ran in the family."

"Yes, on both sides of the family. So, be careful." She winks at me. "Fraternal twins can have twins whereas identical twins usually skip a generation."

"Hmm…I never knew that."

I offer to buy her a coffee and excuse myself a moment, needing to wrap my brain around everything. There's something about her that reminds me of myself when I was in high school and college.

I can't believe my own mother never told me. That's a long time to hold a grudge on someone.

"So…can I be blunt and ask why, after all this time, you decided to contact me?"

After sipping her coffee, she sets it down with a serious expression. "I wanted to meet you one more time."

I give her a puzzling look. "What do you mean one more time? Aren't you getting treatment? I could come down and visit you," I offer.

"They tried treatment, but it spread."

"Okay, so you need something more intensive? We have really great doctors up here. There's a huge specialist hospital in Minnesota. I mean, it's a drive obviously, but they are amazing." I know this because I had an assignment in one of my health and fitness classes that lead me to research MAYO clinic.

"Sweetie, it's inoperable."

"What about chemo?"

"This is my second time getting cancer," she admits. "My body is tired. It's spreading too rapidly. They do surgery and I could die anyway. So I chose against it so I could spend the rest of the time I have with my family. And to see you once again." Her voice is soft, certainty in her tone.

"No," I retort, angry that she's just so easily giving up. "That can't be right. There's treatment. There's ways to fight cancer."

"It's not always that simple, darling."

"Why not?"

"I don't want to waste precious time on something that isn't going to work."

I finally surrender, nodding my head in understanding. "I would've given anything to have just a little more time with my dad. But—" Tears begin surfacing. "It's really not something you tell someone you haven't seen in twenty years." I half-laugh as I wipe the tears away. "Especially, since I didn't have any family growing up. And the one person you looked up to ended up being someone completely different than you thought," I say, referencing my dad.

"That's part of what I wanted to talk about, Cecilia. Your father was my hero."

I sniff, wiping more tears away. "What do you mean?"

"Your dad put me through my first round of treatment when I first got cancer." I lean forward, wanting to hear more. "Your dad and I continued speaking even though your mother forbade it. Once he found out I was sick, he said he would do anything to help me."

Apparently, he literally meant *anything*.

She takes a sip of her coffee and I just continue to stare at her. Ever since learning the truth about his death, I had often wondered what made him go into gambling in the first place.

"You're the reason he joined with Ramiro." It comes out accusingly, but I hadn't meant it to.

"He just called me up one day and said he was sending me money. And the money just kept coming, which meant I could pay for treatment that my insurance wouldn't cover. He never told me how he got it."

I feel my heart racing, the dots finally connecting. "Did you know about Ramiro? Or the gambling? Or the plan?"

"No," she blurts out. "I read his obituary and only what the local papers said online. I never contacted your mom and figured she wouldn't care to hear from me."

"Oh," I say relieved. "He was addicted to gambling," I explain. 'That's how he got the money."

"I never knew."

"Yeah, I didn't know until a couple years ago," I offer softly. It felt weird talking about my dad again, but a part of me felt happy that I still could.

"He killed himself," I say bluntly. "He began losing money and couldn't pay it." I lower my head to avoid seeing his reflection in her face. "He killed himself to keep them away from us. He knew they'd come after us if he couldn't pay up. The insurance money paid them off." The tears come uncontrollably now, and I don't even try to stop them. "I miss him so much."

She rubs the pad of her thumb over my knuckles. "Your dad was a good man, Cecilia."

I smile as I twirl my empty coffee cup in my other hand. "I know. He really was. I always thought of him as my hero when I was a child."

"He saved my life," she says, her words making me lock eyes with her. "However, there isn't any amount of money in the world that can save me now. But just know, no matter how your dad died, he died a hero. He gave me time and that's something I could never get back or could thank him enough for doing. My only regret is not being able to come see him more."

I squeeze her hand in mine, fear obvious in her eyes. "Let's use the time we have now."

ONE MONTH LATER

Ava spent a week with Bentley and me at our house. We Skyped with her husband and sons so I could 'meet' them. I never felt an emotional pain before, but meeting Ava and her family was bittersweet. We promised to keep in touch, but I had an uncanny feeling that this promise wouldn't last long.

After saying goodbye to Ava, it really made me think how I really need to spend time with the people that are important in our lives. It's easy to make excuses when you're busy with work and husbands, but I wanted to make sure I put an extra effort into it now.

Mrs. Leighton and I plan to meet up finally. It's time to finally put this cat pissing fight to rest. I want her involved in our life.

"Cecilia," she says my name as if it's a dirty word.

"Hello, Mrs. Leighton," I say politely, taking a seat across from her. "Thank you for meeting me."

"Well, I do enjoy their lobster," she says blankly.

"Before we order, can I please just say something?" She finally looks at me and nods lightly. "You know I love your son. And I understand you love him just as much. Before I met Bentley or even started thinking of settling down, I never dreamed of a big, white wedding. As you know, I was quite focused on my dad and the past. So when Bentley and I got engaged, we started making plans of what we both like and of what we could combine to each other's tastes. And well, you had other plans, and I didn't know how to tell you."

"What was wrong with my ideas?" she asks cautiously.

"Nothing, honestly. They just weren't what we wanted. You were going for more extravagant and we wanted something more…simple." I make sure to keep my tone neutral. "I'm sorry we left you out of our wedding, but at the end of the day, we just wanted to be able to commit to each other and be husband and wife."

She nods lightly, understanding what I'm telling her. "I'm sorry if I came off as being pushy," she says, moving her silverware around, clearly uncomfortable. "I wasn't trying to be malicious."

"Oh, Mrs. Leighton, I would never think that." I press a palm to my heart. For the first time, I see her actually showing emotion. "I just never knew how to tell you to…back off."

"Well, your email was sufficient in letting me know," she says curtly.

My shoulders slump, wishing I could take that back. "I'm very sorry I sent you that. Bentley told me to just be straightforward with you, and I really should've told you face to face. I understand you just wanted the best for him and that I didn't handle the situation properly."

"Well, thank you, Cecilia. That means a lot to me. I want to have a close relationship with you and Bentley as a couple. It's important to have a close family."

I put a hand over my stomach where a small bump has formed. "I couldn't agree more."

CHAPTER TWENTY-TWO
BENTLEY

"You're sure?"

"Yes."

"How can you know for sure?" I question, pacing the kitchen.

She pulls six white sticks out of her purse and lays them flat out on the counter. "Because six out of six is a pretty good bet."

I lean over and examine them. All saying the exact same thing. Positive.

"Aren't you happy?" she asks, a hint of disappointment in her voice.

I round the counter and cup her face in both hands. I lean in and briefly graze my lips over hers. "I'm ecstatic. Are you happy?"

Her eyes close on contact as I brush a finger over cheek. "Yes. Very."

I just flew back in from L.A. after spending a week there finalizing my contract with several agencies and photographers for Leighton Modeling Co. After discussing my plan with Angie, she went to her boss, who ate the whole thing up. In fact, he even offered to help me get it off the ground with all of his contacts, as well. Now I could work on my own schedule and only have to travel to meet up with joining companies. It's a dream to be my own boss instead of having to answer to someone else. It's still new, and we haven't opened up to prospective clients yet, but we will be in the next six months or so.

"I found out right after you left," she admits. "I almost told your mother when we met up a couple days ago, but I wore a baggy shirt so she wouldn't notice."

"Is it normal to show this early?" I ask with caution.

She scrunches her lips up into a questionable grin. "No, not really. I'd only be about five or six weeks. So, it's probably just bloating."

I raise my brows, feeling very out of my league. "I'm going to have to download some books if I'm going to have any clue on what I'm doing."

She laughs lightly. "You and me both."

I cover her mouth with mine as I soak up her taste and massage my tongue with hers. I stand in between her legs as her arms wrap around me and pull me in closer to her. Her body melts into mine as a moan escapes her lips. Her nails dig into the muscles of my back as I pull her off the barstool and wrap her legs around me.

I walk us to our bedroom, slamming the door shut with my foot. I lay her on the mattress and immediately crawl over her, ripping clothing off that's blocking off any access.

I assist in pulling my pants down and tearing my shirt off. I've missed her all week, but now this was a raw hunger that was making me need her right now.

I stand on the edge of the bed and pull her legs to the edge, letting them hang over the edge. She smiles up at me as I tease her entrance with my cock. I stroke it with one hand as I rub her clit with the other.

I push inside her, deep and forcefully, until I fill her completely. She gasps as I push in even deeper.

"Am I hurting you?" I ask, worried I've somehow hurt the baby.

"No…no, don't stop. Keep going," she pleads. Her eyes roll to the back of her head as I thrust against her upon her request.

I grab both of her wrists with my hands and pin them down on the mattress on each side of her. I keep up with the rhythm as I hold her upper body hostage with my arms and her lower body with my hips. She's completely exposed and vulnerable as I push all the pleasure I can into her.

"Yes, God. Yes."

"Spread your hips wider, baby." She complies, expanding her hips for me. "Relax, sweetheart." Her body eases into the bed, her back lying flat. I pull out of her slightly, letting my cock rest right on her swollen lips before I slam back into her. She gasps, her head falling back as she screams out. "Fucking perfect," I growl.

"Oh, I hope you don't mind, but I've invited the girls over tonight," she says as she rummages through the fridge and freezer, digging out a pre-cut package of cookie dough, a pint of Ben & Jerry's, and a variety of soda. She then walks over to the pantry and grabs two bags of popcorn and a bag of potato chips.

"I hope you plan to share some of that with your guests," I mock. "Or if not—"

She spins around and scowls at me. "Yes, they are for everyone. However, what I call dibs on is none of your business," she teases right back.

"How many people are coming over?" I question, wondering if I'm going to be hiding out in my office all night instead. I can only take so much girl gossip.

"Just Cora, Katelynn, Casey, and my mom. Oh, and I think Casey is bringing Jason. And Katelynn and Brandon are still in that honeymoon planning-the-wedding stage, so I'm sure she'll drag him, too."

I sigh. "Well, at least I won't be the only guy. I might even stick around."

"Good, you should. It's the new season of Celebrity Rehab."

I narrow my brows at her. "You can't be serious."

"Don't make fun of my guilty pleasures." She points a wooden spoon at me as she continues to scowl at me. "Reality TV is my weakness."

"That's an understatement." I laugh.

She throws a bag of popcorn at my face. "Be useful. Pop that in." Her scowl turns into a sweet smile. "I mean...*please.*"

"Is this what I get to look forward to for the next seven to eight months?" I ask, sardonically. "I mean...*enjoy* for the next seven to eight months. I'm going to enjoy every moment." I shoot her an over the top grin.

"You're lucky you're cute, mister."

The doorbell rings and saves me from what I'm sure was going to be me groveling on my hands and knees.

"Hello—" I begin, but am soon interrupted by Cora barging in and walking right passed me. I wave my arm out, now speaking to no one. "Well, come on in."

I hear her walking to the kitchen, apparently eager to talk to Ceci. I shut the door behind me when I hear Ceci squeal.

"Son-of-a-bitch!"

I walk to where they both are hovering over a piece of paper. "What is it?"

She holds up a printed copy of some online tabloid gossip magazine. "How is this possible?"

I grab it from her and read the header, "Bentley and Ceci Leighton expecting! Parents are over-joyed!"

"What the hell?" We haven't had to deal with the press in quite some time. Ever since I stopped modeling all together, they haven't been interested, but now apparently they were. "How's that possible?"

"It's true?" Cora gasps, breaking my stare. And apparently, Ceci hadn't told Cora yet.

"Yes, Cora. It's true. I'm expecting." I pat my stomach, teasing her and getting a smack in the arm in return.

"Shut up, Bentley," she hisses, but I see a hint of a smile on her face. "Are you really?" She turns and faces Ceci who's smiling ear to ear, unable to hide her excitement.

"Yes!" she responds, giddily. "But, I literally only found out a week ago. I have no idea how they even found out." She waves a hand in the air, expressing her annoyance. "I just told Bentley tonight."

"You found out a week ago and didn't tell me?" she scolds. "You took all the fun out of it for me." I laugh, shaking my head. "Hey," Cora groans, pointing a finger at me. "She watched me pee on a stick!"

"I have like two left if you wanna reenact it," Ceci offers, teasingly. "I actually do have to pee." She laughs.

Cora cocks her head to the side. "No, I'll pass on that. But how exciting we're pregnant at the same time!" She wraps her arms around Ceci and hugs her. "Our kids will definitely be best friends."

"I'm going to let you girls have your night and I'll go work in my office," I say, but Cora quickly cuts me off.

"No, you can't. Simon is coming over. The only way I could talk him into it was that I said you'd be here."

I shoot her a disapproving look, but give in already. "All right, fine." I sigh. "I'll make the popcorn." I flash a fake smile. "Oh, who did you have buy the tests for you?" I ask Ceci, pressing the popcorn button on the microwave.

She gives me a puzzling expression, as she slowly answers, "No one. Why?"

"Well, that's probably how they found out. Maybe an employee saw you and leaked it to the press. People will do anything for a dollar," I remind her. "You have to be careful."

Although I wasn't in my old career, people were still obsessed with digging into our private lives. I'm not sure if that's ever going to go away as long as I'm a Leighton.

Our living room is packed with people sitting on the floor and couch as Ceci flips the right channel on.

Since the news was leaked anyway, I tell Ceci she should tell her mom and friends so they aren't finding out like Cora did.

We make eye contact from across the room as I bring in another bowl of popcorn. I nod in agreement with her silent question of if we should say something now or later.

"So," Ceci begins, getting all their attention. I walk over to where she's sitting on the loveseat. "Bentley and I found out some news and we want to be the first ones to tell you before you hear it."

I watch Ceci's mom, her face a mixture of fear and excitement. Although they haven't always had the best relationship, I know it's been a concern of hers that I'd take her daughter out of the state and make it impossible for her to see Ceci. I never wanted that, which was part of the reason for wanting to retire from modeling.

"We found out we're expecting," she finally blurts out.

A mixture of cries and squeals echo the room. Katelynn jumps up almost immediately as tears run down her mom's cheeks.

"Am I the only one not pregnant right now?" Katelynn cries jokingly. I turn and catch Brandon's scared expression.

"Not me!" Ceci's mom says with a smile. "But I'm surely excited you are, baby." She wraps her arms around Ceci. Watching them be close again makes this all more surreal and as if things are starting to fall into place.

"Well, at least I get to be an aunt to two adorable babies now." Katelynn smiles. "Just don't give me the water you two are clearly drinking."

Once everyone has settled from the news, Ceci turns the show back on. Apparently, it's the season premier, and it's when all the new celebrities are announced.

"Oh. My. God!" Ceci all but yells, leaning on the edge of the couch. "Is that...is that freaking Hannah?"

I was barely paying attention before, so when she yells out Hannah's name, my face immediately snaps up.

"Wait, *the* Hannah? Conniving, manipulating, and life ruining—Hannah?" Cora rambles off, her eyes glued to the TV for confirmation.

Simon and Brandon are all sitting back wondering what all the fuss is about when I finally clue them in.

"Yes, that's her."

"How is that possible? She's not famous," Katelynn asks, popping a piece of popcorn in her mouth. "More times than not it's celebs I barely know, but was Hannah ever cast in anything?"

"She did a few times before she got real bad and went into rehab. Once she got addicted, her career nose-dived. That's when she went into rehab."

"And apparently a good one!" Cora chimes in. "Talk about killing two birds with one stone," she says, referencing to the fact that now she was on TV even though she's battling her addiction.

"Well, I hope it helps her at least. I hope she can get clean for her sake," Ceci adds, genuinely. I smile at her, deeply thankful that my wife can be the stronger one and forgive although Hannah doesn't deserve it.

Half way through, the doorbell rings so I get up and greet Casey. "Oh my God, what did I miss?" She barges through me, leaving Jason at the door.

"Is there a sign or something that says ignore the greeter?" I ask although she's long gone. "Hey, man. Come on in. The party's in there." I nod toward the living room. I pat him on the shoulder before adding. "Oh, warning. Ceci's pregnant and Hannah's on Celebrity Rehab. Be prepared for Casey to freak out," I warn and wink at him.

They've been 'casually' dating according to Casey, but from what I hear from Ceci, they spend every free moment together. However, I know this translates into more than just casually dating, which makes me truly happy for them both. It makes me much more comfortable knowing Jason is just her friend and co-worker that she can confide in without any emotions brewing to the surface. And now that I've gotten to know him, I really don't mind him being around. It's good she has both girl and guy friends. Makes me feel a bit less guilty when I still have to travel.

"Oh my God!"

There it is.

I walk in to Casey hugging her sister and squealing obnoxiously.

"Hey, be careful with my wife. That's my baby in there you're squeezing the hell out of."

"Oh, she's fine!" she spits back at me. "She is already rounding out so there's plenty of padding."

"God, Casey," Ceci cries. "Way to be sensitive."

Casey tries to hold in her laughter, but she can't contain it. "Yup, she's pregnant."

CHAPTER TWENTY-THREE
CECILIA

"OH, SHIT. IT'S HOT."

"Mom!" I scold.

"Sorry, but damn, it's humid."

We walk into our hotel that we'll be staying at for the night. I'm a thirteen weeks pregnant now, but Ava's condition has been getting worse, and I want to see her one more time.

"You promised, remember," I remind my mother. She was shocked when I finally told her I knew about Dad's twin sister. She was even more shocked when she found out what Dad was really doing with all that money. She had no idea, and then when I told her I wanted to go visit her one last time, she offered to come with me so they could finally put the past to rest.

"Yes, Cecilia. I know."

My mother can be a tad…intimidating. I made her promise to not drill Ava or even mention money. I wasn't certain she would anyway, but it made me feel at ease knowing she wouldn't.

Once we settled into our room, we grabbed a bite to eat in the hotel restaurant. Mom and I have grown a lot closer over the past couple months. I think it has to do with the fact that I'm carrying her first grandchild, but I'm grateful for it nonetheless. I'd rather build a relationship with her now than never.

"Are you ready?" she asks as I sit in the car in front of her house.

I swallow back the tears that are threatening to surface. The last time

I saw Ava was only months ago, but even in her voice, I could tell she was weaker.

"Yeah." I nod.

My mother holds my hand as we walk to the door. Ava's husband, Adam, answers and greets us.

"Hi, welcome!" He leans in for a hug when I offer him my hand. "It's a pleasure to *officially* meet you."

"Likewise." I introduce him to my mother, and soon, we're being escorted into a room in the back of the house.

"She's back there. She's very excited to see you." Adam nods his head toward the hall, but doesn't follow us down.

I walk softly down the carpeted hallway. I push my hand against the door, opening it slowly. I'm greeted with Ava's smiling face as she pulls herself up against the bedframe.

"Come in, sweetie." Her voice is soft and weak.

I all but run to the side of the bed and wrap my arms around her. "Oh, God, it's so good to see you." I squeeze her lightly, not wanting to put too much pressure on her tiny body.

"You look amazing, Cecilia," she says as she finally gets a better look at me. "Definitely glowing." She smiles wide.

"Sorry, Aunt Ava, but that's not glow. That's sweat. I'm sweating."

She laughs, but shaking her head in disagreement. "Either way, you look gorgeous. Pregnancy agrees with you."

"I brought my mom," I say, changing the subject. Her brows rise as she finally notices my mom is standing behind me. "I hope that's all right."

"Ava…" my mom begins, "I'm sorry. I'm so sorry." She stands next to me. "I never meant to shut you out of our lives for good. I just wanted Brock to see that he wasn't helping you if he was constantly bailing you out. But I should've butt out. You two were family and it wasn't my place."

My mom's confession surprises me, but I couldn't be more appreciative that she comes clean.

"Thank you, Claire. That means a lot to me. I know it's too late now, but your apology means the world to me."

"I'm glad we came," I say sitting on the edge of the bed next to her. The more I study her, the more I see my dad in her face. "It feels right."

"It does." The corners of her lips pull up into a smile. I mold the memory to my brain so I don't ever forget, especially when she's gone.

My mother comes and sits on the other side of the bed. I'm not sure how long we end up staying, but we talk for hours. Adam comes in with food and her meds once before we finally say our goodbyes. I could tell she was exhausted, but she didn't want us to go. She kept insisting she was fine, but I could tell. Her body was breaking down, and soon, she wouldn't be able to eat or breathe on her own. It was only a matter of time.

Jackson and Jamison are in the living room when my mother and I finally make our way out.

"How much time does she have?" I ask, pain in my voice as I say the words aloud.

Both of the boys look tired and stressed. "Doctor says it could be a few days to a few weeks. Once her kidneys go, it'll just be a matter of days then." I nod, not really knowing what else to say.

We stay another hour talking to Jamison and Jackson, since we've only met once on Skype. But soon, we had to leave for good.

Saying goodbye to Ava was one of the hardest things I've had to do. Although I didn't know her long or have a strong lifelong connection to her, it still felt like I was losing a part of me. She resembles my dad so much. I only wish I had been able to meet her sooner.

Ava asked us to stay a few days, but if she only has days left, I didn't want to be greedy when her husband and kids wanted that time with her. Plus, I wasn't sure if I could handle watching her get sicker and sicker.

I'm happy my mother and her were able to make amends before it was too late. I saw the relief on both of their faces when they both agreed to let the past be the past. I will say that my mother has definitely grown since being with Tony. The last couple of years, I've seen her become a better person since he's been in her life.

"So when do you and Tony plan to tie the knot?" I ask as we fly back from Florida to Omaha.

"I'm not sure." She smiles while looking at my stomach. "When do you plan to lose the baby weight so you can fit into a dress?"

"You're always so subtle, Mom."

"Sorry, kid." She laughs lightly. "We've talked about it if that makes you feel better."

"Well, if he can put up with our craziness of a family, I'd say he's a keeper."

She smiles genuinely now. "I agree."

425

CHAPTER TWENTY-FOUR
CECILIA

I was hit with the bad news twelve days after saying goodbye to Ava. Her breathing became too rapid and her kidneys began failing just days after we left. It's bittersweet knowing she's up in Heaven with my dad now. I'm grateful I was able to spend that little time with her and to at least say goodbye. I can feel happy thinking she's looking down on me.

Bentley and I spend the rest of summer and the start of fall preparing the nursery. I help Katelynn with final wedding preparations and Cora with the arrival of her baby girl outside of working. Jason finally got his own office, which I'm grateful for since Casey comes to visit him at lunch and their relationship went from 'casual' to serious.

Bentley's new modeling company officially opens at the beginning of winter, giving us only a few months before I deliver. He spends his time traveling and setting up his new office downtown now before my due date.

Baseball season ended mid-summer, so I transition to something less physical at work since I'm pregnant. I work on a variety of different tasks, anything Coach Tanner asks of me, basically. I don't mind it since I get to rest and sit at my desk mainly. It allows me to Skype with Bentley while he's away.

"You ready?" I ask Katelynn as she stares at herself in the mirror. "You can still run," I lean in and whisper. Her eyes lock with mine in the mirror, a wide smile spread across my face.

"You really suck as matron of honor, you know that?" she says sardonically.

"I'm going to take that as pre-wedding jitters and ignore that last comment."

"You're lucky Cora is still breastfeeding or you would've been tossed out like yesterday's garbage."

"There's the stressed out bride-to-be I know." I grin, fixing her veil. "Reason number thirty-three I eloped!"

"Hey, that's my line!" Cora interrupts, laughing. She has Katie attached to her chest as she walks around the bridal suite.

"You know you can't walk down the aisle like that," Katelynn mocks.

"I can't wait until you're pregnant," she teases.

"No kidding!" I add in. "We get to give all the shit you've given us right back." I smirk, rubbing my belly that's about to pop out of my bridesmaid dress. "Payback's a bitch."

"No problem. I just won't get pregnant." She snarls.

"Have you met your future husband? There's no way you guys are going to keep your hands off each other."

She smiles at the mention of his name. Oh yeah, it won't take long.

The ceremony is perfect. Bentley and I walk down the aisle together in matching red color accents. Katelynn looks stunning as always as she and Brandon promise each other forever. I think back on the memories of when Katelynn and Brandon first met. The whole story is quite funny now that we can look back on it. I really hated hurting Brandon, but knowing he's found his true soul mate makes me think that everything happened for a reason.

The reception and dance are both beautiful and run smoothly. I do my best to participate in all the wedding party shenanigans, but my belly often gets in the way.

Bentley and I dance for most of the evening. Although my feet are swollen and ache, I don't want to let go of this moment we have together. It's only a matter of weeks before our lives change forever.

"You look stunning," he whispers in my ear. "Absolutely gorgeous."

I smile back at him. "Do you regret not having a big, white wedding and reception?"

He looks around and smiles before locking eyes with me again. "No. I love every part of our wedding. I wouldn't change it for anything. Well, maybe that one time I almost got stung by a jellyfish." I laugh at the memory. "But honestly, I think it was perfect."

"I agree. It *was* perfect."

My feet are killing me by the time we leave. We booked a room at the hotel where the reception was so we didn't have to drive all the way home after a long day. We step into the elevator, grinning at each other like a bunch of horny teenagers.

"I know that look, Mr. Leighton."

"Is that so, Mrs. Leighton?" He walks over and pins me to the wall as much as my belly will allow him to. "And what look is that?" He dips his nose into the nape of my neck, trailing kisses up to my ear and jawline.

"It's the look that got me pregnant in the first place," I say matter-of-factly. His lips never part from my skin as he laughs.

"Well, it's a good thing you're already pregnant."

It's practically a race as we finally get the door open of who can get each other's clothes off first. Bentley wins by a landslide with his greedy hands.

His kisses are hungry and raw as he walks us backward toward the bed. My knees buckle when I collide with the bed. He lays me back, worshiping my mouth with his lips and tongue. His hand lands on my breast as he wakes up every nerve sensation in my body, making me eager and practically begging for it.

"Bentley…" I whimper with no other words able to come out as I ache for him.

He kisses down my chest, over my stomach, and down below to my clit. He teases and tortures me before pulling me to stand up.

"Bend over the bed, sweetheart." His lips graze over my ear as I feel his cock pressing into my back. I do just as he says, spreading my legs apart for him.

I feel him walking away, leaving me exposed. I turn to look for him, but I can't see that far back. Fortunately, he returns and kneels in between my legs.

"Hold the bed, baby." I hear the sound of buzzing before I feel it. There's no time to react before Bentley presses a vibrator to my clit.

"Oh my God," I scream. He presses a hand to my back, holding me in place. "W-What are—"

My words are soon lost as he circles it around my pussy, swirling the vibrator up and down my slit.

"Jesus, baby. You're so wet."

"God, Bentley...the sensation is too much."

He pushes just the tip of it inside, allowing me to get use to the foreign feeling. My hips circle on their own accord as he teases my swollen lips. I can feel my own build up as he pushes it deeper inside me.

"Holy shit...you're going to make me go into labor," I say through heavy panting. My fists clench the comforter on the bed. I can barely keep myself up.

"No worries, sweetheart. I looked it up and made sure it was safe for you," he says proudly. "Now relax and let go."

He works the vibrator inside my pussy as his fingers rub against my clit. It's a matter of seconds before I release hard, giving him exactly what he demands.

"Fucking beautiful," he growls. He pulls the vibrator out before standing directly behind me and positioning his cock at my entrance. "Bend lower, baby." He presses a palm to my lower back, guiding my body right where he wants me.

I feel him pushing inside me as my body fully accepts his impressive length. The raw feeling of his cock working my pussy is almost too much, but I try to hold back until he's closer. I arch my back more and widen my hips, giving him perfect access to thrust deeper inside.

"Yes. God, yes," I moan, urging him on. "Harder, Bentley. Faster."

"God, sweetheart. I love when you're desperate and needy for me." He leans down and grips my shoulder as he pulsates deeper and faster per my request. His animalistic growls put me over the edge, releasing hard all around him.

He comes hard within seconds after I do, jerking fiercely inside me before we finally both come down. He pulls out and grabs me from behind so I'm now standing. He swings me around and collides with my mouth instantly. His kisses are filled with passion and love, fast and eager.

"God, I love you, Ceci."

I smile against his lips. I can hear the intensity in his tone. "I love you, Bentley."

He lowers his lips and kisses down my neck and in between my breasts before landing on my stomach. "And daddy loves you."

EPILOGUE
CECILIA

"Come on, hurry!" I call out as I wait for Bentley to come into the living room. "It's almost on."

"Coming!" I hear him yell from his office.

I get comfortable on the couch as a new episode of CSI is about to start.

"Got the popcorn," I announce as I hear him walk in.

"It's weird that you have a whole set up thing, you know?"

I pop a piece into my mouth and smile. "No, it's not. I get to see Hannah get slaughtered to death. She gets her fame, and I get to feel a tiny bit better by watching her guts explode all over the screen."

"That's gross." He grabs a fistful of popcorn and begins shoving them into his mouth.

"Hey, we all have our quirks. Don't judge."

"Whatever makes you feel better. But she's not really getting slaughtered to death..."

I punch him playfully in the shoulder. "Don't ruin it for me!"

As much as I've forgiven Hannah for all the shit she's pulled on Bentley and me, it doesn't mean I won't enjoy her character dying.

After she finished Celebrity Rehab, she was picked up by a new agent, who immediately started getting her auditions for parts in popular TV shows. This is her third episode where her character finally dies.

"Oh my God!" I laugh as her eyes bulge out of her face the moment she realizes she's about to die. Her character is side-swiped by a huge bus, the film effects showing body pieces and guts flying every which way. "C'mon." I nudge Bentley in the ribs. "That shit is funny."

"That amuses you, sweetheart." He shakes his head at me. "However—"

"Holy shit!" I cut him off, holding my stomach with both hands. "My water just broke. Or I peed. Like a lot. Oh my God," I ramble off frantically.

He stands up, ready to follow orders, but I'm not even exactly sure what to do. "What do you need? Should I call the doctor? Is it coming out right now?"

"Bentley!" I scream, snapping him out of it. "Get me towels. And some new pants. And my shoes. And then grab my overnight bag. I'll call the doctor." I try to remain calm now because I know that's the only way he'll remain calm.

"Right. Okay, on it."

In less than fifteen minutes, Bentley's driving through the Saturday night traffic. Everyone and their mom is out tonight apparently.

I text my mom and Casey, letting them know we're on our way. They've been helping me prepare for weeks.

We finally arrive—in one piece thankfully. He helps me through the Emergency Room entrance and quickly grabs me a wheel chair. I feel and look like a whale. I haven't seen my feet in weeks, and I'm not even sure I slipped my sandals on at this point.

"Ready?"

"Yes, hurry please. These contractions are getting more intense." My head falls back as more pain ripples through me. "Oh, shit. Oh, fuck. Oh my God."

Bentley rushes me in and immediately takes the elevator up to labor and delivery. He flags down a nurse and follows her into the nearest room available.

Once I'm settled in and comfortable, Casey and my mom walk in. They look like a bunch of crazed lunatics with their messy hair and frantic expressions.

"Oh my God, did we make it?"

I narrow my brows at them. "Do you see me holding a baby?"

"It's going to be a while," one of the nurses interrupts.

"How long is a while?" I ask, really not sure how much longer I can take this. "Are we talking like an hour or two?" I ask hopeful.

She smirks, hiding her face, but I see the look she's giving me. "Depends, Mrs. Leighton. But you're only dilated to a two. We've got some time, so get comfortable."

"Oh my God. Only a two?"

"Only a two what?" Casey speaks up.

"Centimeters."

"Oh, right."

"Are you all right?"

"Yes, it's just…blood freaks me out."

"You better not pass out!" I scold, pointing my finger at her.

"Anyone that's going to faint with the sight of blood needs to stay above the waist," the nurse chimes in again.

"Casey, no fainting."

"I'm not going to faint. I'm fine," she insists, although I'm not sure who she's trying to convince.

Bentley stands next to me, gripping my hand in one hand while rubbing my head with the other. I'm already sweating, and I haven't even started pushing yet.

"It's been six hours. Oh my God," I whine as the nurse checks my stats. "Is this normal? Shouldn't I have popped already?"

She grins as she continues reading my contractions graph. "Oh, honey. I've had women in here that were in labor for days."

"DAYS?" I gasp, nearly waking Casey and my mom up who passed out on the couch two hours ago.

"Afraid so. We try to make you as comfortable as possible."

The nurse checks me again and finally tells me the news I've been dying to hear. "Ok, Ceci. You're at ten. It's time to push."

The pain meds have worked well so far. I'm already anticipating some discomfort, but either way, I'm squeezing Bentley's hand the entire time.

"Are you ready for this?" he whispers, his eyes filled with passion and excitement.

"I hope so. Are you?"

"Yes. I've been ready. Having the most gorgeous woman on Earth have my children, what else could I ask for?" He leans down and softly grazes my lips. "You can do this."

I nod fiercely, hoping to convince myself as beads of sweat cover my forehead. My mom and Casey finally wake up as the nurses and doctor begin prepping. They both stand on one side as Bentley stands on the other.

"All right, Ceci. It's time to push."

I nod, letting them adjust my legs how they need them. God, this is so uncomfortable. I lean forward, and as soon as the nurse tells me, I begin to push.

I push with every contraction and pray to God that this is the one that gets a baby out of me.

"You're doing amazing, sweetheart." Bentley focuses on me, keeping me on track.

"C'mon, Celia, you're a West. Push that baby out already," my sister calls out like it's a game of football. I glare at her, mentally reminding myself to kick her ass later.

"I see the head. One more big push. Come on," the nurse informs me. I watch as she starts handing the doctor gadgets and tools. I lean forward one more time and push with every ounce of energy I have.

My body finally relaxes at the sound of a baby crying. Tears begin strolling down my cheeks as I get a glimpse of my new baby.

"It's a girl!"

"Oh my God," I whimper out. "Is she okay?"

I watch as one of the nurses holds her up briefly for me to see before taking it away.

"She's just fine, Cecilia." I hear the nurse call out. Relief floods through me as her screams get louder and stronger.

"You're incredible." Bentley covers my mouth with his. "So amazing."

"All right, Cecilia. Not much time to rest. Baby number two is right behind and ready."

I watch as my mother and Casey's jaws drop.

Surprise.

BREAKING NEWS!

Bentley and Ceci Leighton welcome two precious bundles of joy!

Omaha, NE has two new residents as the iconic couple officially become parents early Sunday morning. The couple evidentially kept the news of expecting twins under wraps as their own friends and family were stunned by the announcement that Ceci had delivered two healthy babies, a boy and a girl.

A source close to the couple has reported that the parents and babies are doing exceptional and the new parents are beyond words ecstatic at their growing family. Congrats to the Leighton family!

BIRTH ANNOUNCEMENT

Bentley & Cecilia Leighton are pleased to announce the births of Ava
Claire, 5 lbs. 3 oz. and Brock William, Jr. 5 lbs. 1 oz. on
March 10th at 2:35 a.m. and 2:38 a.m.

Ava has her mother's facial features and Brock has his father's temper.

All four are home and well.

And of course, they all lived happily ever after.

If you enjoyed this forbidden and emotional romance, then you'll love SHOULDN'T WANT YOU

I shouldn't want him—my older fiancé's *son*.
He's arrogant, unapologetic, and annoying as hell.

Keeping my distance is easier than it sounds, especially now that he's moved in with us. He's constantly in my space, invading my boundaries, and taunting me with his good looks and devilish charm.

I want to hate him. To push him away.
To confess our secret and forget what happened.

But then the rug gets ripped out from underneath me and my life gets turned around.
Except this time, there's no going back.

If you enjoyed this forbidden and emotional romance, then you'll love PUSHING THE LIMITS

He's my art professor.
I'm his student.
With an electric connection and undeniable chemistry,
I know it won't be long until one of us cracks.

When the opportunity arises to pose naked for the entire art class, I can't help the thrill of knowing he'll be watching me.
While they all look past me with their eyes narrowed and concentrated, drawing only the lines and angles of my body, he sees right through me down to my vulnerability.

He sees more than just the physical aspects—*he sees me.*

That's when I see the struggle in his features as he tries to stay in control.

How do we keep our distance when everything seems to be pulling us together?
What feels so right can only go wrong if we keep *pushing the limits.*

ABOUT THE AUTHOR

Brooke Cumberland is a *USA Today* Bestselling author who wears many hats on any given day. She co-wrote under the *USA Today* Bestselling duo, Kennedy Fox for six years before going back to solo writing. She lives in the frozen tundra of Packer Nation with her husband, wild teenager, and four dogs. When she's not writing, you can find her reading, watching ASMR and reading vlogs on YouTube, or binge-watching a TV show she's most likely behind on. Brooke's addicted to iced coffee, leggings, and naps. She found her passion for telling stories during winter break one year in grad school—and she hasn't stopped since.

Find her on her website at www.BrookeWritesRomance.com and follow her on social media:

facebook.com/brookewritesromance

instagram.com/brookewritesromance

amazon.com/author/brookecumberland

tiktok.com/@brookewritesromance

goodreads.com/brookecumberland

Written under Brooke Cumberland:

The Intern Trilogy

The Spark series

Pushing the Limits

Shouldn't Want You

Someone Like You

Written under Kennedy Fox:

Checkmate Duet series

Roommate Duet series

Lawton Ridge Duet series

Only One series

Bishop Brothers series

Circle B Ranch series

Love in Isolation series

Make Me series

Printed in the USA
CPSIA information can be obtained
at www.ICGtesting.com
LVHW092250230324
775354LV00008B/282